PROPHET™

PROPHET, VOL. 1: REMISSION TP
ISBN#: 978-1-60706-611-8
First printing

IMAGE COMICS, INC.
Robert Kirkman - chief operating officer
Erik Larsen - chief financial officer
Todd McFarlane - president
Marc Silvestri - chief executive officer
Jim Valentino - vice-president

Eric Stephenson - publisher
Todd Martinez - sales & licensing coordinator
Jennifer de Guzman - pr & marketing director
Branwyn Bigglestone - accounts manager
Emily Miller - administrative assistant
Jamie Parreno - marketing assistant
Sarah deLaine - events coordinator
Kevin Yuen - digital rights coordinator
Tyler Shainline - production manager
Drew Gill - art director
Jonathan Chan - design director
Monica Garcia - production artist
Vincent Kukua - production artist
Jana Cook - production artist
www.imagecomics.com

STORY Brandon Graham
with Simon Roy (chapters 1-3)
with Farel Dalrymple (chapter 4)
with Giannis Milonogiannis
and Simon Roy (chapter 6)

ART Simon Roy (chapters 1-3)
Farel Dalrymple (chapter 4)
Brandon Graham (chapter 5)
Giannis Milonogiannis (chapter 6)
Marian Churchland (chapter 1 title page)

COLORS Richard Ballermann (chapters 1-3)
Joseph Bergin III (chapter 4, 6)
Brandon Graham (chapter 5)
Jason Wordie (chapter 2 title page)

LETTERS Ed Brisson

EDITS Eric Stephenson

COVER Simon Roy

COIL: A CLONE STORY backup story by Emma Rios

PROPHET created by Rob Liefeld

1

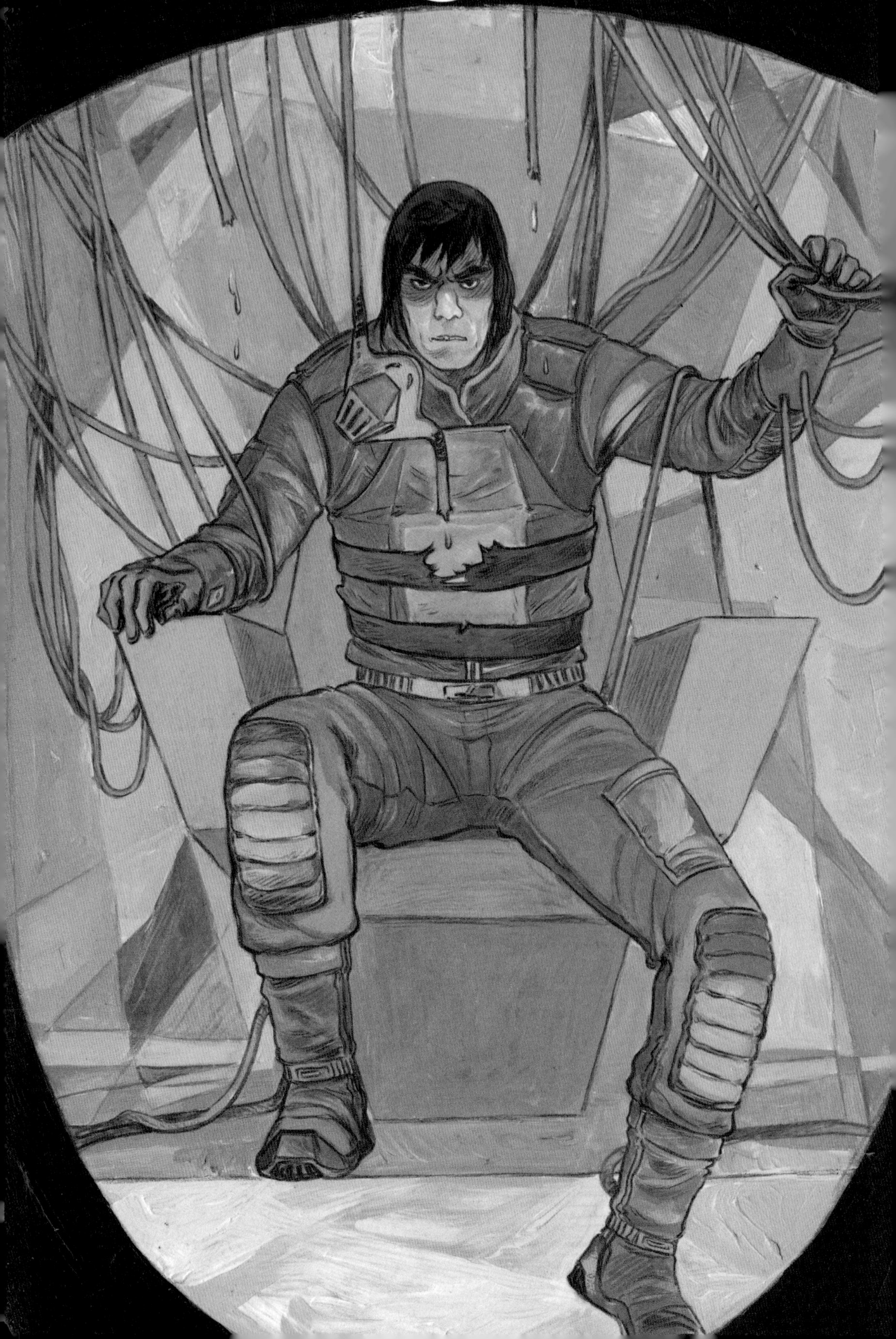

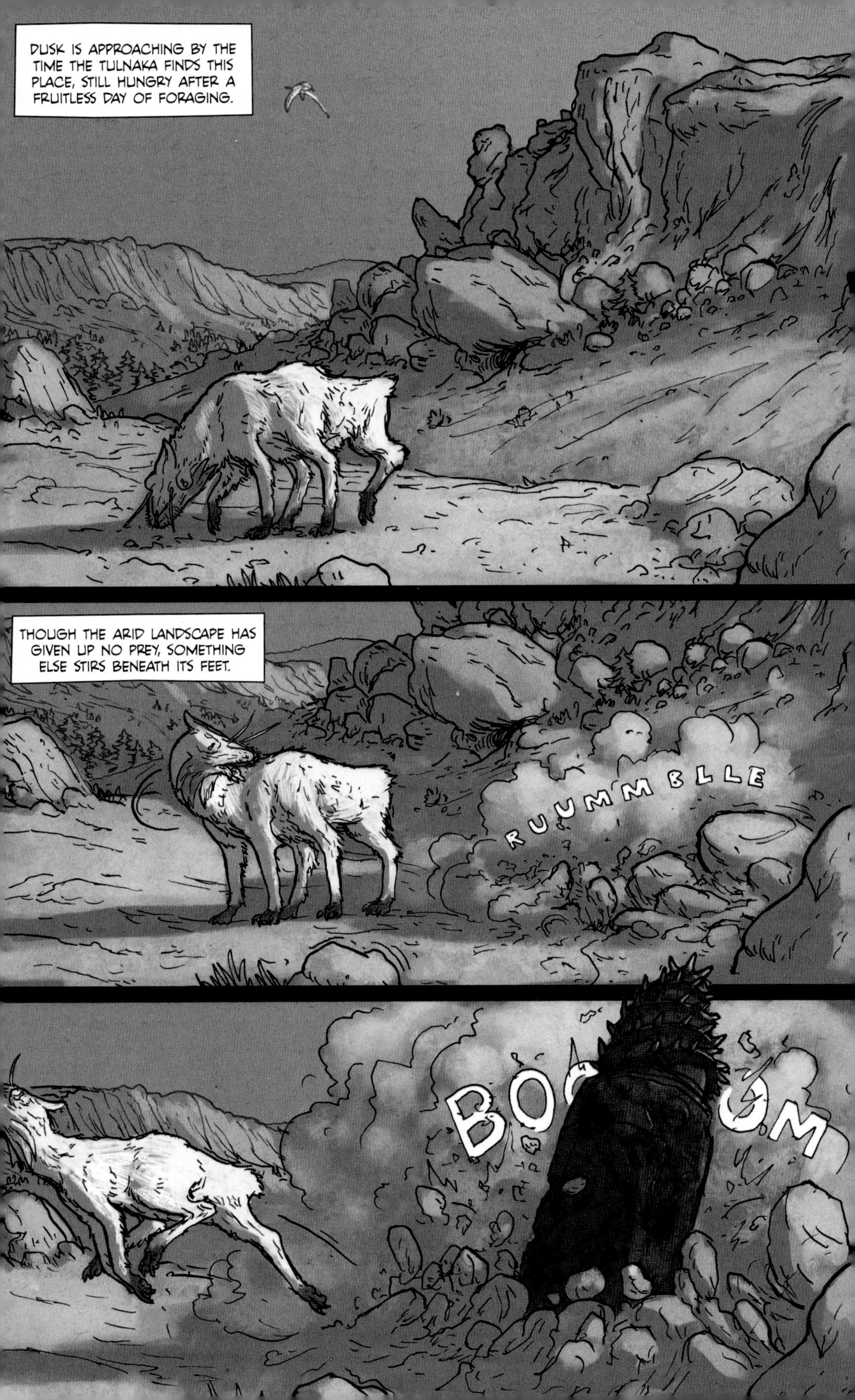
DUSK IS APPROACHING BY THE TIME THE TULNAKA FINDS THIS PLACE, STILL HUNGRY AFTER A FRUITLESS DAY OF FORAGING.
THOUGH THE ARID LANDSCAPE HAS GIVEN UP NO PREY, SOMETHING ELSE STIRS BENEATH ITS FEET.
RUUMMBLLE
BOOOM

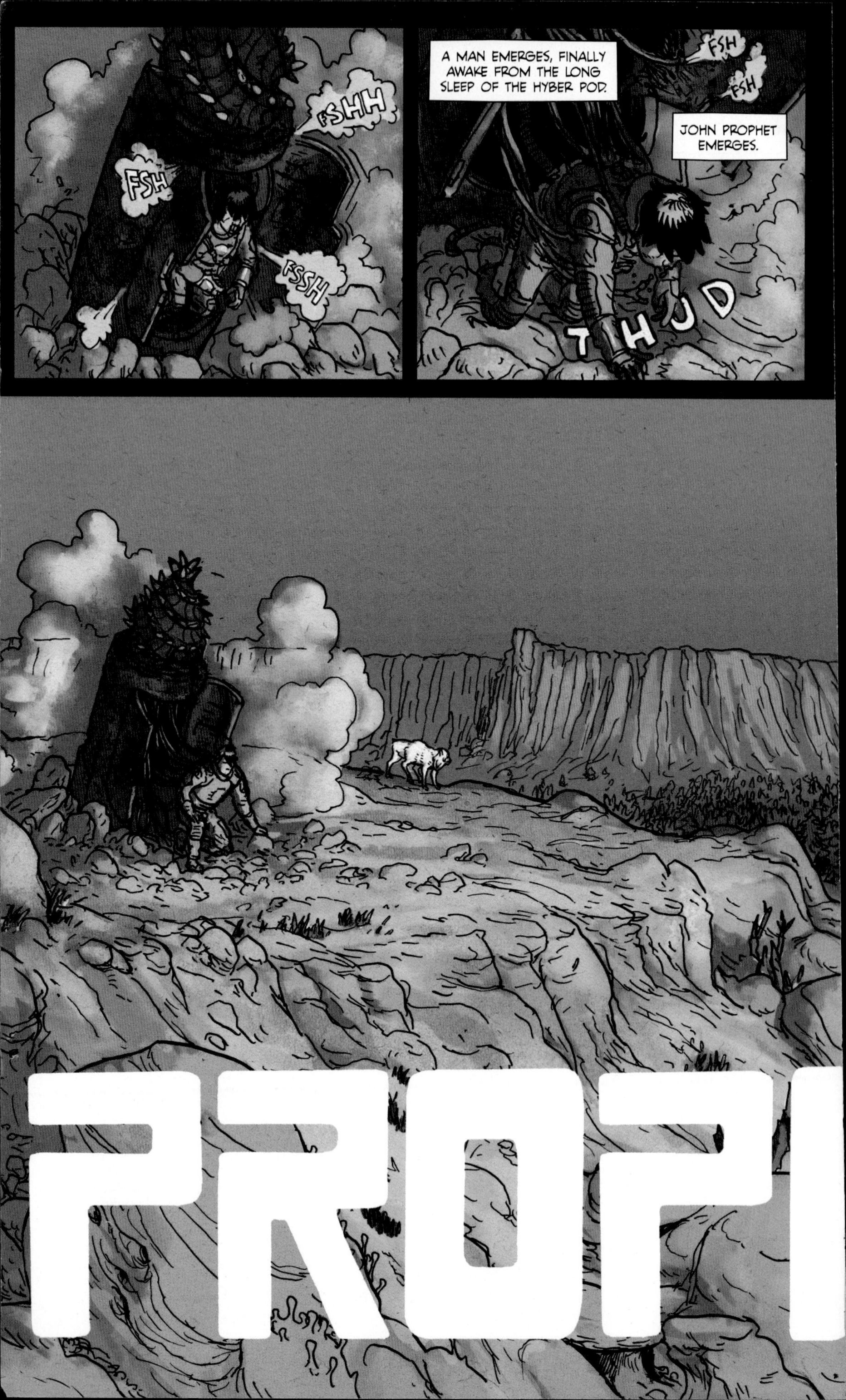
FSHH
FSH
FSSH
A MAN EMERGES, FINALLY AWAKE FROM THE LONG SLEEP OF THE HYBER POD.
FSH
FSH
JOHN PROPHET EMERGES.
THUD
PROPH

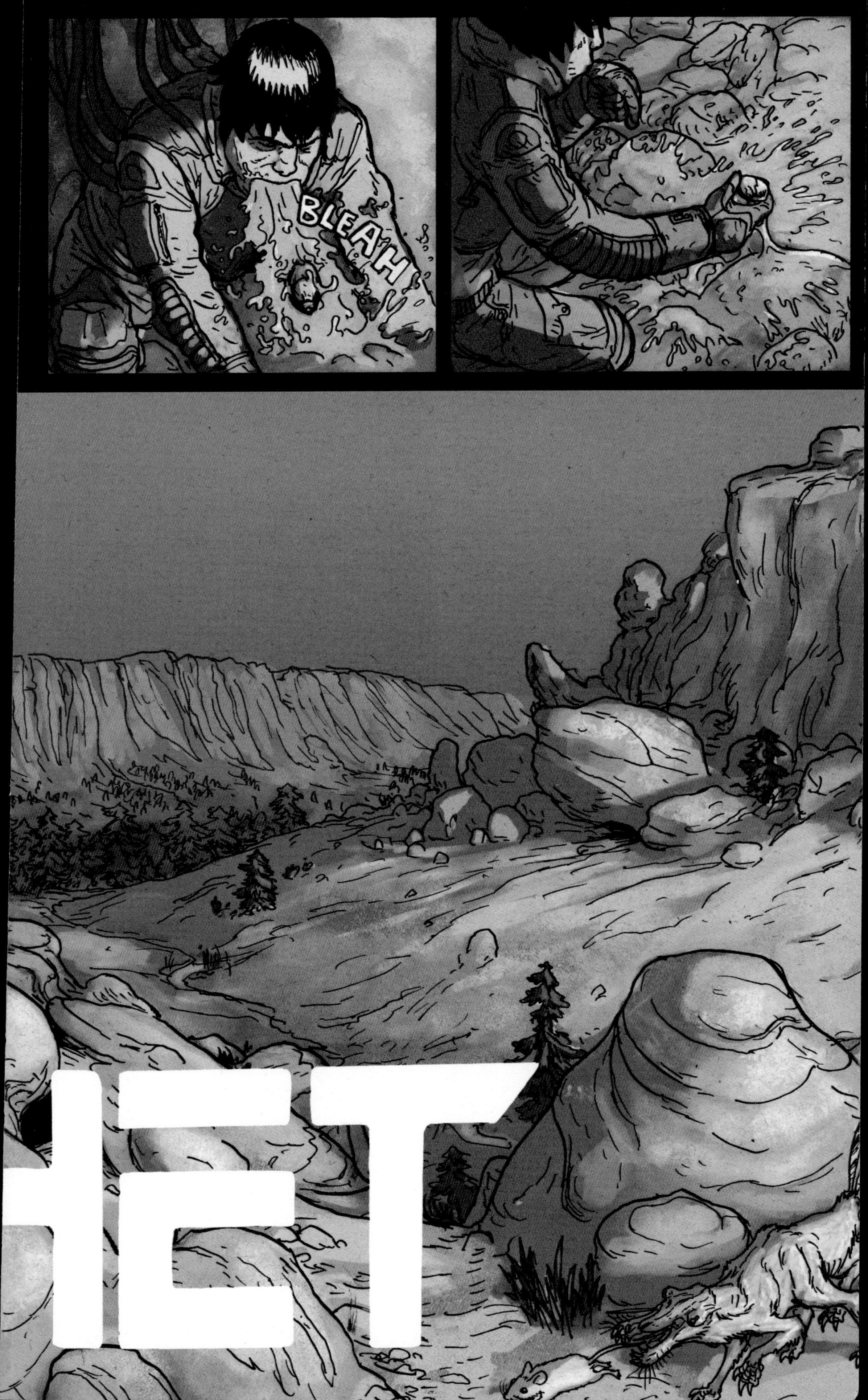
BLEAH
HET

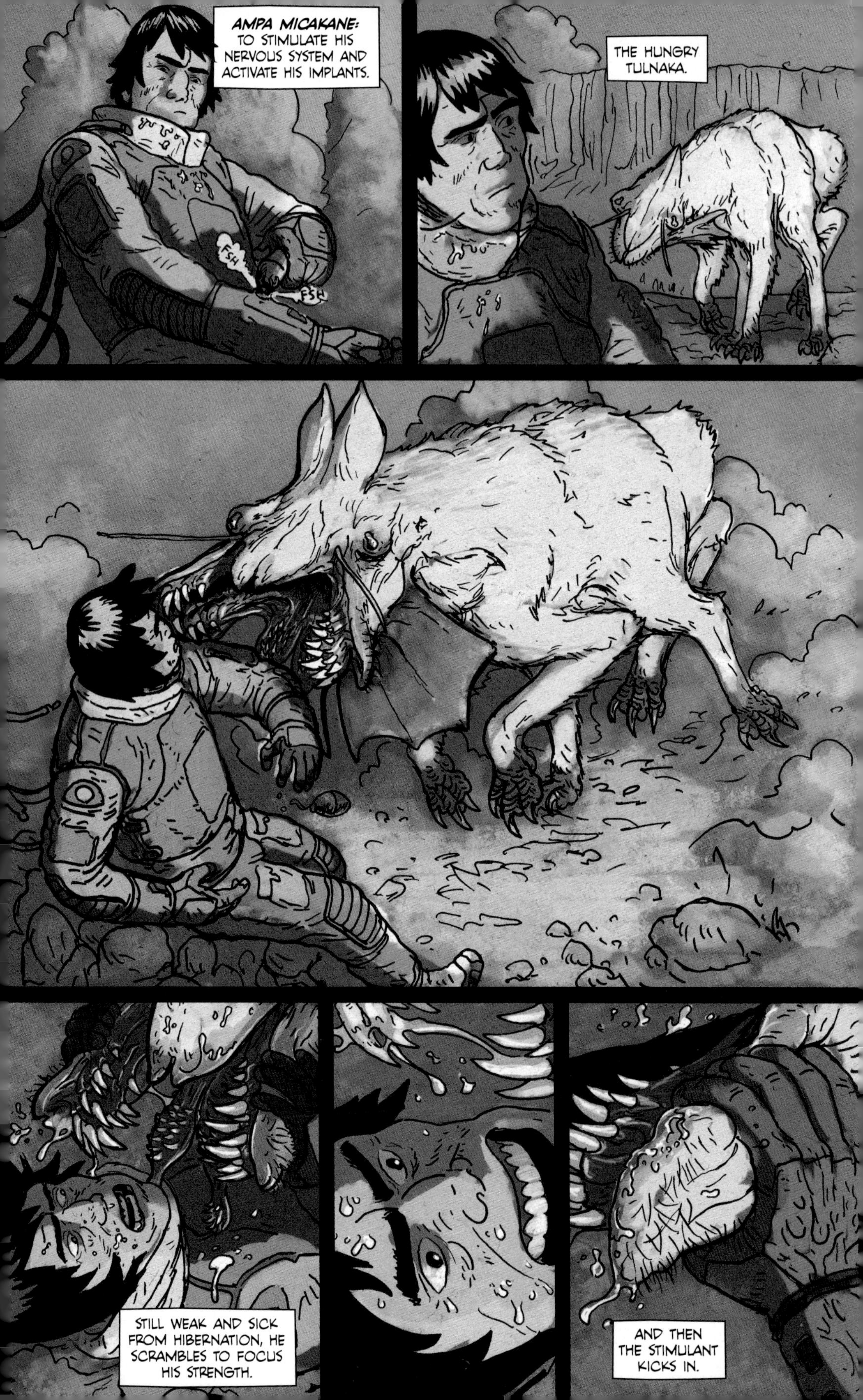
AMPA MICAKANE: TO STIMULATE HIS NERVOUS SYSTEM AND ACTIVATE HIS IMPLANTS.
FSH
FSH
THE HUNGRY TULNAKA.
STILL WEAK AND SICK FROM HIBERNATION, HE SCRAMBLES TO FOCUS HIS STRENGTH.
AND THEN THE STIMULANT KICKS IN.

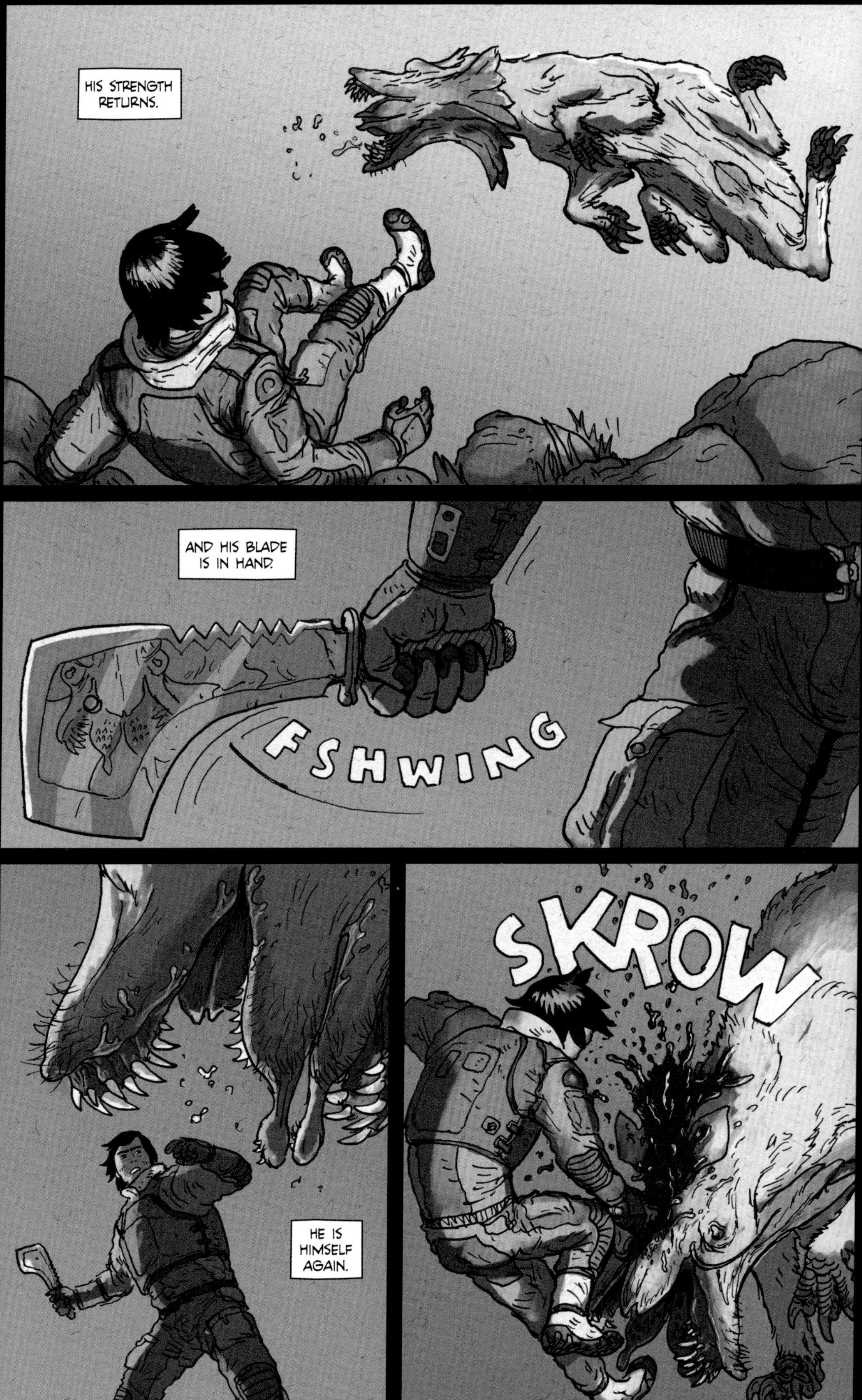
HIS STRENGTH RETURNS.
AND HIS BLADE IS IN HAND.
FSHWING
HE IS HIMSELF AGAIN.
SKROW

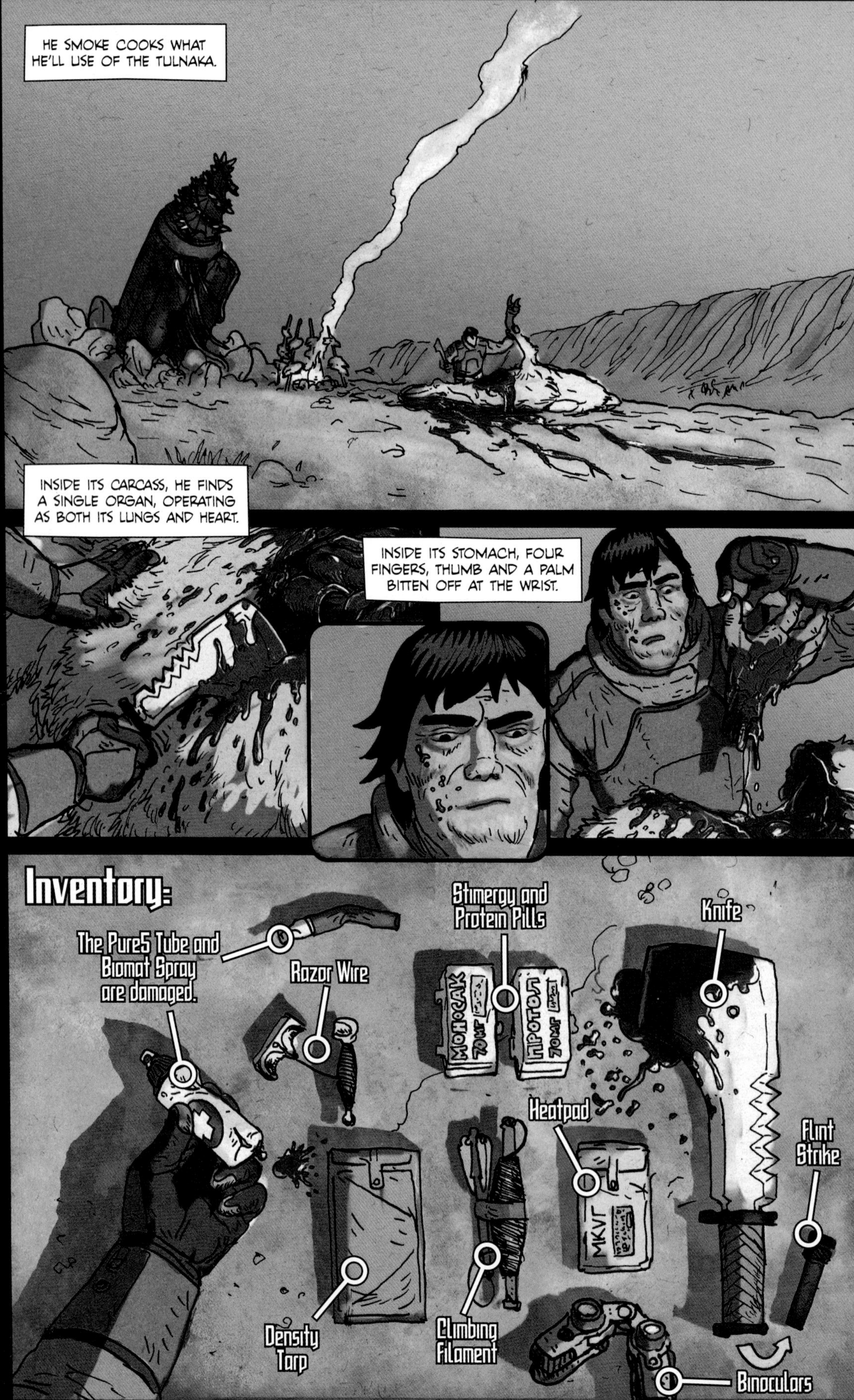

HE SMOKE COOKS WHAT HE'LL USE OF THE TULNAKA.
INSIDE ITS CARCASS, HE FINDS A SINGLE ORGAN, OPERATING AS BOTH ITS LUNGS AND HEART.
INSIDE ITS STOMACH, FOUR FINGERS, THUMB AND A PALM BITTEN OFF AT THE WRIST.
Inventory:
The Pure5 Tube and Biomat Spray are damaged.
Razor Wire
Stimergy and Protein Pills
Knife
Heatpad
Flint Strike
Density Tarp
Climbing Filament
Binoculars

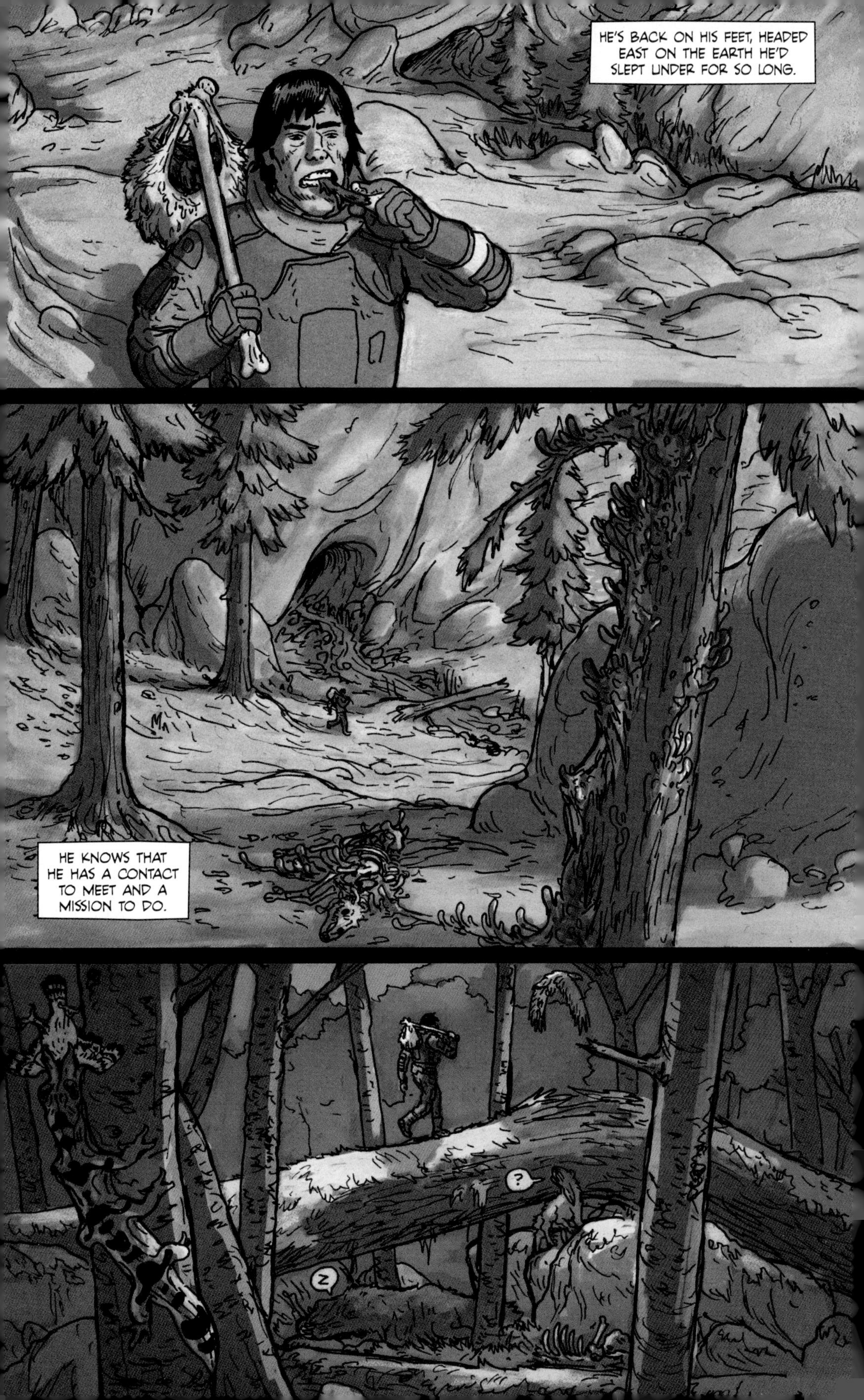
HE'S BACK ON HIS FEET, HEADED EAST ON THE EARTH HE'D SLEPT UNDER FOR SO LONG.
HE KNOWS THAT HE HAS A CONTACT TO MEET AND A MISSION TO DO.
?
Z

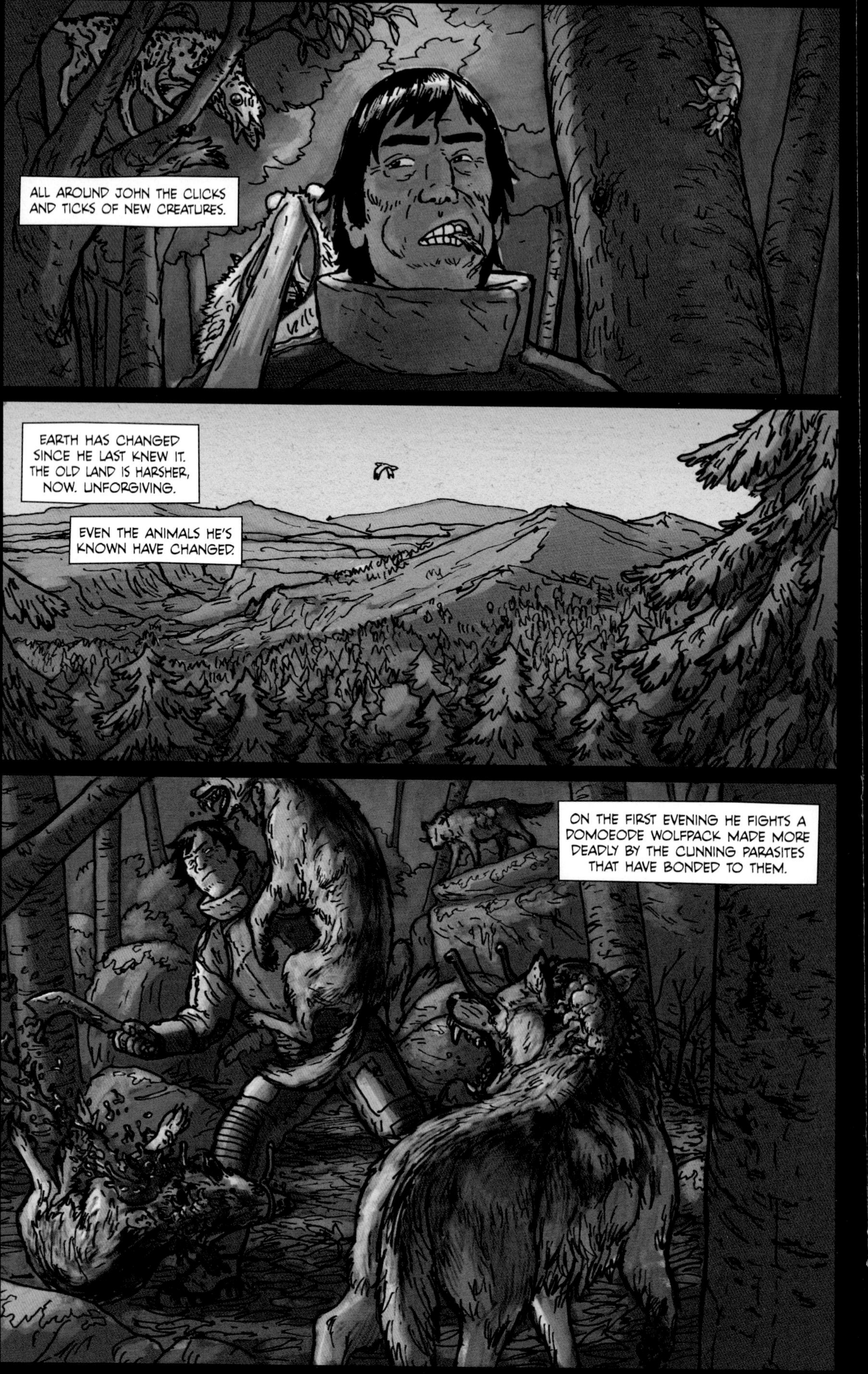
ALL AROUND JOHN THE CLICKS AND TICKS OF NEW CREATURES.
EARTH HAS CHANGED SINCE HE LAST KNEW IT. THE OLD LAND IS HARSHER, NOW. UNFORGIVING.
EVEN THE ANIMALS HE'S KNOWN HAVE CHANGED.
ON THE FIRST EVENING HE FIGHTS A DOMOEODE WOLFPACK MADE MORE DEADLY BY THE CUNNING PARASITES THAT HAVE BONDED TO THEM.

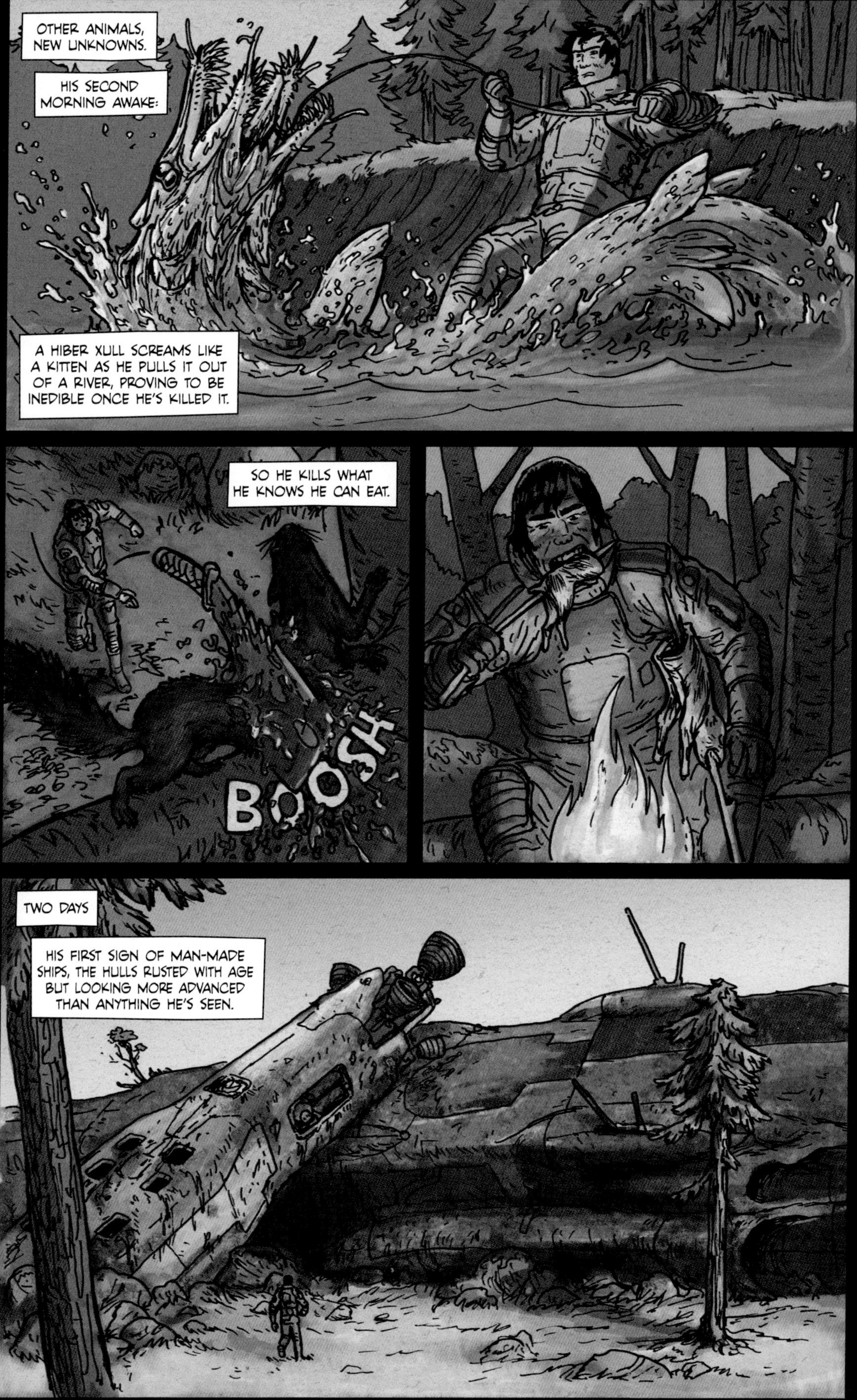
OTHER ANIMALS, NEW UNKNOWNS.
HIS SECOND MORNING AWAKE:
A HIBER XULL SCREAMS LIKE A KITTEN AS HE PULLS IT OUT OF A RIVER, PROVING TO BE INEDIBLE ONCE HE'S KILLED IT.
SO HE KILLS WHAT HE KNOWS HE CAN EAT.
BOOSH
TWO DAYS
HIS FIRST SIGN OF MAN-MADE SHIPS, THE HULLS RUSTED WITH AGE BUT LOOKING MORE ADVANCED THAN ANYTHING HE'S SEEN.

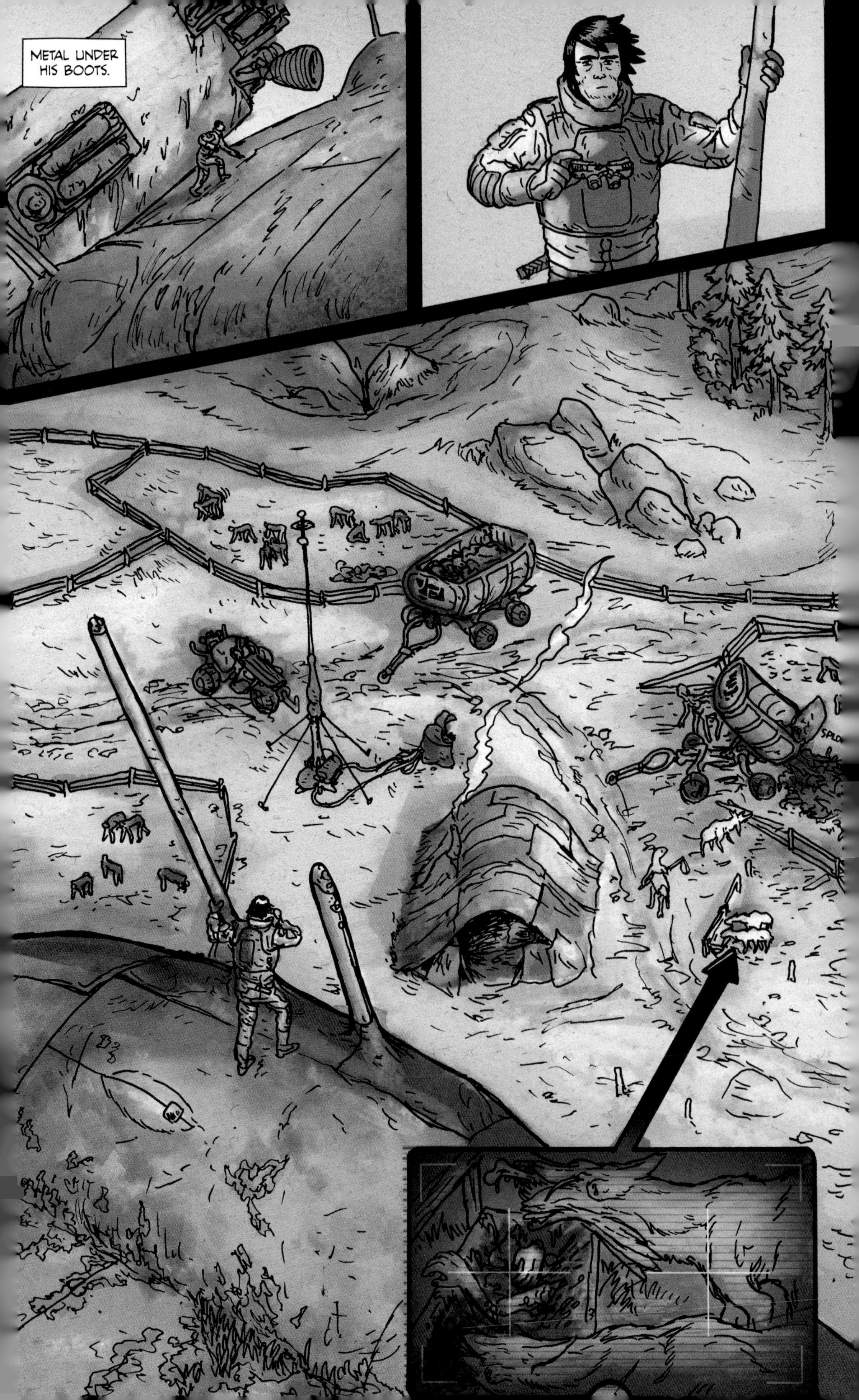
METAL UNDER HIS BOOTS.

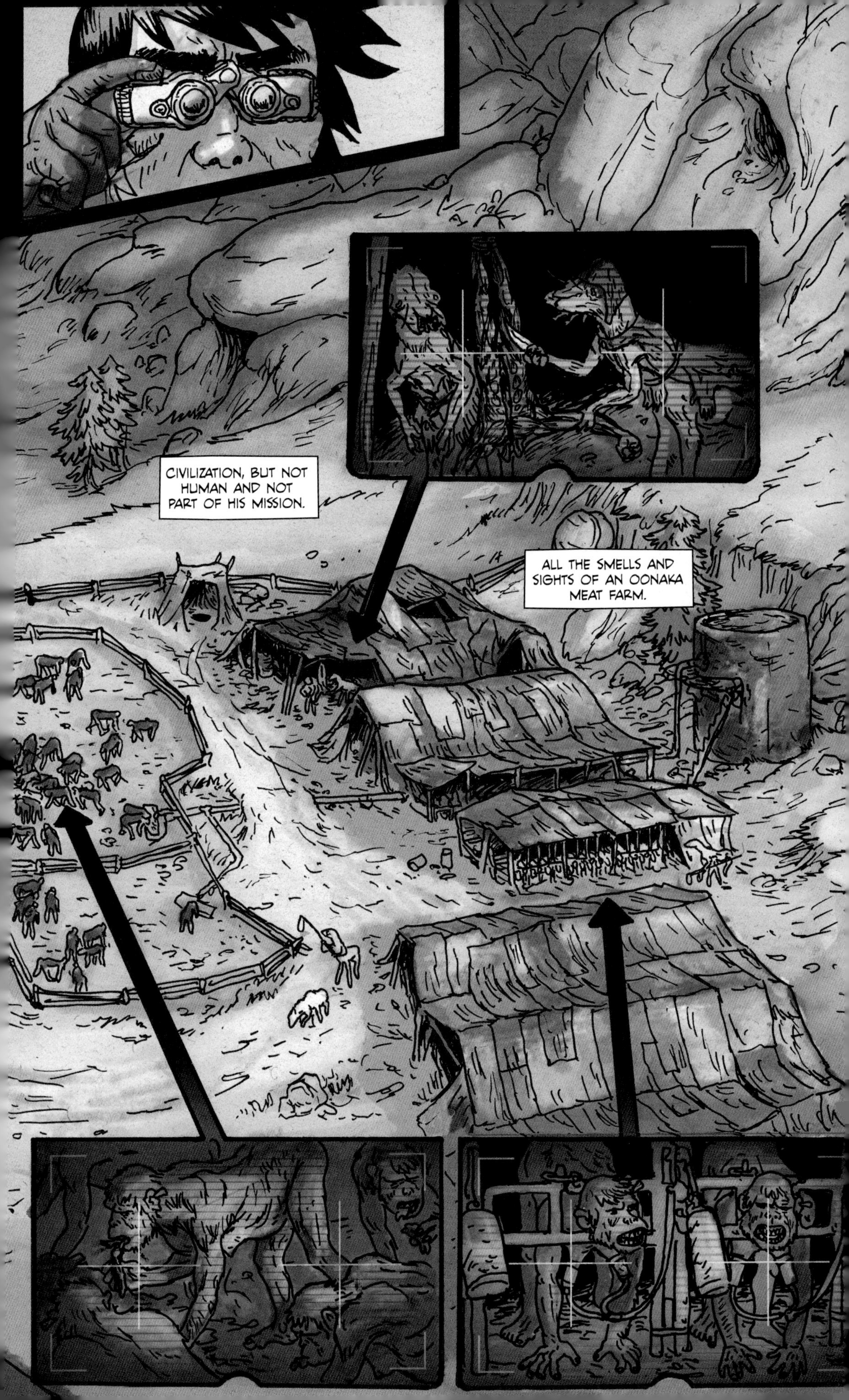
CIVILIZATION, BUT NOT HUMAN AND NOT PART OF HIS MISSION.
ALL THE SMELLS AND SIGHTS OF AN OONAKA MEAT FARM.

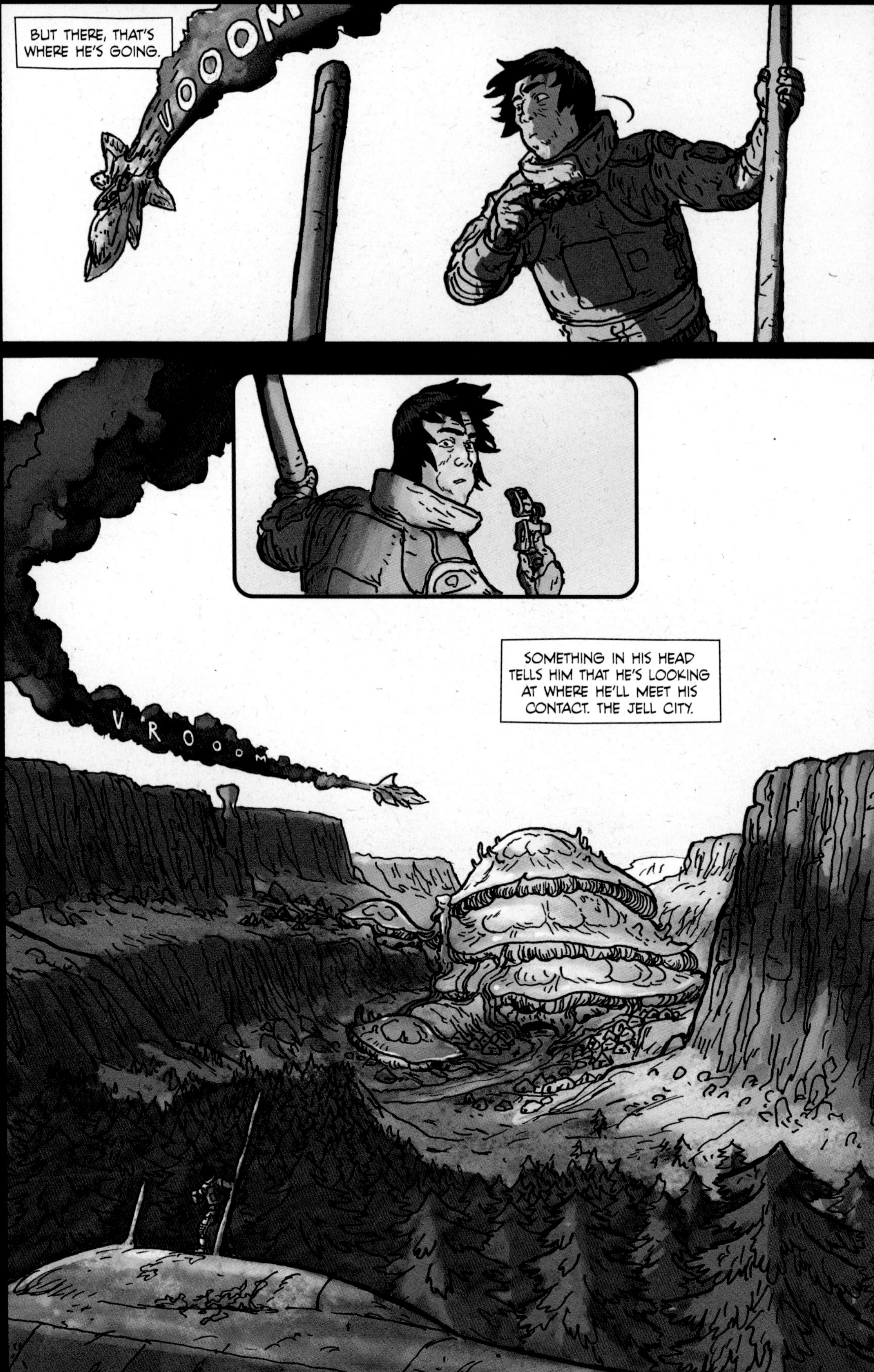
BUT THERE, THAT'S WHERE HE'S GOING.
VOOOM
SOMETHING IN HIS HEAD TELLS HIM THAT HE'S LOOKING AT WHERE HE'LL MEET HIS CONTACT. THE JELL CITY.
VROOOM

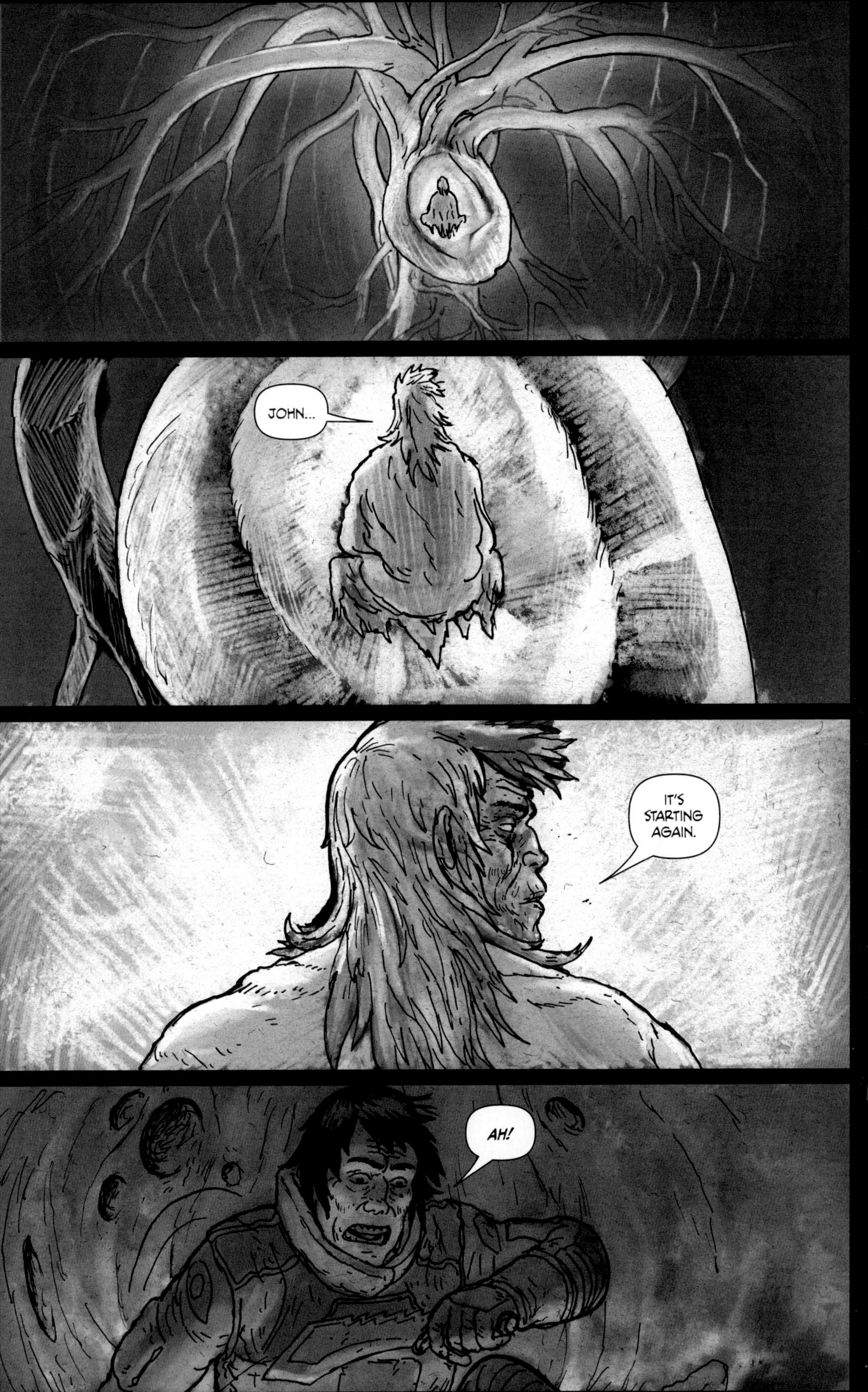
JOHN...
IT'S STARTING AGAIN.
AH!

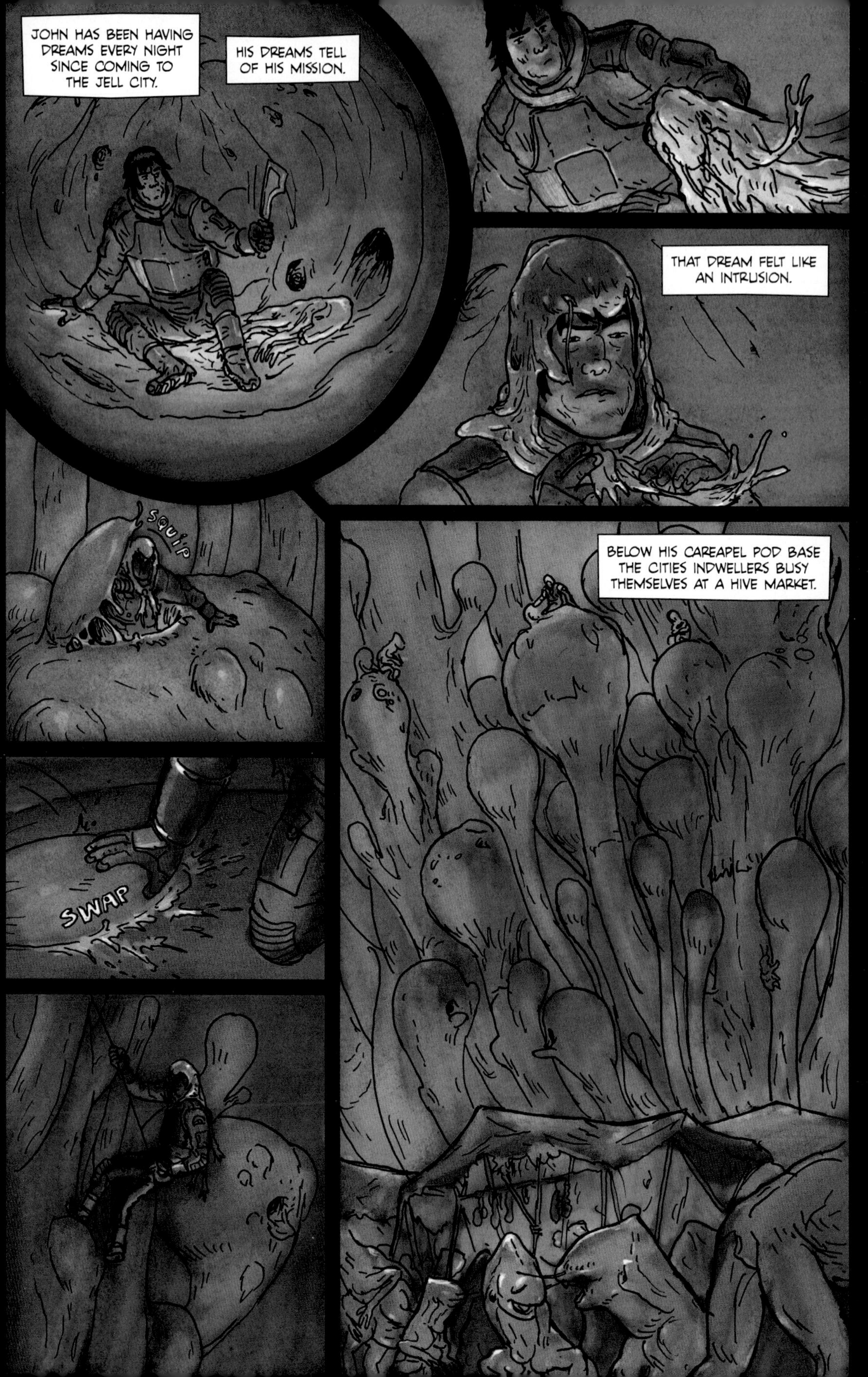
JOHN HAS BEEN HAVING DREAMS EVERY NIGHT SINCE COMING TO THE JELL CITY.
HIS DREAMS TELL OF HIS MISSION.
THAT DREAM FELT LIKE AN INTRUSION.
SQUIP
SWAP
BELOW HIS CAREAPEL POD BASE THE CITIES INDWELLERS BUSY THEMSELVES AT A HIVE MARKET.

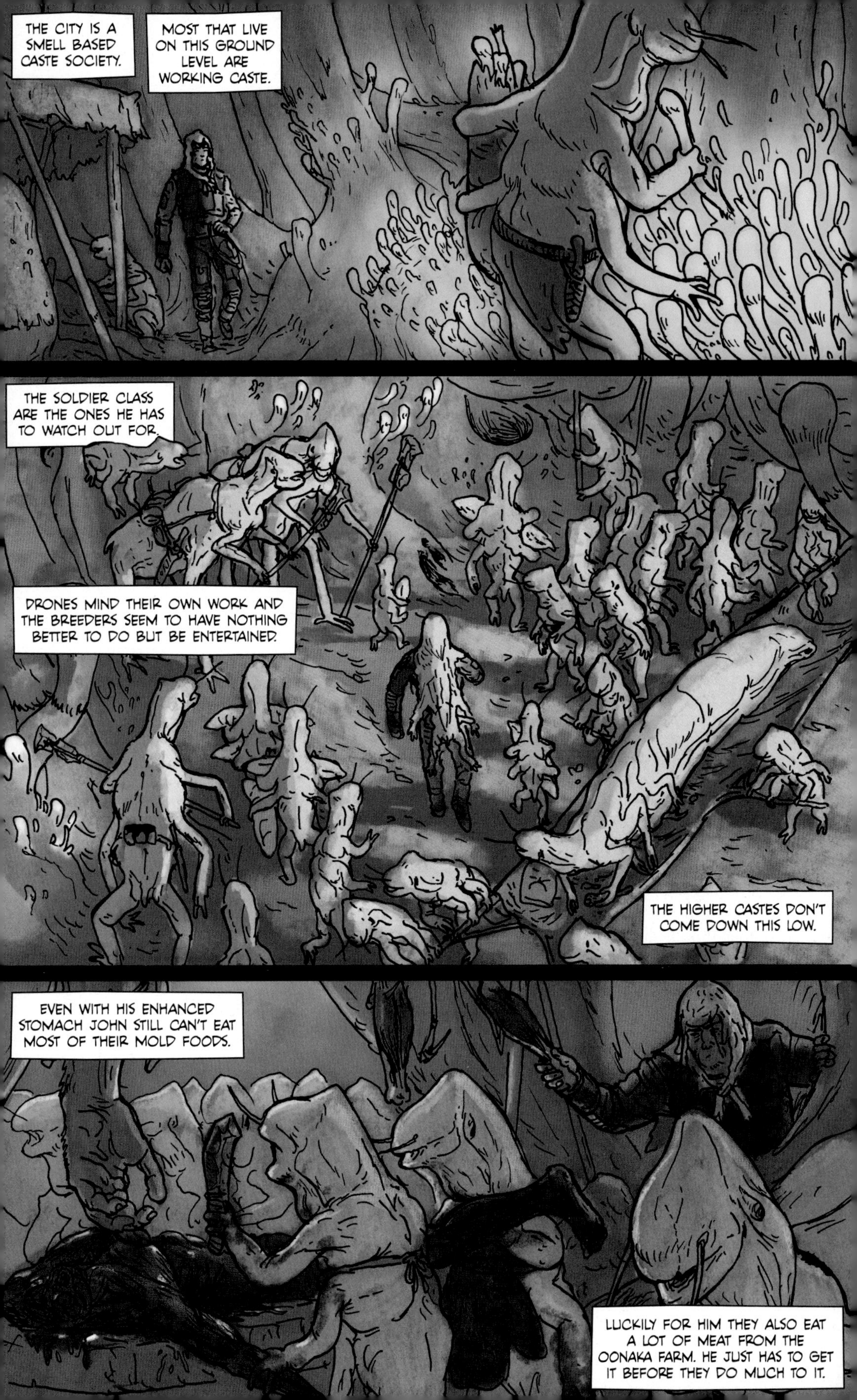
THE CITY IS A SMELL BASED CASTE SOCIETY.
MOST THAT LIVE ON THIS GROUND LEVEL ARE WORKING CASTE.
THE SOLDIER CLASS ARE THE ONES HE HAS TO WATCH OUT FOR.
DRONES MIND THEIR OWN WORK AND THE BREEDERS SEEM TO HAVE NOTHING BETTER TO DO BUT BE ENTERTAINED.
THE HIGHER CASTES DON'T COME DOWN THIS LOW.
EVEN WITH HIS ENHANCED STOMACH JOHN STILL CAN'T EAT MOST OF THEIR MOLD FOODS.
LUCKILY FOR HIM THEY ALSO EAT A LOT OF MEAT FROM THE OONAKA FARM. HE JUST HAS TO GET IT BEFORE THEY DO MUCH TO IT.

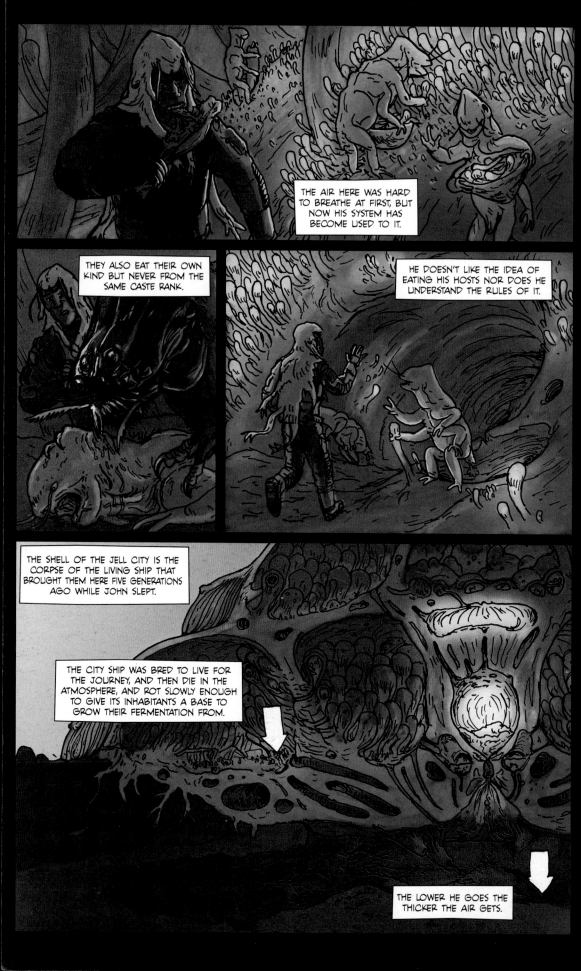

THE AIR HERE WAS HARD TO BREATHE AT FIRST, BUT NOW HIS SYSTEM HAS BECOME USED TO IT.

THEY ALSO EAT THEIR OWN KIND BUT NEVER FROM THE SAME CASTE RANK.

HE DOESN'T LIKE THE IDEA OF EATING HIS HOSTS NOR DOES HE UNDERSTAND THE RULES OF IT.

THE SHELL OF THE JELL CITY IS THE CORPSE OF THE LIVING SHIP THAT BROUGHT THEM HERE FIVE GENERATIONS AGO WHILE JOHN SLEPT.

THE CITY SHIP WAS BRED TO LIVE FOR THE JOURNEY, AND THEN DIE IN THE ATMOSPHERE, AND ROT SLOWLY ENOUGH TO GIVE ITS INHABITANTS A BASE TO GROW THEIR FERMENTATION FROM.

THE LOWER HE GOES THE THICKER THE AIR GETS.

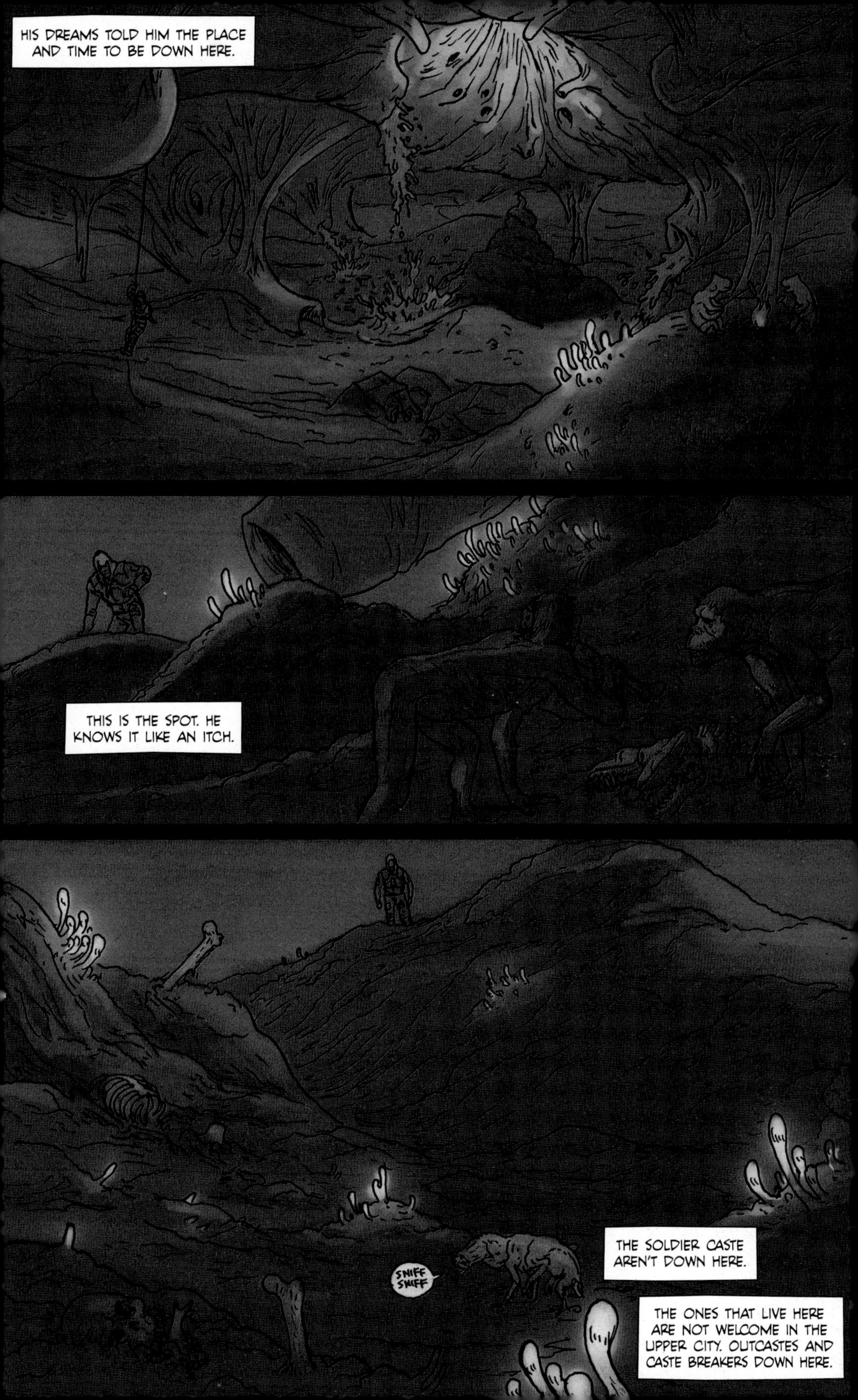
HIS DREAMS TOLD HIM THE PLACE AND TIME TO BE DOWN HERE.
THIS IS THE SPOT. HE KNOWS IT LIKE AN ITCH.
SNIFF SNIFF
THE SOLDIER CASTE AREN'T DOWN HERE.
THE ONES THAT LIVE HERE ARE NOT WELCOME IN THE UPPER CITY. OUTCASTES AND CASTE BREAKERS DOWN HERE.

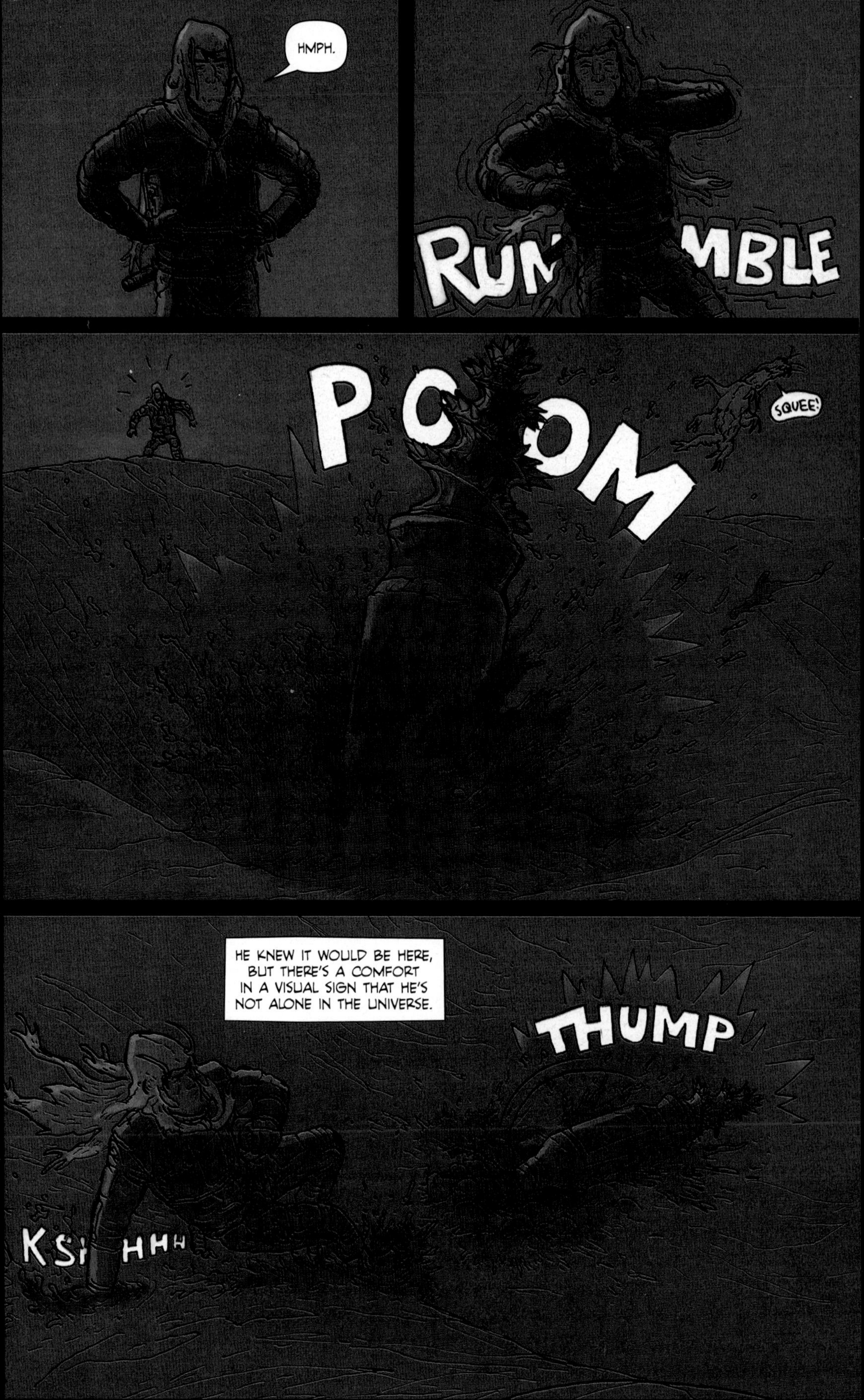
HMPH.
RUM MBLE
POOM
SQUEE!
HE KNEW IT WOULD BE HERE, BUT THERE'S A COMFORT IN A VISUAL SIGN THAT HE'S NOT ALONE IN THE UNIVERSE.
THUMP
KS HHH

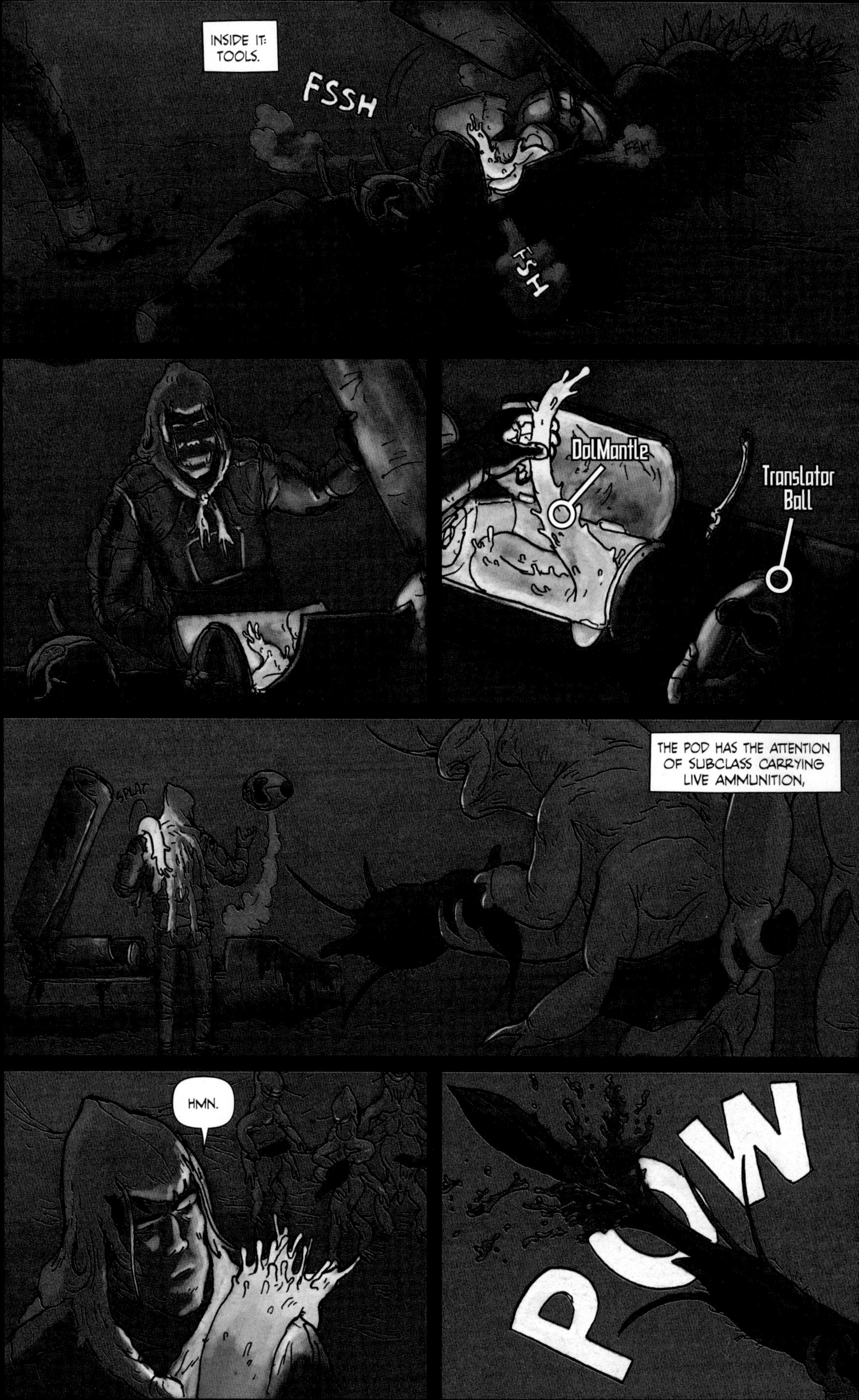
INSIDE IT: TOOLS.
FSSH
FSH
FSH
DolMantle
Translator Ball
THE POD HAS THE ATTENTION OF SUBCLASS CARRYING LIVE AMMUNITION,
SPLAT
HMN.
POW

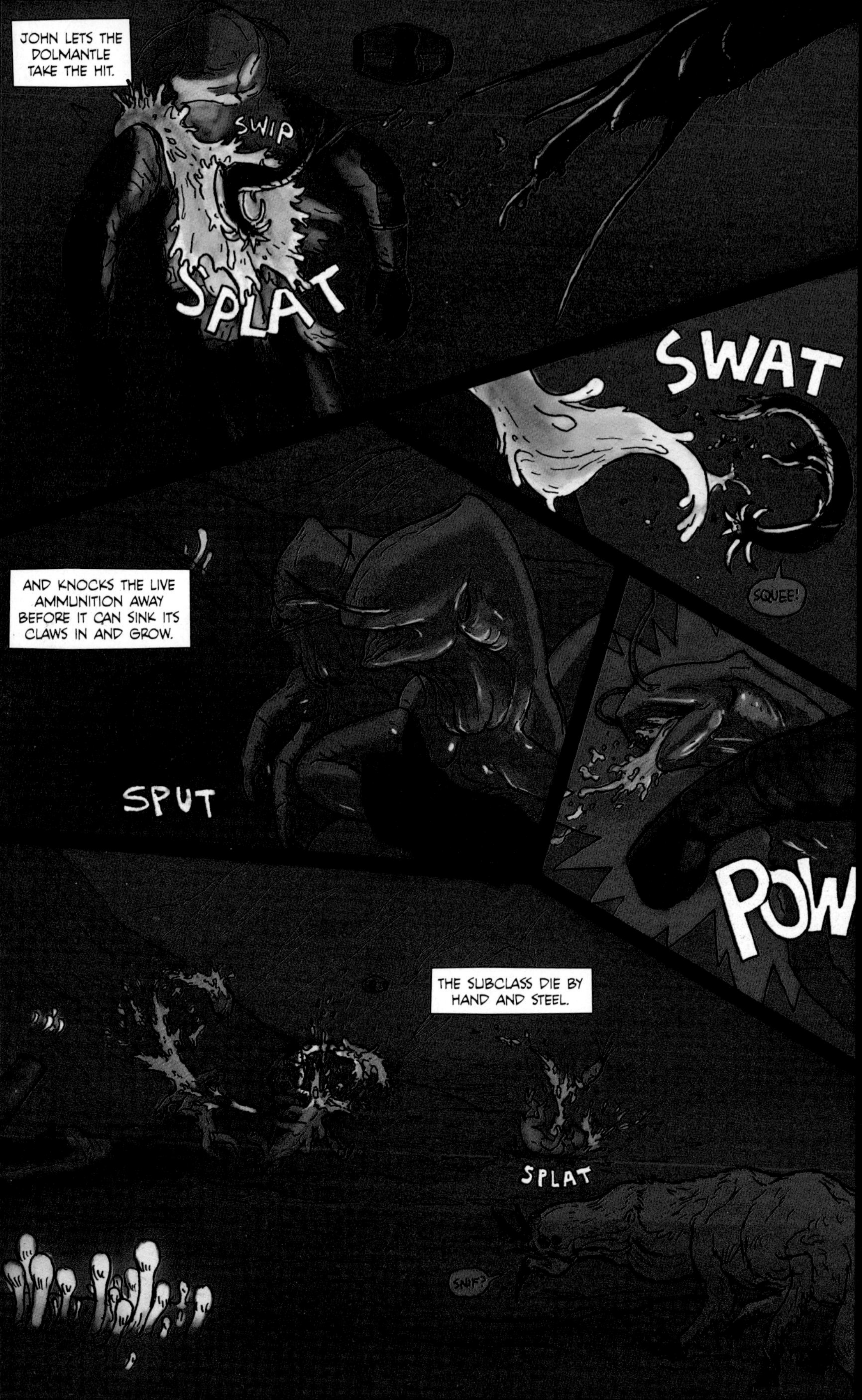
JOHN LETS THE DOLMANTLE TAKE THE HIT.
SWIP
SPLAT
SWAT
SQUEE!
AND KNOCKS THE LIVE AMMUNITION AWAY BEFORE IT CAN SINK ITS CLAWS IN AND GROW.
SPUT
POW
THE SUBCLASS DIE BY HAND AND STEEL.
SPLAT
SNIF?

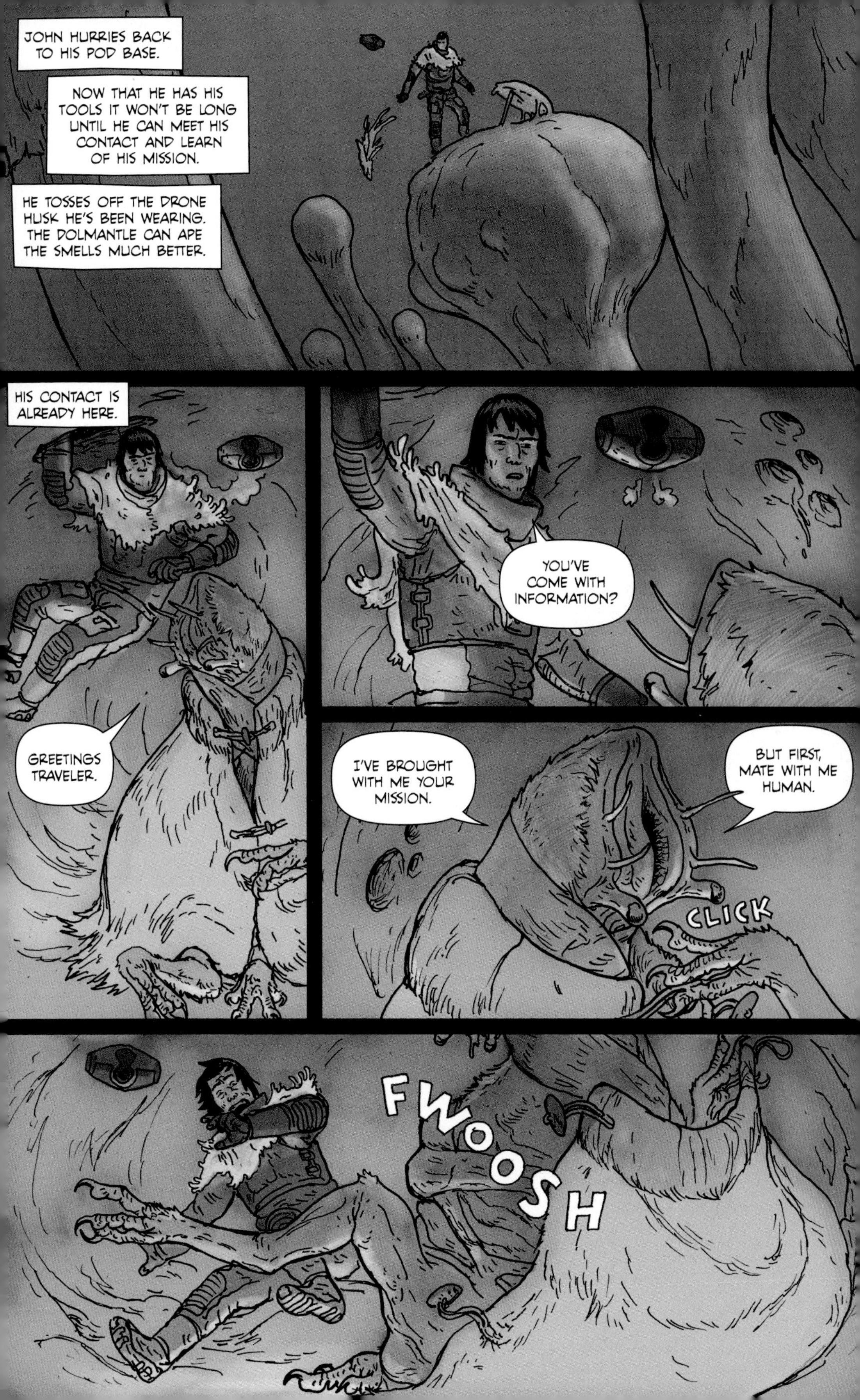
JOHN HURRIES BACK TO HIS POD BASE.
NOW THAT HE HAS HIS TOOLS IT WON'T BE LONG UNTIL HE CAN MEET HIS CONTACT AND LEARN OF HIS MISSION.
HE TOSSES OFF THE DRONE HUSK HE'S BEEN WEARING. THE DOLMANTLE CAN APE THE SMELLS MUCH BETTER.
HIS CONTACT IS ALREADY HERE.
GREETINGS TRAVELER.
YOU'VE COME WITH INFORMATION?
I'VE BROUGHT WITH ME YOUR MISSION.
BUT FIRST, MATE WITH ME HUMAN.
CLICK
FWOOSH

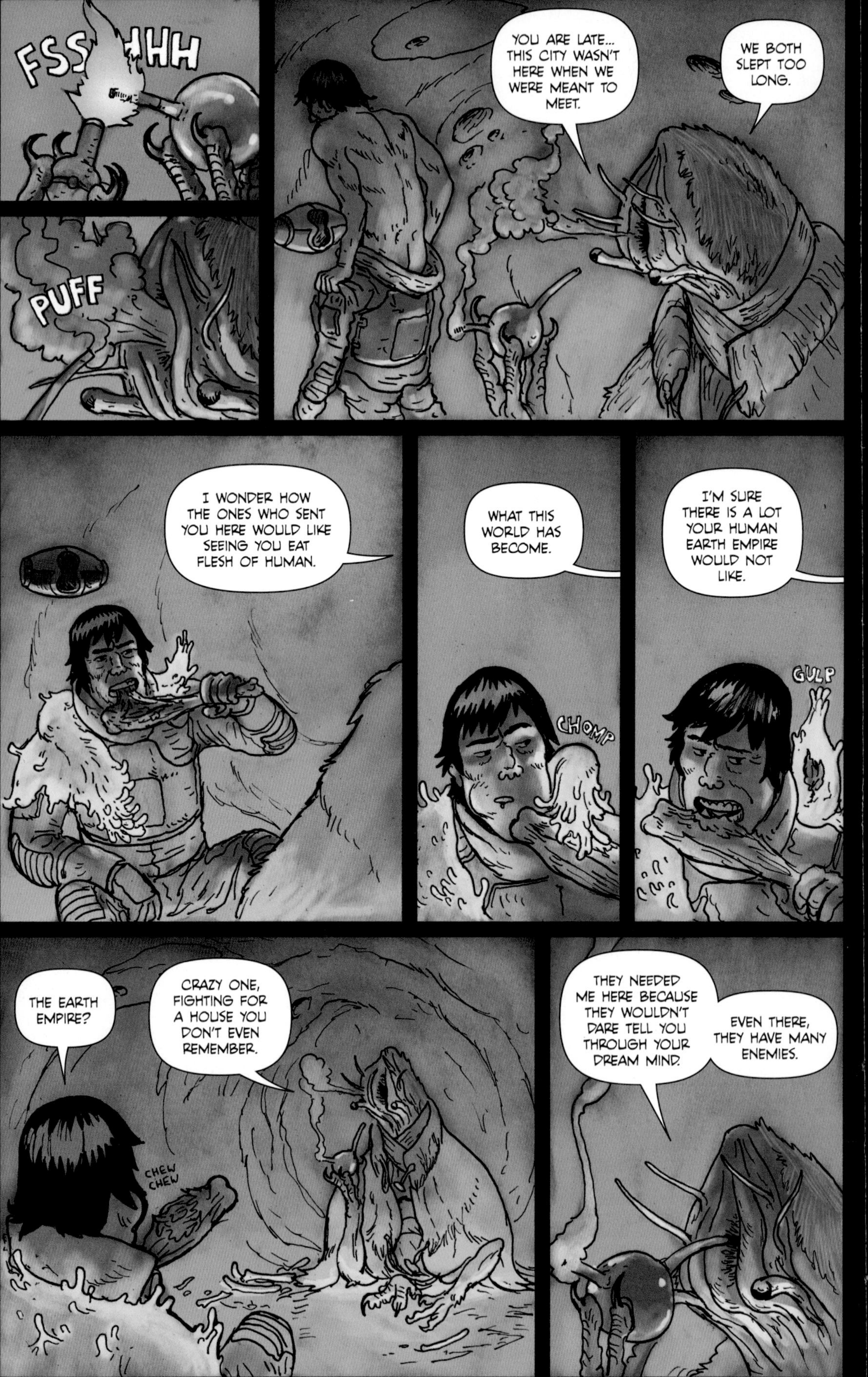
FSSHHH
PUFF
YOU ARE LATE... THIS CITY WASN'T HERE WHEN WE WERE MEANT TO MEET.
WE BOTH SLEPT TOO LONG.
I WONDER HOW THE ONES WHO SENT YOU HERE WOULD LIKE SEEING YOU EAT FLESH OF HUMAN.
WHAT THIS WORLD HAS BECOME.
CHOMP
I'M SURE THERE IS A LOT YOUR HUMAN EARTH EMPIRE WOULD NOT LIKE.
GULP
THE EARTH EMPIRE?
CRAZY ONE, FIGHTING FOR A HOUSE YOU DON'T EVEN REMEMBER.
CHEW CHEW
THEY NEEDED ME HERE BECAUSE THEY WOULDN'T DARE TELL YOU THROUGH YOUR DREAM MIND.
EVEN THERE, THEY HAVE MANY ENEMIES.

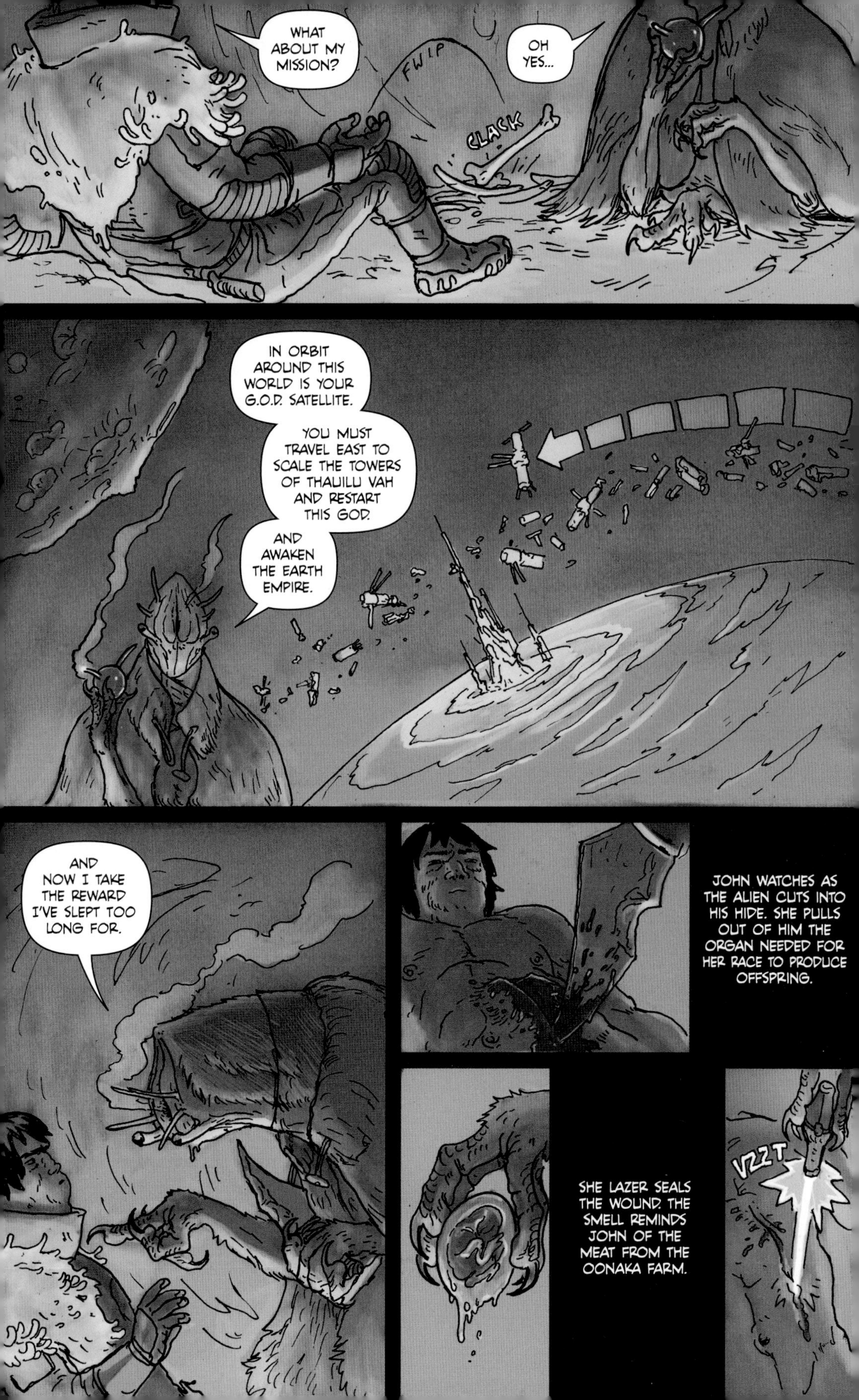
WHAT ABOUT MY MISSION?
FWIP
OH YES...
CLACK
IN ORBIT AROUND THIS WORLD IS YOUR G.O.D. SATELLITE.
YOU MUST TRAVEL EAST TO SCALE THE TOWERS OF THAUILU VAH AND RESTART THIS GOD.
AND AWAKEN THE EARTH EMPIRE.
AND NOW I TAKE THE REWARD I'VE SLEPT TOO LONG FOR.
JOHN WATCHES AS THE ALIEN CUTS INTO HIS HIDE. SHE PULLS OUT OF HIM THE ORGAN NEEDED FOR HER RACE TO PRODUCE OFFSPRING.
SHE LAZER SEALS THE WOUND. THE SMELL REMINDS JOHN OF THE MEAT FROM THE OONAKA FARM.
VZZT

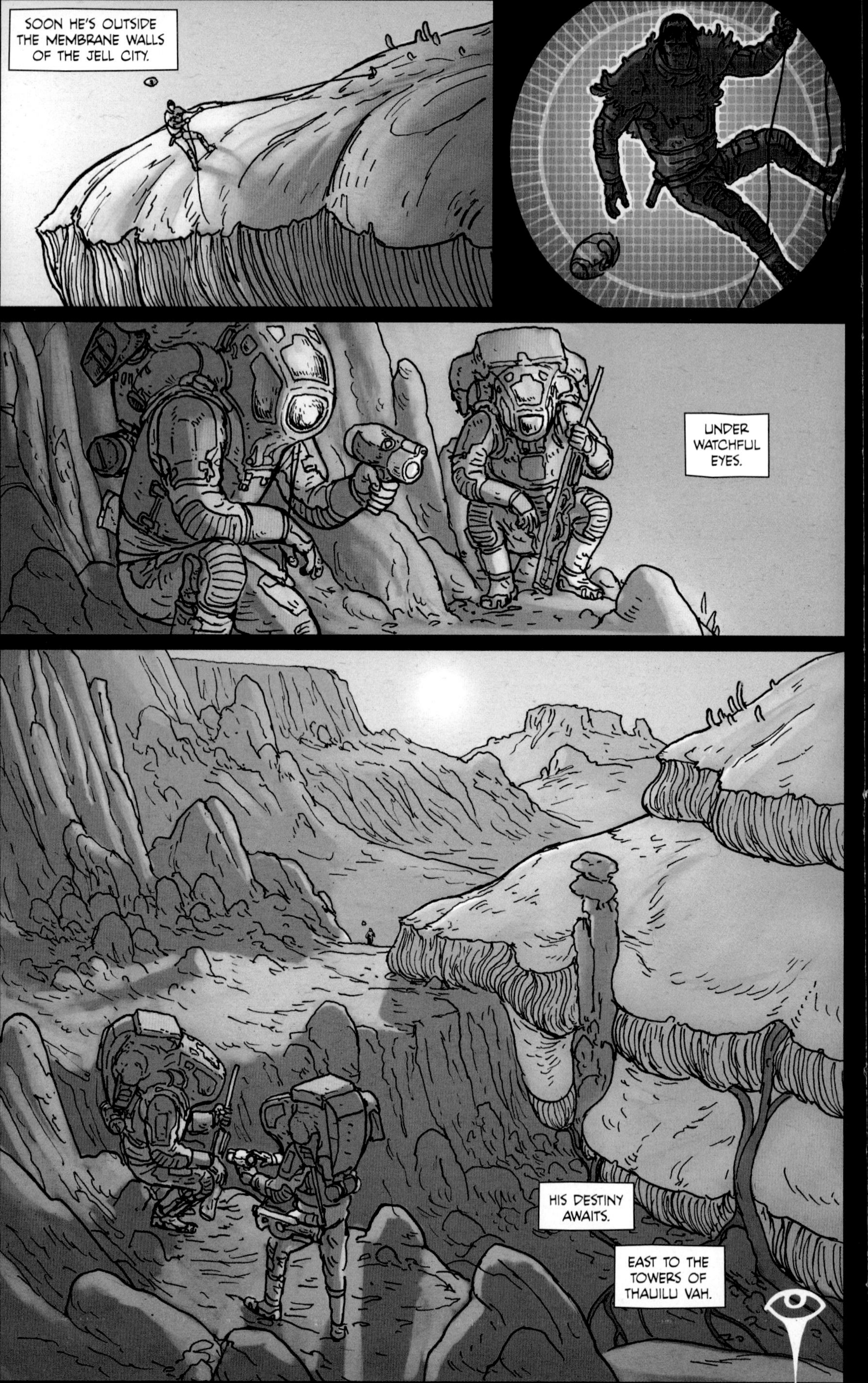
SOON HE'S OUTSIDE THE MEMBRANE WALLS OF THE JELL CITY.
UNDER WATCHFUL EYES.
HIS DESTINY AWAITS.
EAST TO THE TOWERS OF THAUILU VAH.

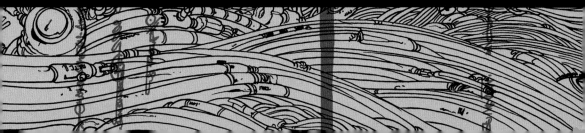

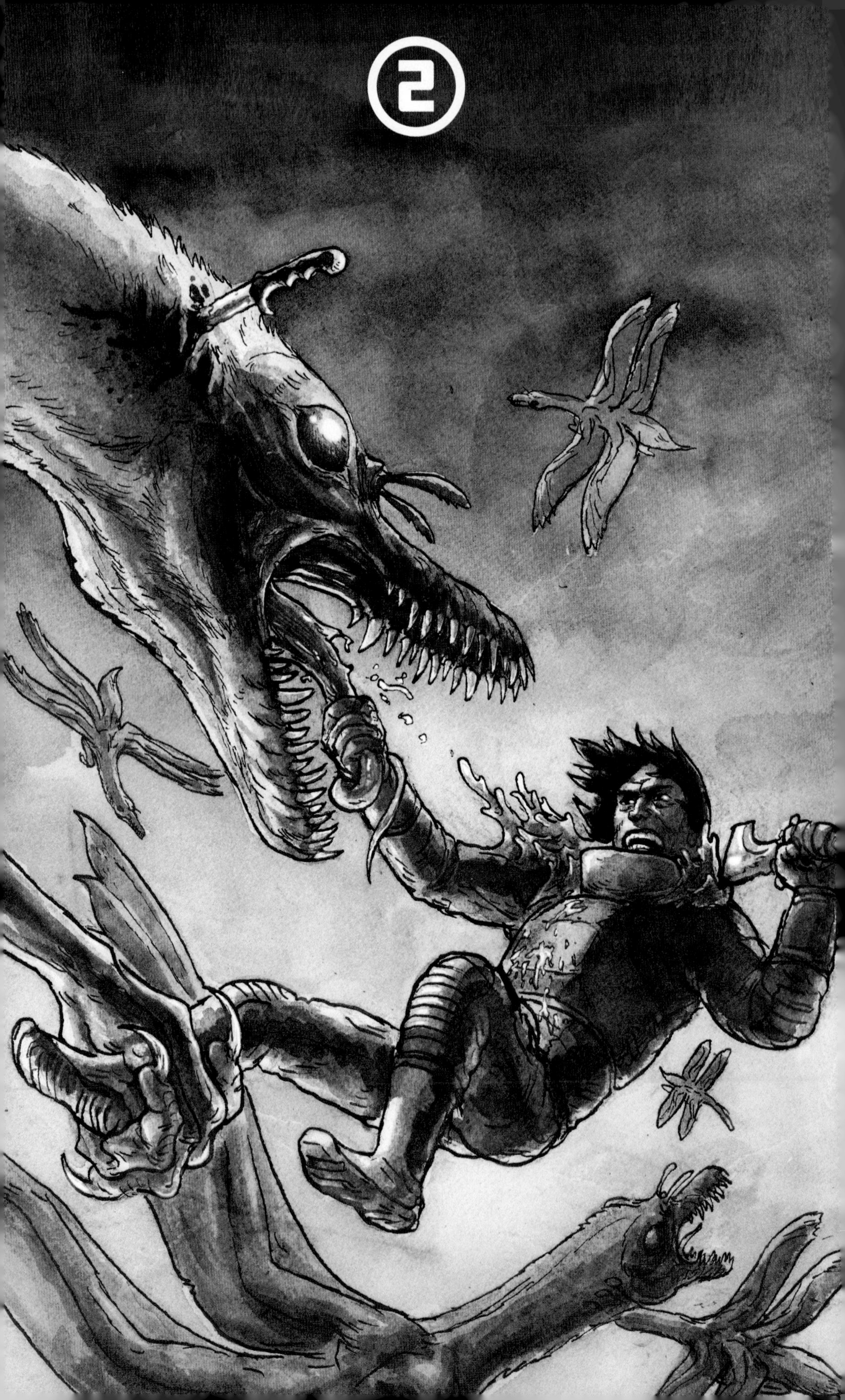
2

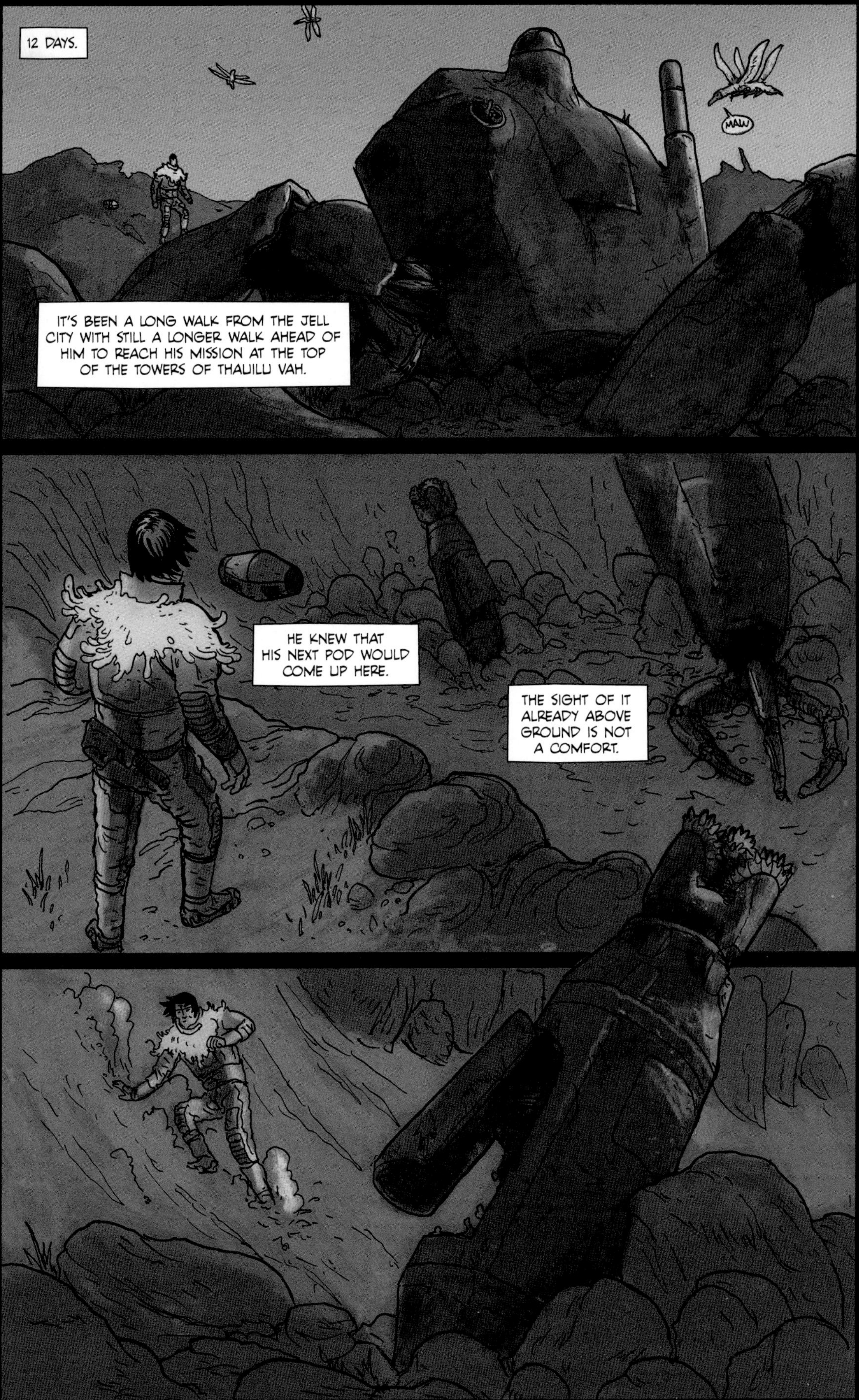
12 DAYS.
MAW
IT'S BEEN A LONG WALK FROM THE JELL CITY WITH STILL A LONGER WALK AHEAD OF HIM TO REACH HIS MISSION AT THE TOP OF THE TOWERS OF THAUILU VAH.
HE KNEW THAT HIS NEXT POD WOULD COME UP HERE.
THE SIGHT OF IT ALREADY ABOVE GROUND IS NOT A COMFORT.

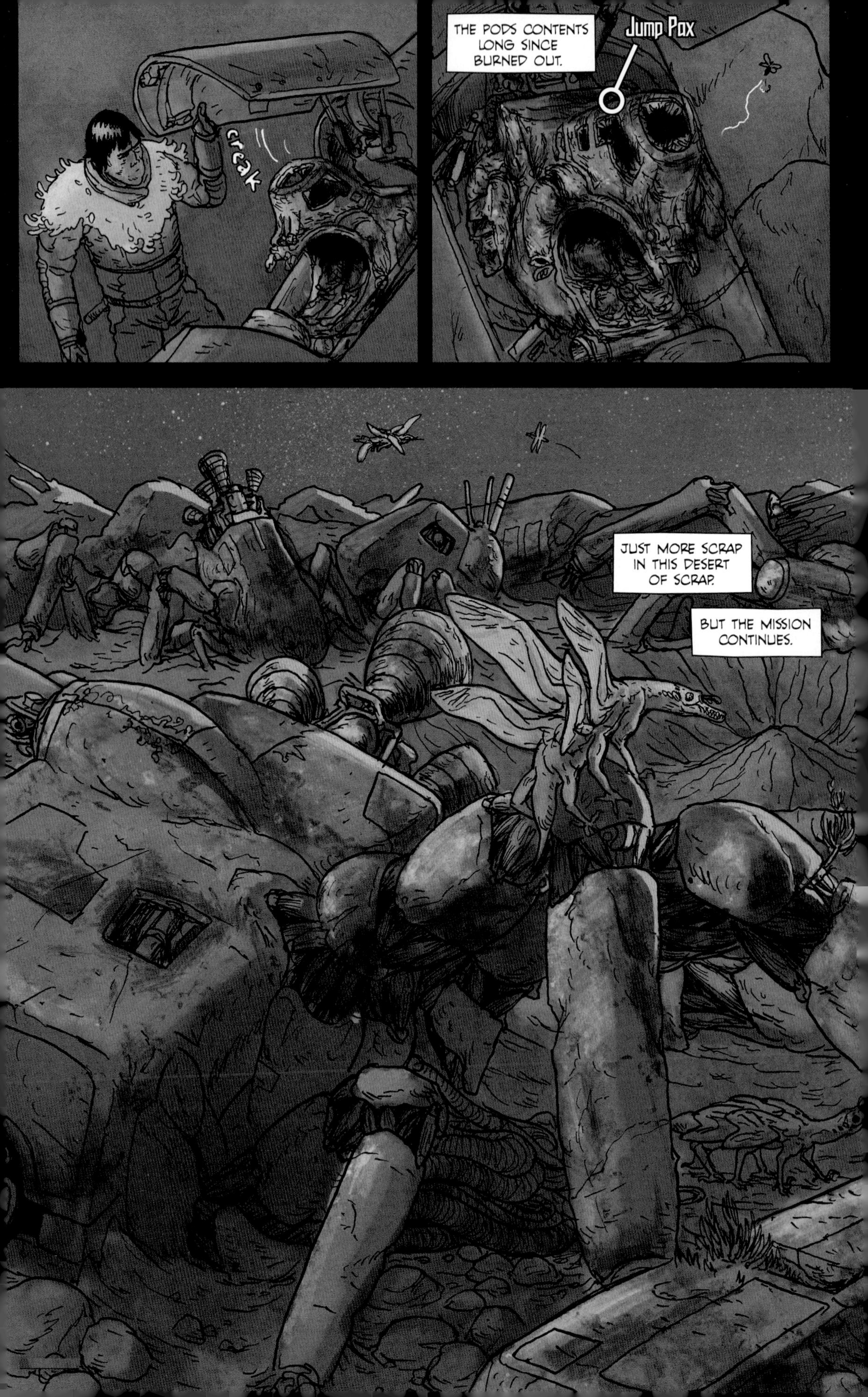
creak
THE PODS CONTENTS LONG SINCE BURNED OUT.
Jump Pax
JUST MORE SCRAP IN THIS DESERT OF SCRAP.
BUT THE MISSION CONTINUES.

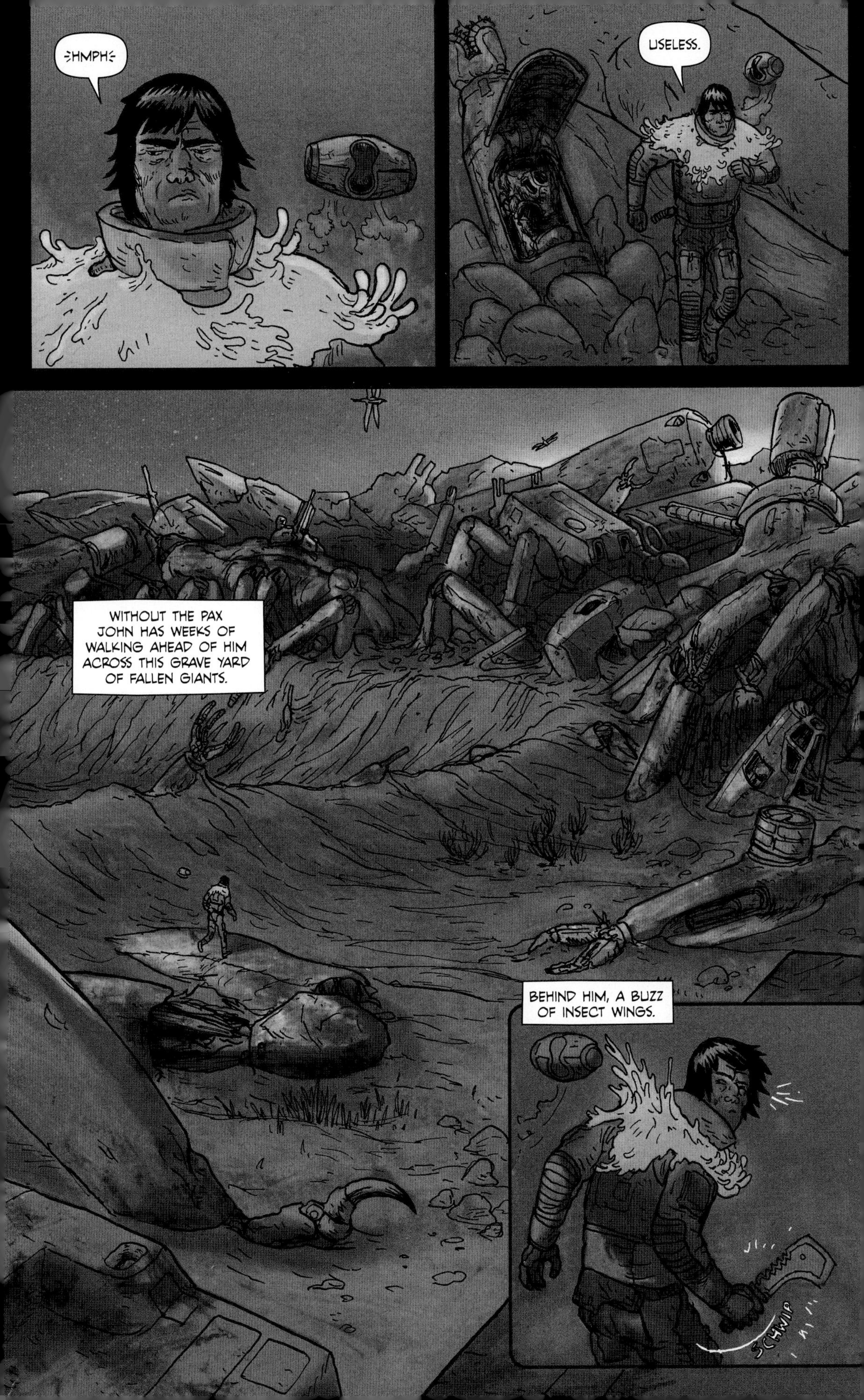

HMPH
USELESS.
WITHOUT THE PAX JOHN HAS WEEKS OF WALKING AHEAD OF HIM ACROSS THIS GRAVE YARD OF FALLEN GIANTS.
BEHIND HIM, A BUZZ OF INSECT WINGS.
SCHWIP

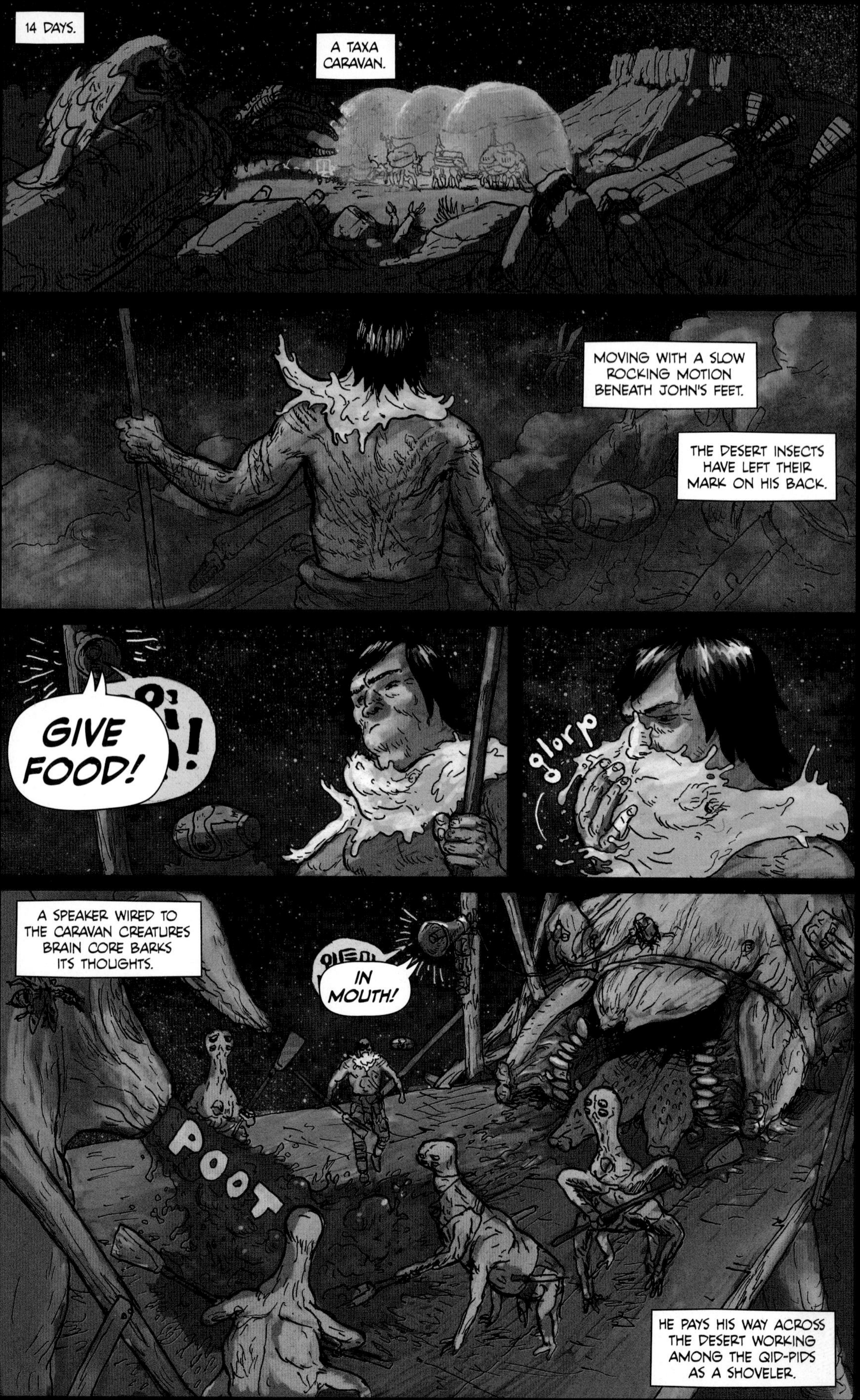
14 DAYS.
A TAXA CARAVAN.
MOVING WITH A SLOW ROCKING MOTION BENEATH JOHN'S FEET.
THE DESERT INSECTS HAVE LEFT THEIR MARK ON HIS BACK.
GIVE FOOD!
glorp
A SPEAKER WIRED TO THE CARAVAN CREATURES BRAIN CORE BARKS ITS THOUGHTS.
IN MOUTH!
POOT
HE PAYS HIS WAY ACROSS THE DESERT WORKING AMONG THE QID-PIDS AS A SHOVELER.

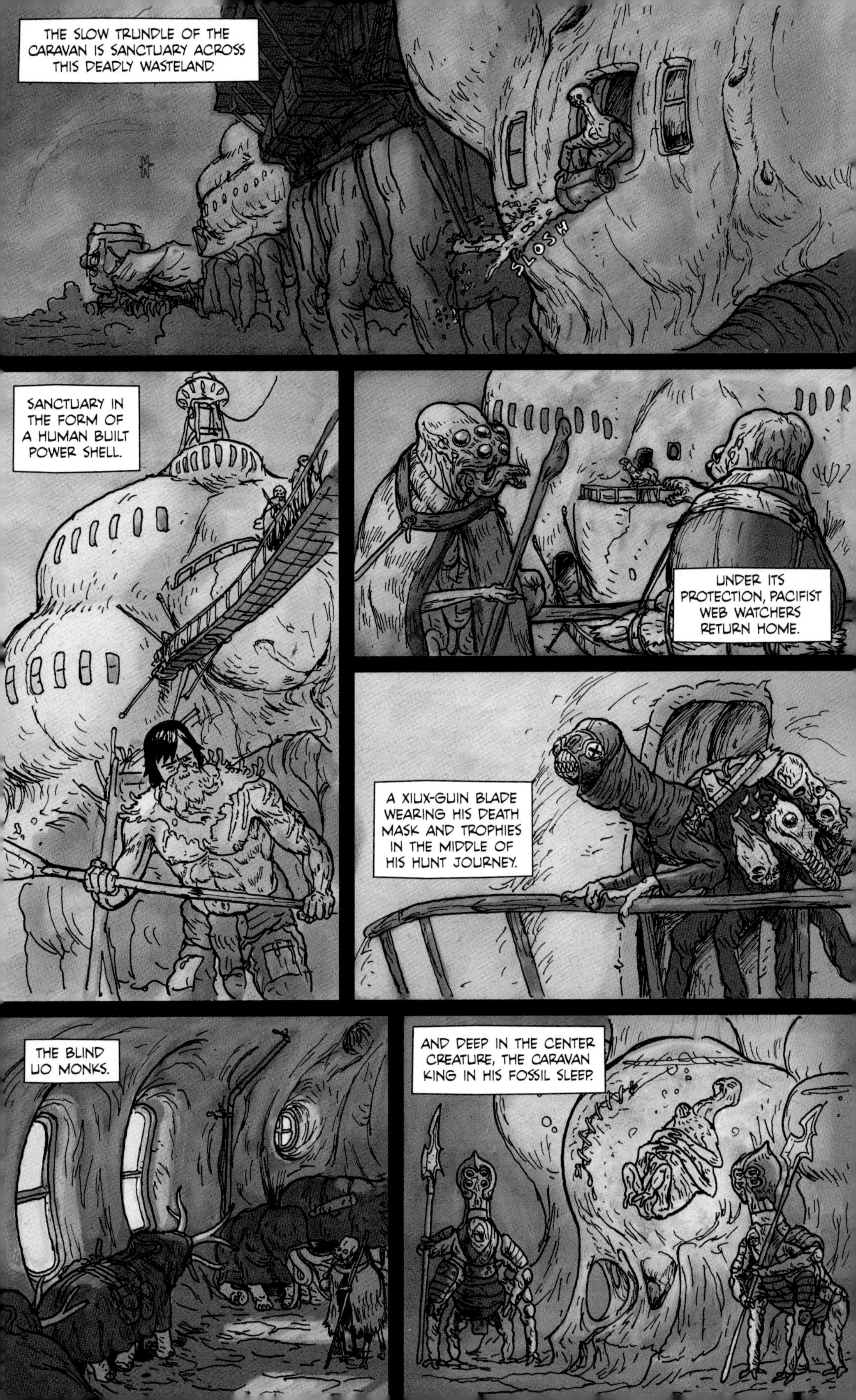

THE SLOW TRUNDLE OF THE CARAVAN IS SANCTUARY ACROSS THIS DEADLY WASTELAND.
SLOSH
SANCTUARY IN THE FORM OF A HUMAN BUILT POWER SHELL.
UNDER ITS PROTECTION, PACIFIST WEB WATCHERS RETURN HOME.
A XIUX-GUIN BLADE WEARING HIS DEATH MASK AND TROPHIES IN THE MIDDLE OF HIS HUNT JOURNEY.
THE BLIND UO MONKS.
AND DEEP IN THE CENTER CREATURE, THE CARAVAN KING IN HIS FOSSIL SLEEP.

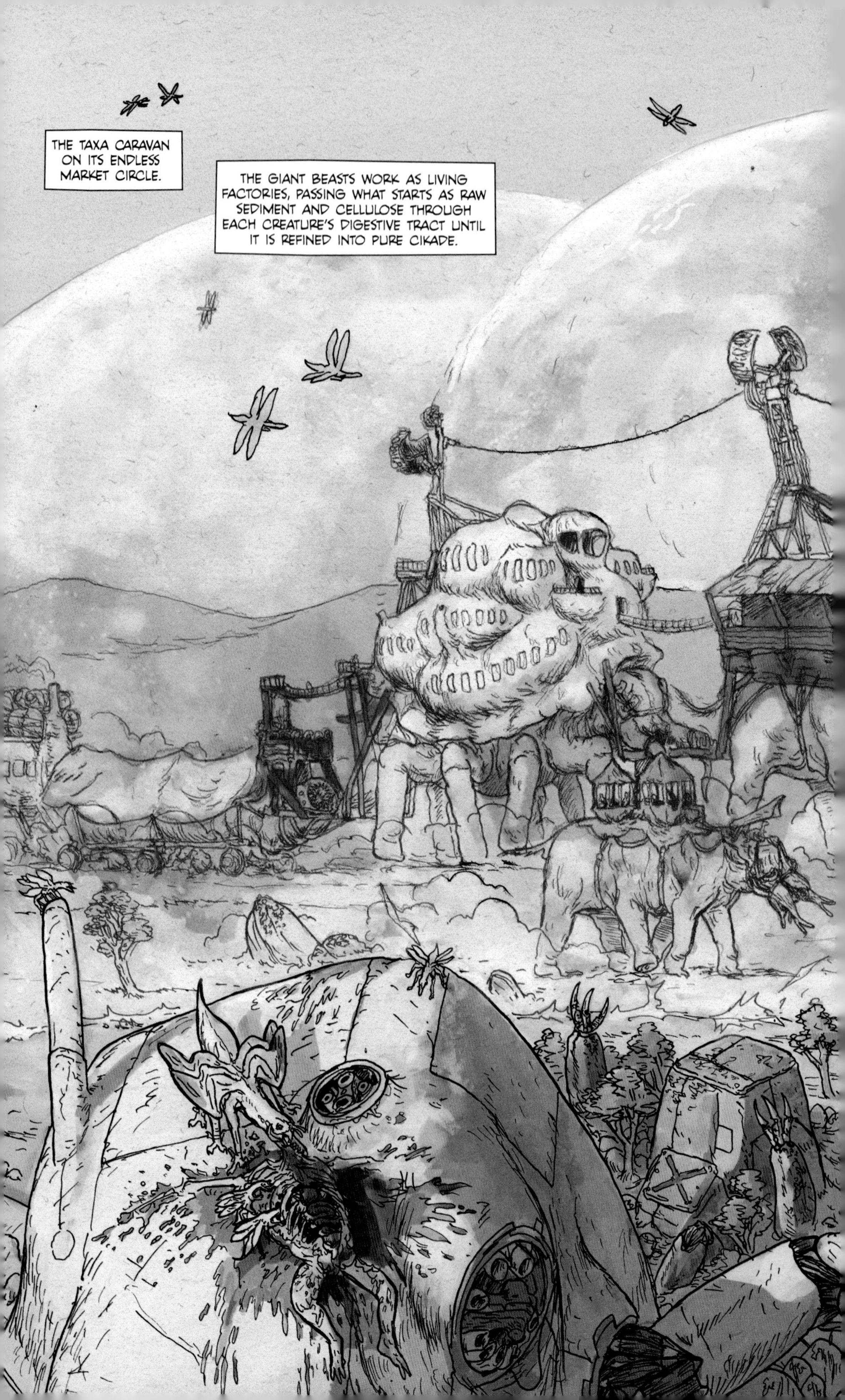
THE TAXA CARAVAN ON ITS ENDLESS MARKET CIRCLE.
THE GIANT BEASTS WORK AS LIVING FACTORIES, PASSING WHAT STARTS AS RAW SEDIMENT AND CELLULOSE THROUGH EACH CREATURE'S DIGESTIVE TRACT UNTIL IT IS REFINED INTO PURE CIKADE.

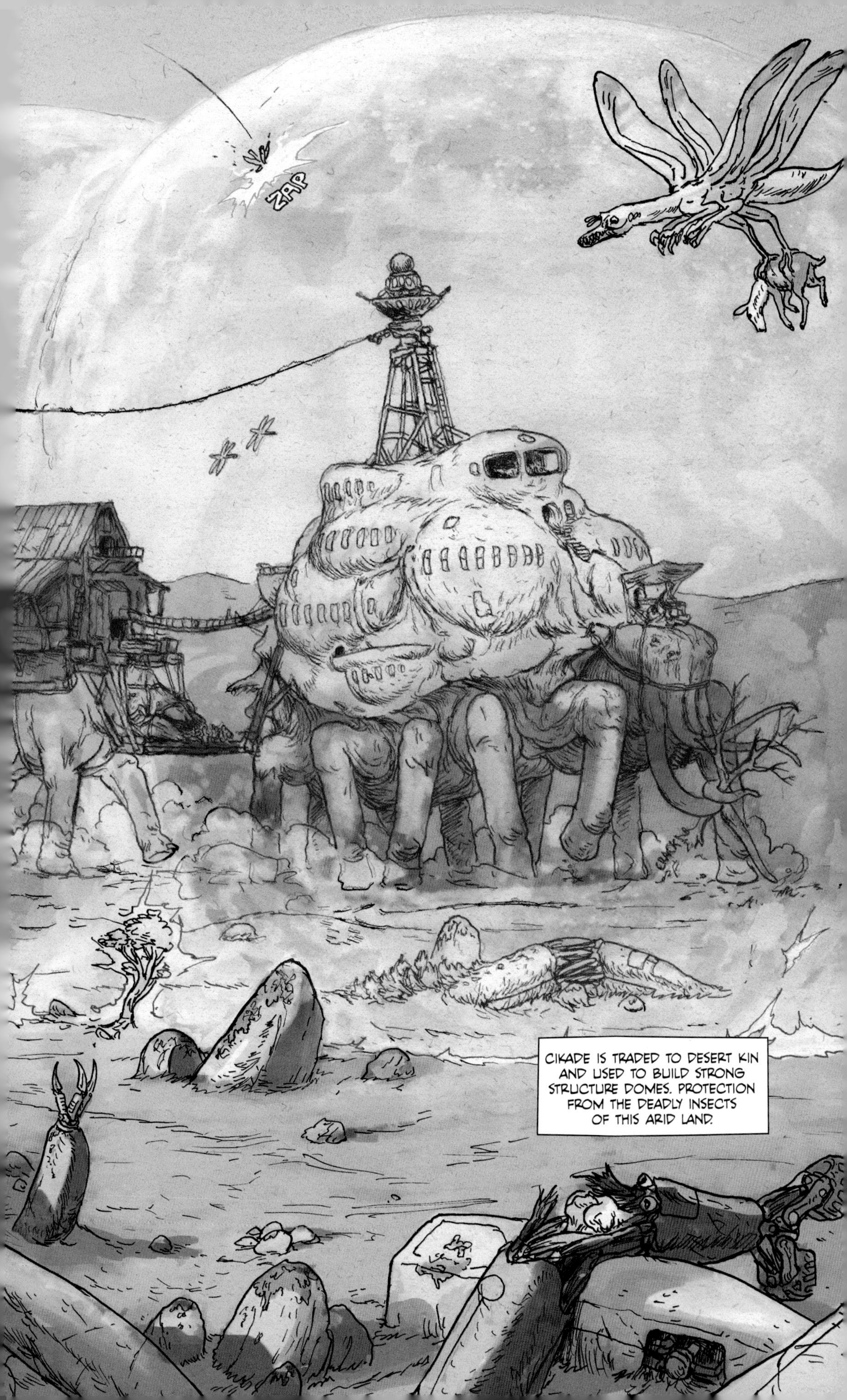
ZAP
CIKADE IS TRADED TO DESERT KIN AND USED TO BUILD STRONG STRUCTURE DOMES. PROTECTION FROM THE DEADLY INSECTS OF THIS ARID LAND.

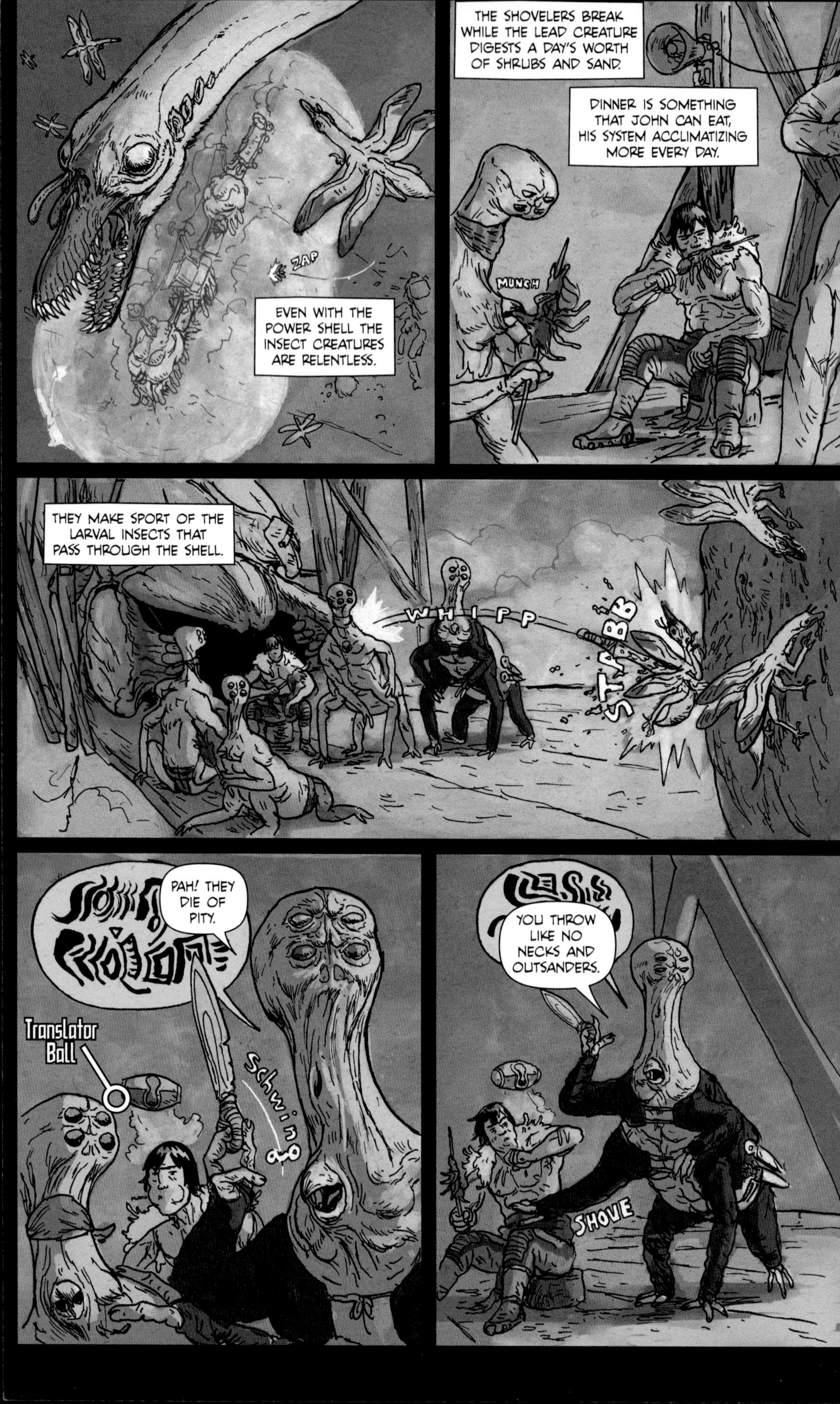
ZAP
EVEN WITH THE POWER SHELL THE INSECT CREATURES ARE RELENTLESS.
THE SHOVELERS BREAK WHILE THE LEAD CREATURE DIGESTS A DAY'S WORTH OF SHRUBS AND SAND.
DINNER IS SOMETHING THAT JOHN CAN EAT, HIS SYSTEM ACCLIMATIZING MORE EVERY DAY.
MUNCH
THEY MAKE SPORT OF THE LARVAL INSECTS THAT PASS THROUGH THE SHELL.
WHIPP
STABB
PAH! THEY DIE OF PITY.
Translator Ball
Schwing
YOU THROW LIKE NO NECKS AND OUTSANDERS.
SHOVE

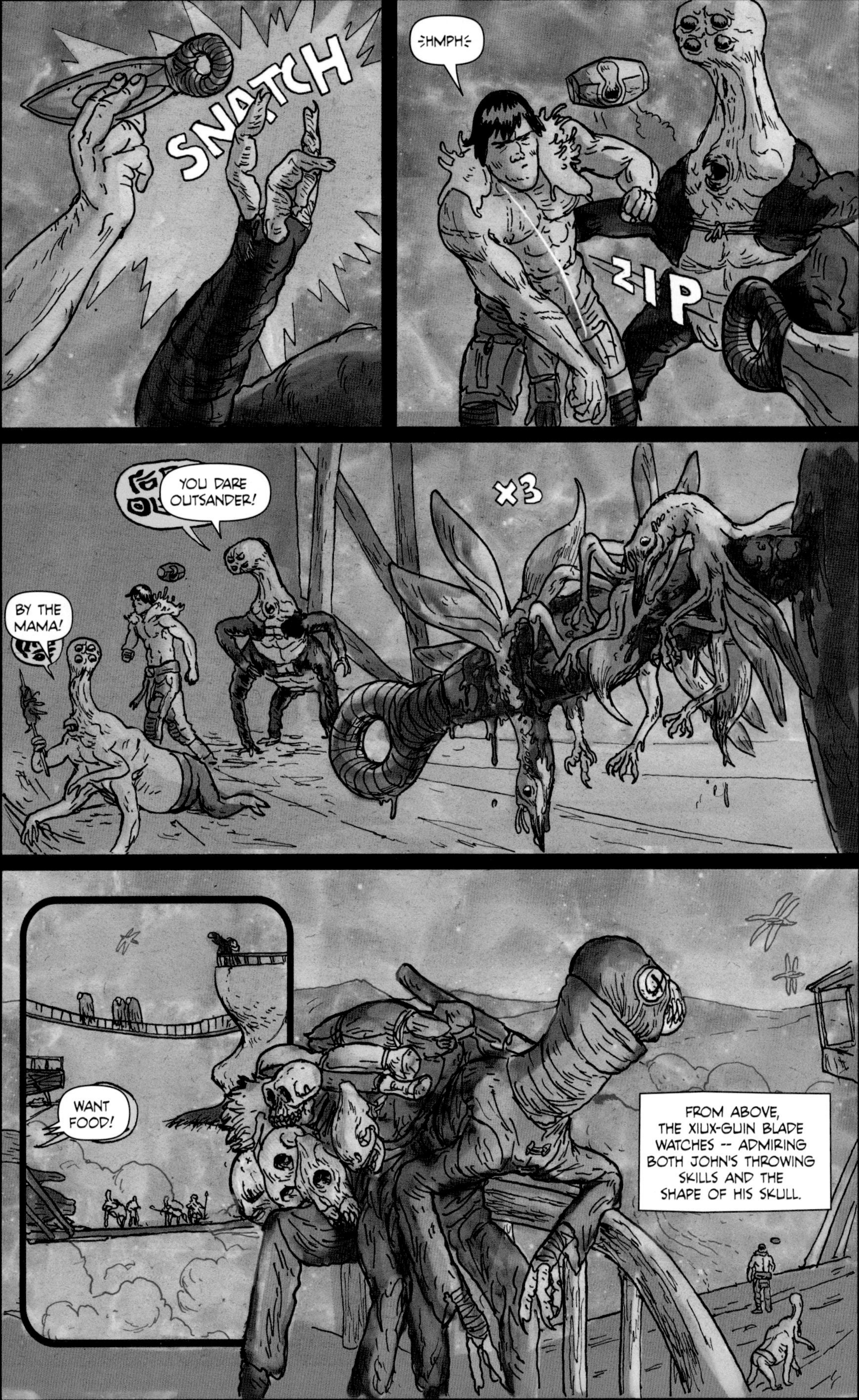
SNATCH
HMPH
ZIP
YOU DARE OUTSANDER!
BY THE MAMA!
×3
WANT FOOD!
FROM ABOVE, THE XIUX-GUIN BLADE WATCHES -- ADMIRING BOTH JOHN'S THROWING SKILLS AND THE SHAPE OF HIS SKULL.

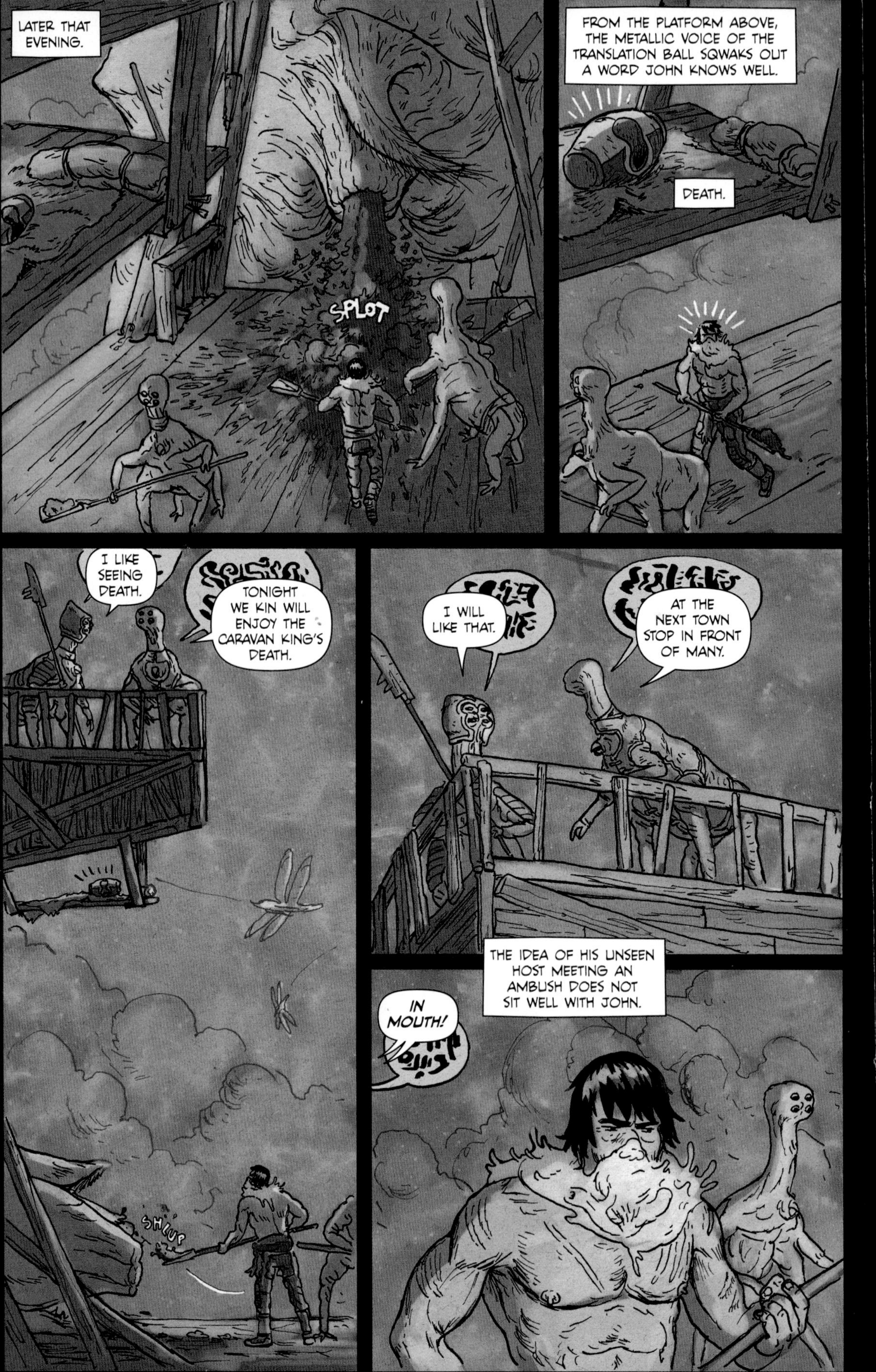
LATER THAT EVENING.
SPLOT
FROM THE PLATFORM ABOVE, THE METALLIC VOICE OF THE TRANSLATION BALL SQWAKS OUT A WORD JOHN KNOWS WELL.
DEATH.
I LIKE SEEING DEATH.
TONIGHT WE KIN WILL ENJOY THE CARAVAN KING'S DEATH.
SHLUP
I WILL LIKE THAT.
AT THE NEXT TOWN STOP IN FRONT OF MANY.
THE IDEA OF HIS UNSEEN HOST MEETING AN AMBUSH DOES NOT SIT WELL WITH JOHN.
IN MOUTH!

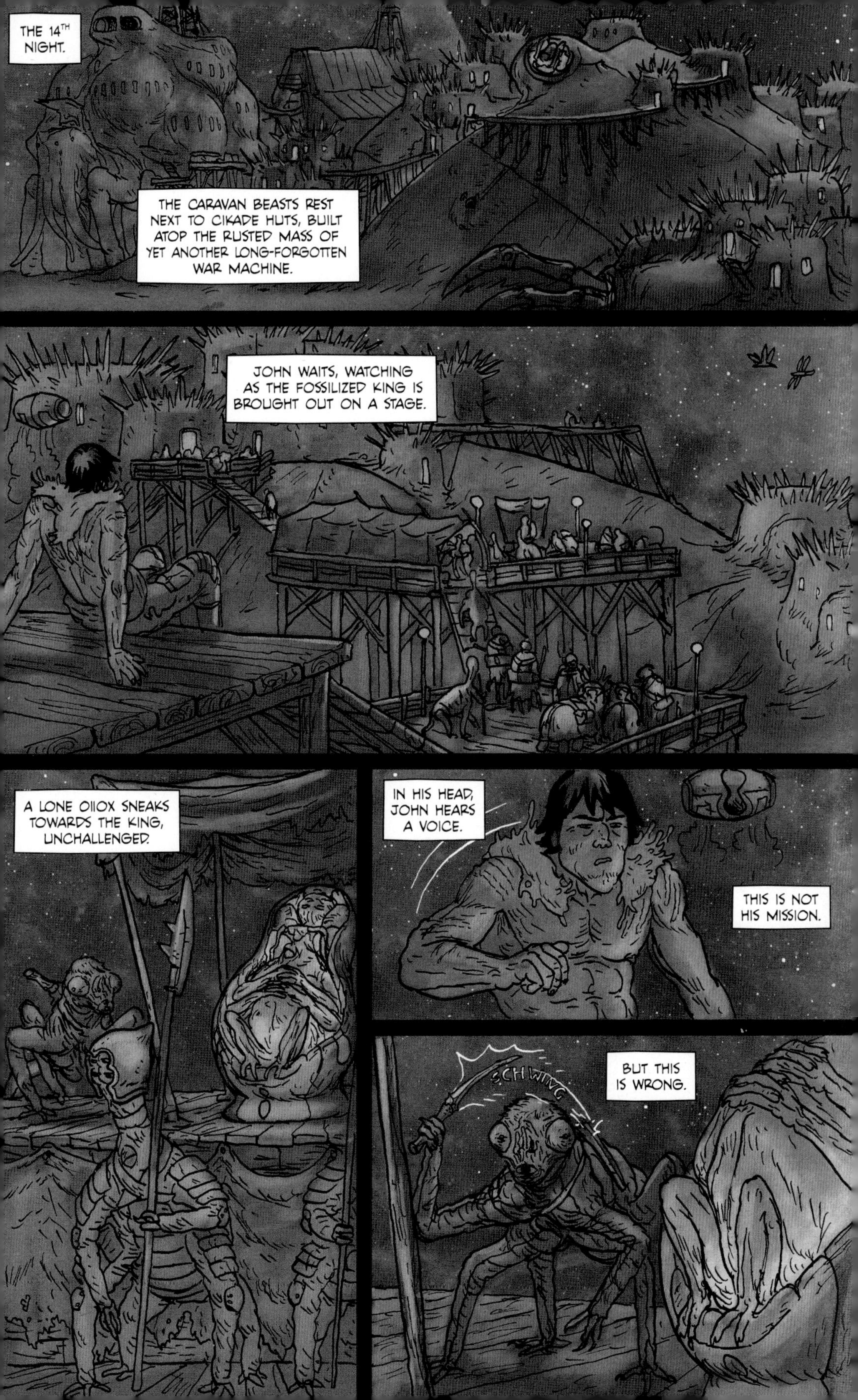
THE 14TH NIGHT.
THE CARAVAN BEASTS REST NEXT TO CIKADE HUTS, BUILT ATOP THE RUSTED MASS OF YET ANOTHER LONG-FORGOTTEN WAR MACHINE.
JOHN WAITS, WATCHING AS THE FOSSILIZED KING IS BROUGHT OUT ON A STAGE.
A LONE OIIOX SNEAKS TOWARDS THE KING, UNCHALLENGED.
IN HIS HEAD, JOHN HEARS A VOICE.
THIS IS NOT HIS MISSION.
SCHWING
BUT THIS IS WRONG.

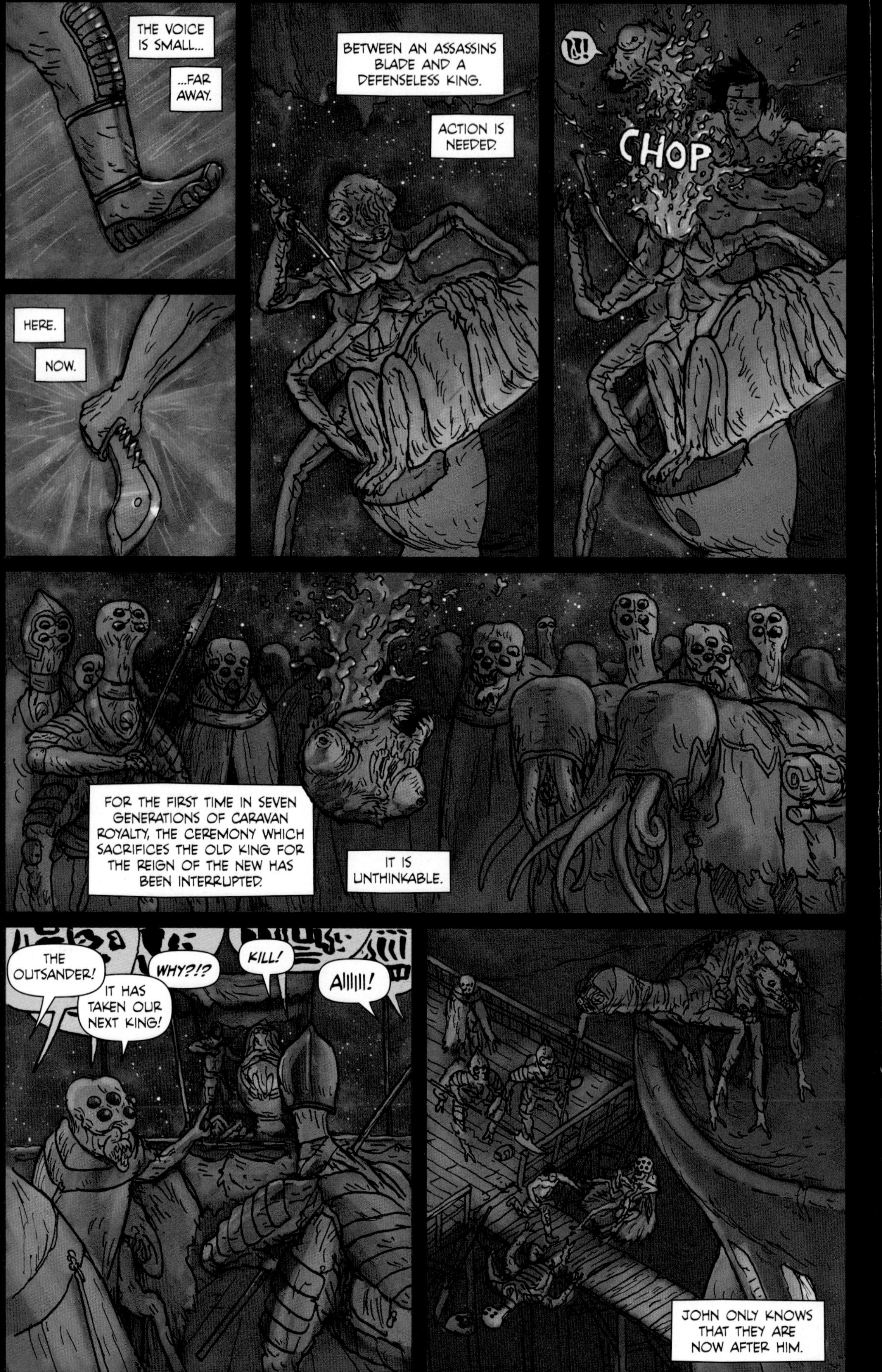
THE VOICE IS SMALL...
...FAR AWAY.
BETWEEN AN ASSASSINS BLADE AND A DEFENSELESS KING.
ACTION IS NEEDED.
?!!
CHOP
HERE.
NOW.
FOR THE FIRST TIME IN SEVEN GENERATIONS OF CARAVAN ROYALTY, THE CEREMONY WHICH SACRIFICES THE OLD KING FOR THE REIGN OF THE NEW HAS BEEN INTERRUPTED.
IT IS UNTHINKABLE.
THE OUTSANDER!
IT HAS TAKEN OUR NEXT KING!
WHY?!?
KILL!
AIIIII!
JOHN ONLY KNOWS THAT THEY ARE NOW AFTER HIM.

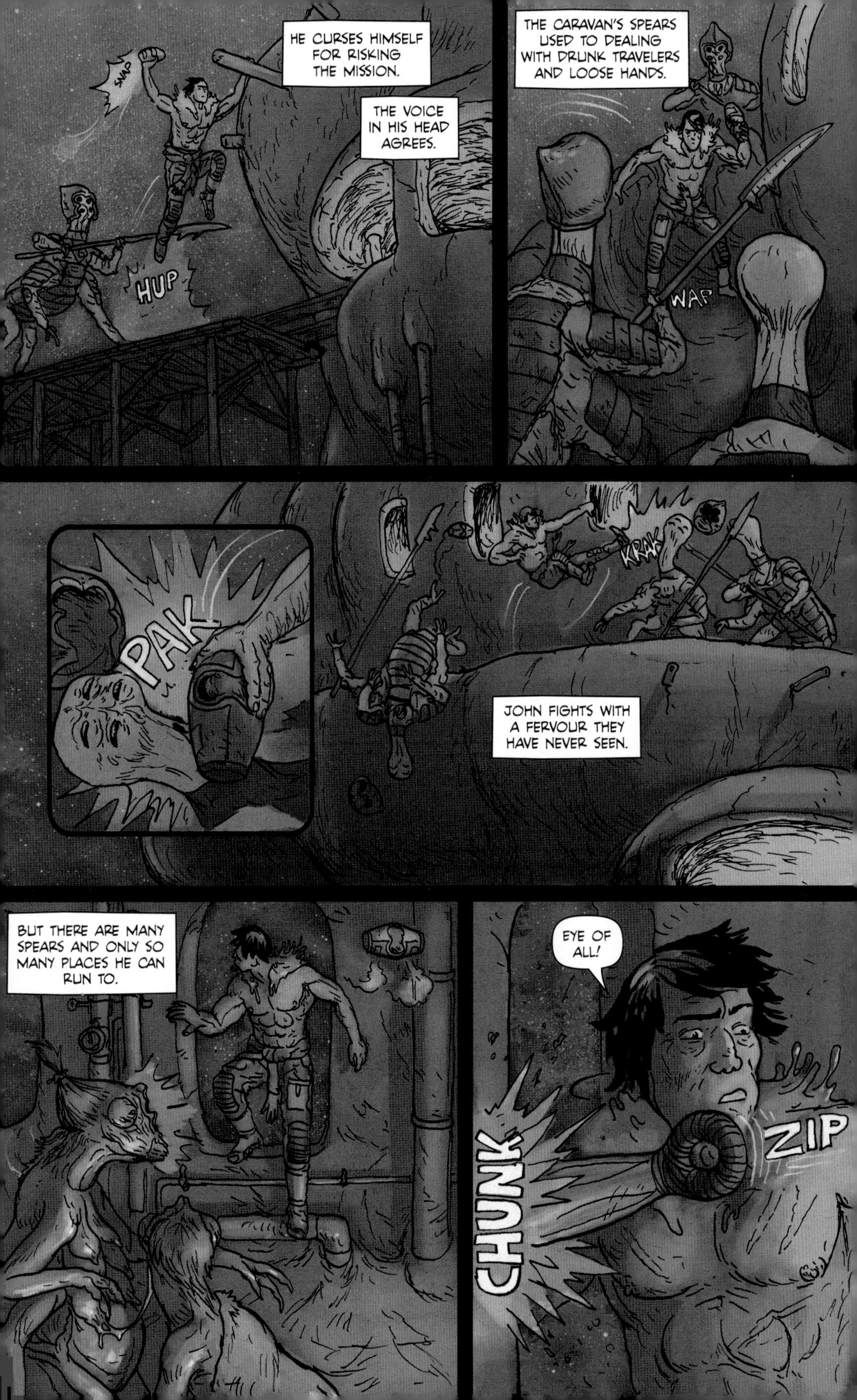
SNAP
HE CURSES HIMSELF FOR RISKING THE MISSION.
THE VOICE IN HIS HEAD AGREES.
HUP
THE CARAVAN'S SPEARS USED TO DEALING WITH DRUNK TRAVELERS AND LOOSE HANDS.
WAP
PAK
KRAK
JOHN FIGHTS WITH A FERVOUR THEY HAVE NEVER SEEN.
BUT THERE ARE MANY SPEARS AND ONLY SO MANY PLACES HE CAN RUN TO.
EYE OF ALL!
CHUNK
ZIP

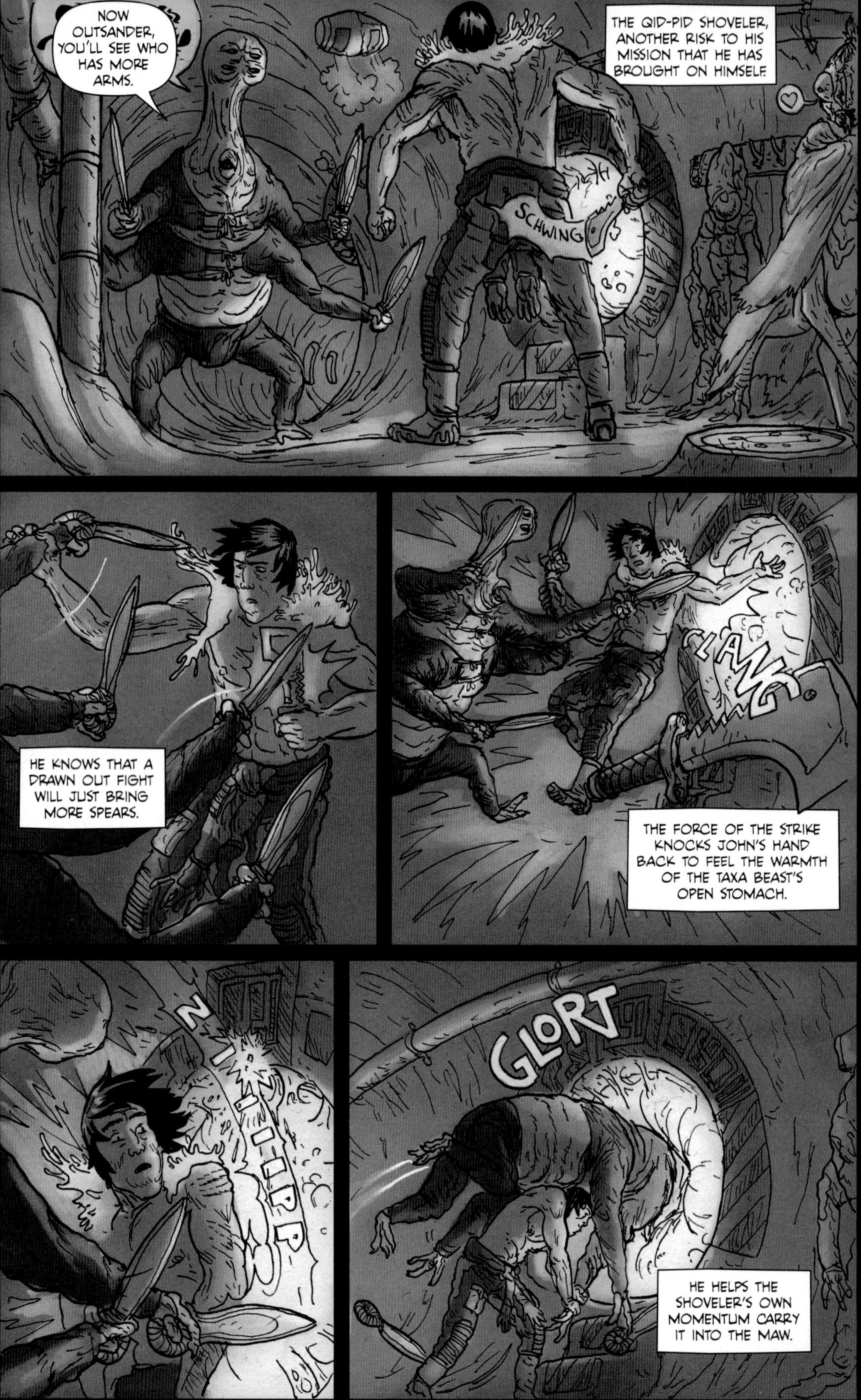

NOW OUTSANDER, YOU'LL SEE WHO HAS MORE ARMS.
THE QID-PID SHOVELER, ANOTHER RISK TO HIS MISSION THAT HE HAS BROUGHT ON HIMSELF.
SCHWING
HE KNOWS THAT A DRAWN OUT FIGHT WILL JUST BRING MORE SPEARS.
CLANG
THE FORCE OF THE STRIKE KNOCKS JOHN'S HAND BACK TO FEEL THE WARMTH OF THE TAXA BEAST'S OPEN STOMACH.
GLORT
HE HELPS THE SHOVELER'S OWN MOMENTUM CARRY IT INTO THE MAW.

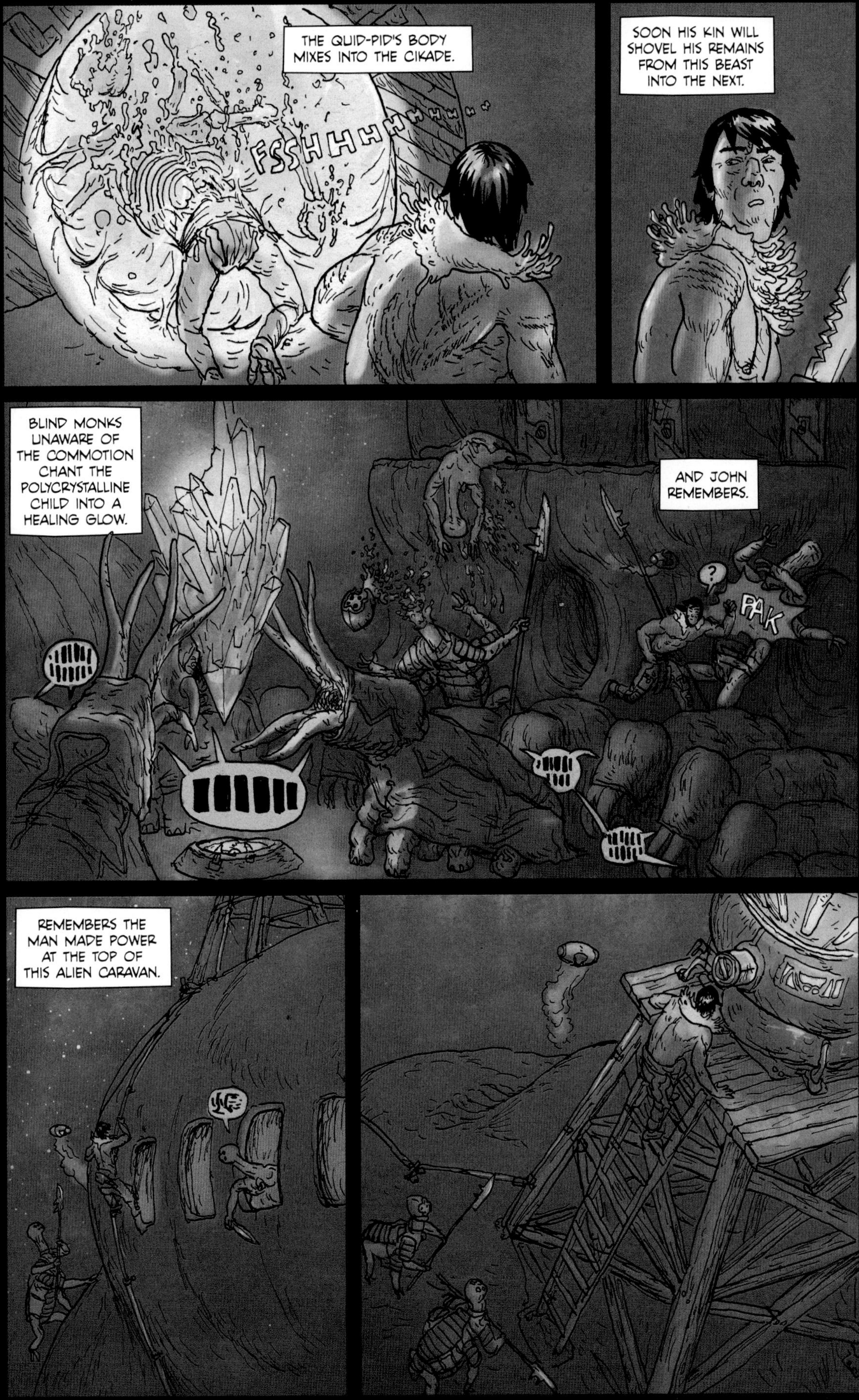
THE QUID-PID'S BODY MIXES INTO THE CIKADE.
FSSHHHHHHHHHHH
SOON HIS KIN WILL SHOVEL HIS REMAINS FROM THIS BEAST INTO THE NEXT.
BLIND MONKS UNAWARE OF THE COMMOTION CHANT THE POLYCRYSTALLINE CHILD INTO A HEALING GLOW.
AND JOHN REMEMBERS.
?
PAK
REMEMBERS THE MAN MADE POWER AT THE TOP OF THIS ALIEN CARAVAN.

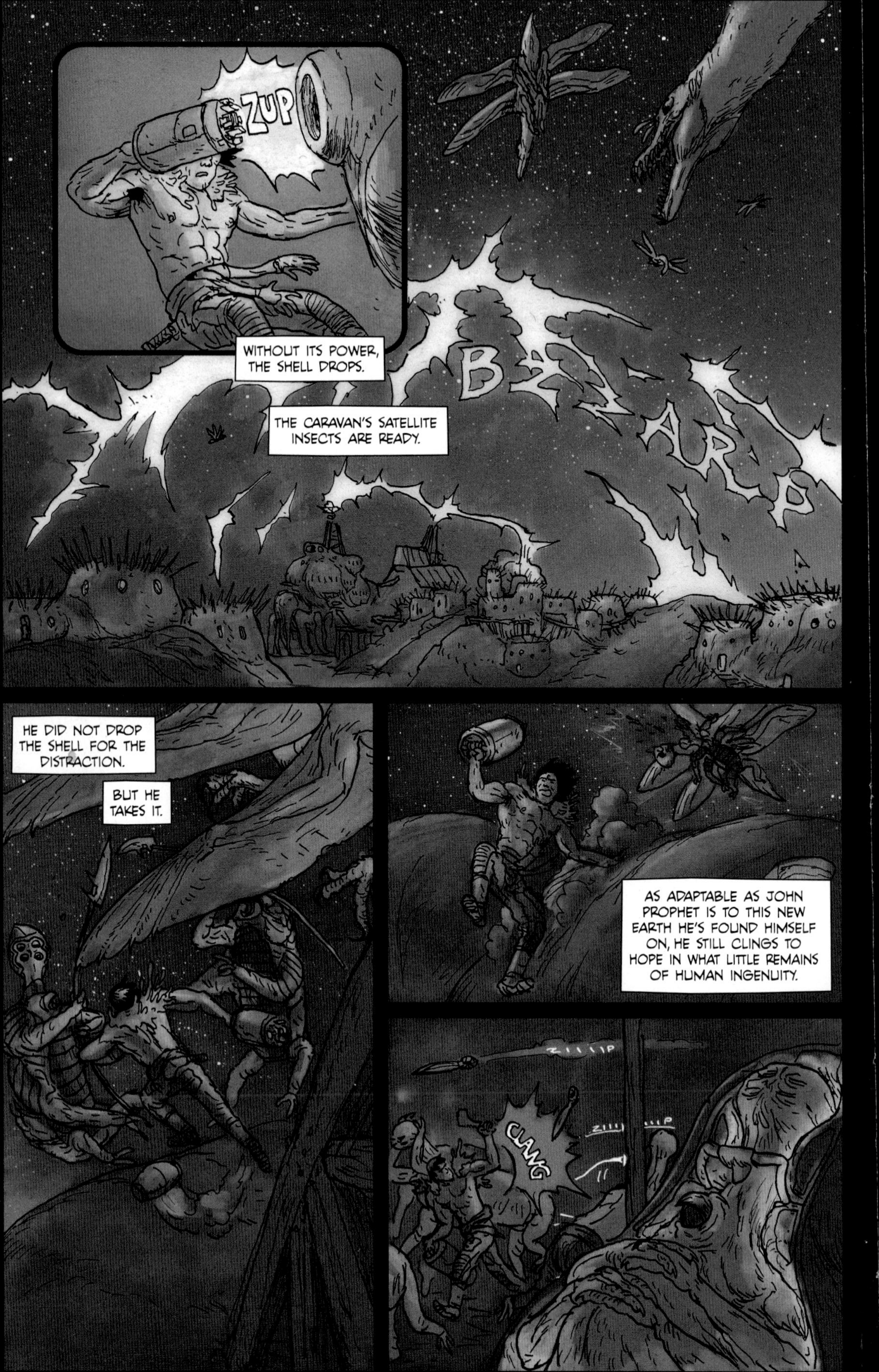
ZUP
WITHOUT ITS POWER, THE SHELL DROPS.
THE CARAVAN'S SATELLITE INSECTS ARE READY.
BZZARP
HE DID NOT DROP THE SHELL FOR THE DISTRACTION.
BUT HE TAKES IT.
AS ADAPTABLE AS JOHN PROPHET IS TO THIS NEW EARTH HE'S FOUND HIMSELF ON, HE STILL CLINGS TO HOPE IN WHAT LITTLE REMAINS OF HUMAN INGENUITY.
ZIIIIP
CLANG
ZIIIIIIP

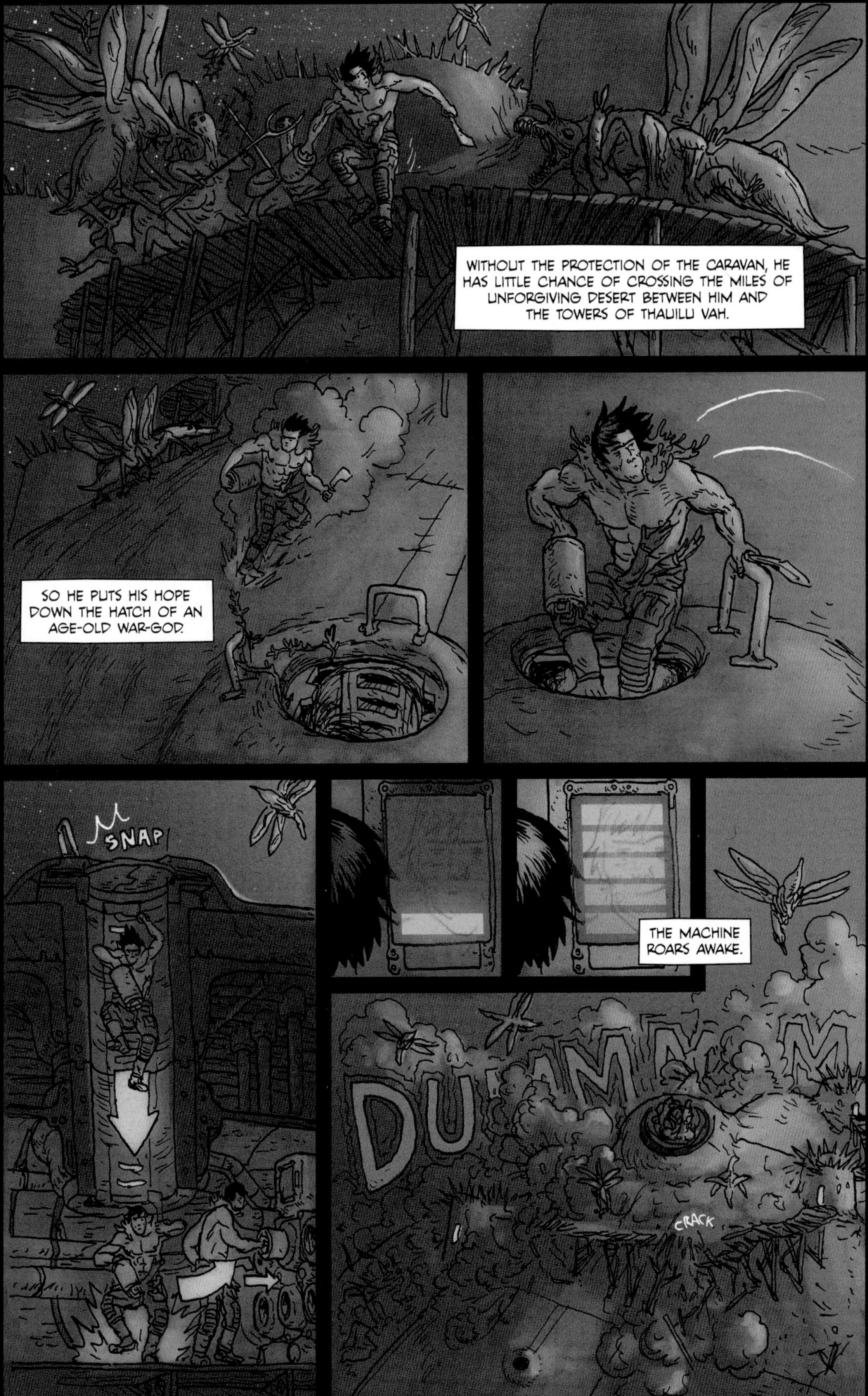
WITHOUT THE PROTECTION OF THE CARAVAN, HE HAS LITTLE CHANCE OF CROSSING THE MILES OF UNFORGIVING DESERT BETWEEN HIM AND THE TOWERS OF THAUILU VAH.
SO HE PUTS HIS HOPE DOWN THE HATCH OF AN AGE-OLD WAR-GOD.
SNAP
THE MACHINE ROARS AWAKE.
CRACK

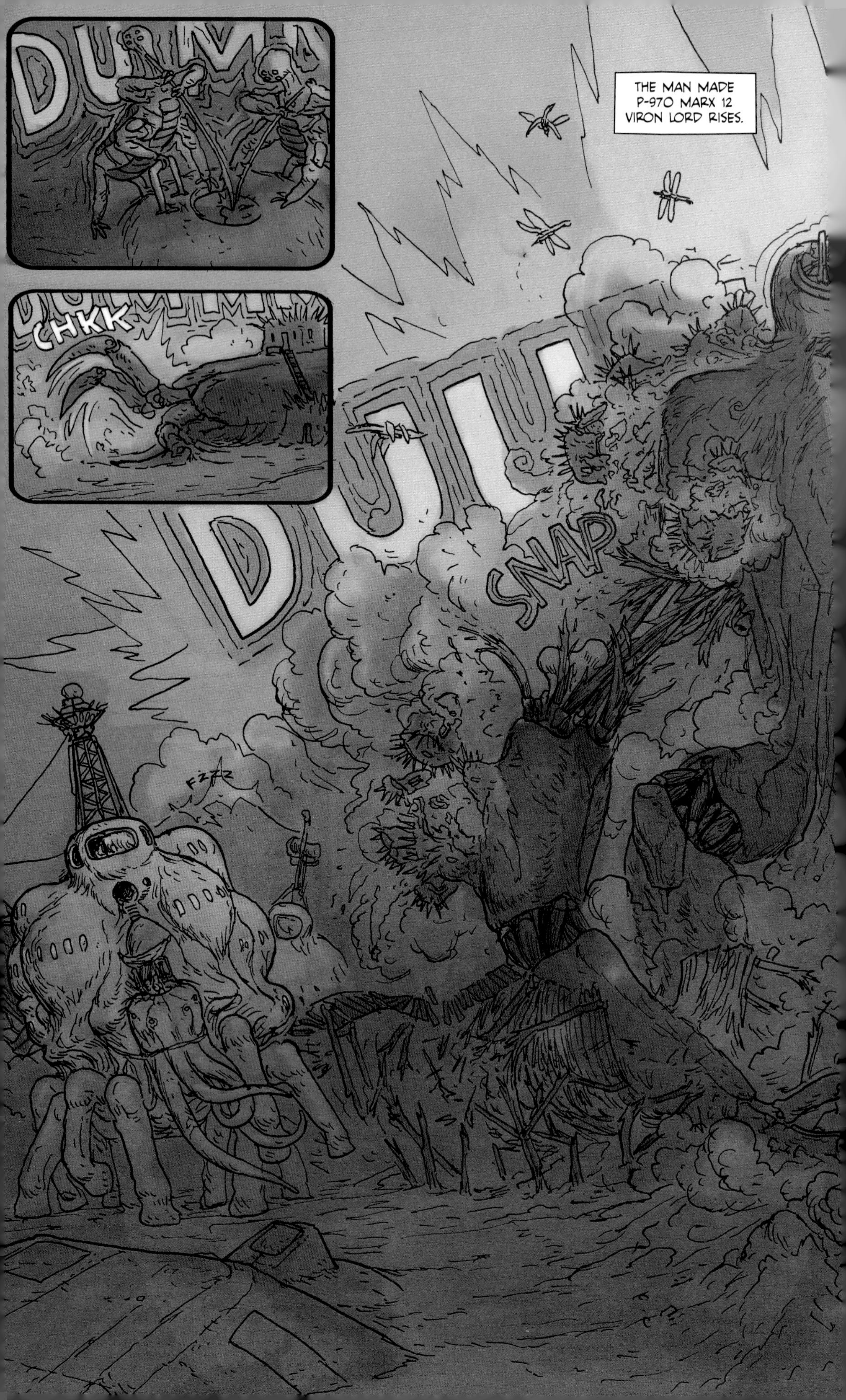
DUM
CHKK
THE MAN MADE P-970 MARX 12 VIRON LORD RISES.
DUM
SNAP
FZZZ

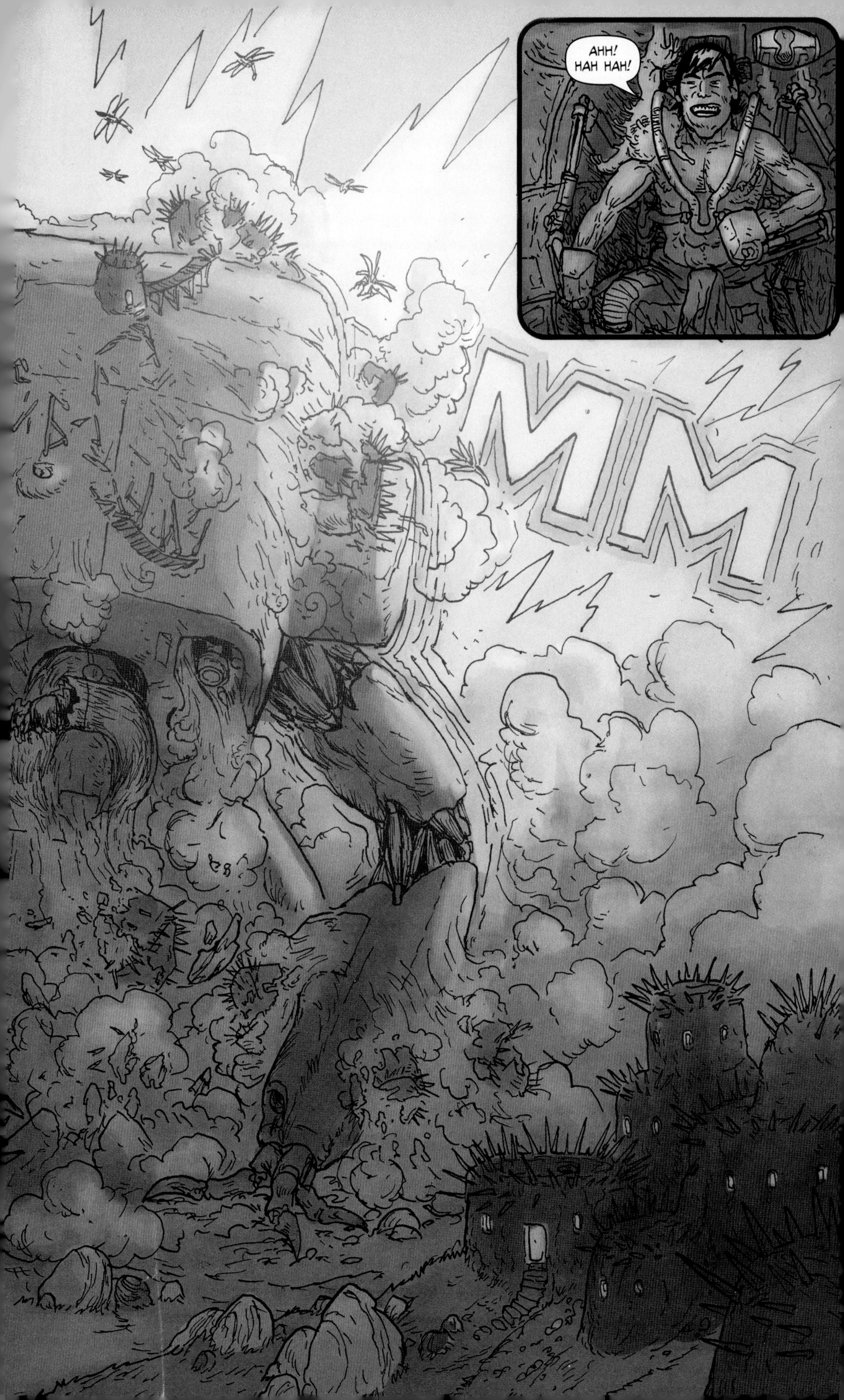
AHH! HAH HAH!
MM

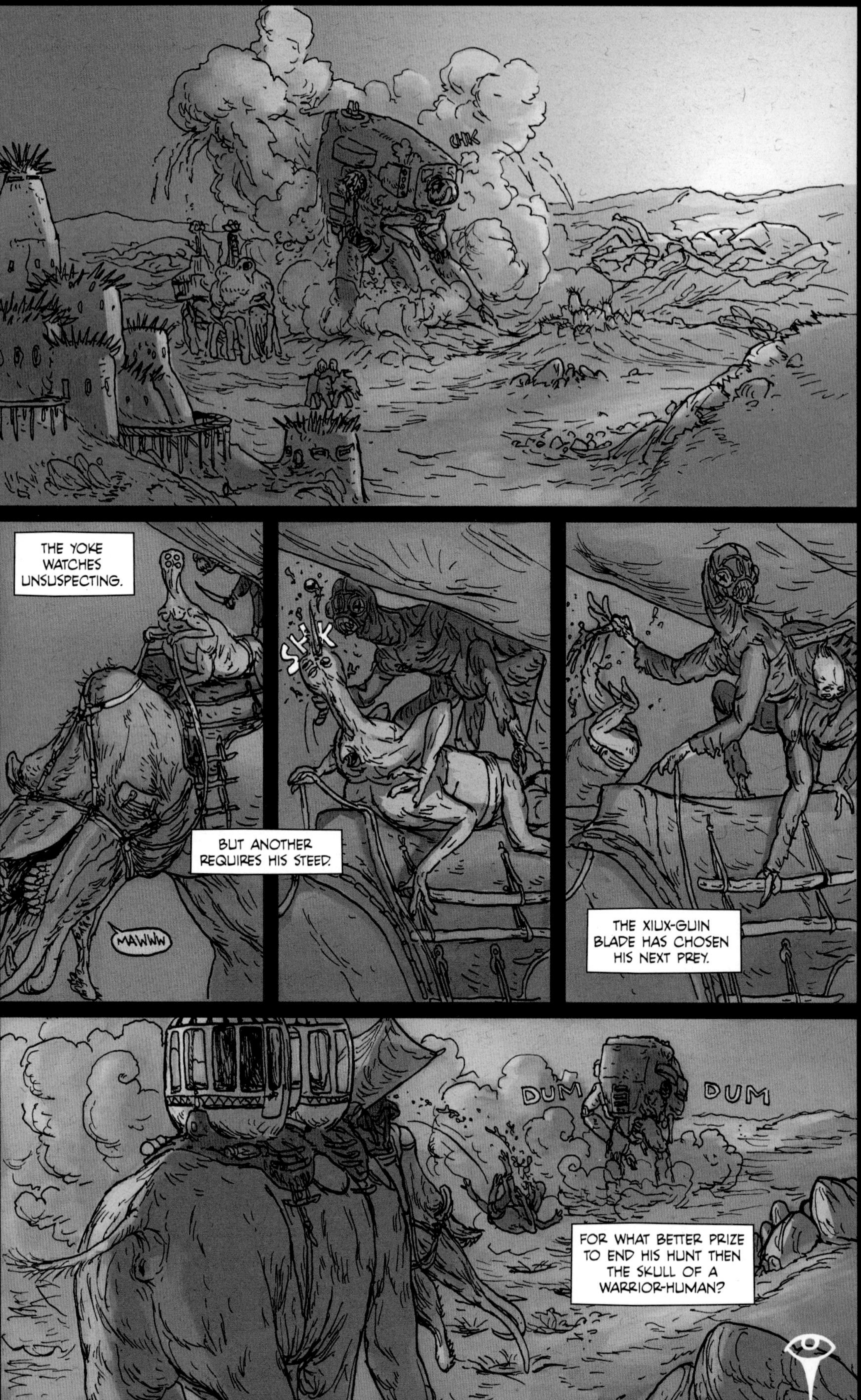
CHIK
THE YOKE WATCHES UNSUSPECTING.
BUT ANOTHER REQUIRES HIS STEED.
MAWWW
SHK
THE XIUX-GUIN BLADE HAS CHOSEN HIS NEXT PREY.
DUM
DUM
FOR WHAT BETTER PRIZE TO END HIS HUNT THEN THE SKULL OF A WARRIOR-HUMAN?

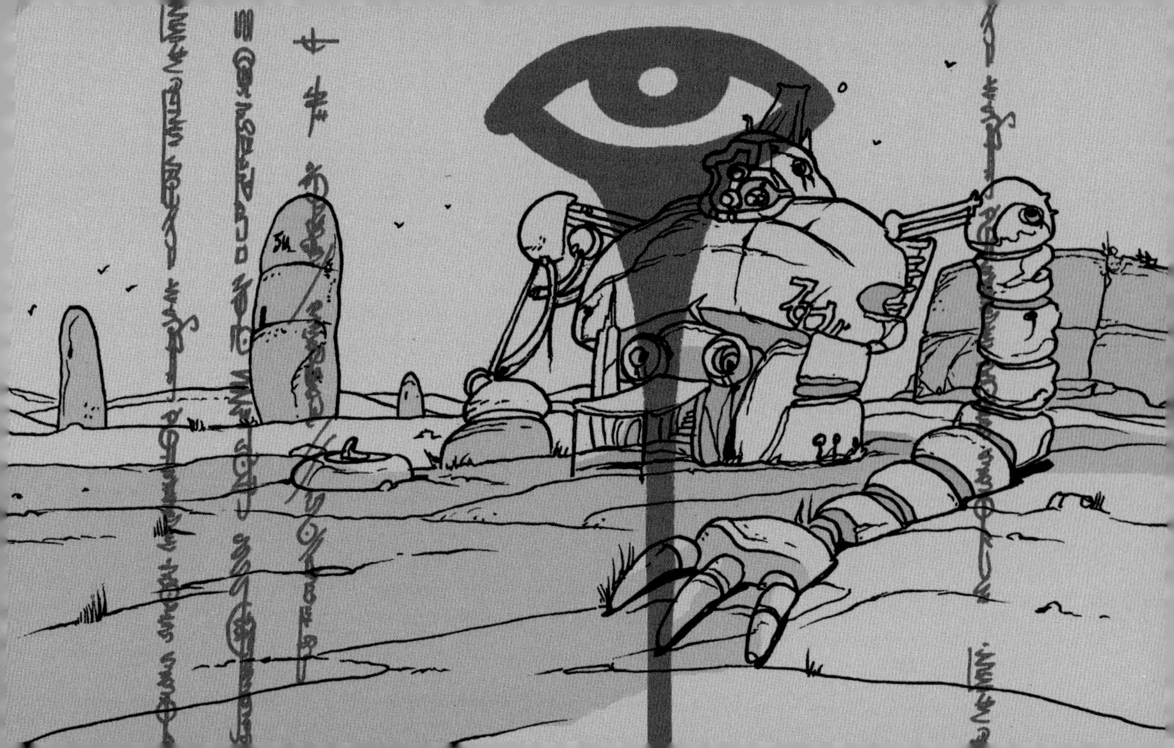

3

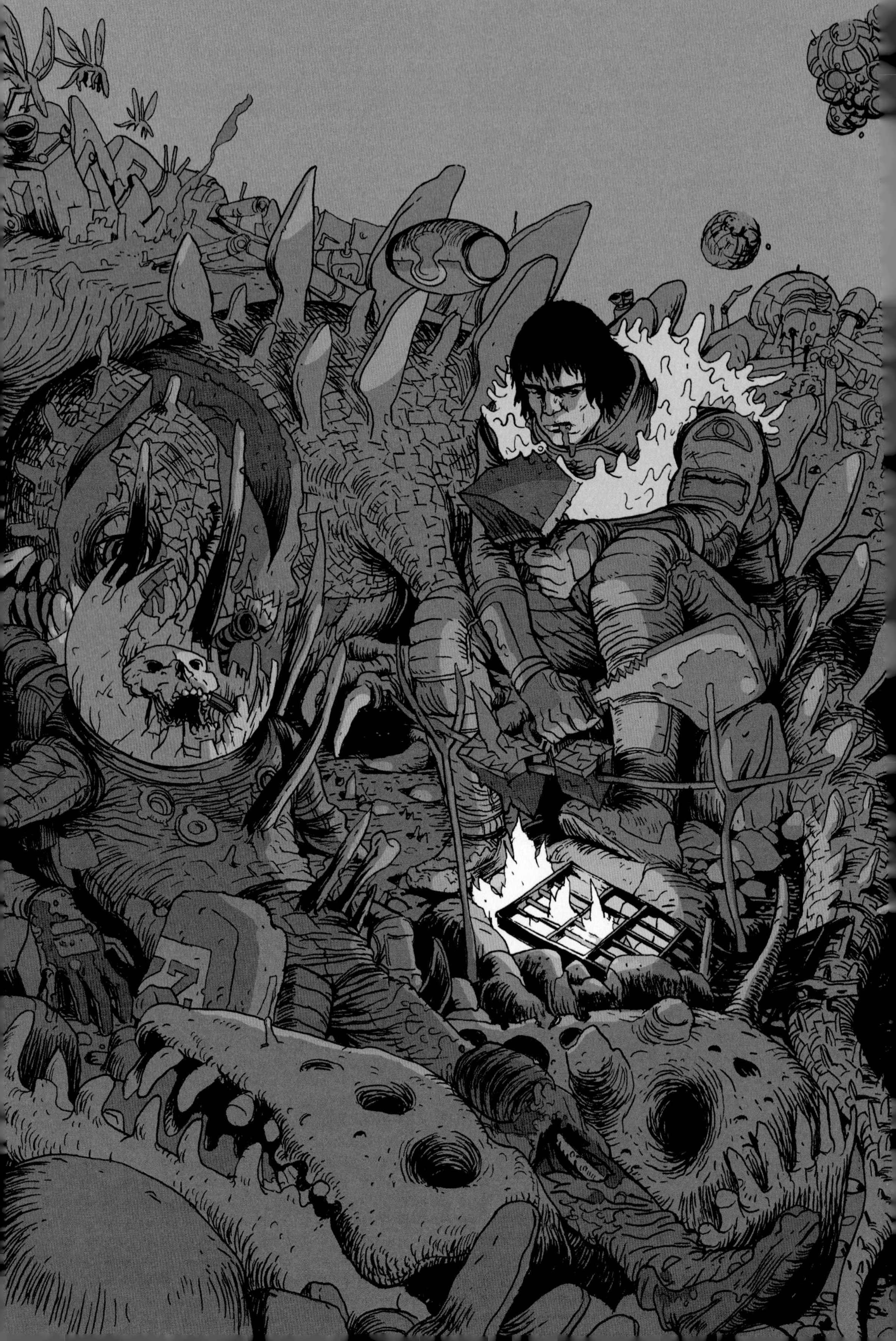

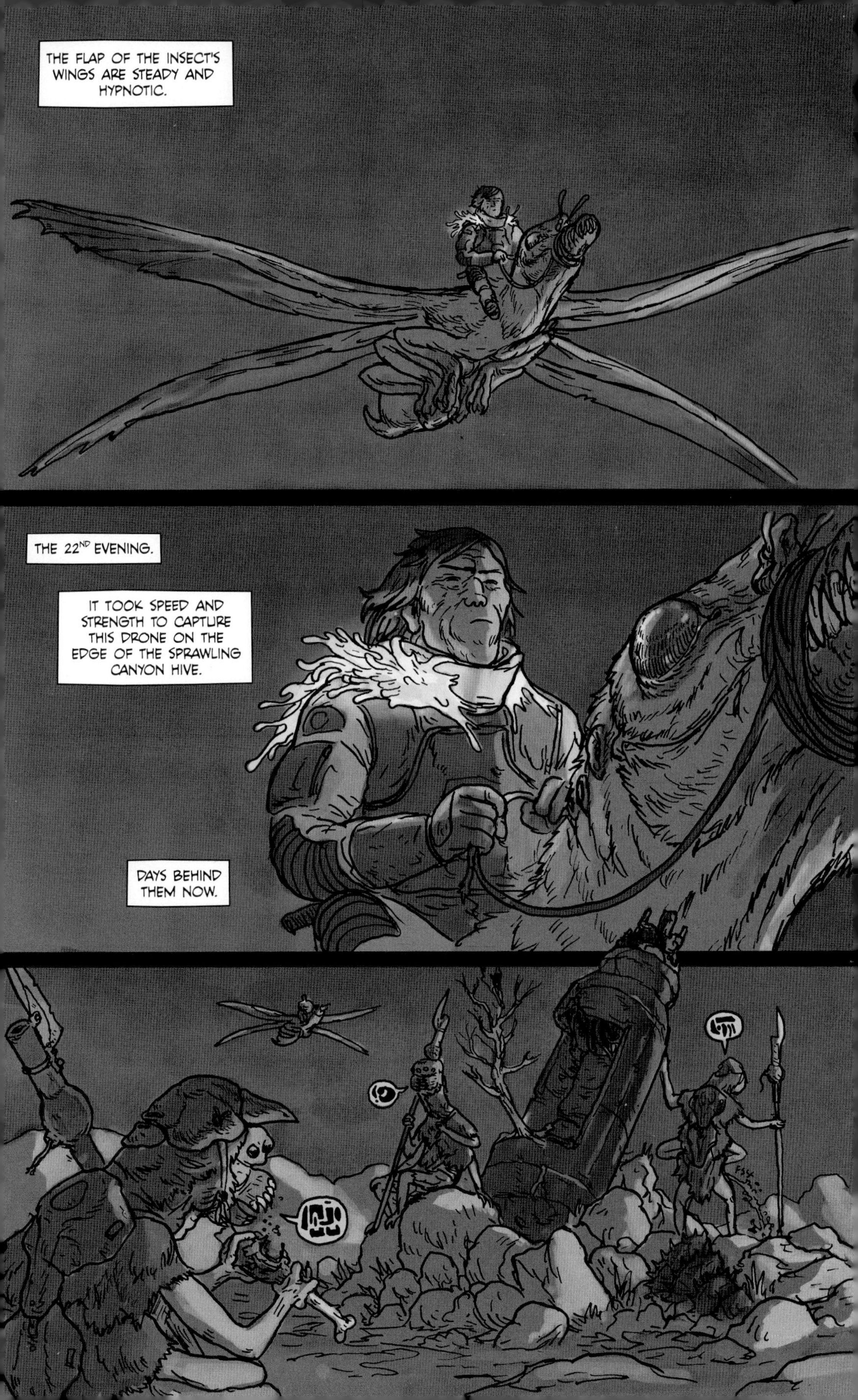
THE FLAP OF THE INSECT'S WINGS ARE STEADY AND HYPNOTIC.
THE 22ND EVENING.
IT TOOK SPEED AND STRENGTH TO CAPTURE THIS DRONE ON THE EDGE OF THE SPRAWLING CANYON HIVE.
DAYS BEHIND THEM NOW.

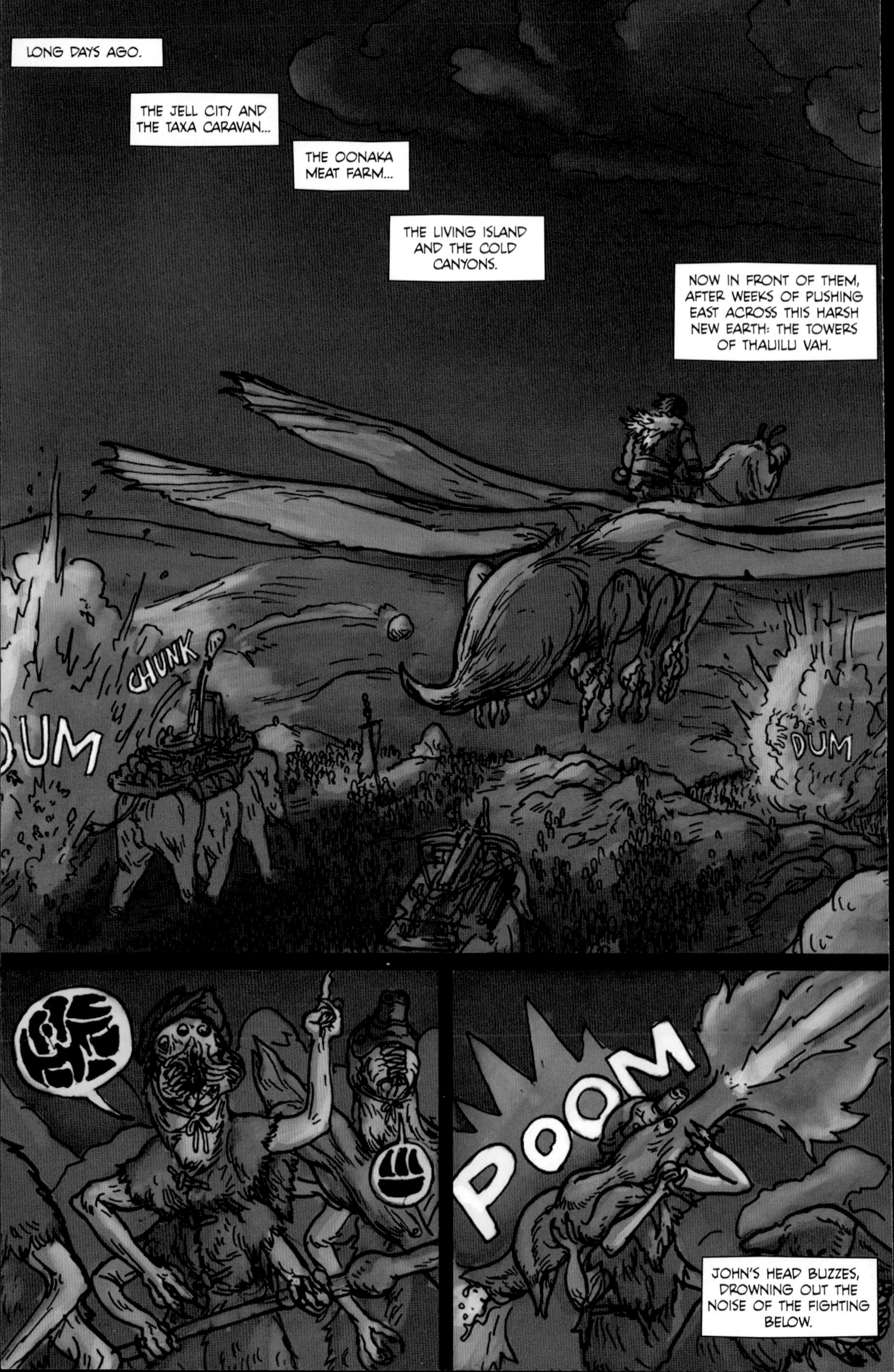
LONG DAYS AGO.
THE JELL CITY AND THE TAXA CARAVAN...
THE OONAKA MEAT FARM...
THE LIVING ISLAND AND THE COLD CANYONS.
NOW IN FRONT OF THEM, AFTER WEEKS OF PUSHING EAST ACROSS THIS HARSH NEW EARTH: THE TOWERS OF THAUILU VAH.
CHUNK
DUM
DUM
POOM
JOHN'S HEAD BUZZES, DROWNING OUT THE NOISE OF THE FIGHTING BELOW.

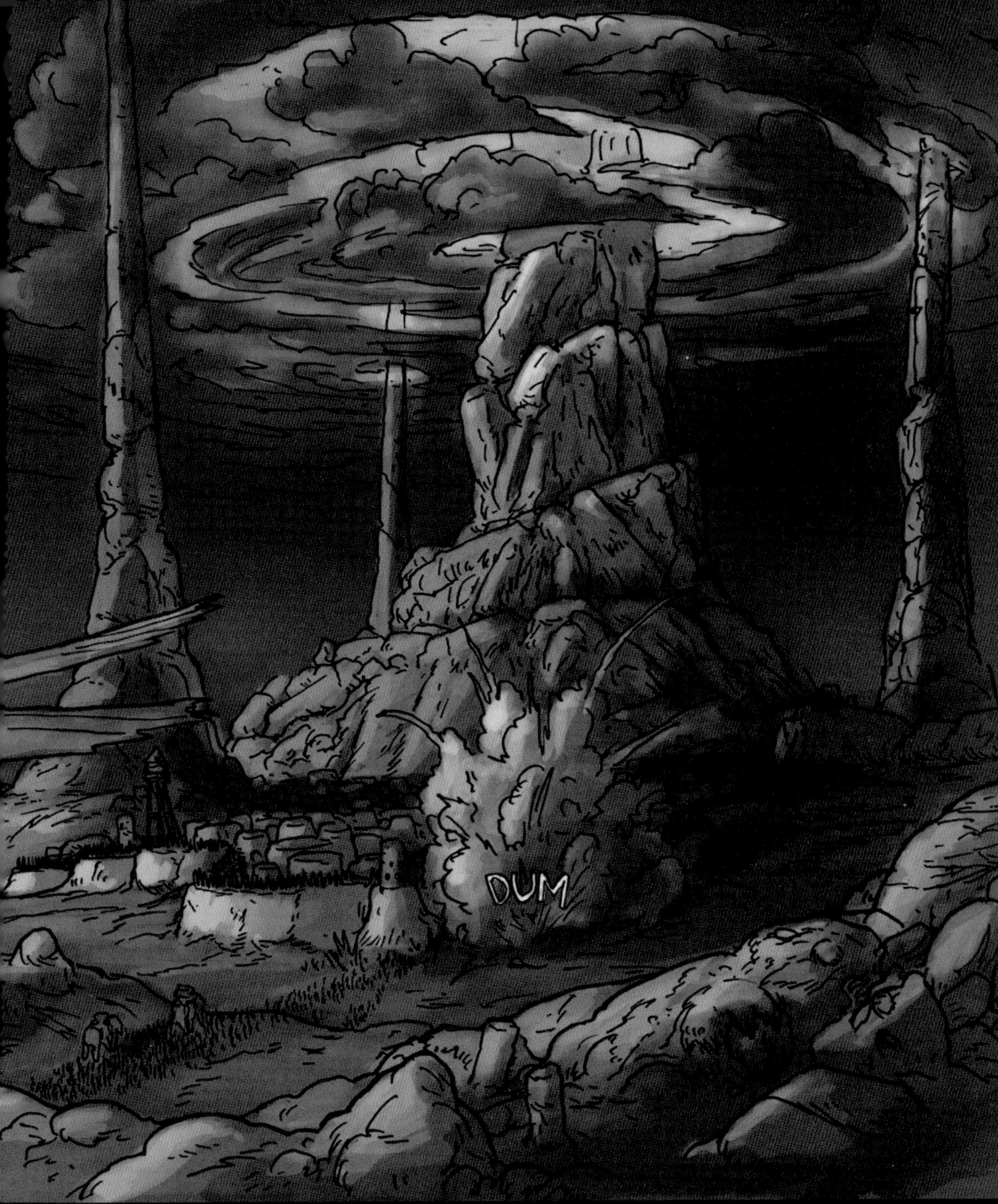
DUM

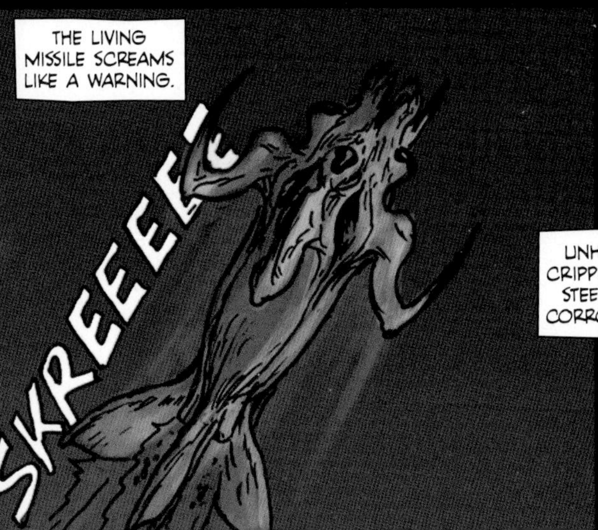
THE LIVING MISSILE SCREAMS LIKE A WARNING.
SKREEEEE

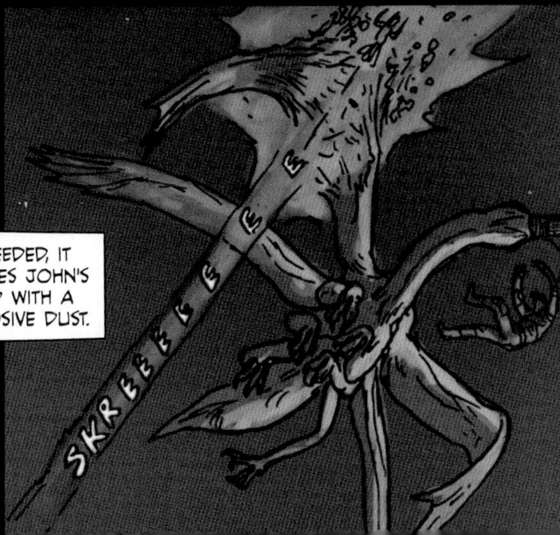
UNHEEDED, IT CRIPPLES JOHN'S STEED WITH A CORROSIVE DUST.
SKREEEEEEE

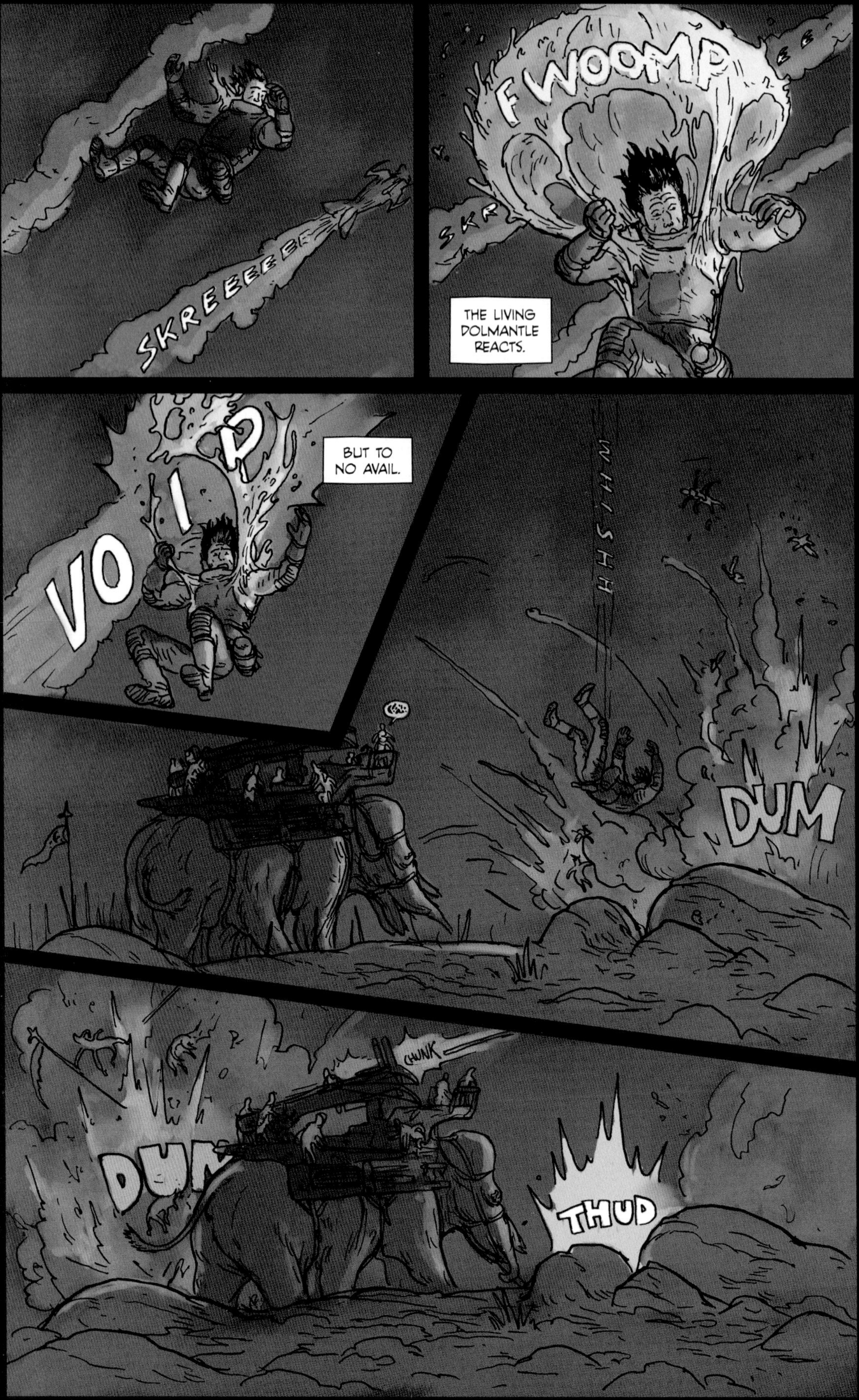
SKREEEEEE
FWOOMP
SKR
THE LIVING DOLMANTLE REACTS.
VOID
BUT TO NO AVAIL.
WHISHH
DUM
CHUNK
DUM
THUD

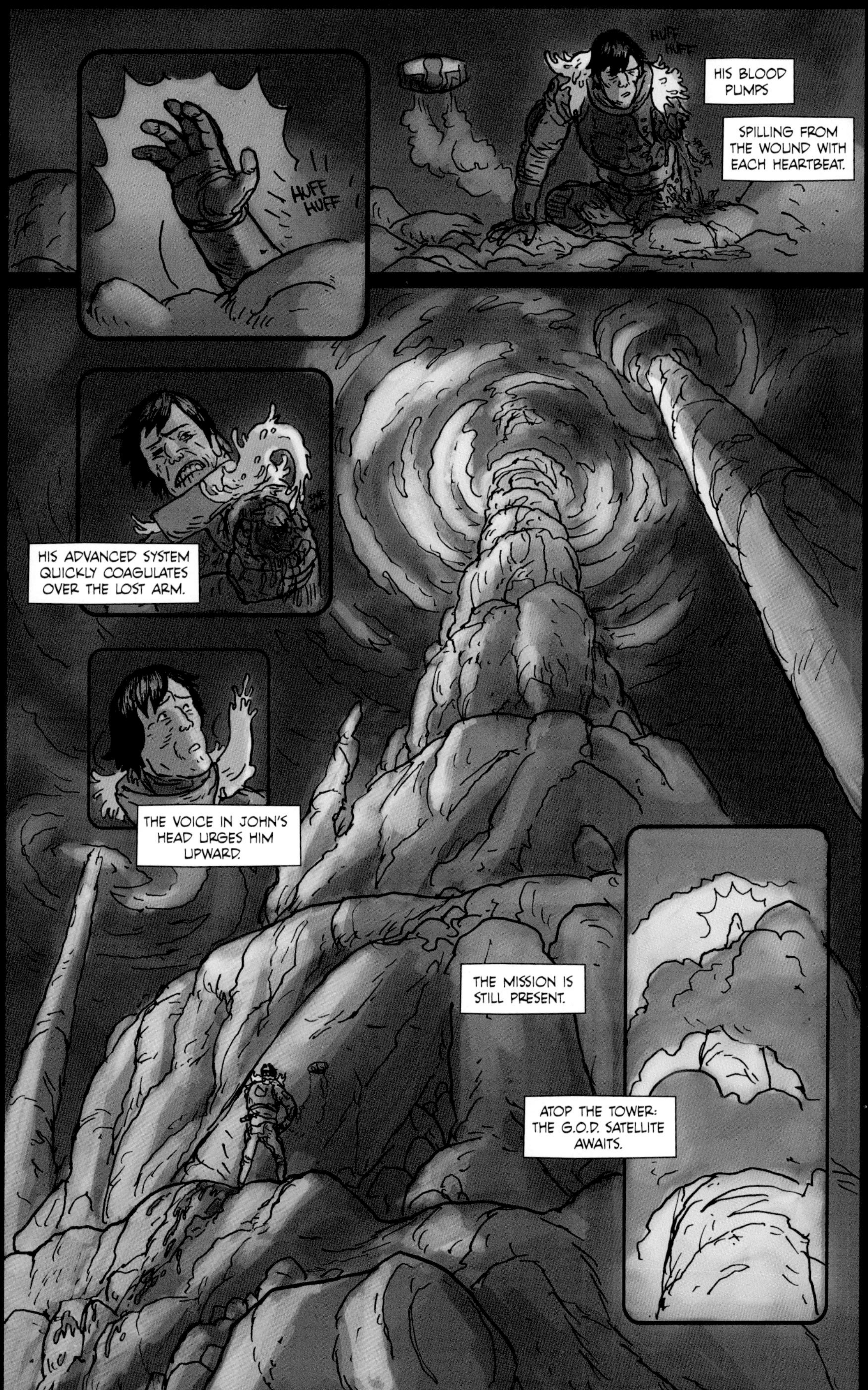
HUFF HUFF
HUFF HUFF
HIS BLOOD PUMPS
SPILLING FROM THE WOUND WITH EACH HEARTBEAT.
HIS ADVANCED SYSTEM QUICKLY COAGULATES OVER THE LOST ARM.
THE VOICE IN JOHN'S HEAD URGES HIM UPWARD.
THE MISSION IS STILL PRESENT.
ATOP THE TOWER: THE G.O.D. SATELLITE AWAITS.

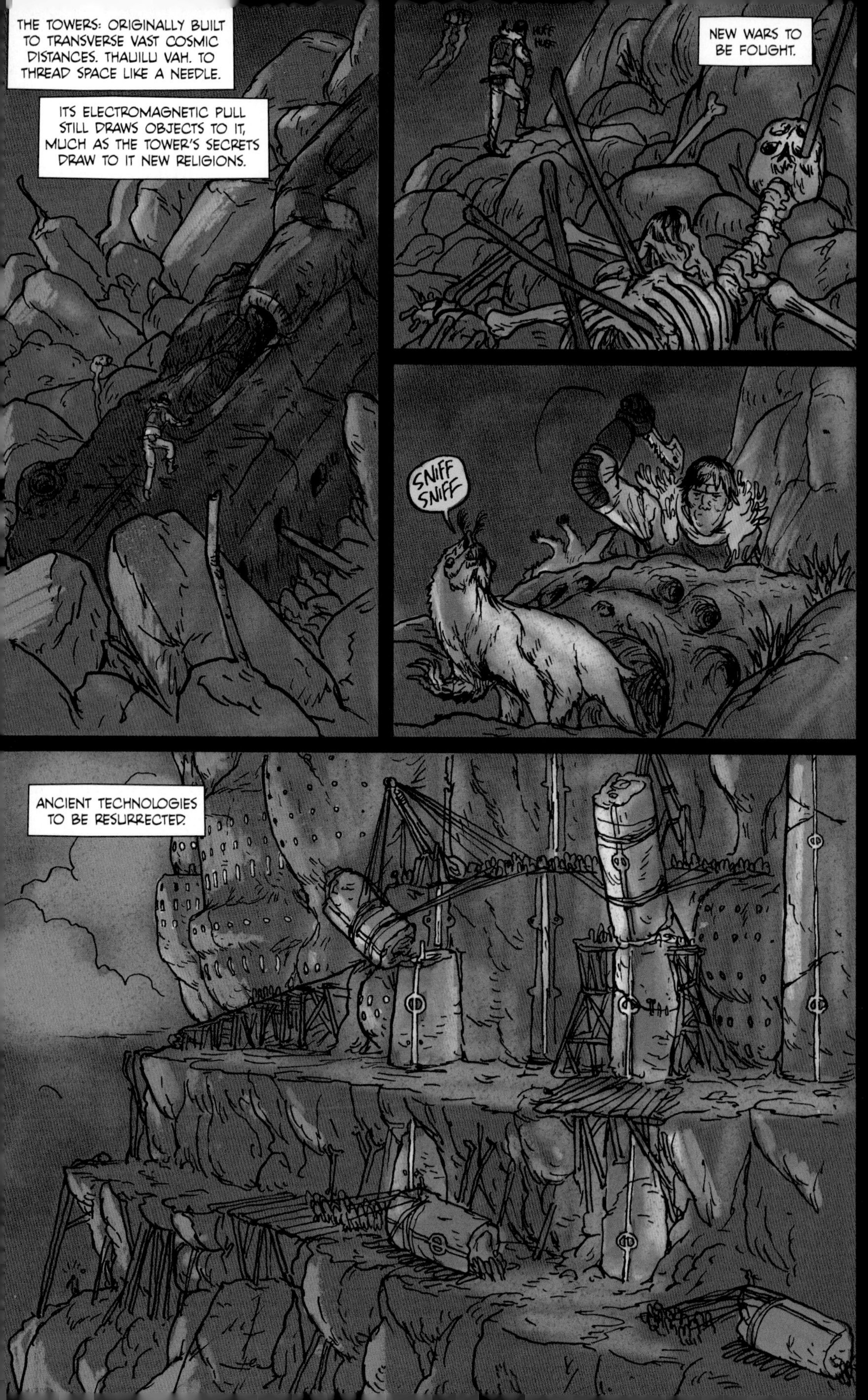
THE TOWERS: ORIGINALLY BUILT TO TRANSVERSE VAST COSMIC DISTANCES. THAUILU VAH. TO THREAD SPACE LIKE A NEEDLE.
ITS ELECTROMAGNETIC PULL STILL DRAWS OBJECTS TO IT, MUCH AS THE TOWER'S SECRETS DRAW TO IT NEW RELIGIONS.
NEW WARS TO BE FOUGHT.
SNIFF SNIFF
ANCIENT TECHNOLOGIES TO BE RESURRECTED.

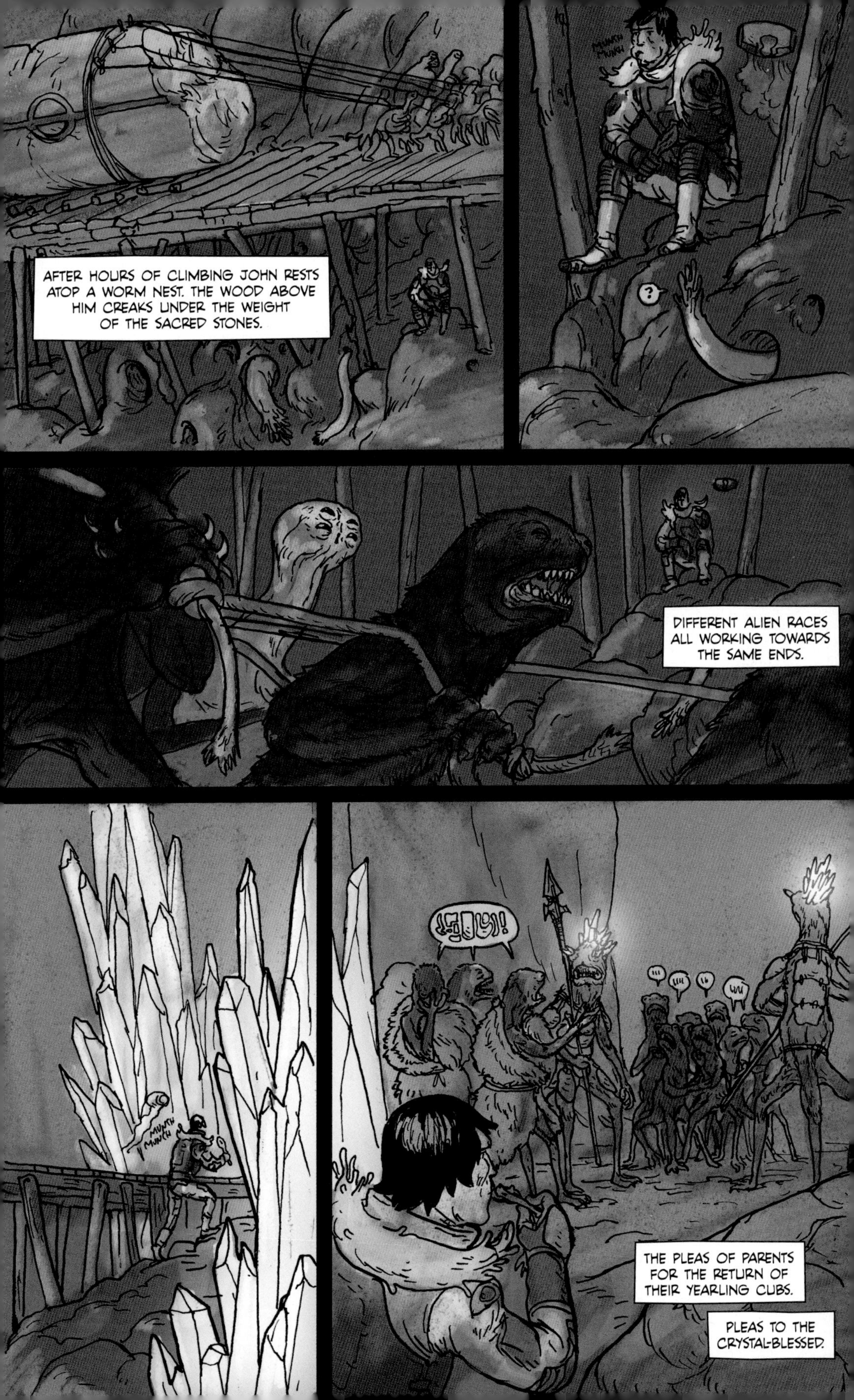

AFTER HOURS OF CLIMBING JOHN RESTS ATOP A WORM NEST. THE WOOD ABOVE HIM CREAKS UNDER THE WEIGHT OF THE SACRED STONES.
MUNCH MUNCH
?
DIFFERENT ALIEN RACES ALL WORKING TOWARDS THE SAME ENDS.
MUNCH MUNCH
THE PLEAS OF PARENTS FOR THE RETURN OF THEIR YEARLING CUBS.
PLEAS TO THE CRYSTAL-BLESSED.

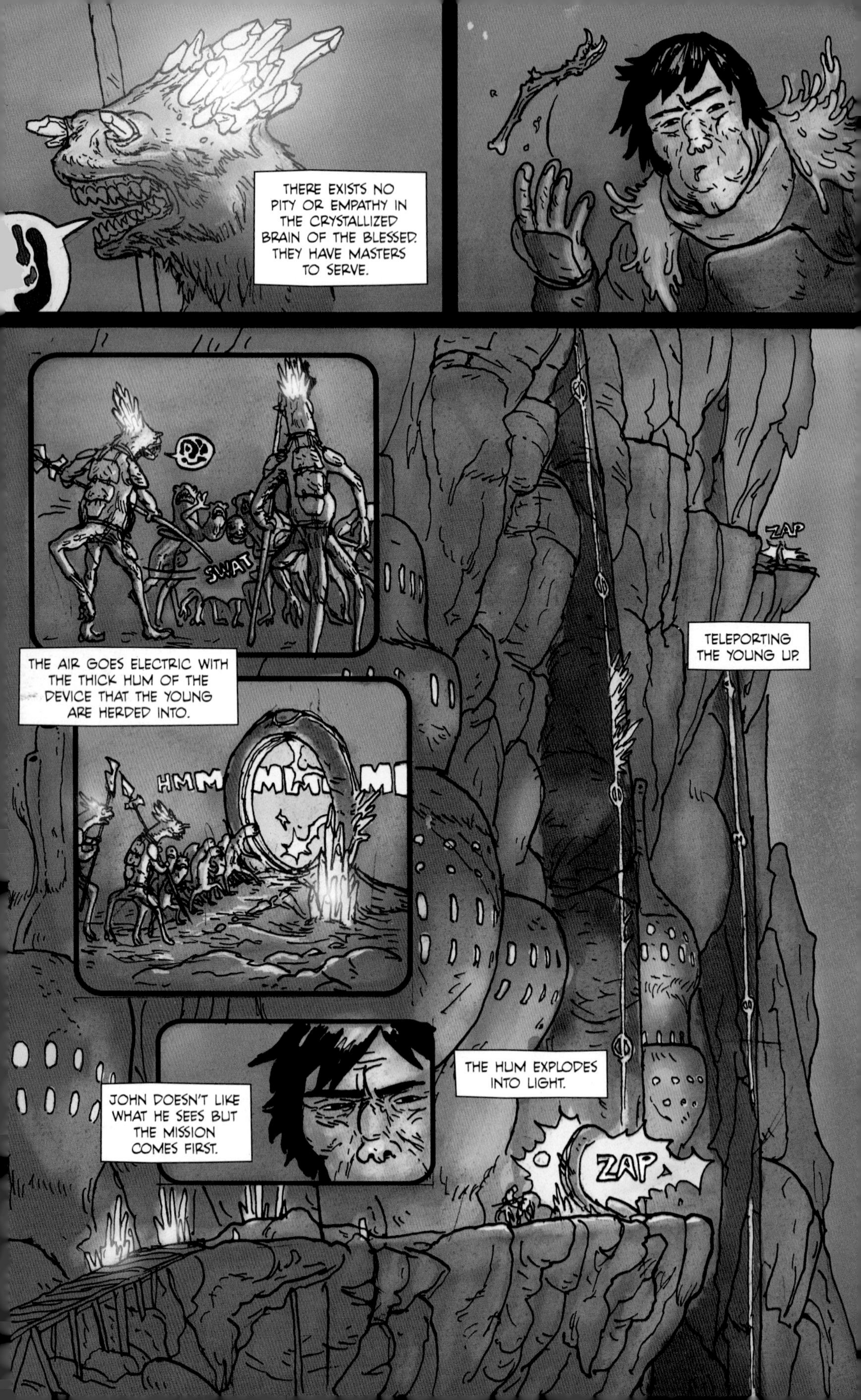
THERE EXISTS NO PITY OR EMPATHY IN THE CRYSTALLIZED BRAIN OF THE BLESSED. THEY HAVE MASTERS TO SERVE.
SWAT
THE AIR GOES ELECTRIC WITH THE THICK HUM OF THE DEVICE THAT THE YOUNG ARE HERDED INTO.
HMMMMMMMMM
ZAP
TELEPORTING THE YOUNG UP.
JOHN DOESN'T LIKE WHAT HE SEES BUT THE MISSION COMES FIRST.
THE HUM EXPLODES INTO LIGHT.
ZAP

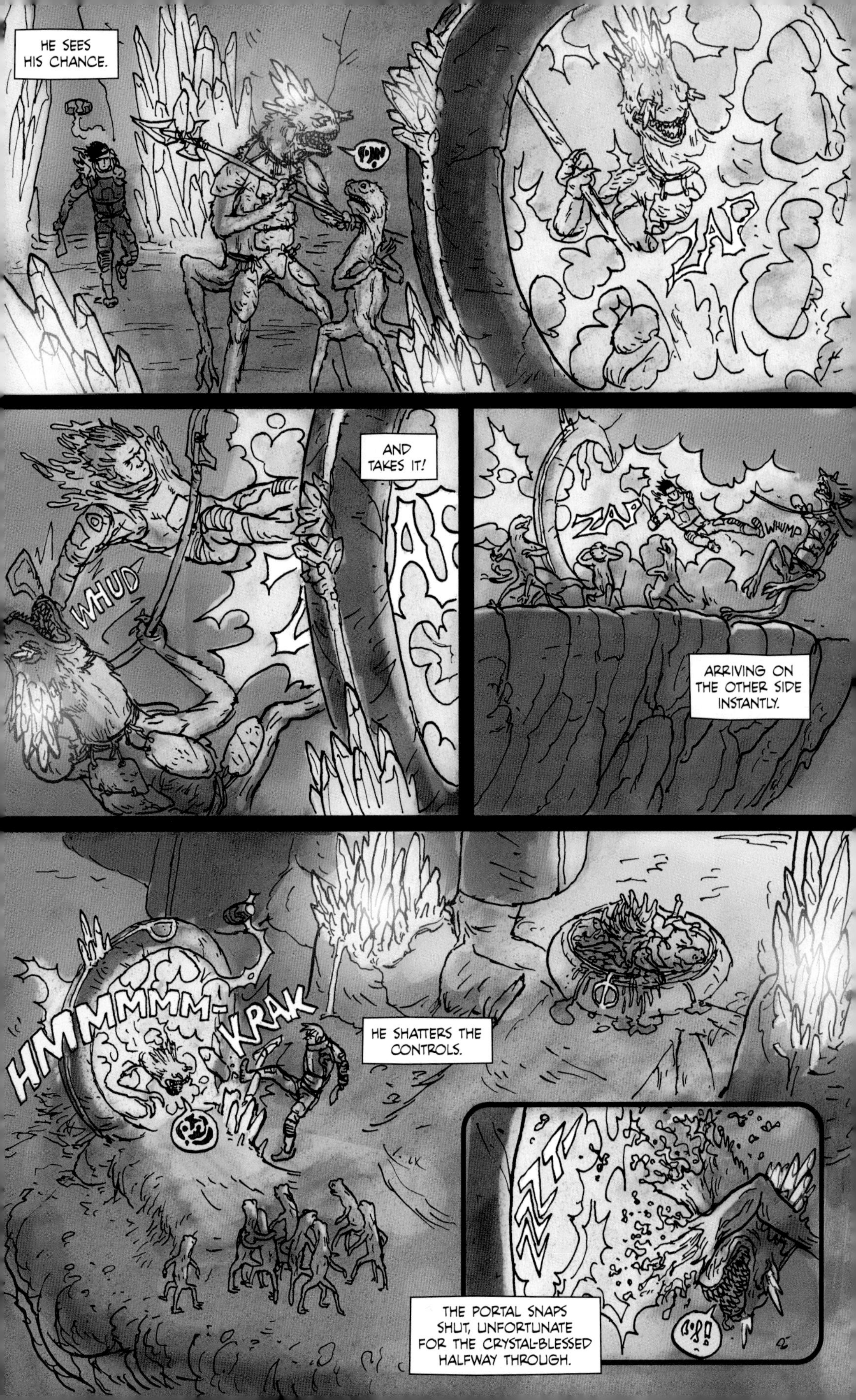
HE SEES HIS CHANCE.
ZAP
AND TAKES IT!
WHUD
ZAP
WHUMP
ARRIVING ON THE OTHER SIDE INSTANTLY.
HMMMMM-KRAK
HE SHATTERS THE CONTROLS.
ZZT
THE PORTAL SNAPS SHUT, UNFORTUNATE FOR THE CRYSTAL-BLESSED HALFWAY THROUGH.

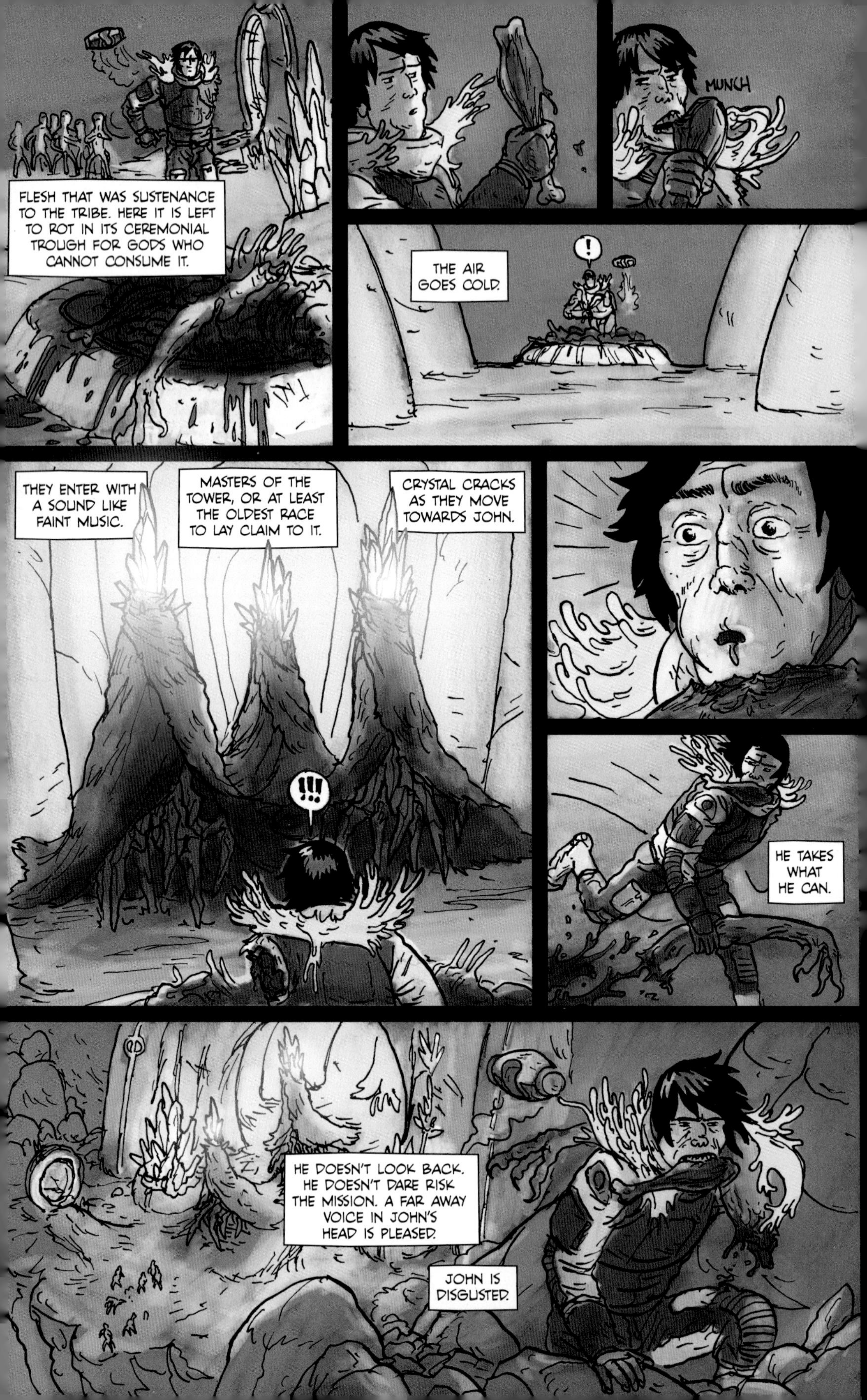

FLESH THAT WAS SUSTENANCE TO THE TRIBE. HERE IT IS LEFT TO ROT IN ITS CEREMONIAL TROUGH FOR GODS WHO CANNOT CONSUME IT.
MUNCH
THE AIR GOES COLD.
!
THEY ENTER WITH A SOUND LIKE FAINT MUSIC.
MASTERS OF THE TOWER, OR AT LEAST THE OLDEST RACE TO LAY CLAIM TO IT.
CRYSTAL CRACKS AS THEY MOVE TOWARDS JOHN.
!!!
HE TAKES WHAT HE CAN.
HE DOESN'T LOOK BACK. HE DOESN'T DARE RISK THE MISSION. A FAR AWAY VOICE IN JOHN'S HEAD IS PLEASED.
JOHN IS DISGUSTED.

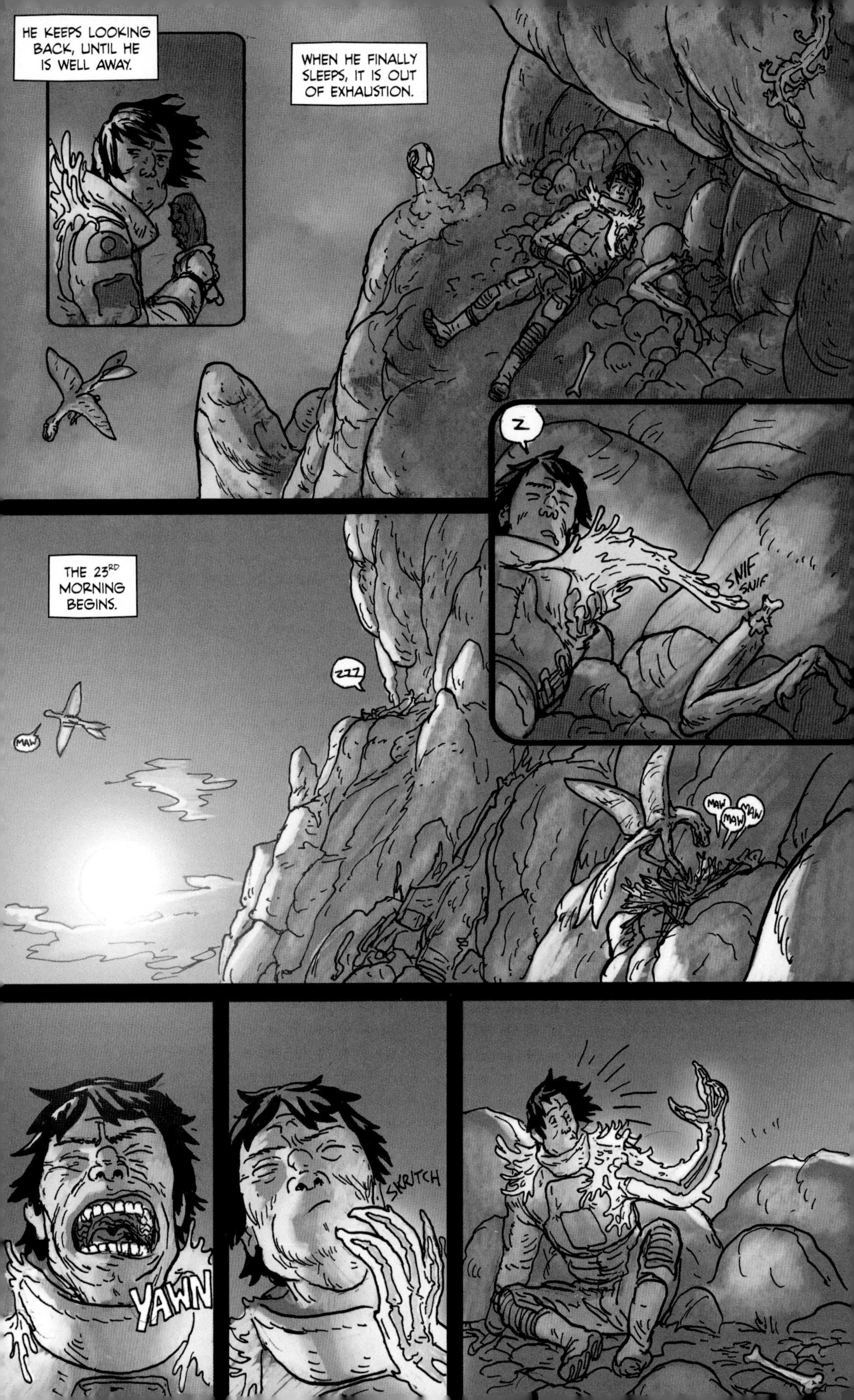
HE KEEPS LOOKING BACK, UNTIL HE IS WELL AWAY.
WHEN HE FINALLY SLEEPS, IT IS OUT OF EXHAUSTION.
Z
SNIF
SNIF
THE 23RD MORNING BEGINS.
ZZZ
MAW
MAW
MAW
MAW
YAWN
SKRITCH

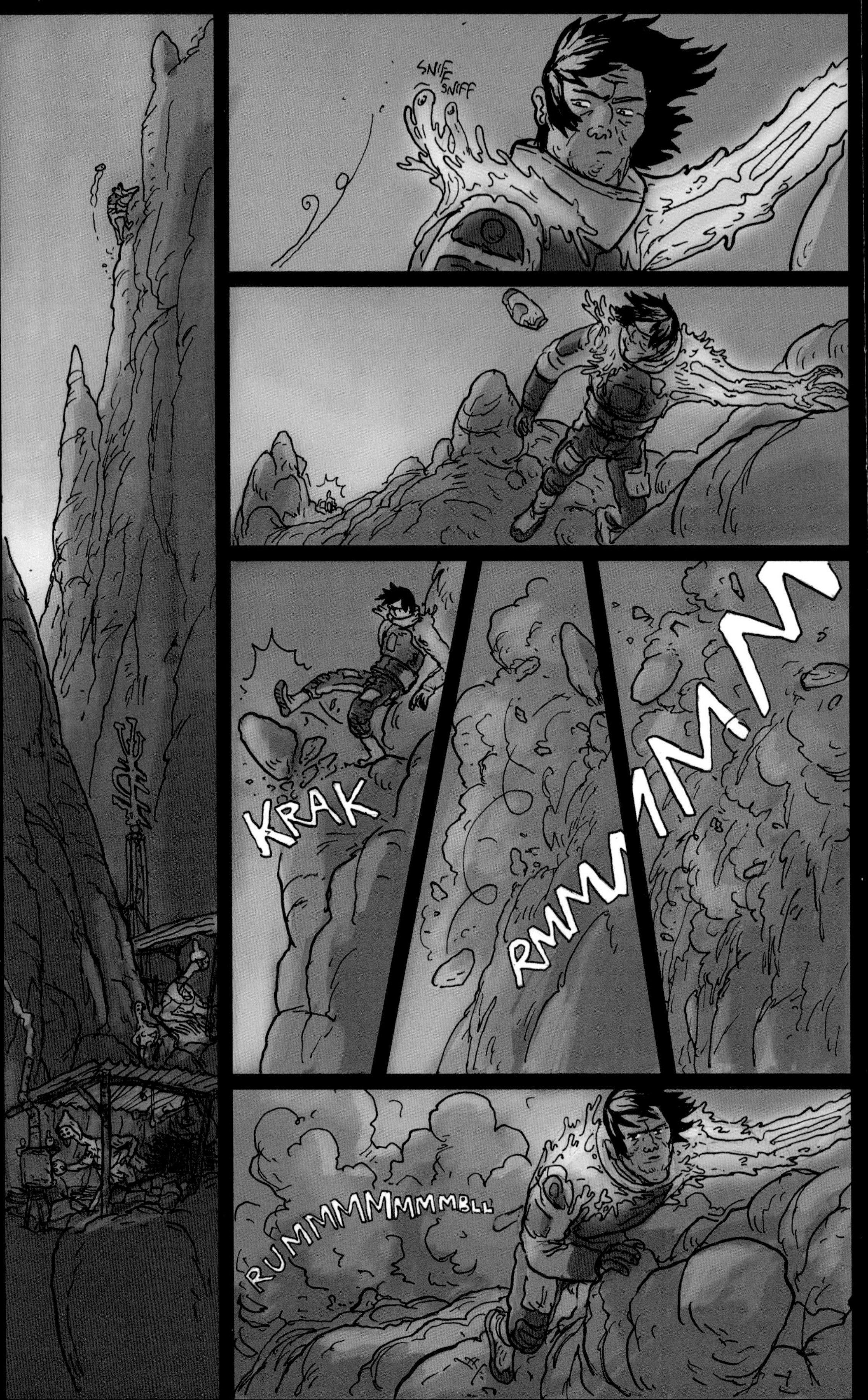

SNIFF SNIFF
KRAK
RMMMMMM
RUMMMMMMMMMBLL

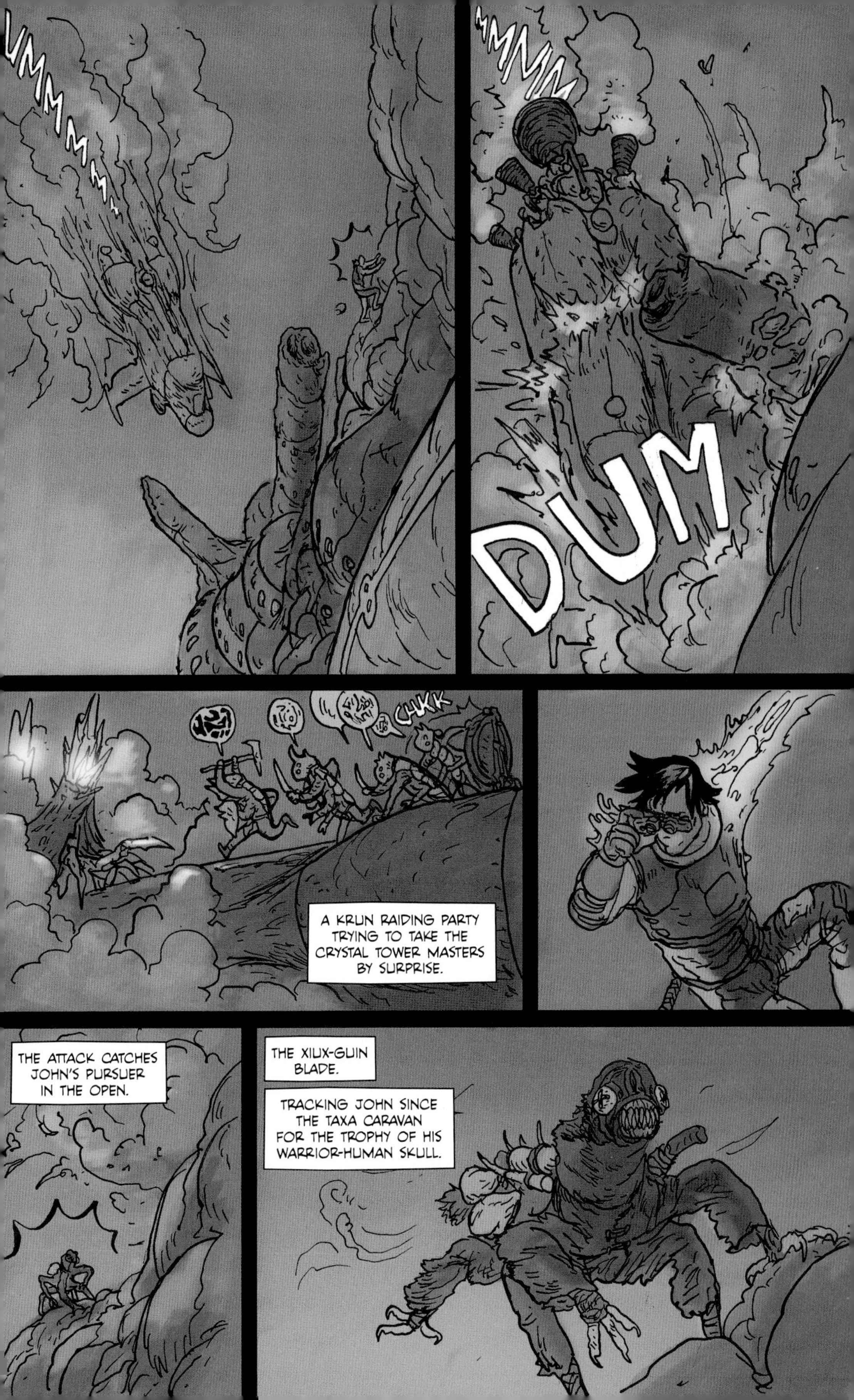
UMMMMMMM
MMNM
DUM
CHKK
A KRUN RAIDING PARTY TRYING TO TAKE THE CRYSTAL TOWER MASTERS BY SURPRISE.
THE ATTACK CATCHES JOHN'S PURSUER IN THE OPEN.
THE XIUX-GUIN BLADE.
TRACKING JOHN SINCE THE TAXA CARAVAN FOR THE TROPHY OF HIS WARRIOR-HUMAN SKULL.

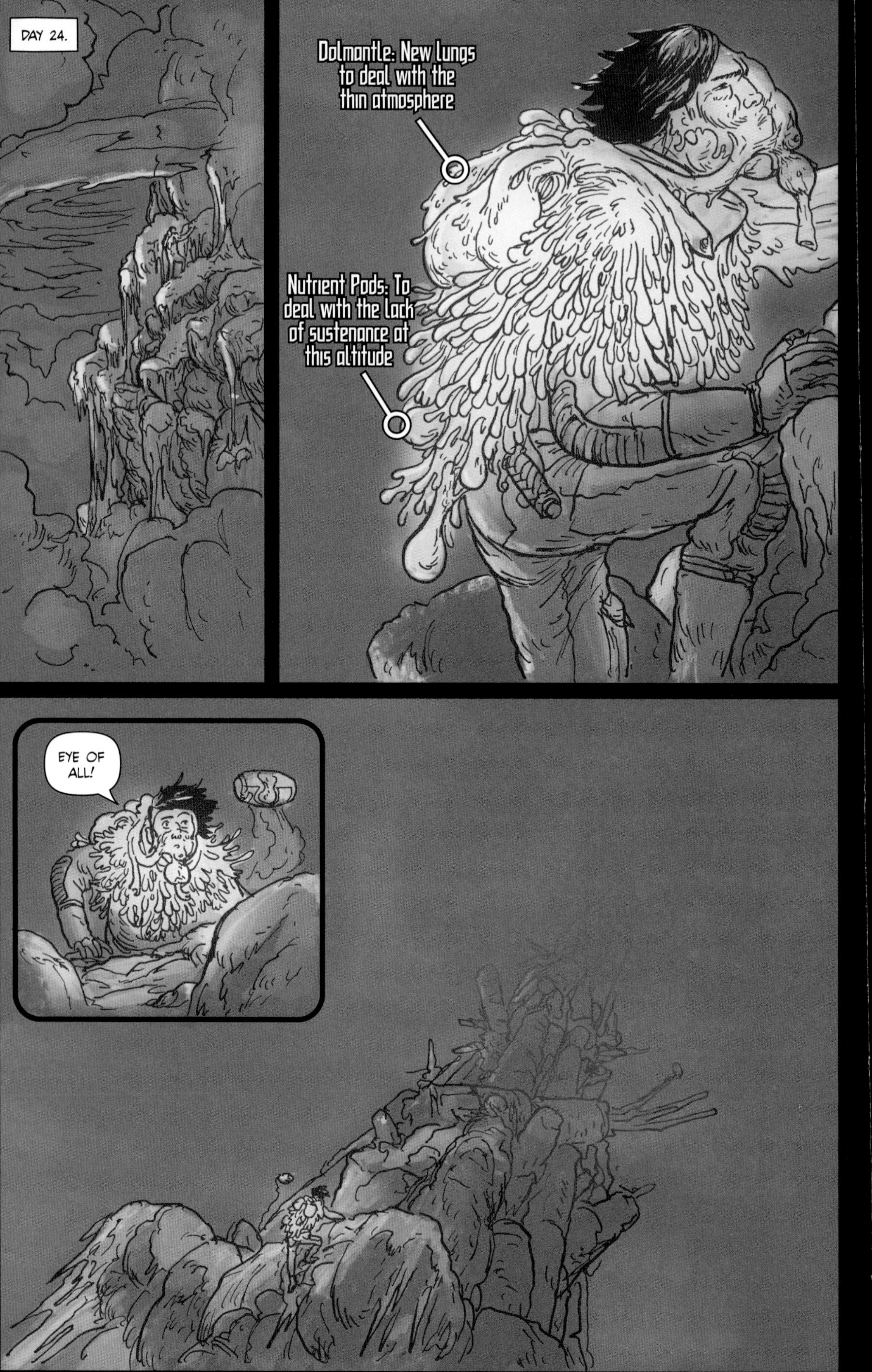
DAY 24.
Dolmantle: New lungs to deal with the thin atmosphere
Nutrient Pods: To deal with the lack of sustenance at this altitude
EYE OF ALL!

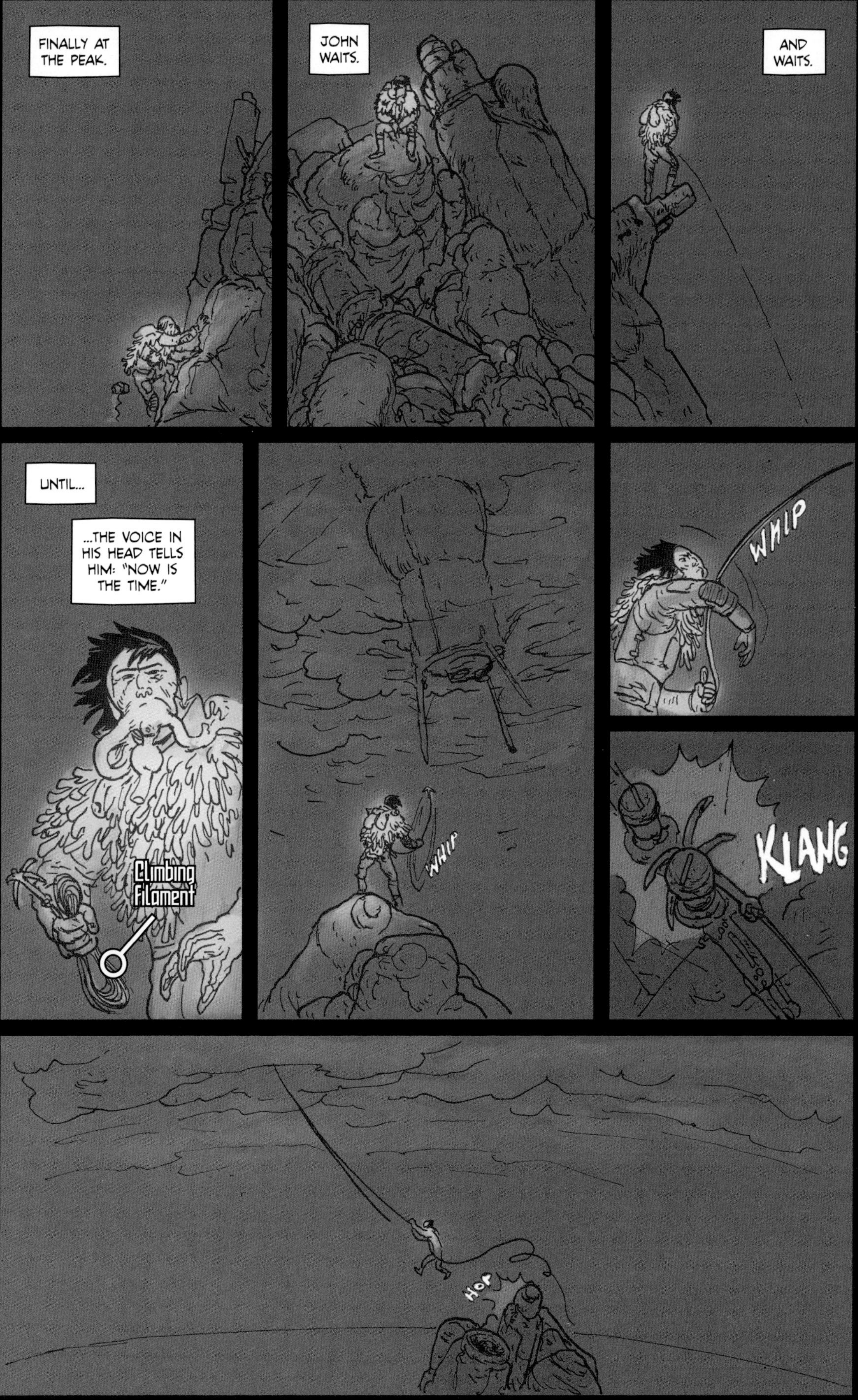
FINALLY AT THE PEAK.
JOHN WAITS.
AND WAITS.
UNTIL...
...THE VOICE IN HIS HEAD TELLS HIM: "NOW IS THE TIME."
Climbing Filament
WHIP
WHIP
KLANG
HOP

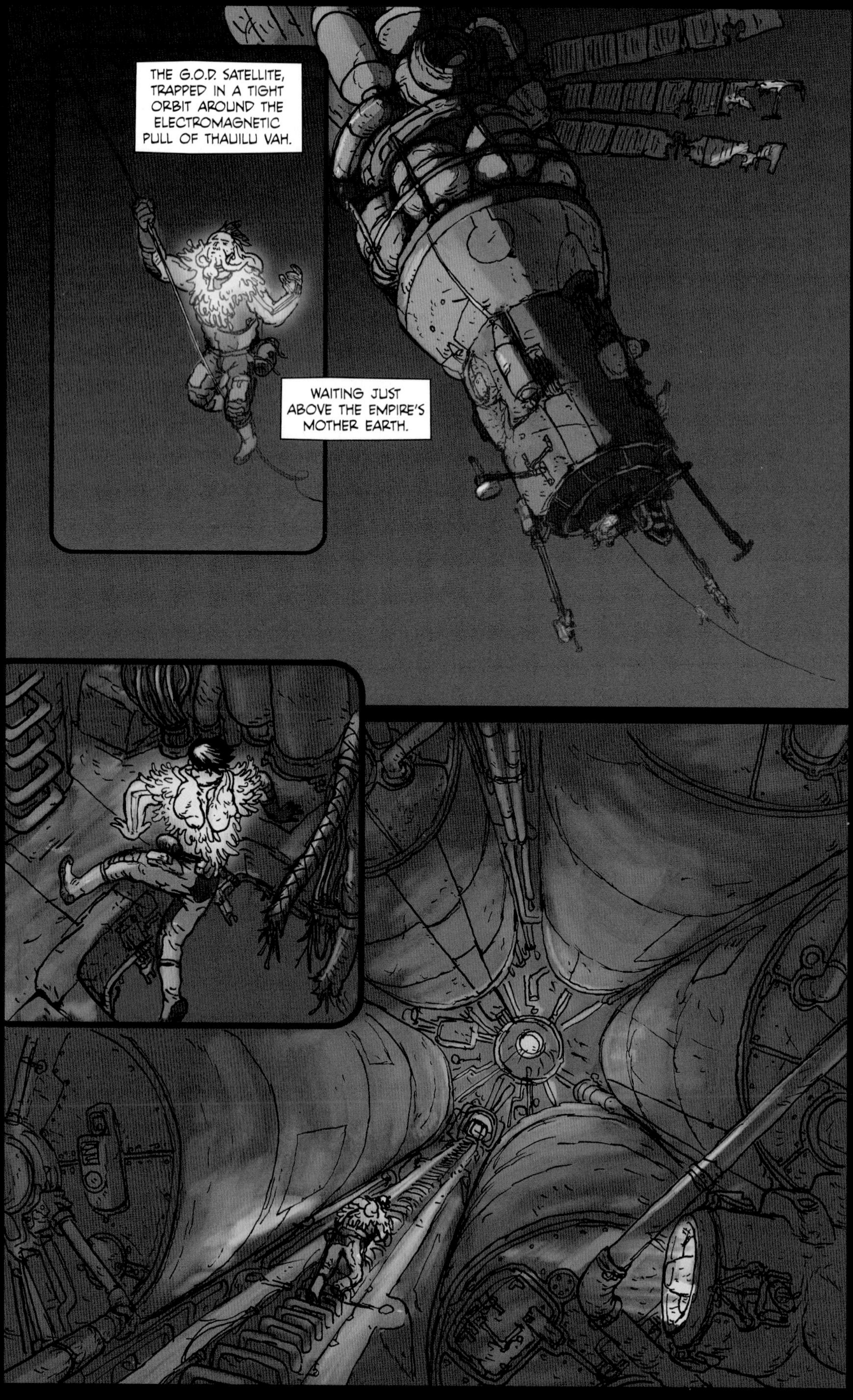
THE G.O.D. SATELLITE, TRAPPED IN A TIGHT ORBIT AROUND THE ELECTROMAGNETIC PULL OF THAVILU VAH.
WAITING JUST ABOVE THE EMPIRE'S MOTHER EARTH.

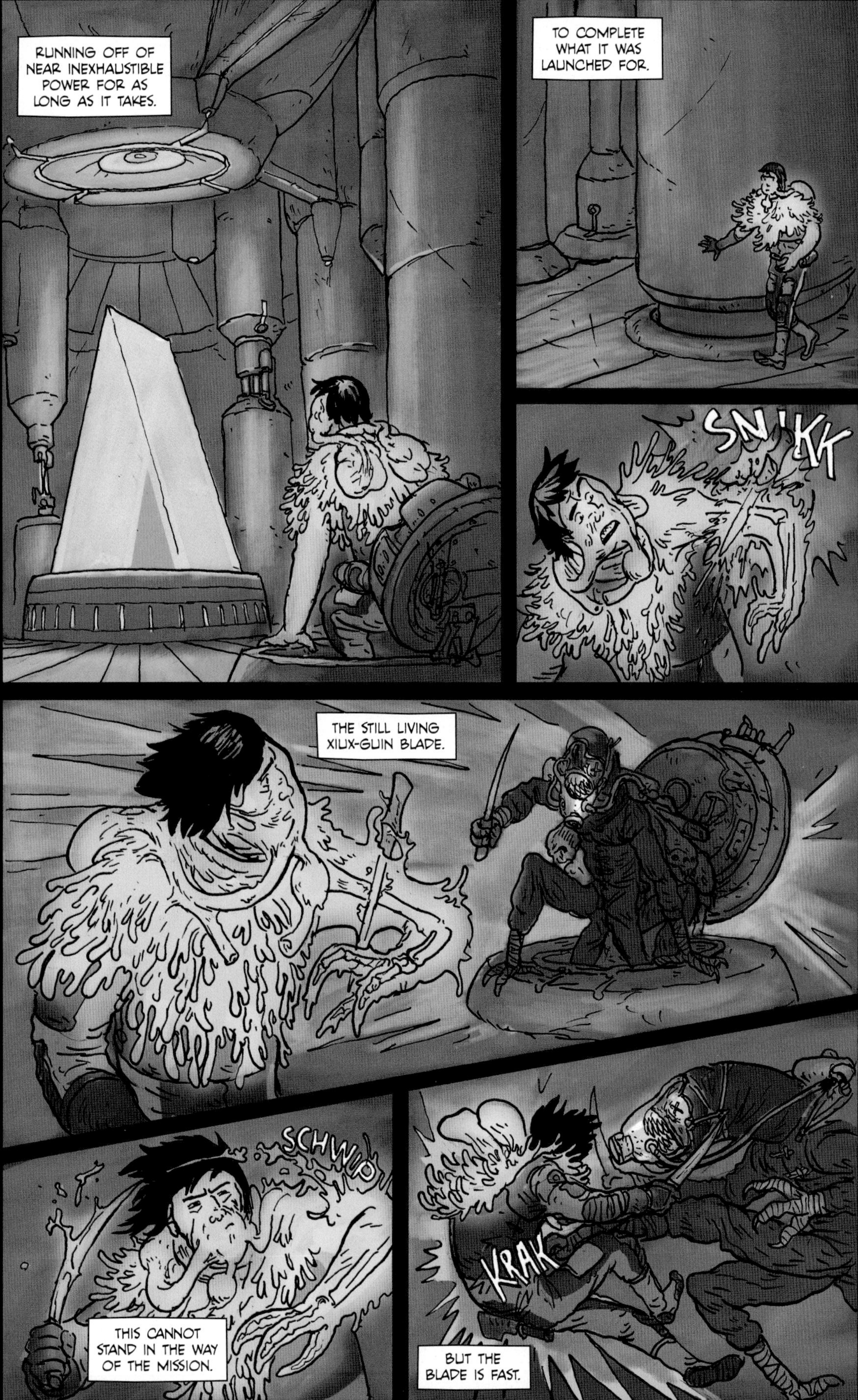
RUNNING OFF OF NEAR INEXHAUSTIBLE POWER FOR AS LONG AS IT TAKES.
TO COMPLETE WHAT IT WAS LAUNCHED FOR.
SNIKK
THE STILL LIVING XIUX-GUIN BLADE.
SCHWIP
THIS CANNOT STAND IN THE WAY OF THE MISSION.
KRAK
BUT THE BLADE IS FAST.

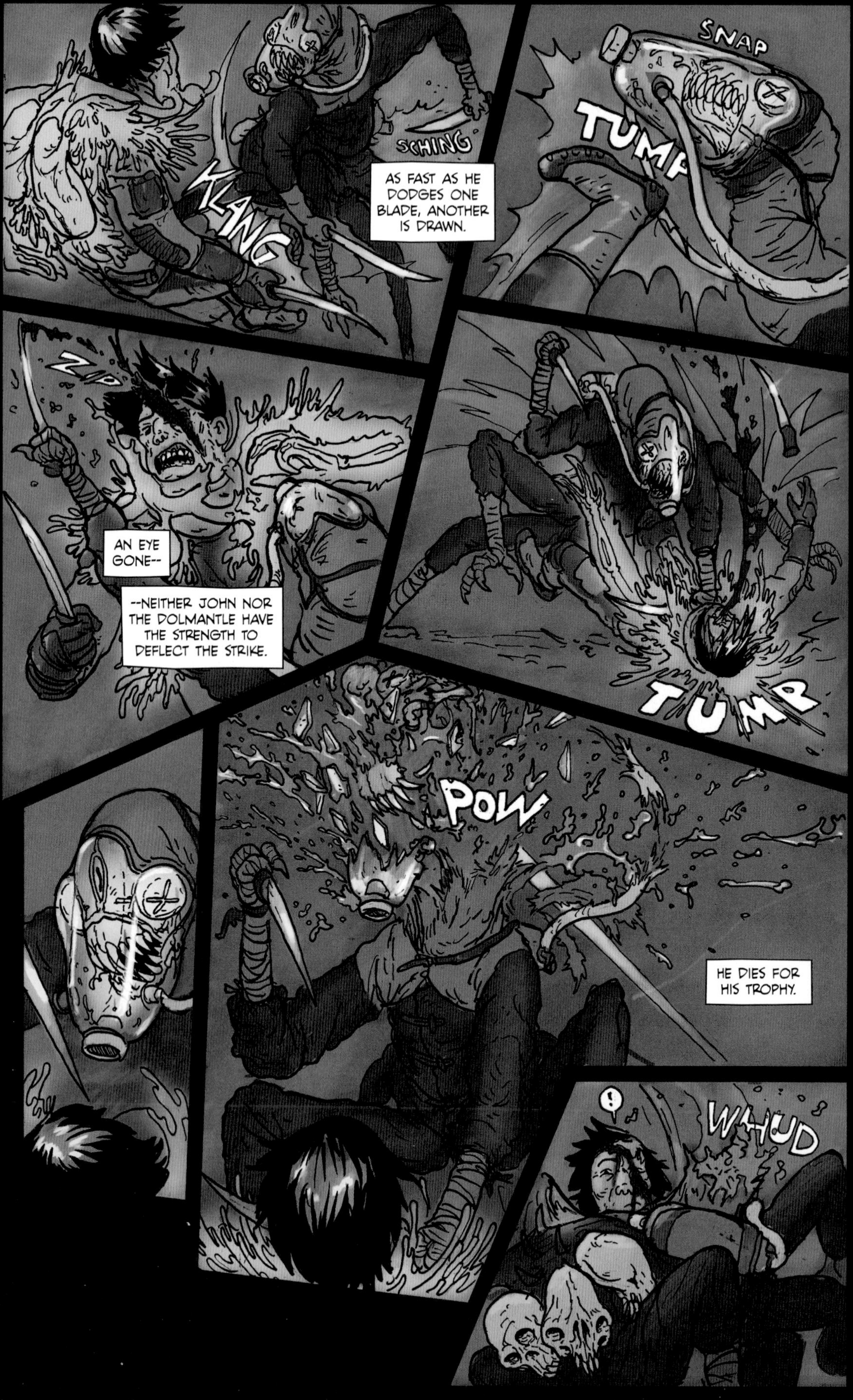
KLANG
SCHING
AS FAST AS HE DODGES ONE BLADE, ANOTHER IS DRAWN.
SNAP
TUMP
ZIP
AN EYE GONE--
--NEITHER JOHN NOR THE DOLMANTLE HAVE THE STRENGTH TO DEFLECT THE STRIKE.
TUMP
POW
HE DIES FOR HIS TROPHY.
!
WHUD

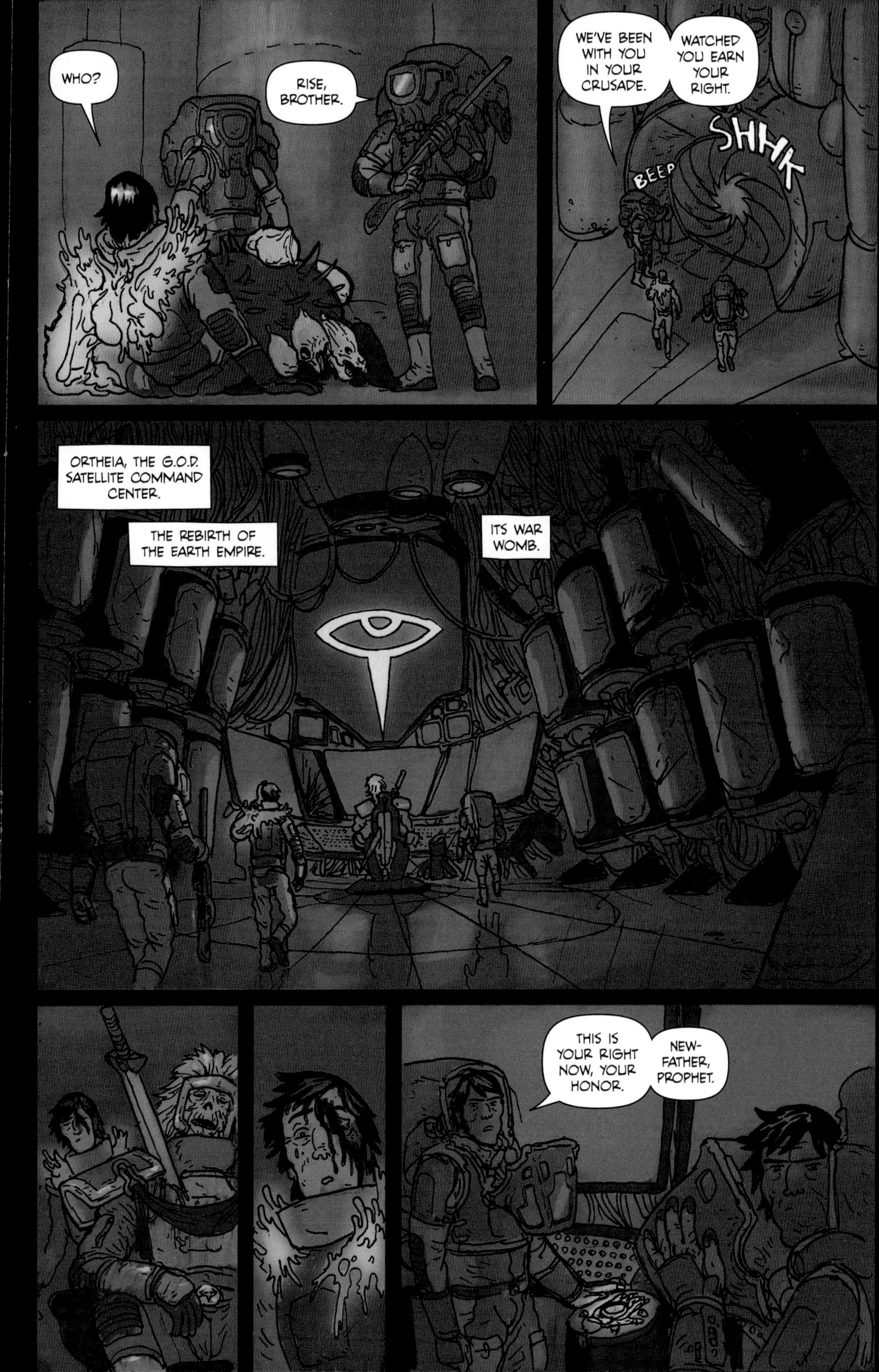
WHO?
RISE, BROTHER.
WE'VE BEEN WITH YOU IN YOUR CRUSADE.
WATCHED YOU EARN YOUR RIGHT.
BEEP
SHHK
ORTHEIA, THE G.O.D. SATELLITE COMMAND CENTER.
THE REBIRTH OF THE EARTH EMPIRE.
ITS WAR WOMB.
THIS IS YOUR RIGHT NOW, YOUR HONOR.
NEW-FATHER, PROPHET.

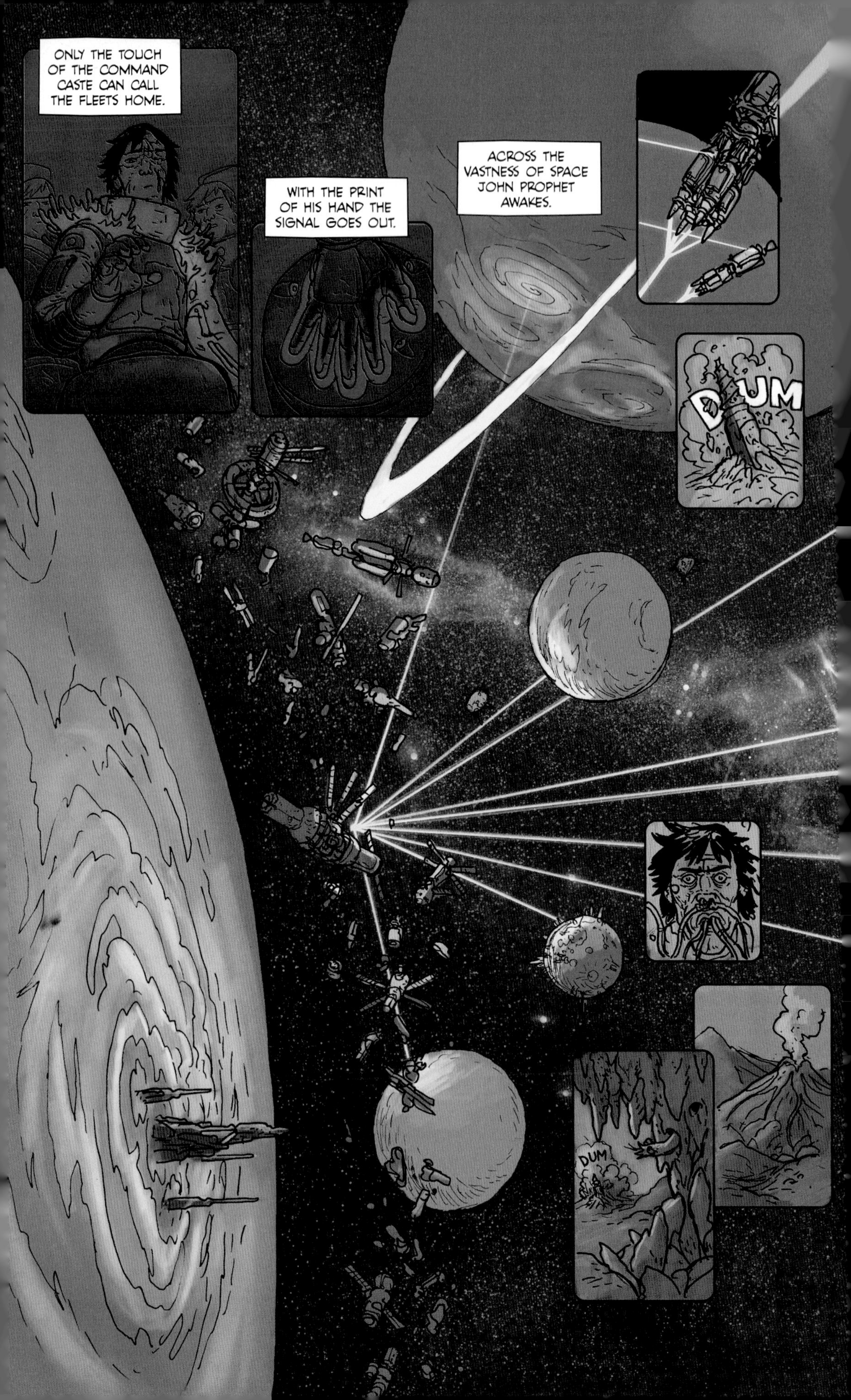
ONLY THE TOUCH OF THE COMMAND CASTE CAN CALL THE FLEETS HOME.
WITH THE PRINT OF HIS HAND THE SIGNAL GOES OUT.
ACROSS THE VASTNESS OF SPACE JOHN PROPHET AWAKES.
DUM
DUM

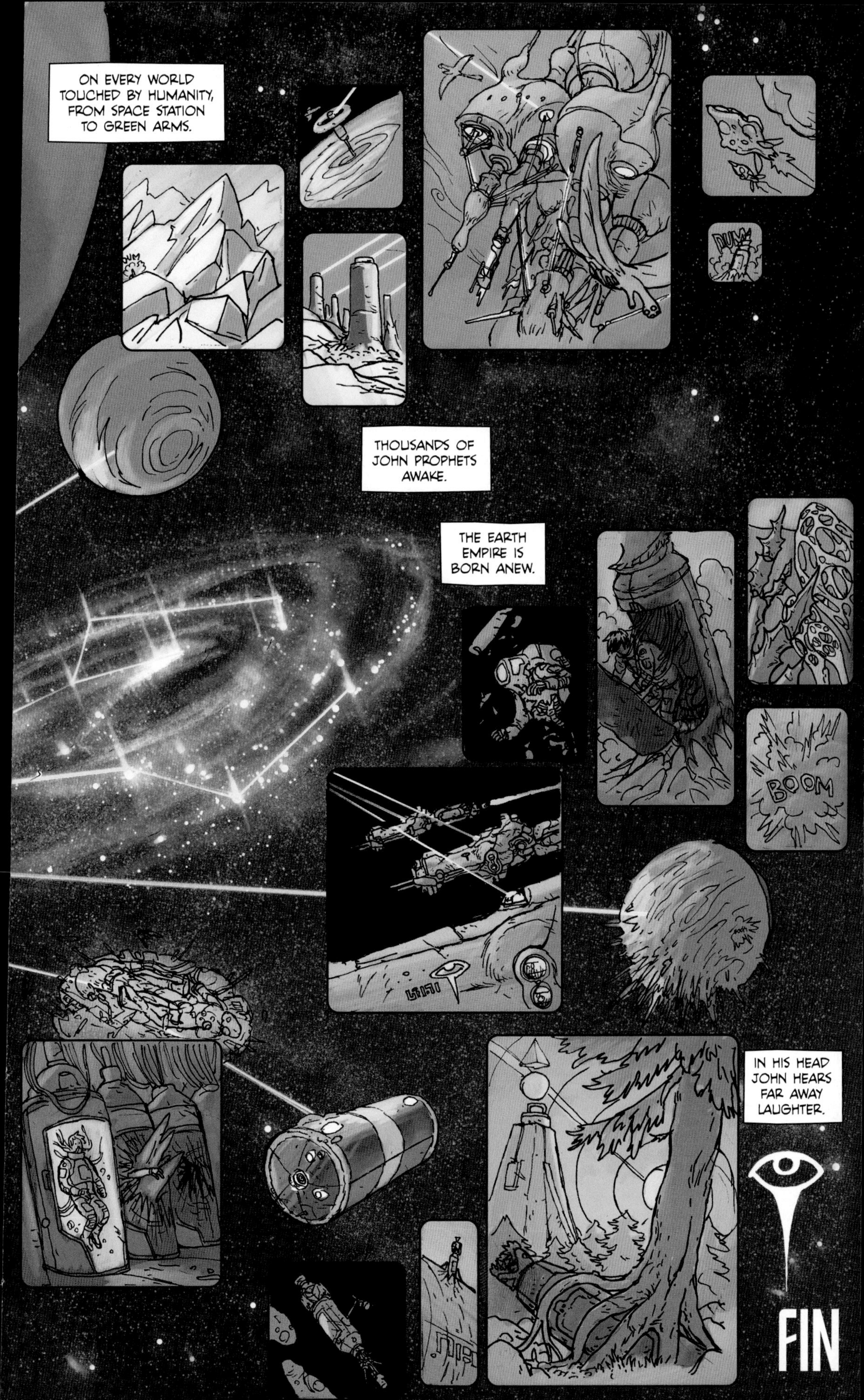
ON EVERY WORLD TOUCHED BY HUMANITY, FROM SPACE STATION TO GREEN ARMS.
DUM
THOUSANDS OF JOHN PROPHETS AWAKE.
THE EARTH EMPIRE IS BORN ANEW.
BOOM
IN HIS HEAD JOHN HEARS FAR AWAY LAUGHTER.
FIN

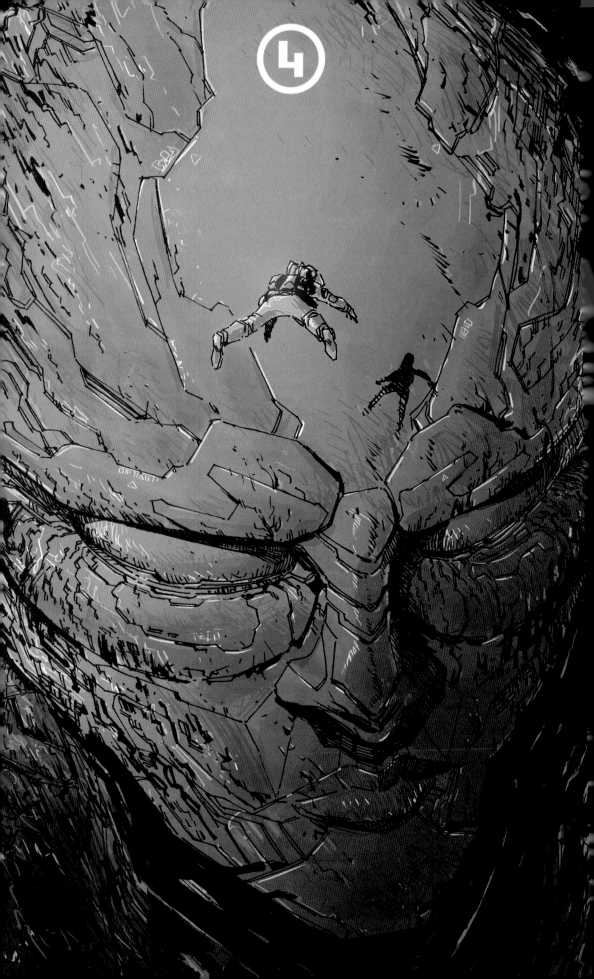

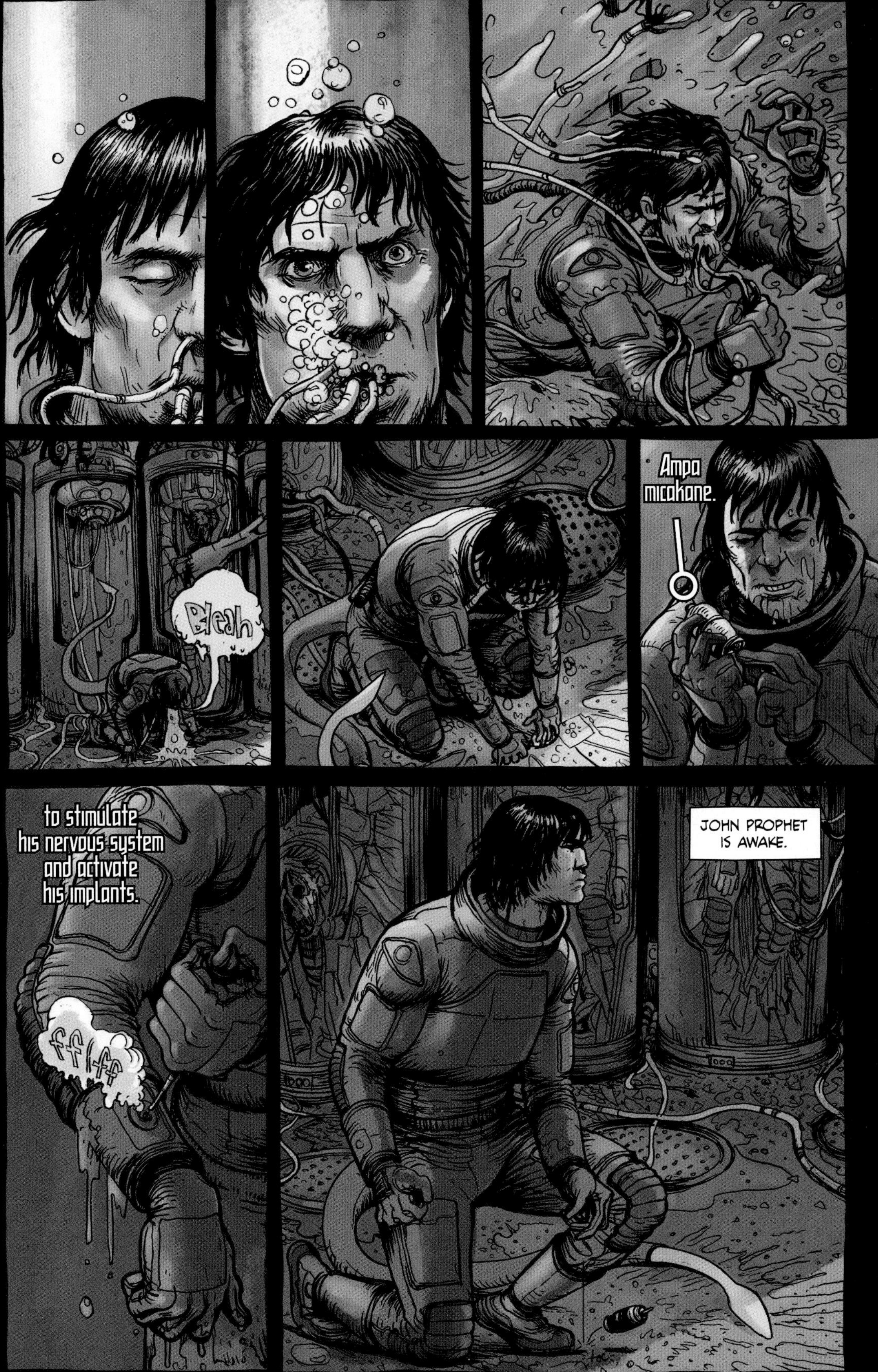
Bleah
Ampa micakane.
to stimulate his nervous system and activate his implants.
fflff
JOHN PROPHET IS AWAKE.

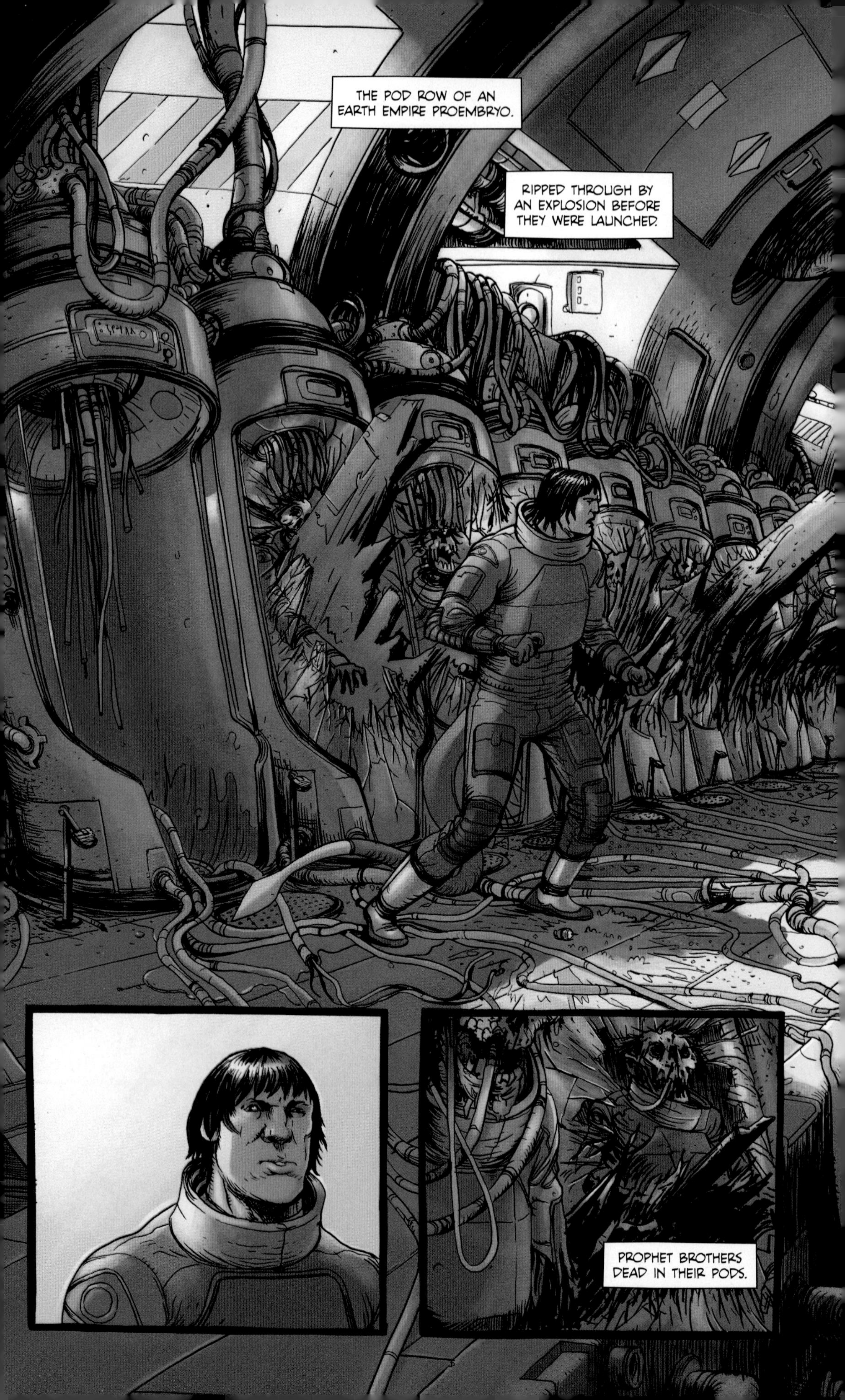
THE POD ROW OF AN EARTH EMPIRE PROEMBRYO.
RIPPED THROUGH BY AN EXPLOSION BEFORE THEY WERE LAUNCHED.
PROPHET BROTHERS DEAD IN THEIR PODS.

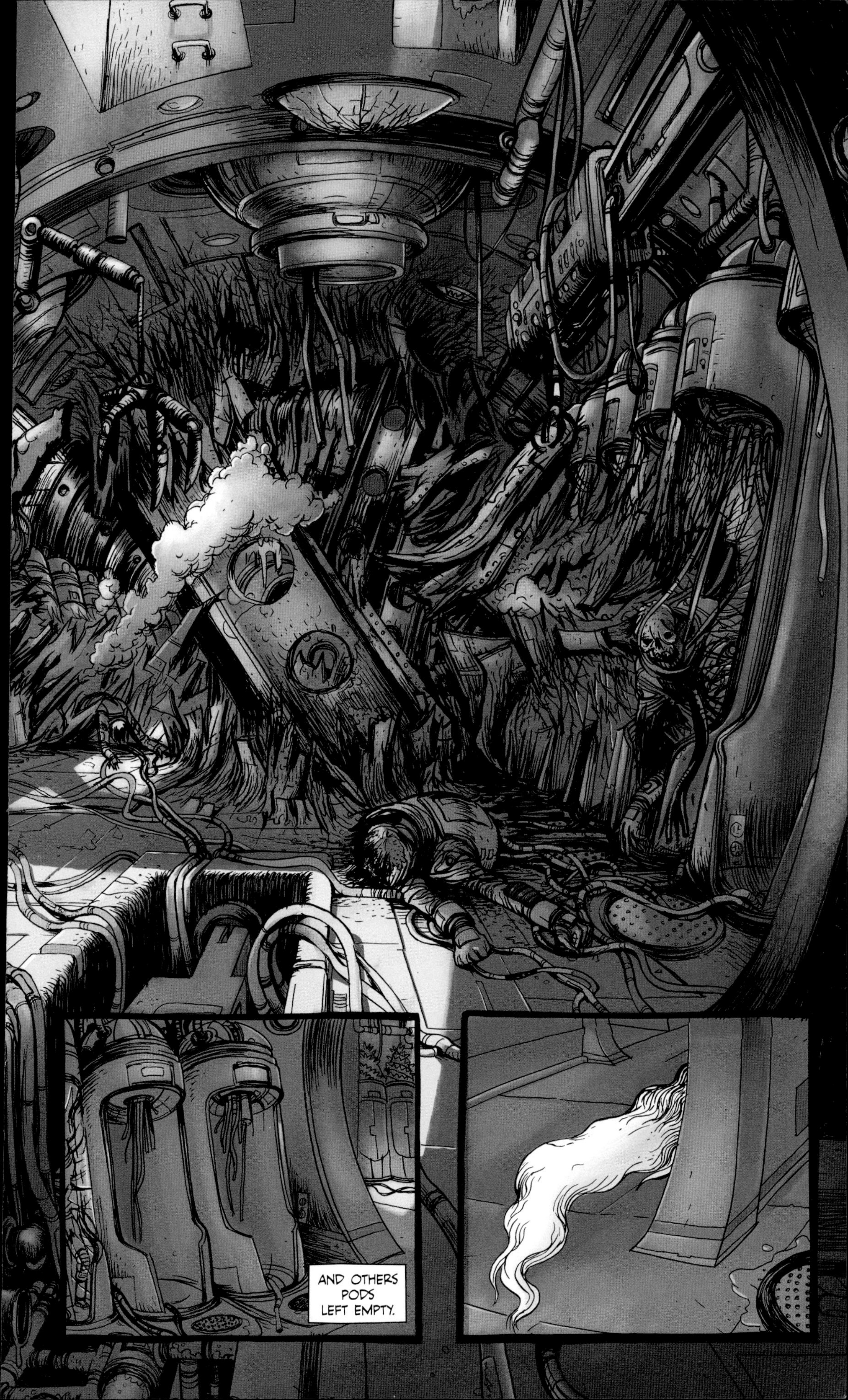
AND OTHERS
PODS
LEFT EMPTY.

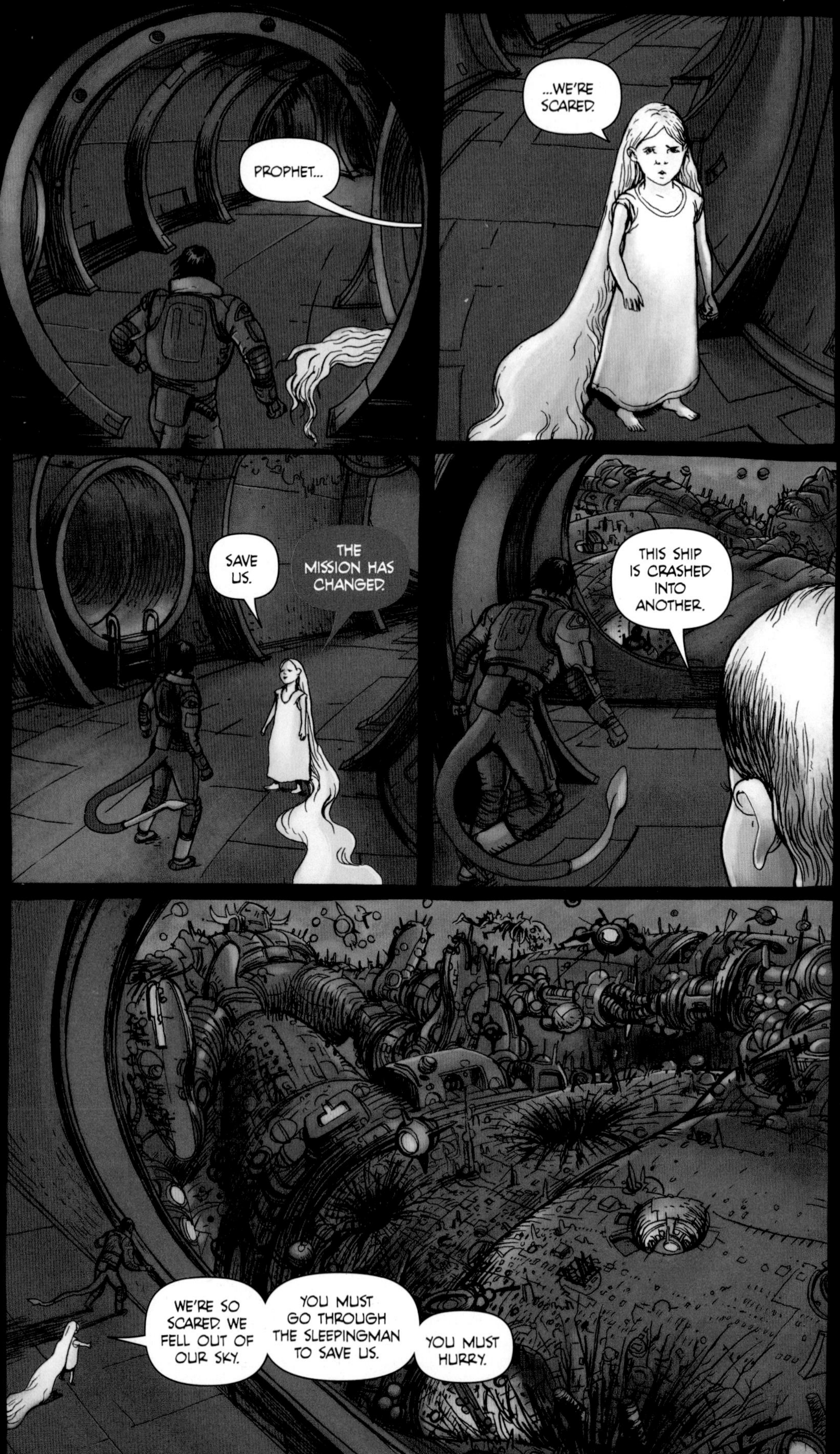
PROPHET...
...WE'RE SCARED.
SAVE US.
THE MISSION HAS CHANGED.
THIS SHIP IS CRASHED INTO ANOTHER.
WE'RE SO SCARED. WE FELL OUT OF OUR SKY.
YOU MUST GO THROUGH THE SLEEPINGMAN TO SAVE US.
YOU MUST HURRY.

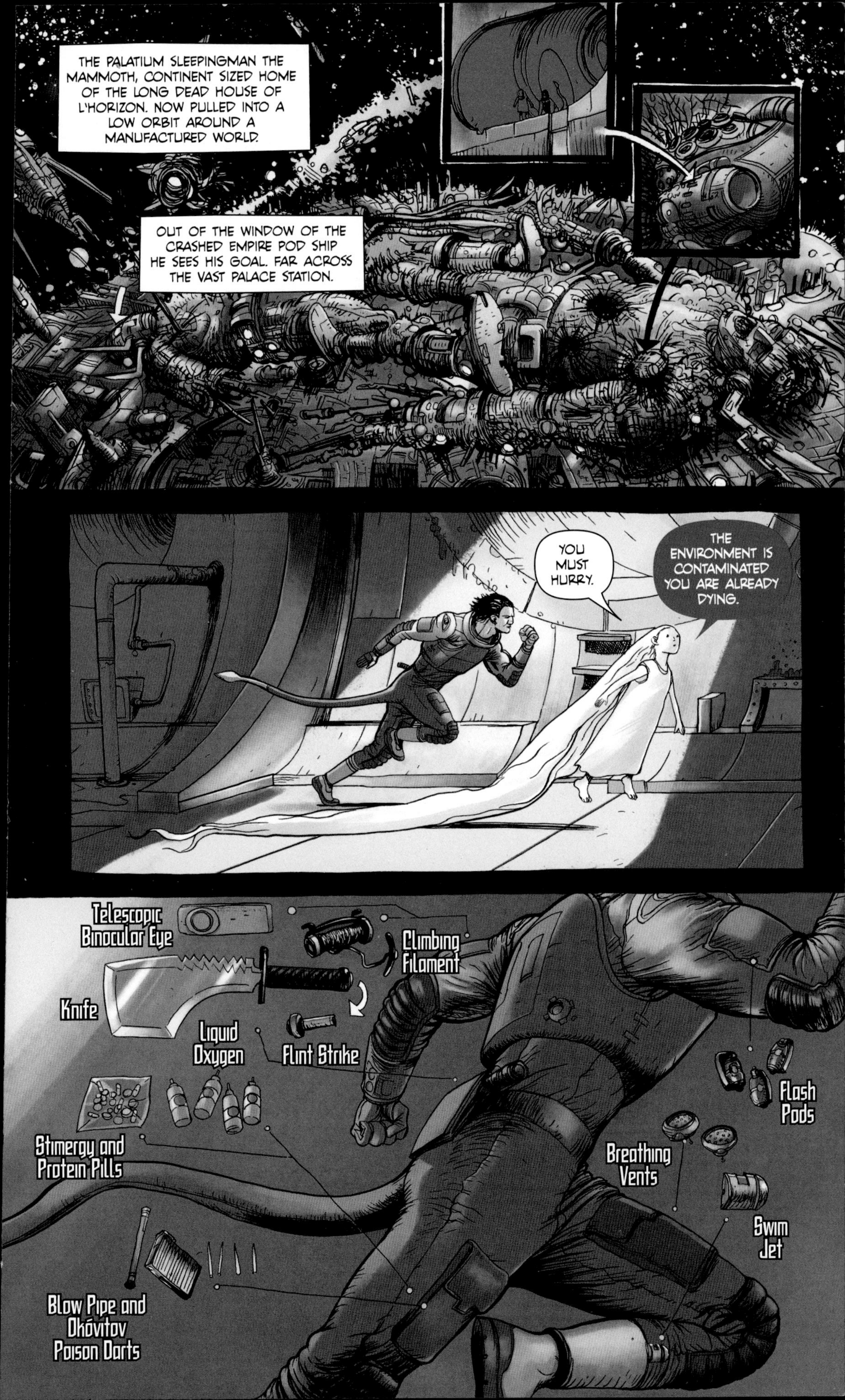
THE PALATIUM SLEEPINGMAN THE MAMMOTH, CONTINENT SIZED HOME OF THE LONG DEAD HOUSE OF L'HORIZON. NOW PULLED INTO A LOW ORBIT AROUND A MANUFACTURED WORLD.
OUT OF THE WINDOW OF THE CRASHED EMPIRE POD SHIP HE SEES HIS GOAL. FAR ACROSS THE VAST PALACE STATION.
YOU MUST HURRY.
THE ENVIRONMENT IS CONTAMINATED YOU ARE ALREADY DYING.
Telescopic Binocular Eye
Climbing Filament
Knife
Liquid Oxygen
Flint Strike
Flash Pods
Stimergy and Protein Pills
Breathing Vents
Swim Jet
Blow Pipe and Okóvitov Poison Darts

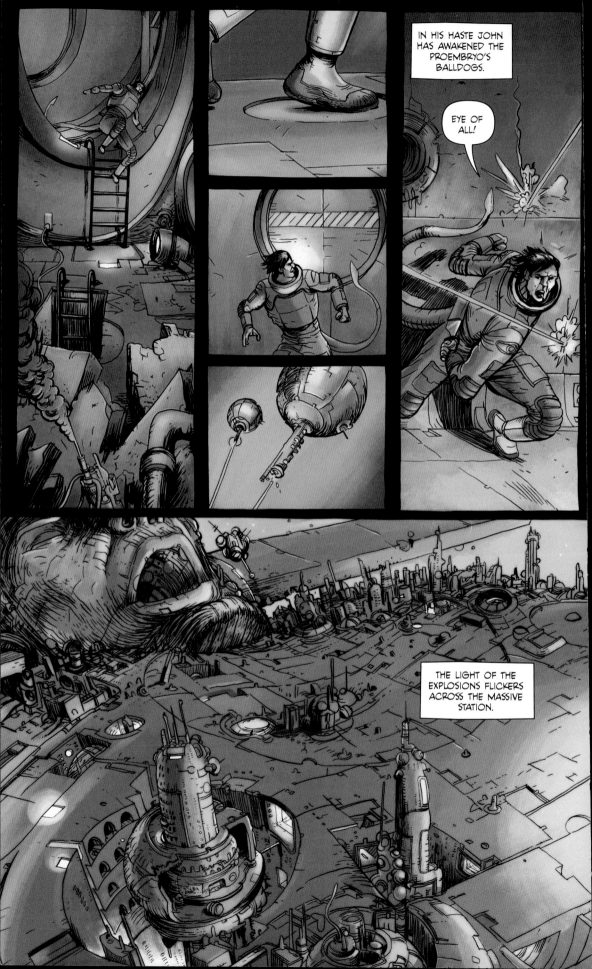

IN HIS HASTE JOHN HAS AWAKENED THE PROEMBRYO'S BALLDOGS.

EYE OF ALL!

THE LIGHT OF THE EXPLOSIONS FLICKERS ACROSS THE MASSIVE STATION.

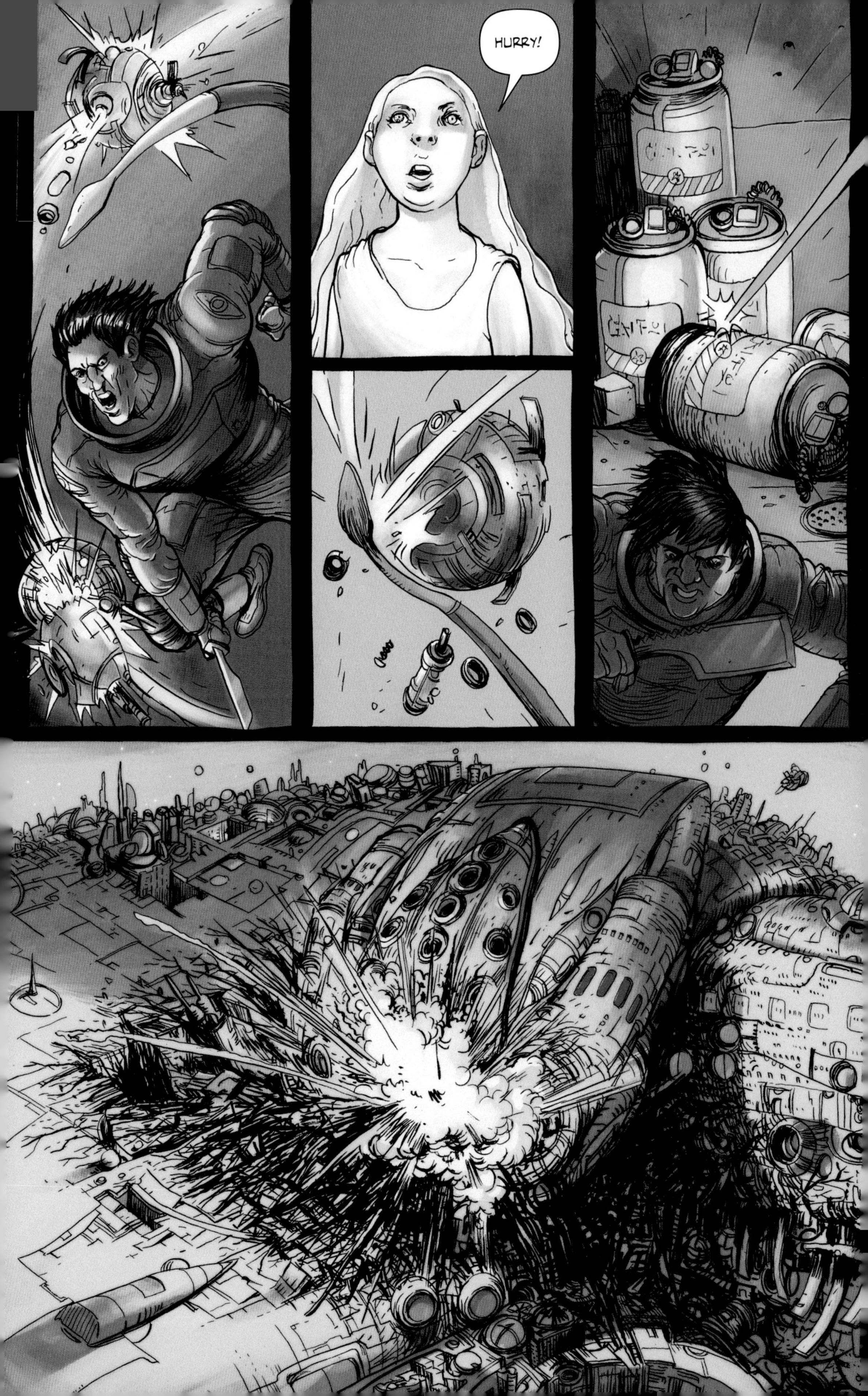
HURRY!

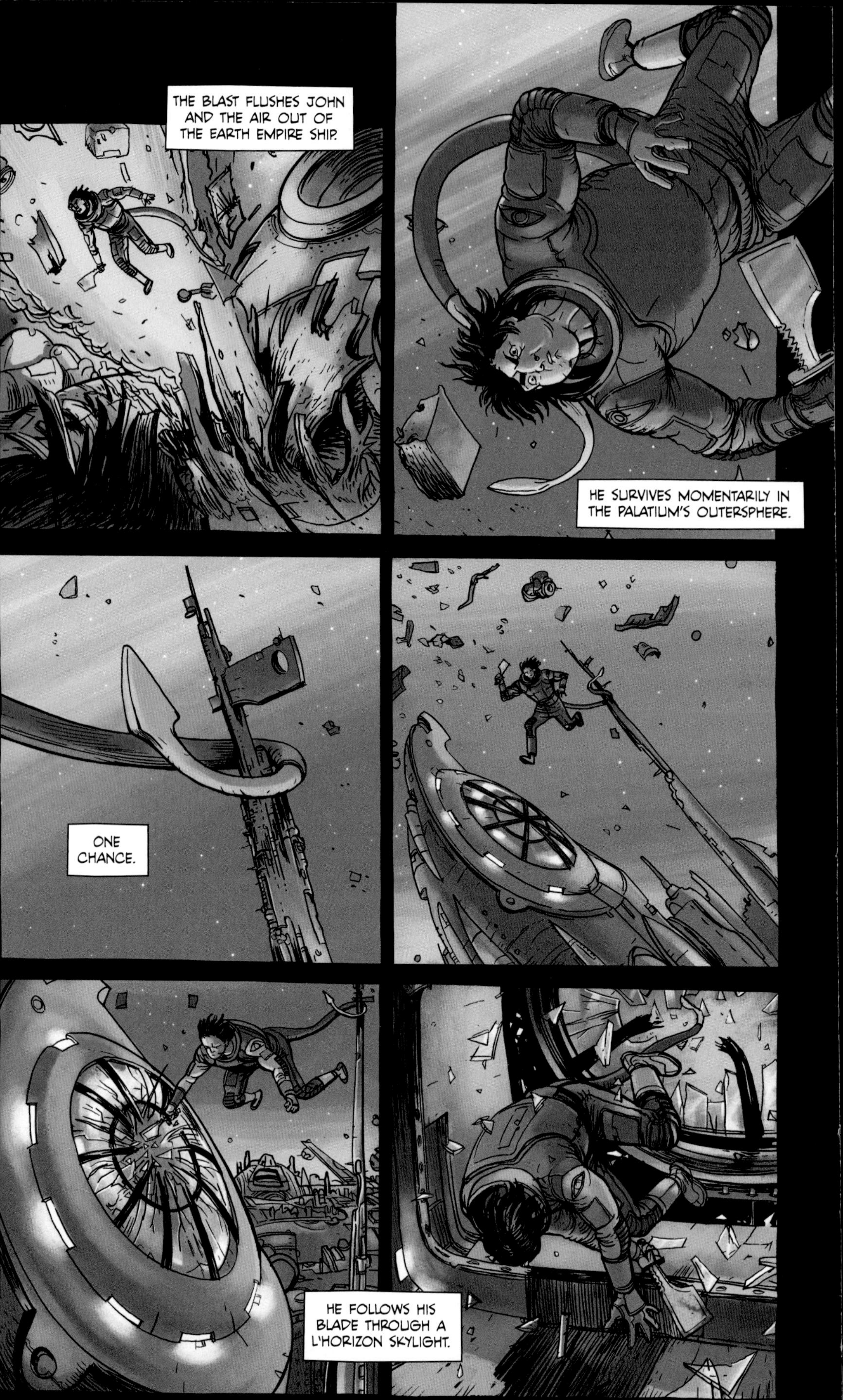
THE BLAST FLUSHES JOHN AND THE AIR OUT OF THE EARTH EMPIRE SHIP.
HE SURVIVES MOMENTARILY IN THE PALATIUM'S OUTERSPHERE.
ONE CHANCE.
HE FOLLOWS HIS BLADE THROUGH A L'HORIZON SKYLIGHT.

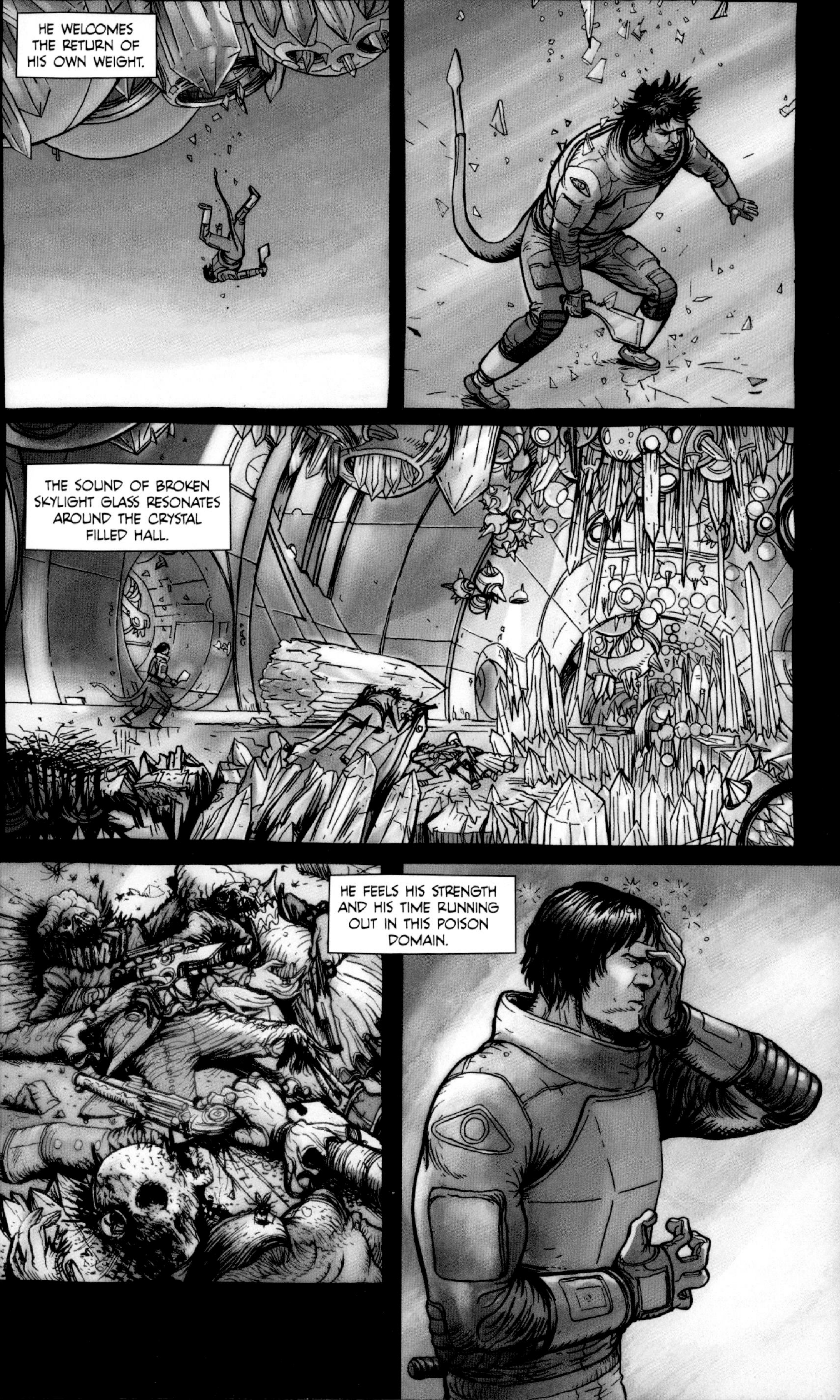
HE WELCOMES THE RETURN OF HIS OWN WEIGHT.
THE SOUND OF BROKEN SKYLIGHT GLASS RESONATES AROUND THE CRYSTAL FILLED HALL.
HE FEELS HIS STRENGTH AND HIS TIME RUNNING OUT IN THIS POISON DOMAIN.

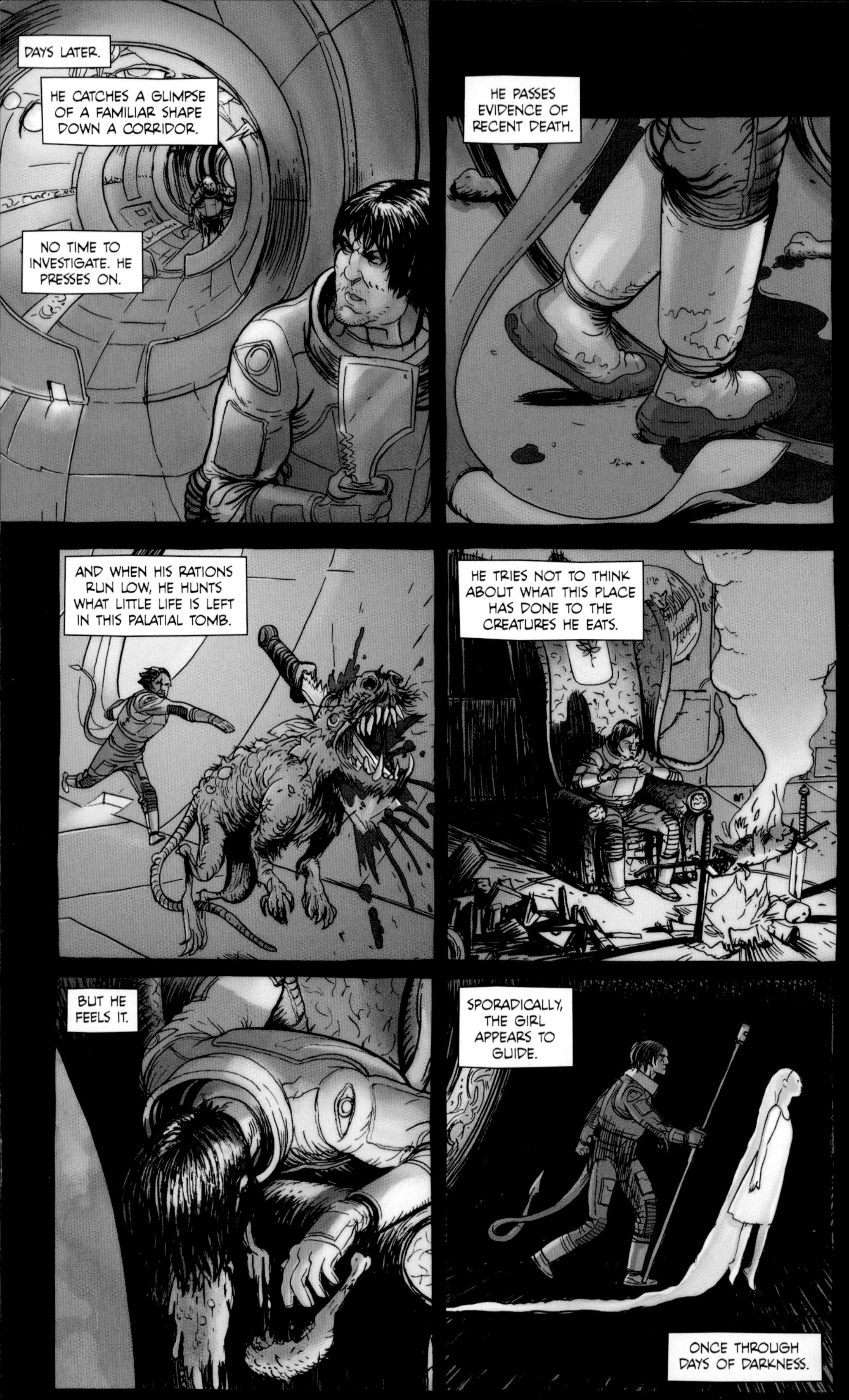
DAYS LATER.
HE CATCHES A GLIMPSE OF A FAMILIAR SHAPE DOWN A CORRIDOR.
NO TIME TO INVESTIGATE. HE PRESSES ON.
HE PASSES EVIDENCE OF RECENT DEATH.
AND WHEN HIS RATIONS RUN LOW, HE HUNTS WHAT LITTLE LIFE IS LEFT IN THIS PALATIAL TOMB.
HE TRIES NOT TO THINK ABOUT WHAT THIS PLACE HAS DONE TO THE CREATURES HE EATS.
BUT HE FEELS IT.
SPORADICALLY, THE GIRL APPEARS TO GUIDE.
ONCE THROUGH DAYS OF DARKNESS.

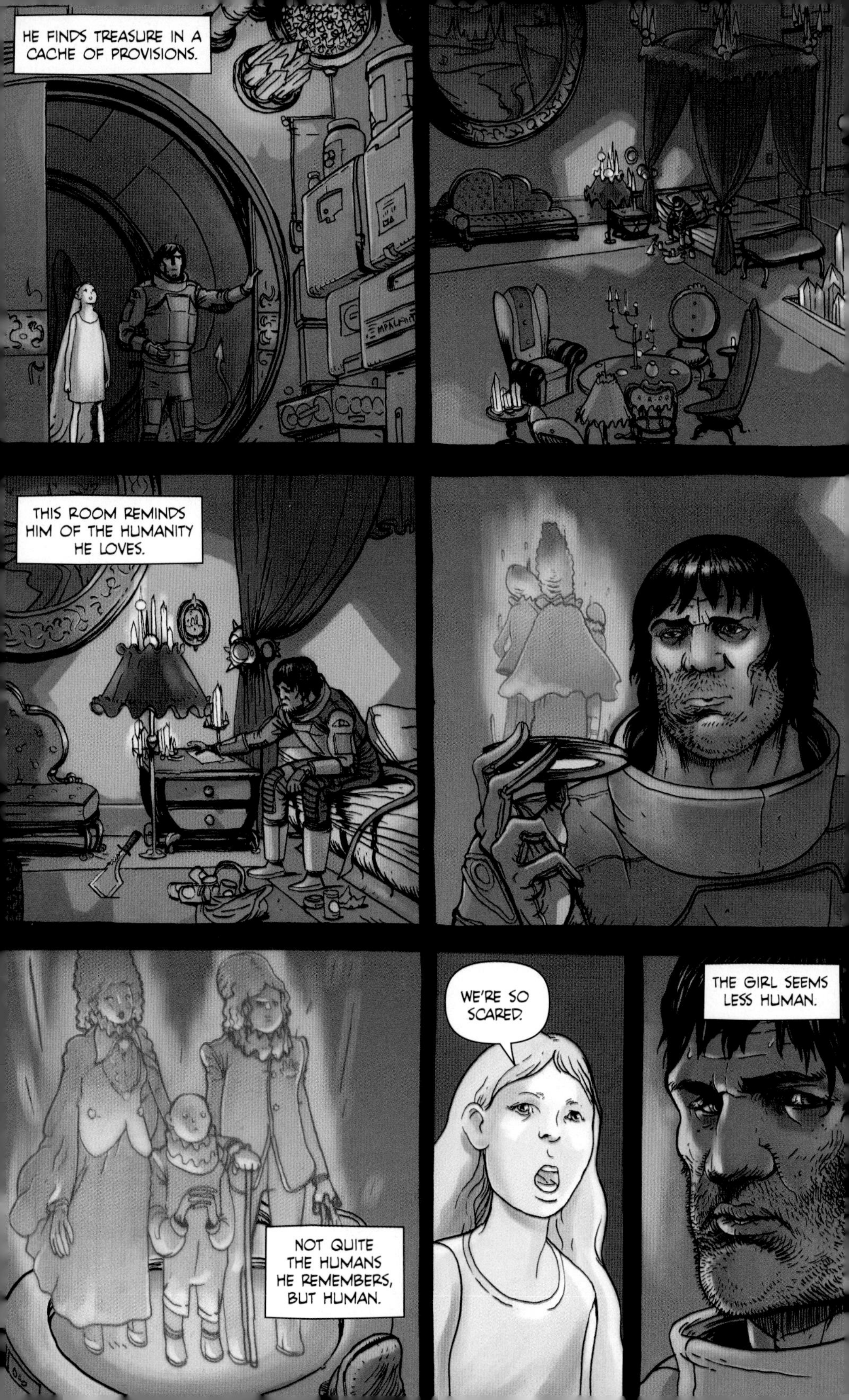
HE FINDS TREASURE IN A CACHE OF PROVISIONS.
THIS ROOM REMINDS HIM OF THE HUMANITY HE LOVES.
NOT QUITE THE HUMANS HE REMEMBERS, BUT HUMAN.
WE'RE SO SCARED.
THE GIRL SEEMS LESS HUMAN.

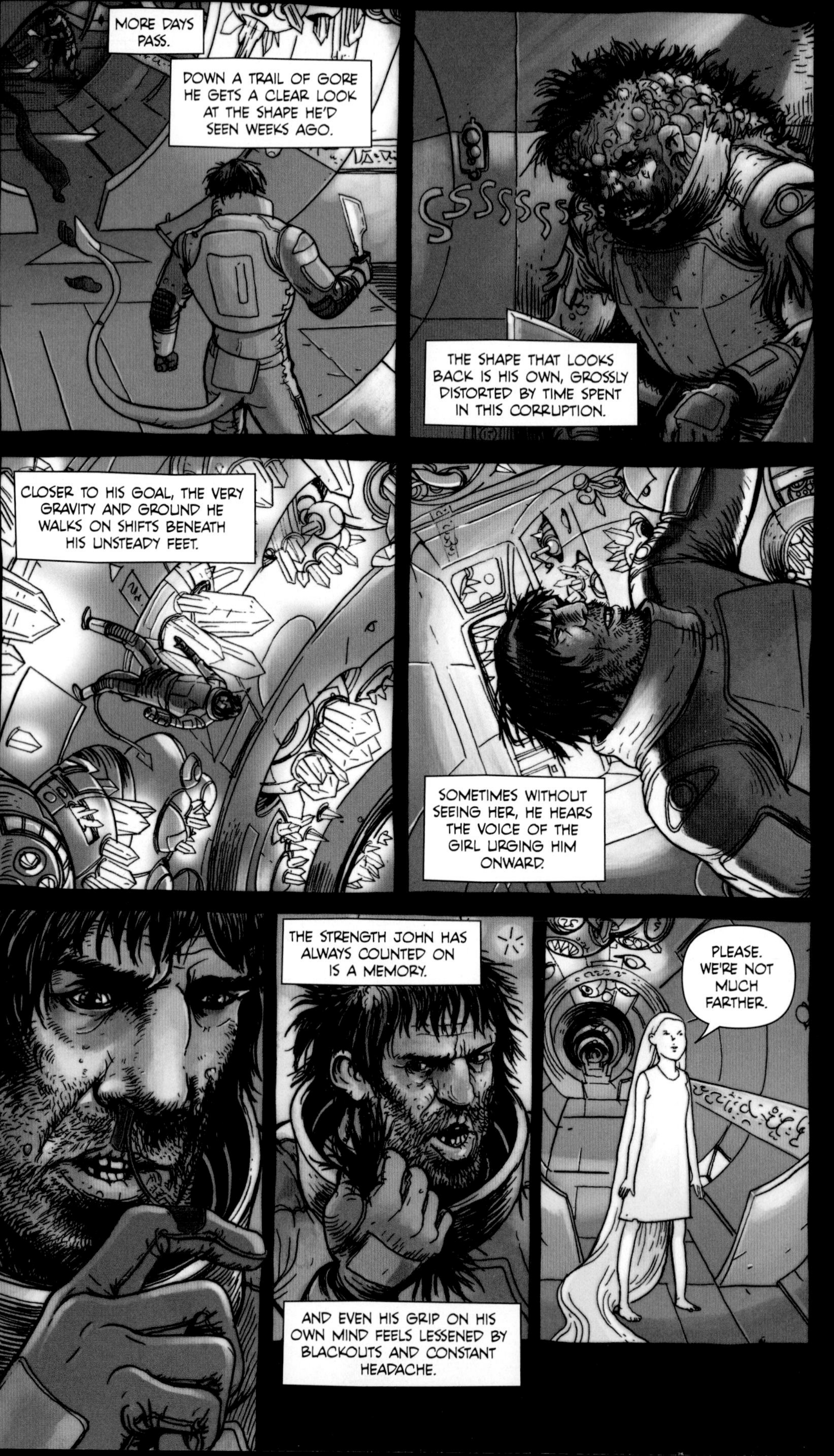
MORE DAYS PASS.
DOWN A TRAIL OF GORE HE GETS A CLEAR LOOK AT THE SHAPE HE'D SEEN WEEKS AGO.
SSSSSSS
THE SHAPE THAT LOOKS BACK IS HIS OWN, GROSSLY DISTORTED BY TIME SPENT IN THIS CORRUPTION.
CLOSER TO HIS GOAL, THE VERY GRAVITY AND GROUND HE WALKS ON SHIFTS BENEATH HIS UNSTEADY FEET.
SOMETIMES WITHOUT SEEING HER, HE HEARS THE VOICE OF THE GIRL URGING HIM ONWARD.
THE STRENGTH JOHN HAS ALWAYS COUNTED ON IS A MEMORY.
AND EVEN HIS GRIP ON HIS OWN MIND FEELS LESSENED BY BLACKOUTS AND CONSTANT HEADACHE.
PLEASE. WE'RE NOT MUCH FARTHER.

WALKING HAS BECOME A TREMENDOUS FEAT BY THE TIME HIS DOPPELGANGER DECIDES TO STRIKE.

THE BLADE THAT JOHN KNOWS SO WELL NOW TURNED AGAINST HIM.

JOHN PULLS HIS BROTHER'S WEAPON FROM HIS WOUND.

AND RETURNS IT TO HIM.

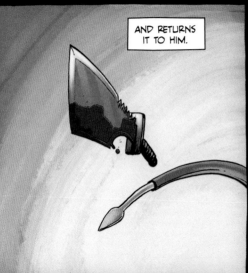

AND THEN RETURNS TO THE TASK OF WALKING.

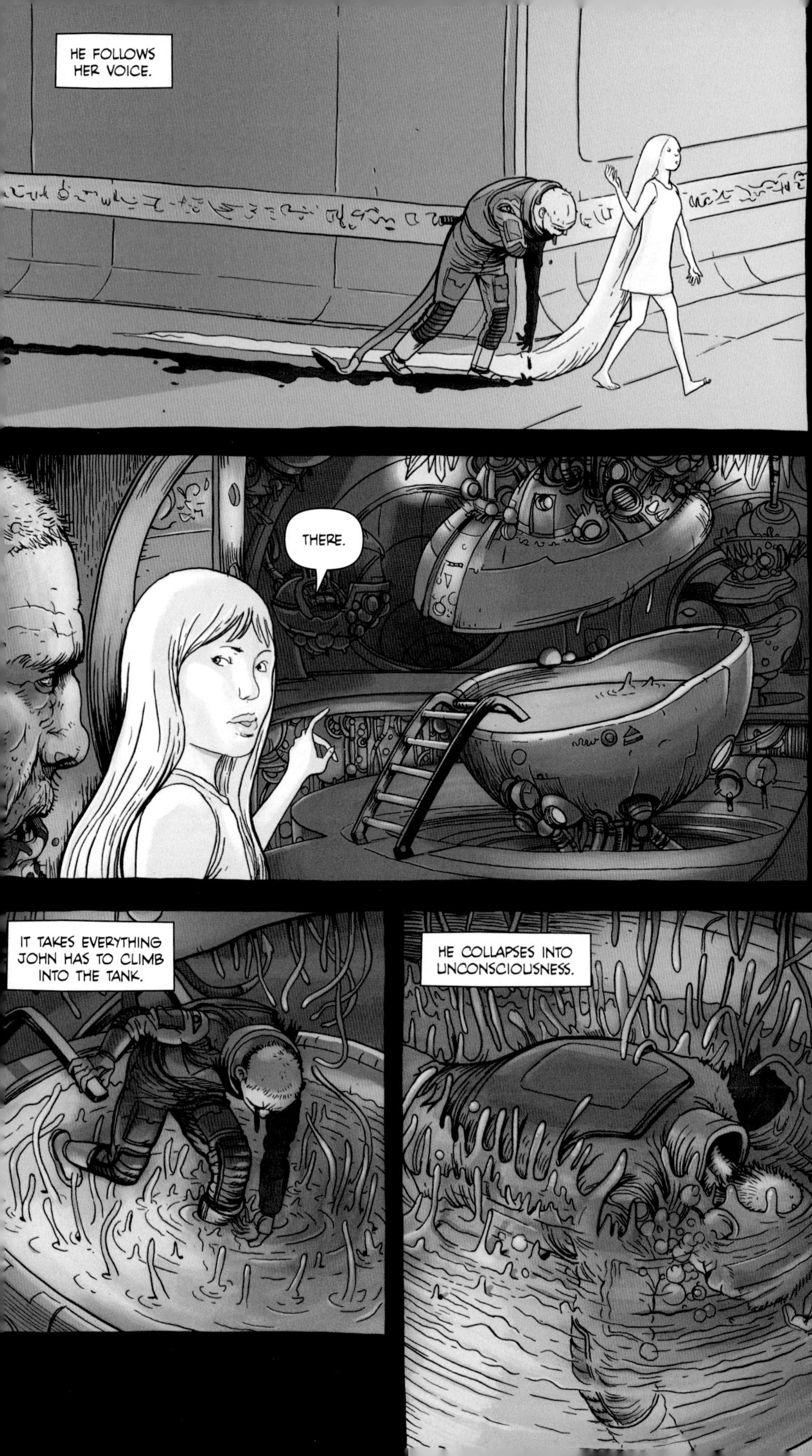
HE FOLLOWS HER VOICE.
THERE.
IT TAKES EVERYTHING JOHN HAS TO CLIMB INTO THE TANK.
HE COLLAPSES INTO UNCONSCIOUSNESS.

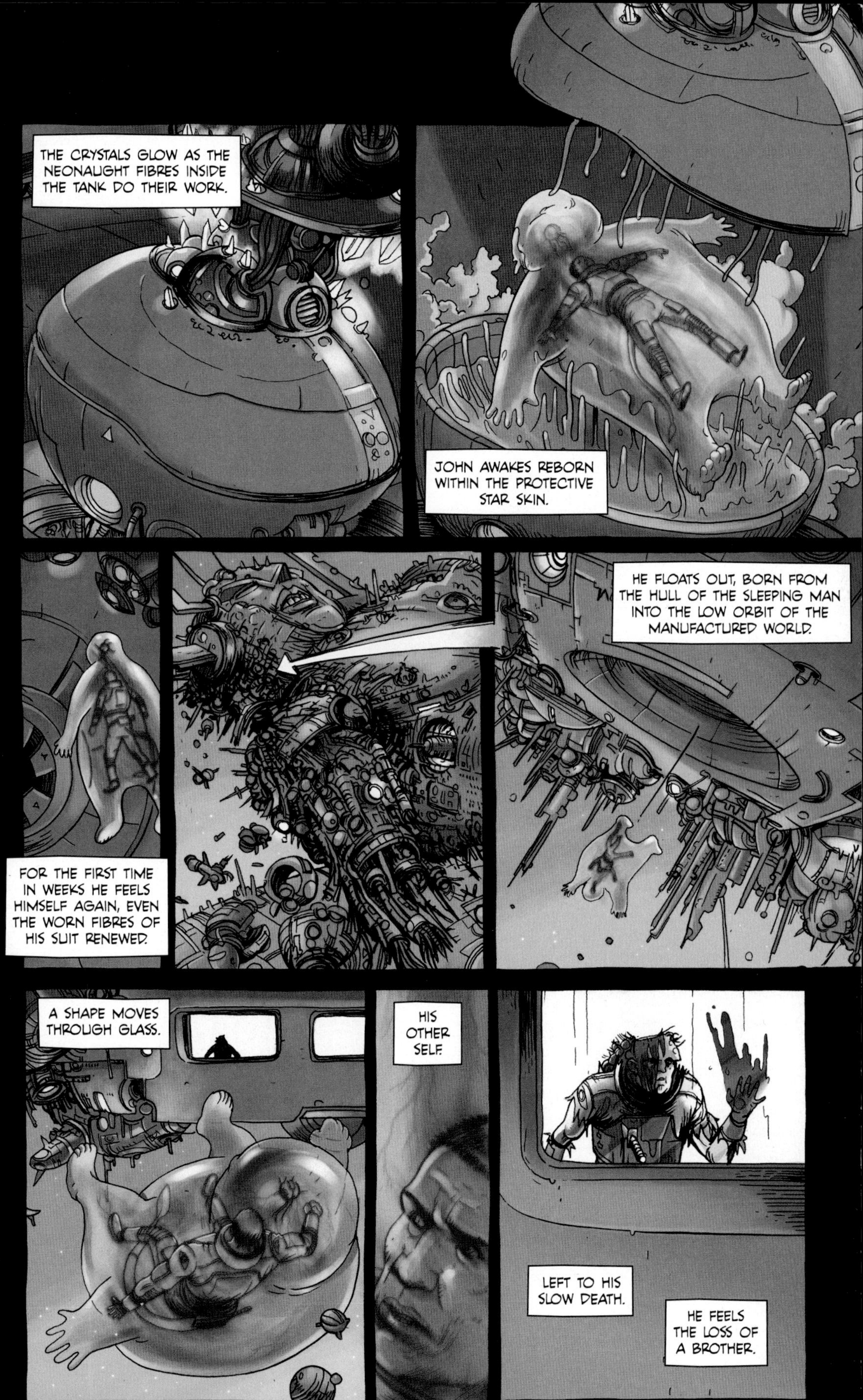
THE CRYSTALS GLOW AS THE NEONAUGHT FIBRES INSIDE THE TANK DO THEIR WORK.
JOHN AWAKES REBORN WITHIN THE PROTECTIVE STAR SKIN.
HE FLOATS OUT, BORN FROM THE HULL OF THE SLEEPING MAN INTO THE LOW ORBIT OF THE MANUFACTURED WORLD.
FOR THE FIRST TIME IN WEEKS HE FEELS HIMSELF AGAIN, EVEN THE WORN FIBRES OF HIS SUIT RENEWED.
A SHAPE MOVES THROUGH GLASS.
HIS OTHER SELF.
LEFT TO HIS SLOW DEATH.
HE FEELS THE LOSS OF A BROTHER.

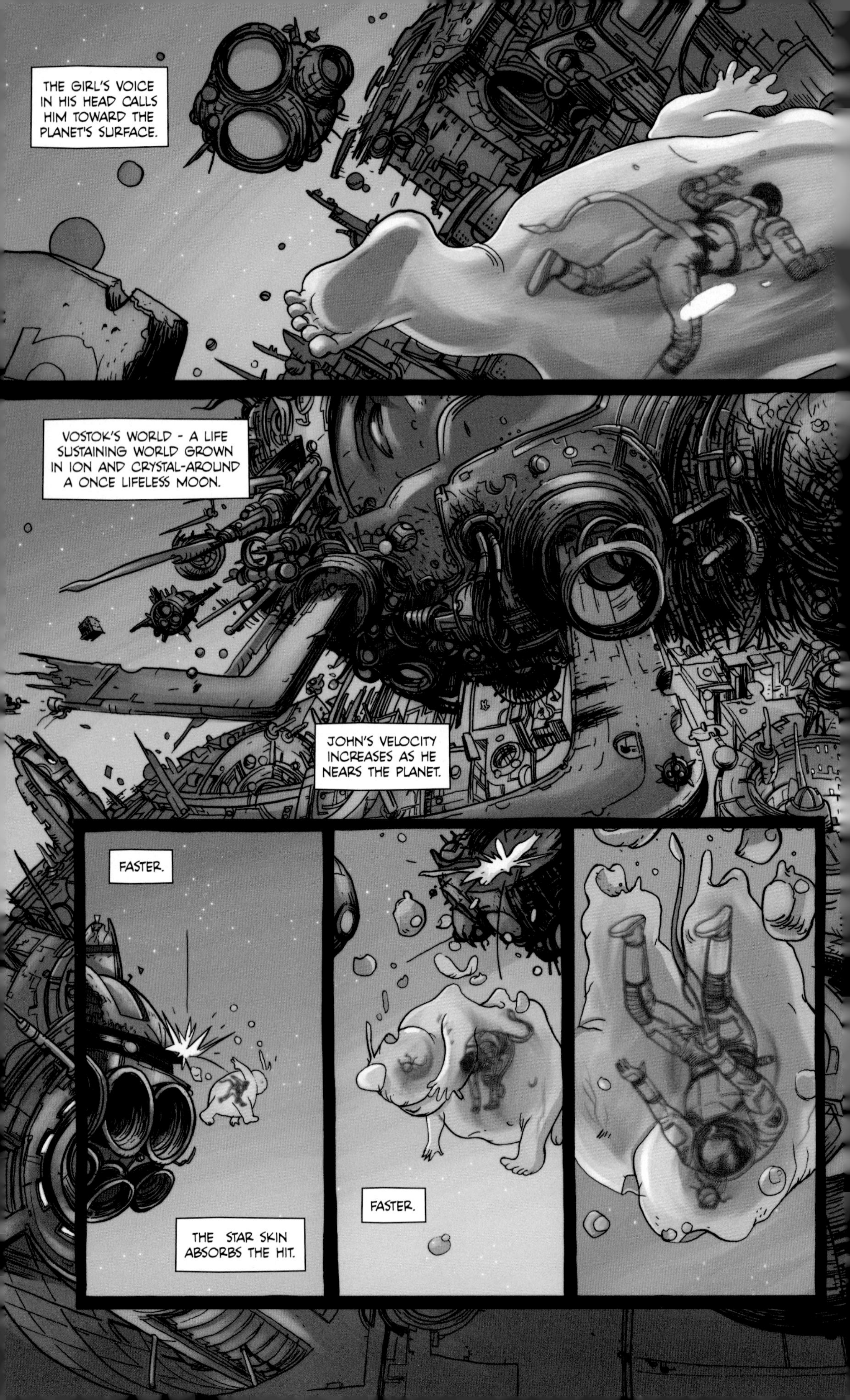
THE GIRL'S VOICE IN HIS HEAD CALLS HIM TOWARD THE PLANET'S SURFACE.
VOSTOK'S WORLD - A LIFE SUSTAINING WORLD GROWN IN ION AND CRYSTAL-AROUND A ONCE LIFELESS MOON.
JOHN'S VELOCITY INCREASES AS HE NEARS THE PLANET.
FASTER.
THE STAR SKIN ABSORBS THE HIT.
FASTER.

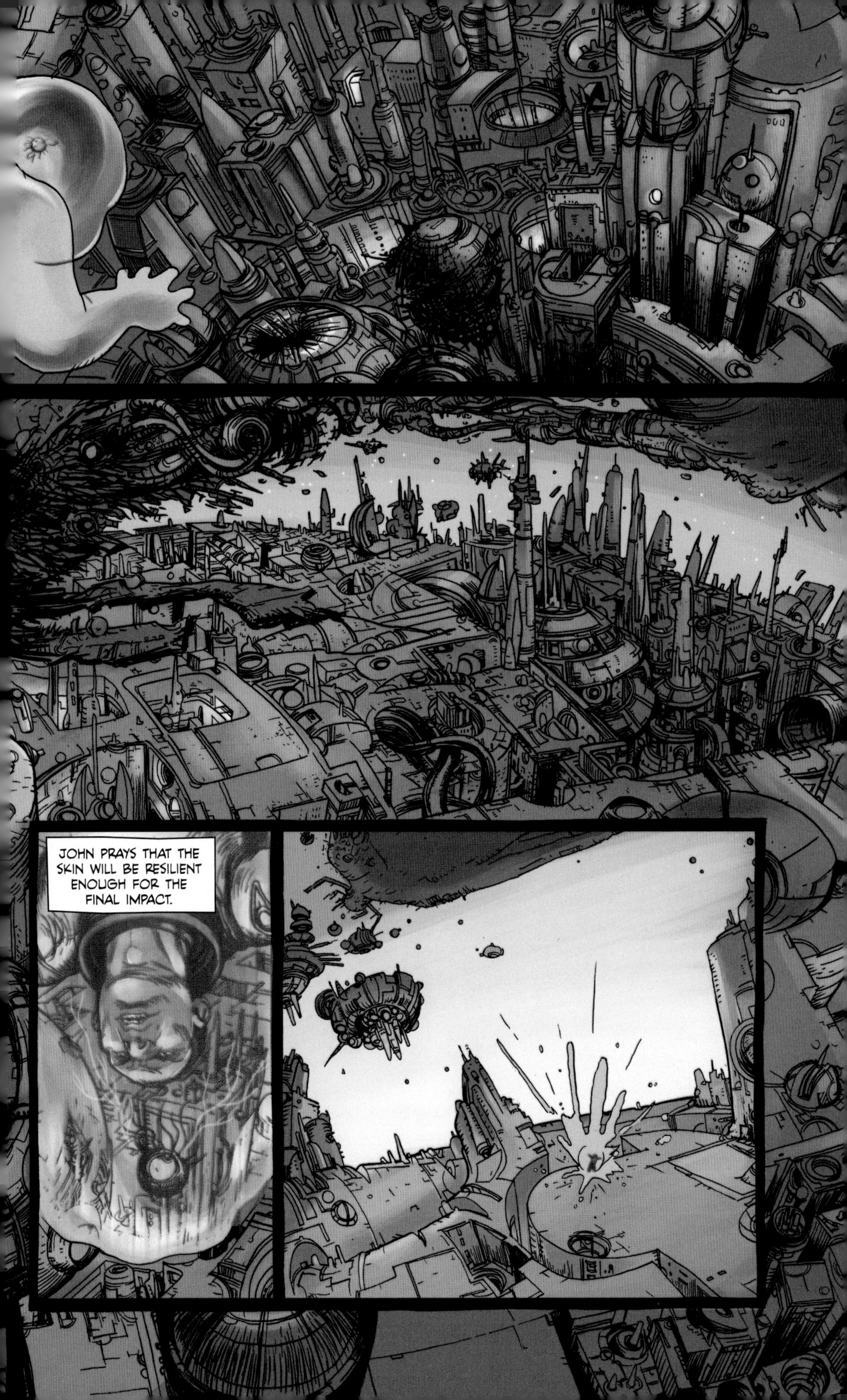
JOHN PRAYS THAT THE SKIN WILL BE RESILIENT ENOUGH FOR THE FINAL IMPACT.

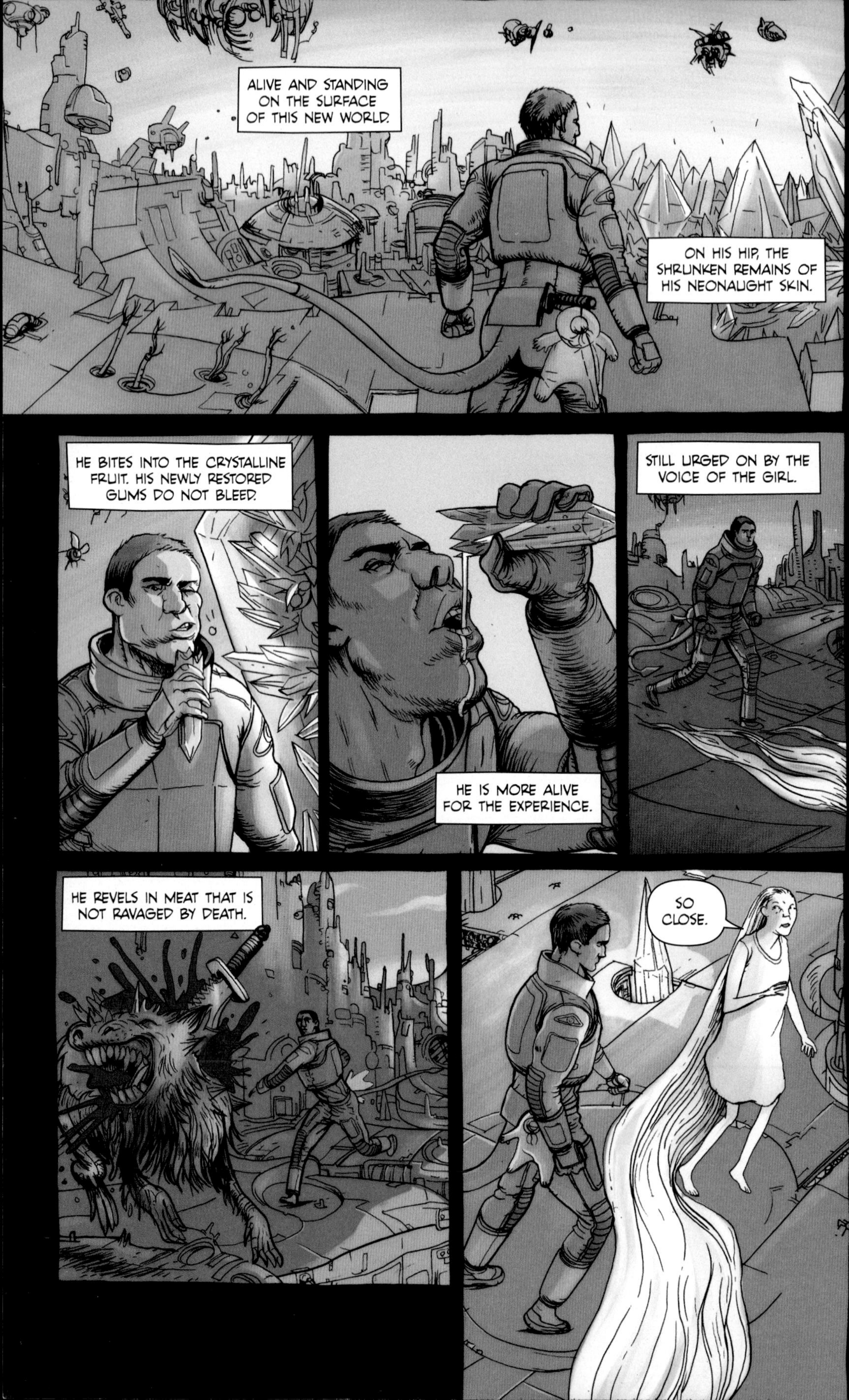
ALIVE AND STANDING ON THE SURFACE OF THIS NEW WORLD.
ON HIS HIP, THE SHRUNKEN REMAINS OF HIS NEONAUGHT SKIN.
HE BITES INTO THE CRYSTALLINE FRUIT. HIS NEWLY RESTORED GUMS DO NOT BLEED.
HE IS MORE ALIVE FOR THE EXPERIENCE.
STILL URGED ON BY THE VOICE OF THE GIRL.
HE REVELS IN MEAT THAT IS NOT RAVAGED BY DEATH.
SO CLOSE.

PART OF THE SLEEPING MAN FALLEN TO THE SURFACE.

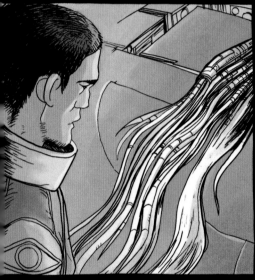

HE CAN FEEL HIS GOAL JUST AHEAD.

IT IS AN ITCH THAT MUST BE SCRATCHED.

WE ARE HERE.

EYE OF ALL!

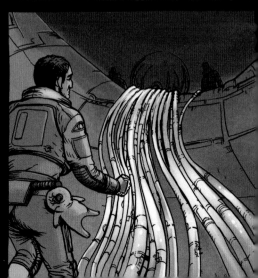

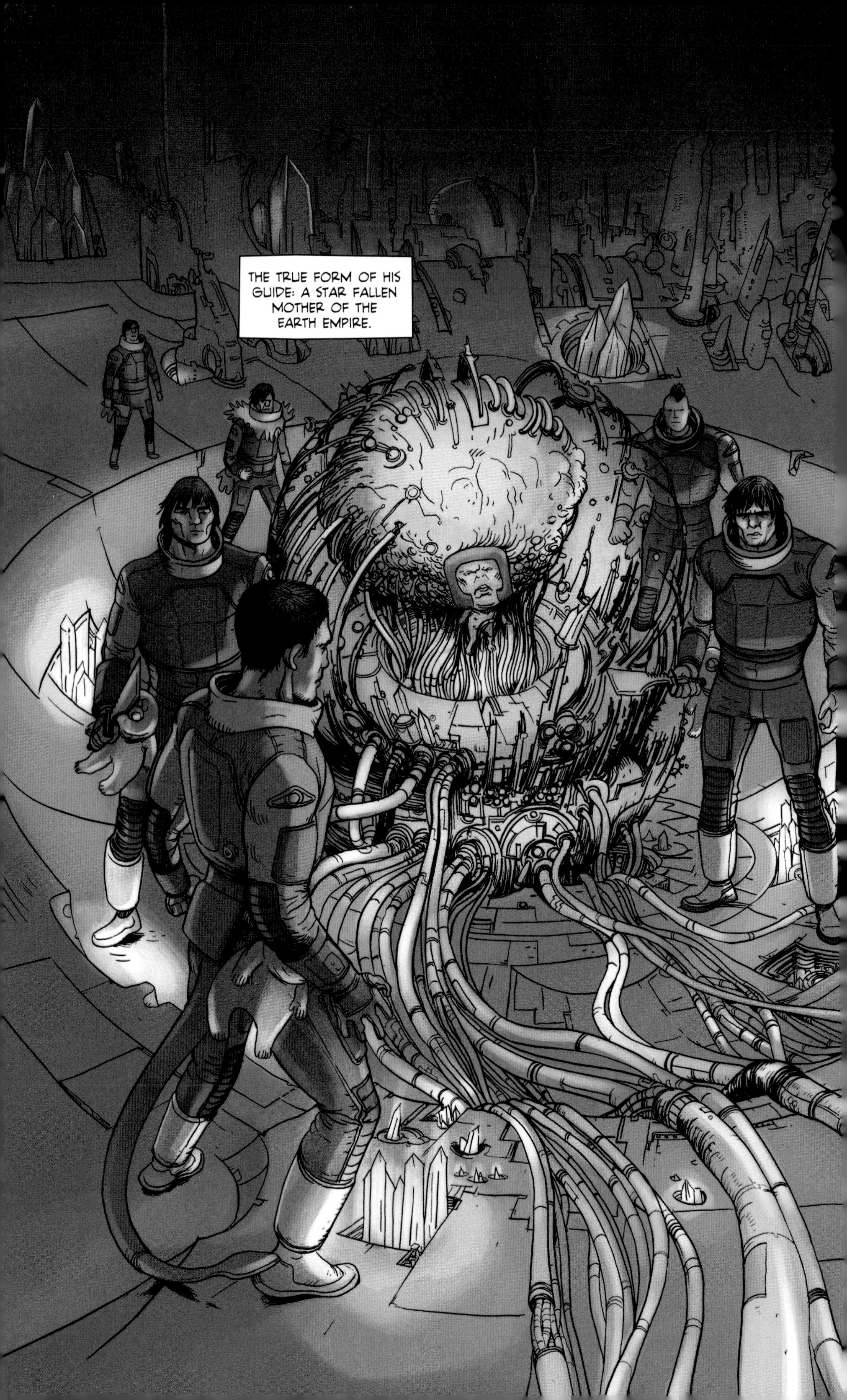
THE TRUE FORM OF HIS GUIDE: A STAR FALLEN MOTHER OF THE EARTH EMPIRE.

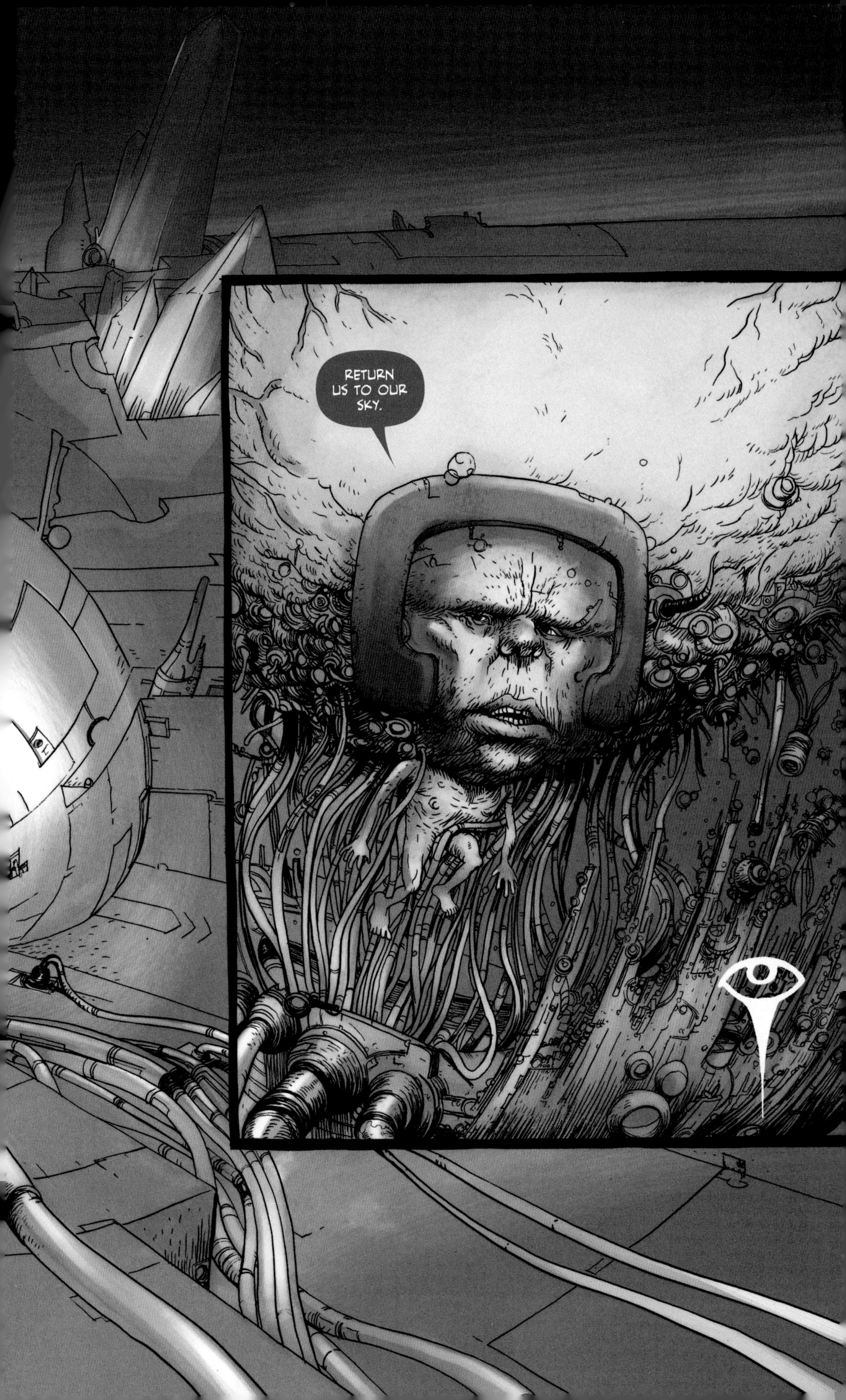
RETURN US TO OUR SKY.

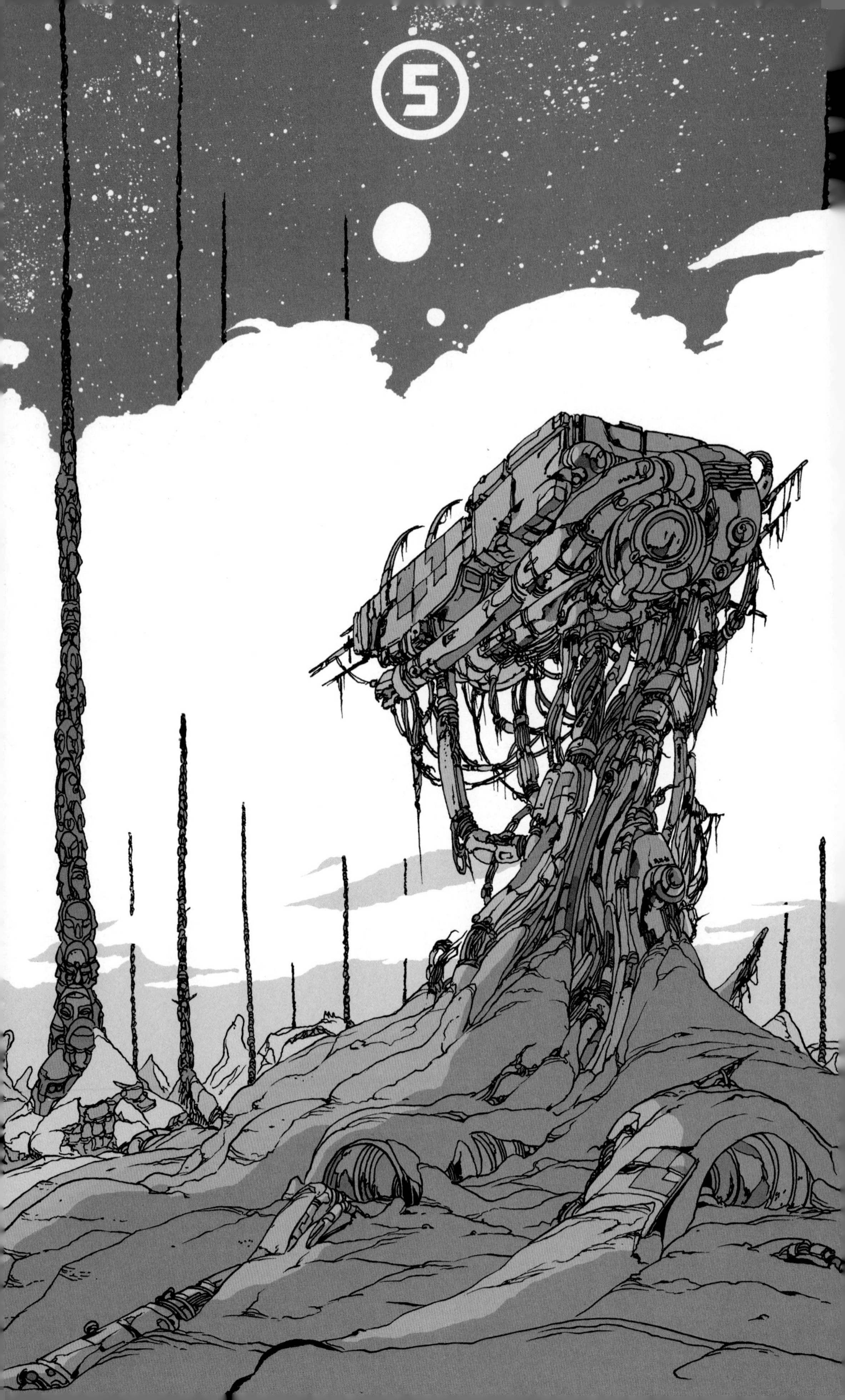
5

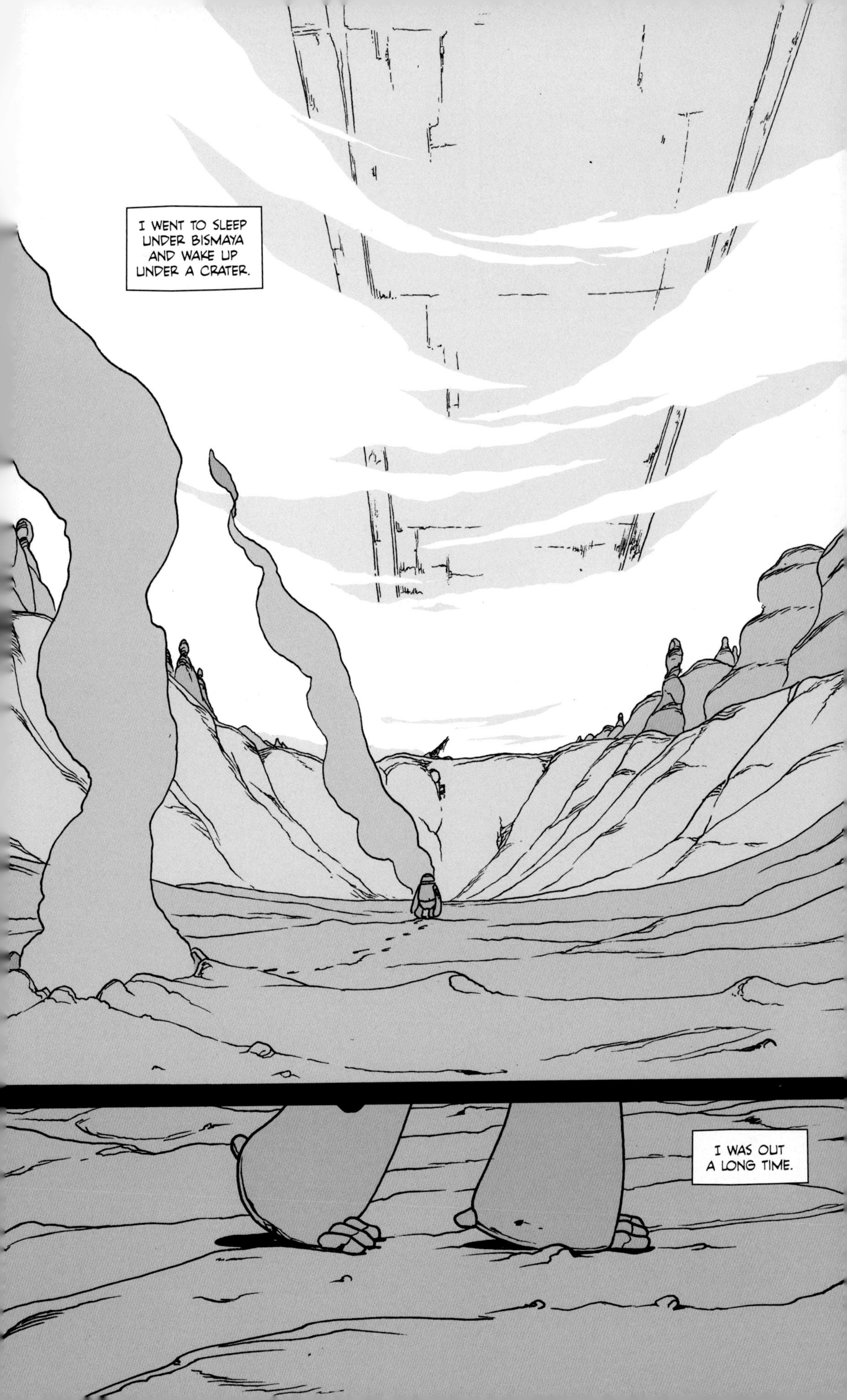
I WENT TO SLEEP UNDER BISMAYA AND WAKE UP UNDER A CRATER.
I WAS OUT A LONG TIME.

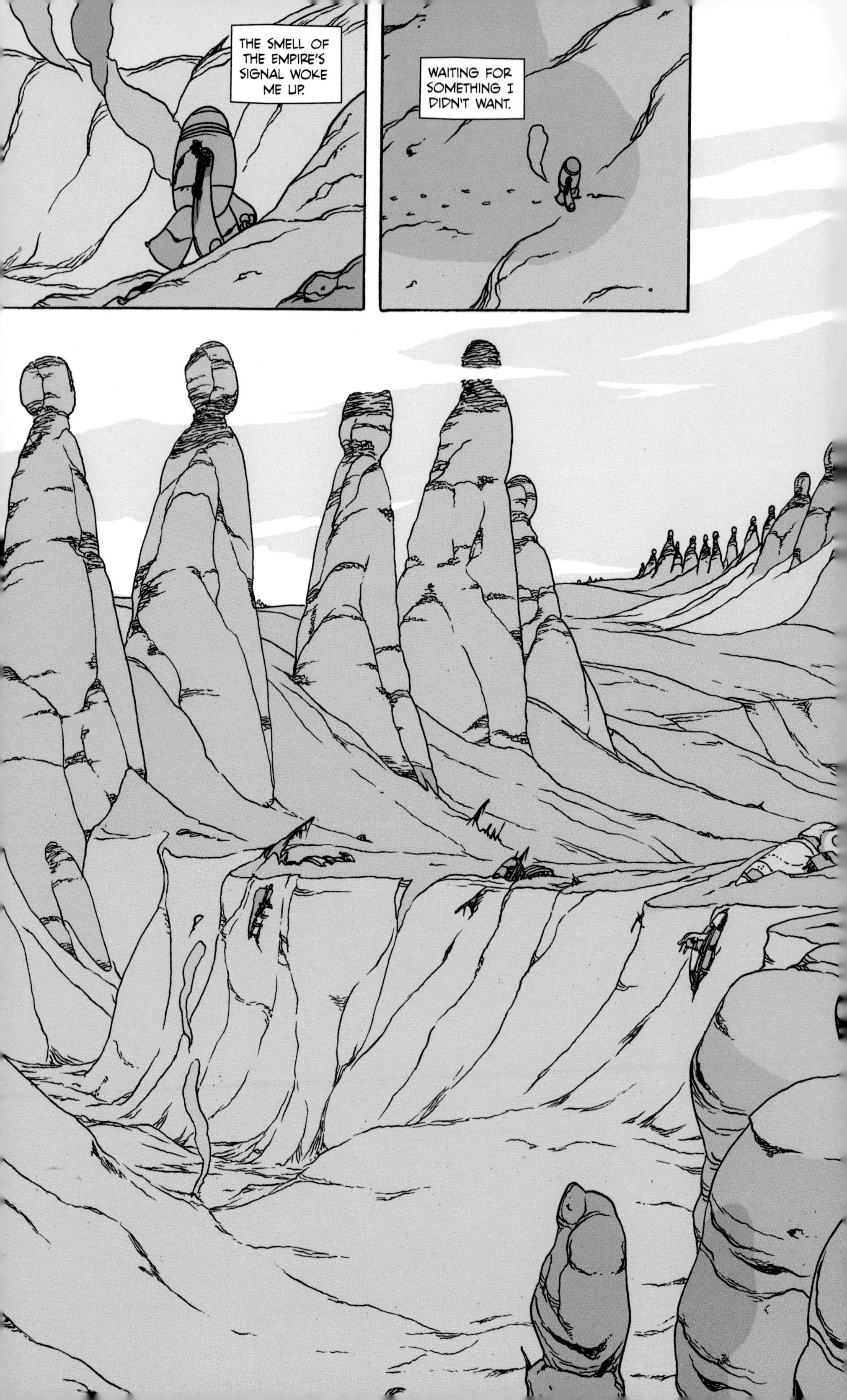
THE SMELL OF THE EMPIRE'S SIGNAL WOKE ME UP.
WAITING FOR SOMETHING I DIDN'T WANT.

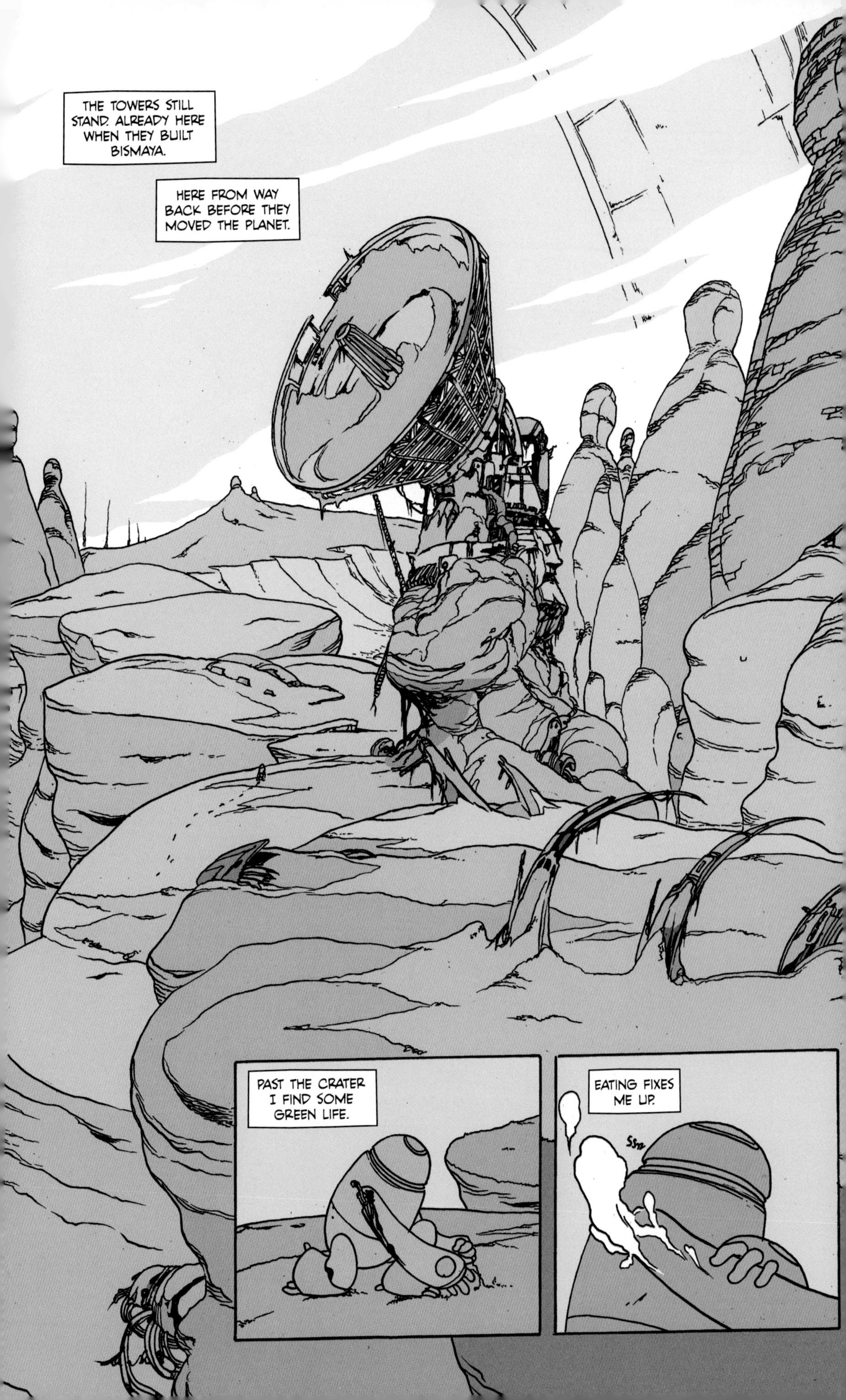
THE TOWERS STILL STAND. ALREADY HERE WHEN THEY BUILT BISMAYA.
HERE FROM WAY BACK BEFORE THEY MOVED THE PLANET.
PAST THE CRATER I FIND SOME GREEN LIFE.
EATING FIXES ME UP.

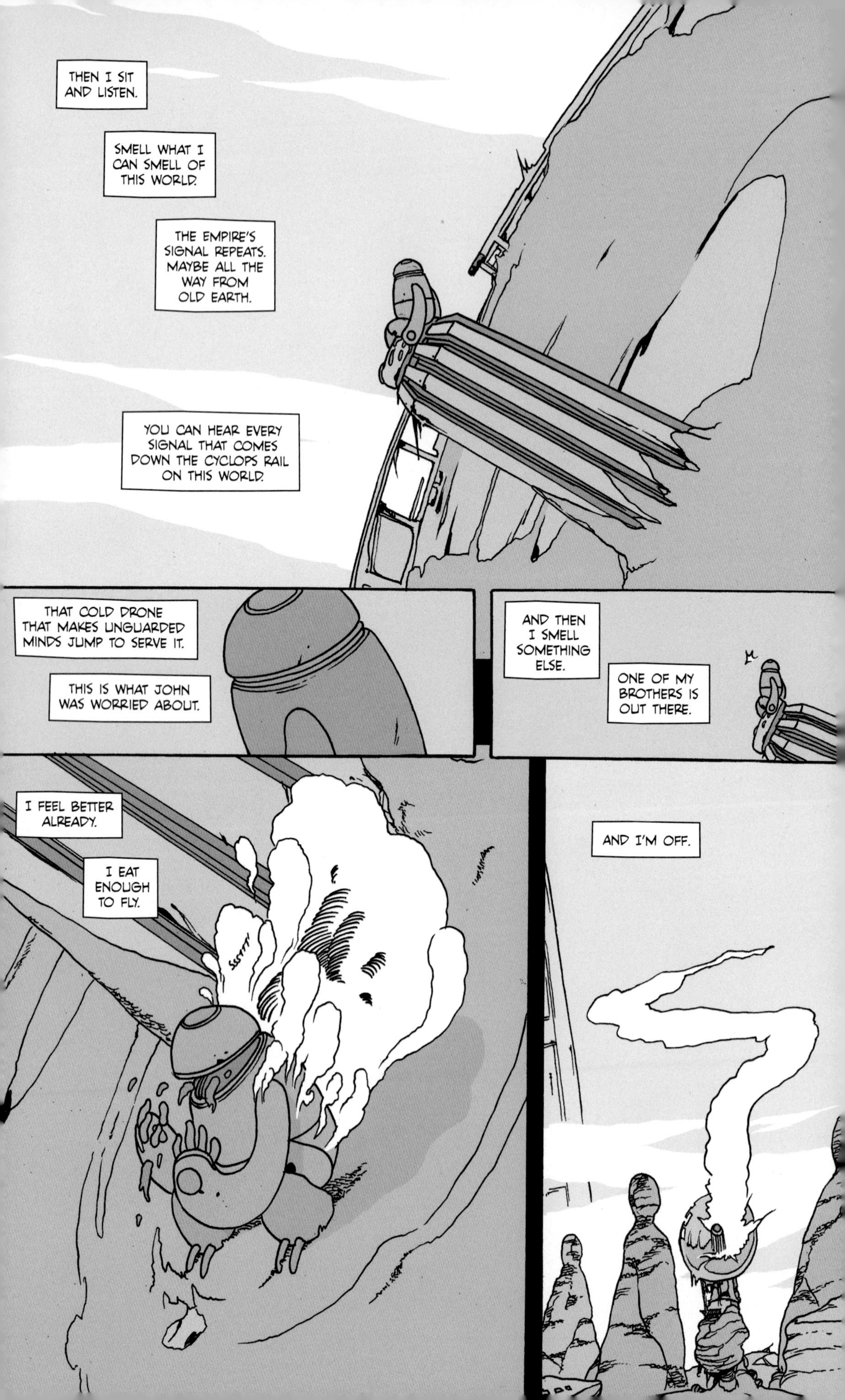
THEN I SIT AND LISTEN.
SMELL WHAT I CAN SMELL OF THIS WORLD.
THE EMPIRE'S SIGNAL REPEATS. MAYBE ALL THE WAY FROM OLD EARTH.
YOU CAN HEAR EVERY SIGNAL THAT COMES DOWN THE CYCLOPS RAIL ON THIS WORLD.
THAT COLD DRONE THAT MAKES UNGUARDED MINDS JUMP TO SERVE IT.
THIS IS WHAT JOHN WAS WORRIED ABOUT.
AND THEN I SMELL SOMETHING ELSE.
ONE OF MY BROTHERS IS OUT THERE.
I FEEL BETTER ALREADY.
I EAT ENOUGH TO FLY.
AND I'M OFF.

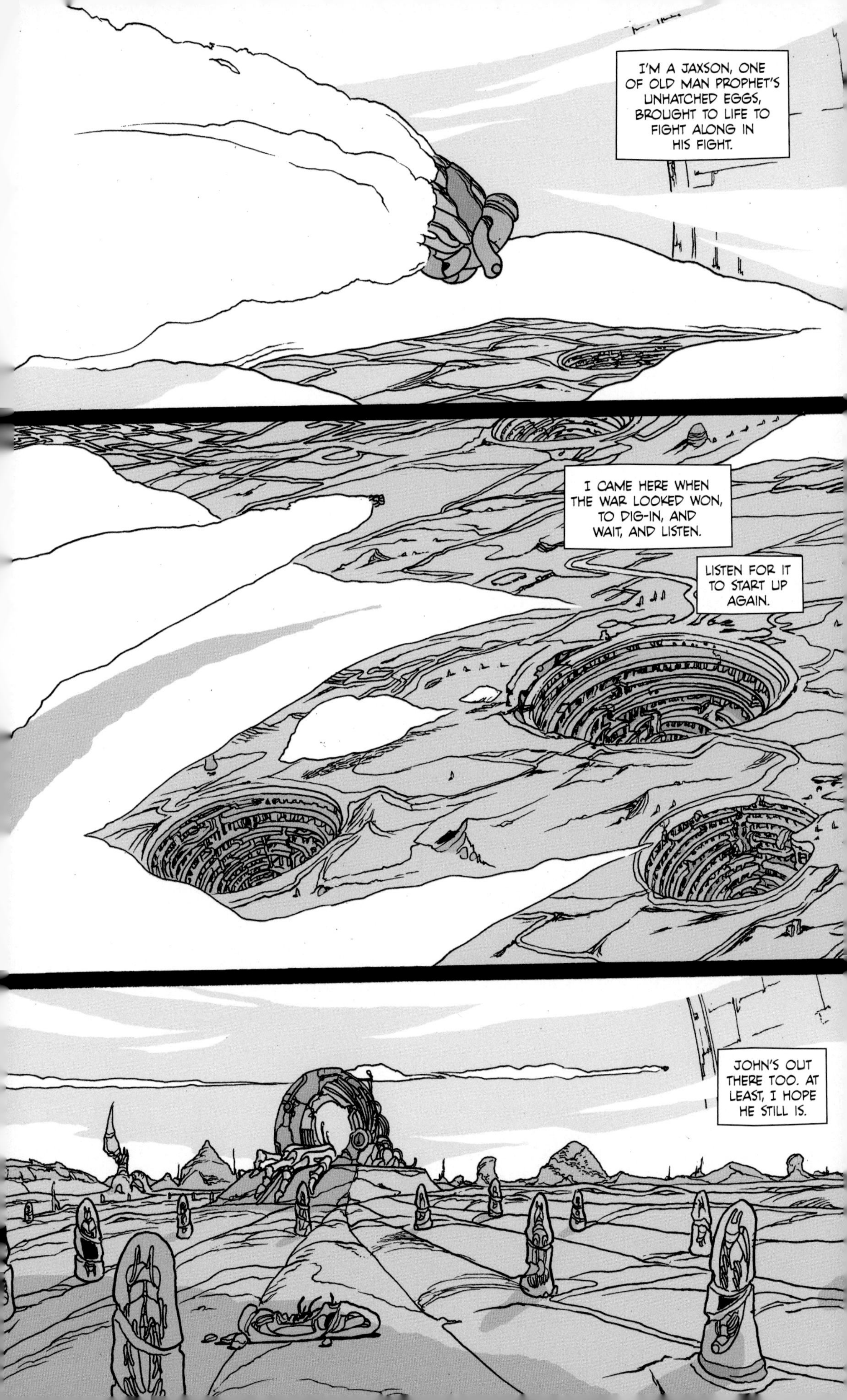
I'M A JAXSON, ONE OF OLD MAN PROPHET'S UNHATCHED EGGS, BROUGHT TO LIFE TO FIGHT ALONG IN HIS FIGHT.
I CAME HERE WHEN THE WAR LOOKED WON, TO DIG-IN, AND WAIT, AND LISTEN.
LISTEN FOR IT TO START UP AGAIN.
JOHN'S OUT THERE TOO. AT LEAST, I HOPE HE STILL IS.

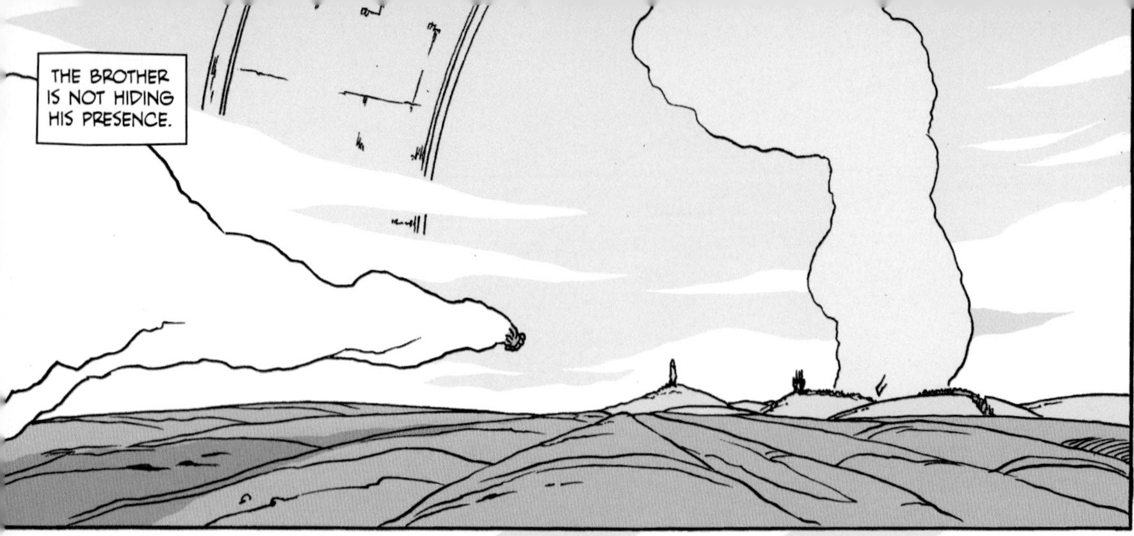
THE BROTHER IS NOT HIDING HIS PRESENCE.

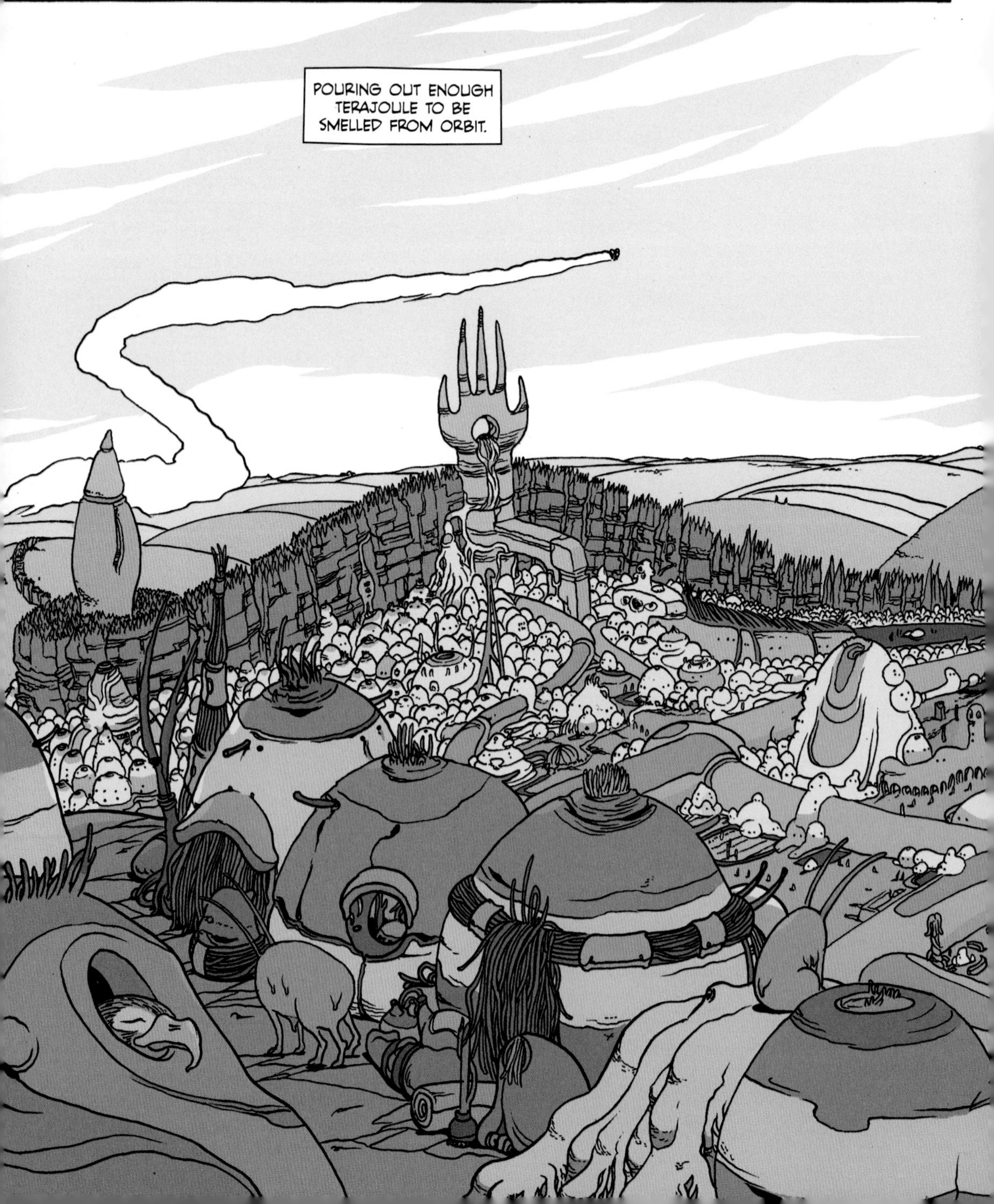
POURING OUT ENOUGH TERAJOULE TO BE SMELLED FROM ORBIT.

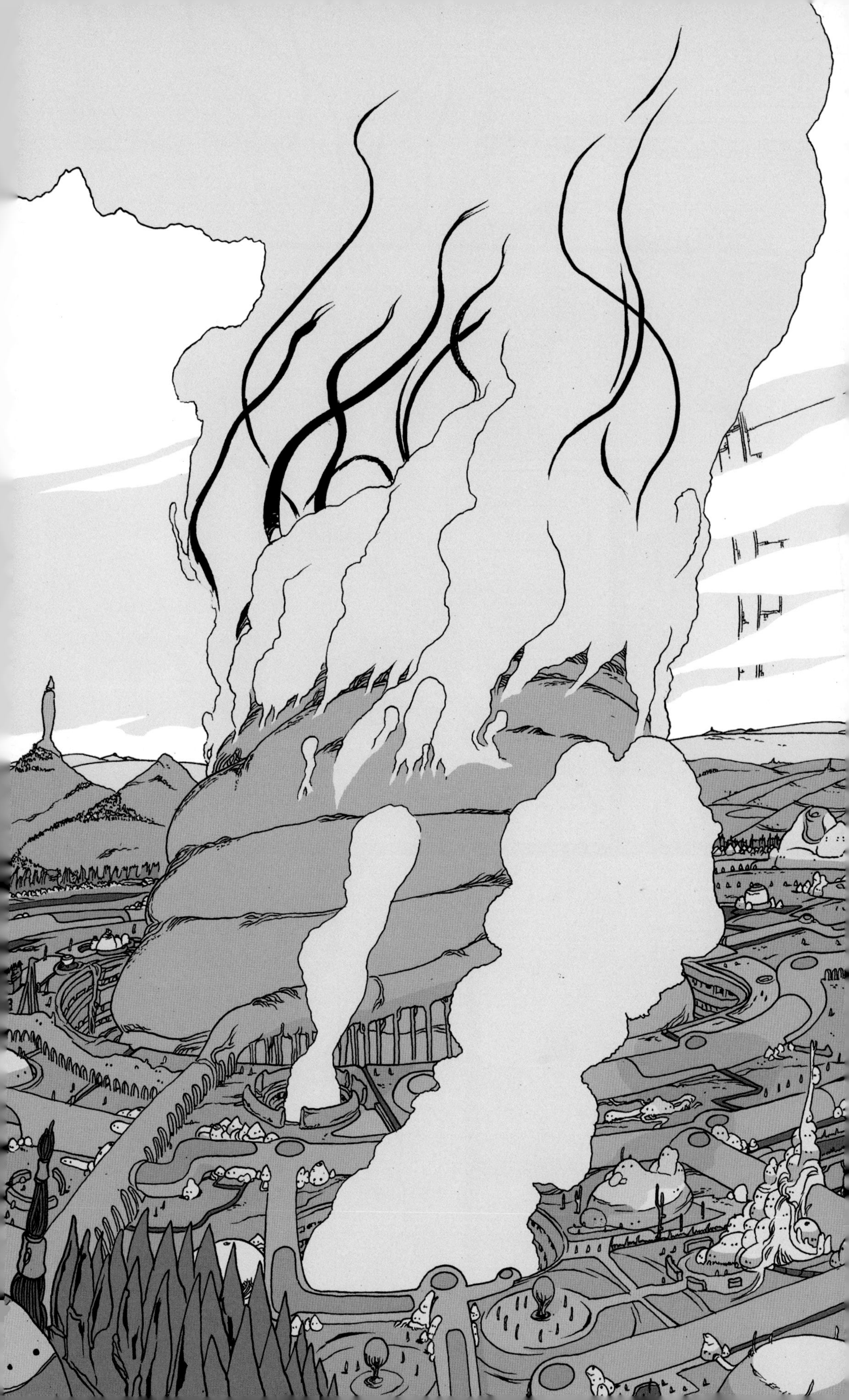

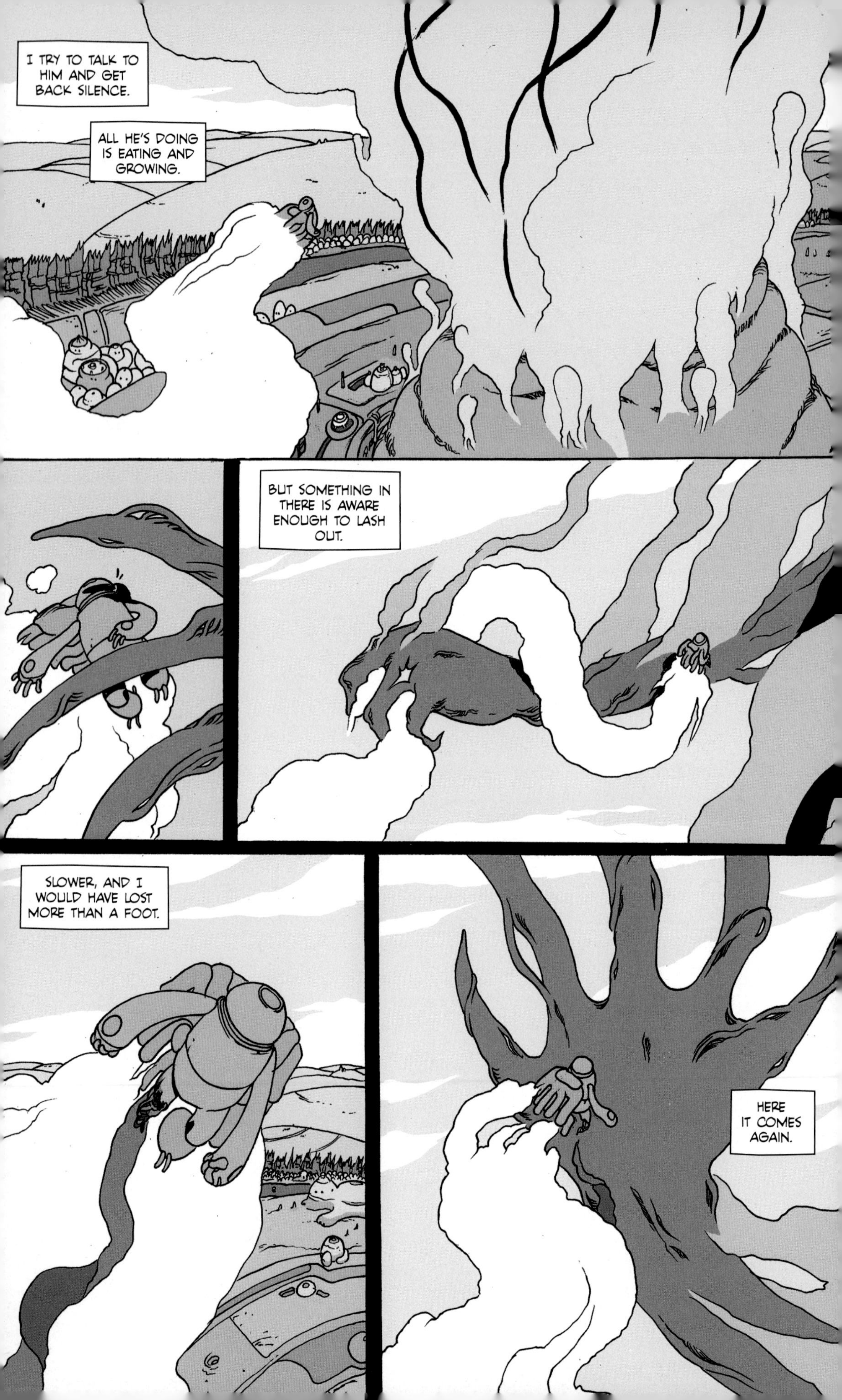

I TRY TO TALK TO HIM AND GET BACK SILENCE.
ALL HE'S DOING IS EATING AND GROWING.
BUT SOMETHING IN THERE IS AWARE ENOUGH TO LASH OUT.
SLOWER, AND I WOULD HAVE LOST MORE THAN A FOOT.
HERE IT COMES AGAIN.

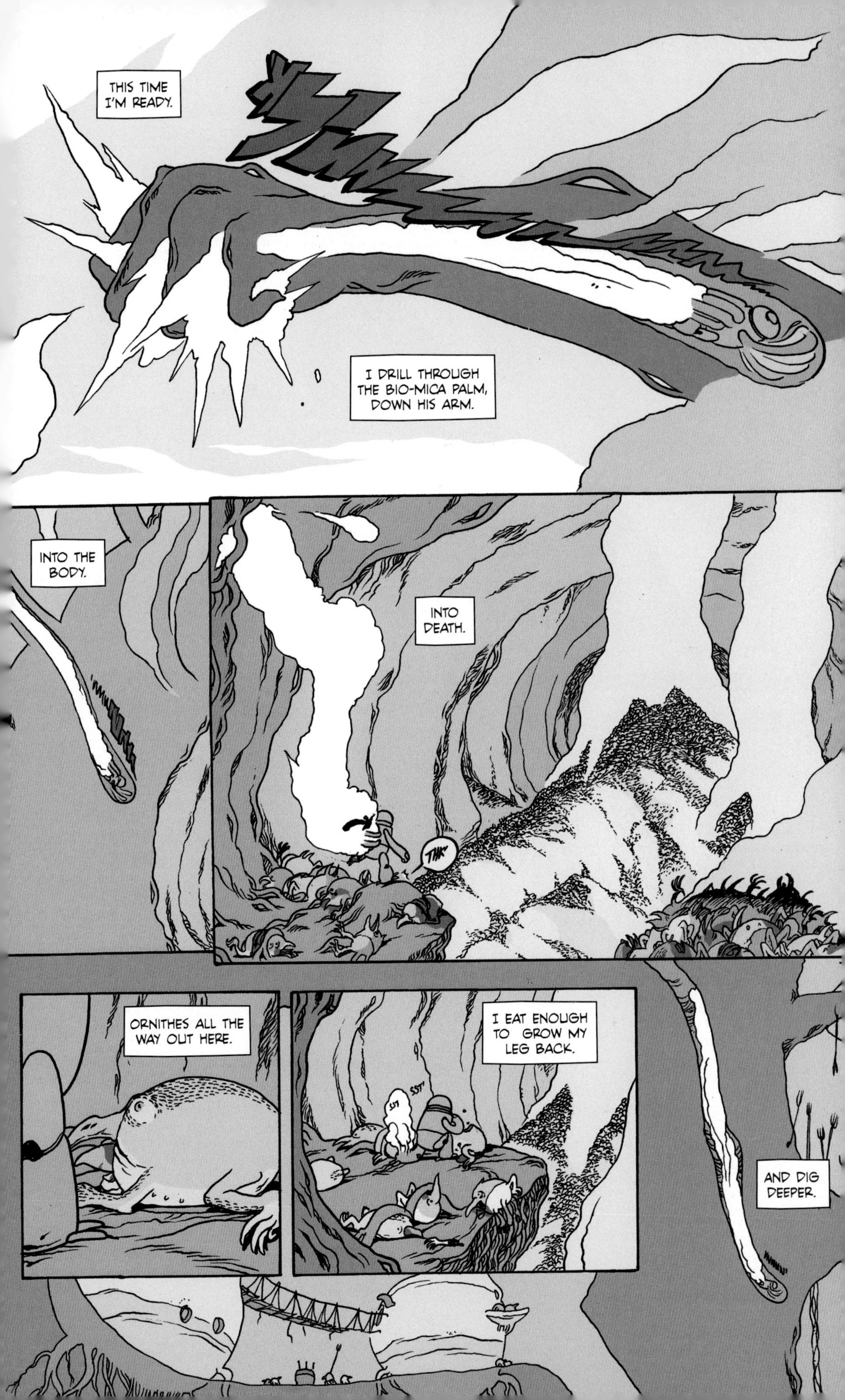
THIS TIME I'M READY.
I DRILL THROUGH THE BIO-MICA PALM, DOWN HIS ARM.
INTO THE BODY.
INTO DEATH.
THK'
ORNITHES ALL THE WAY OUT HERE.
I EAT ENOUGH TO GROW MY LEG BACK.
SST
SST'
AND DIG DEEPER.

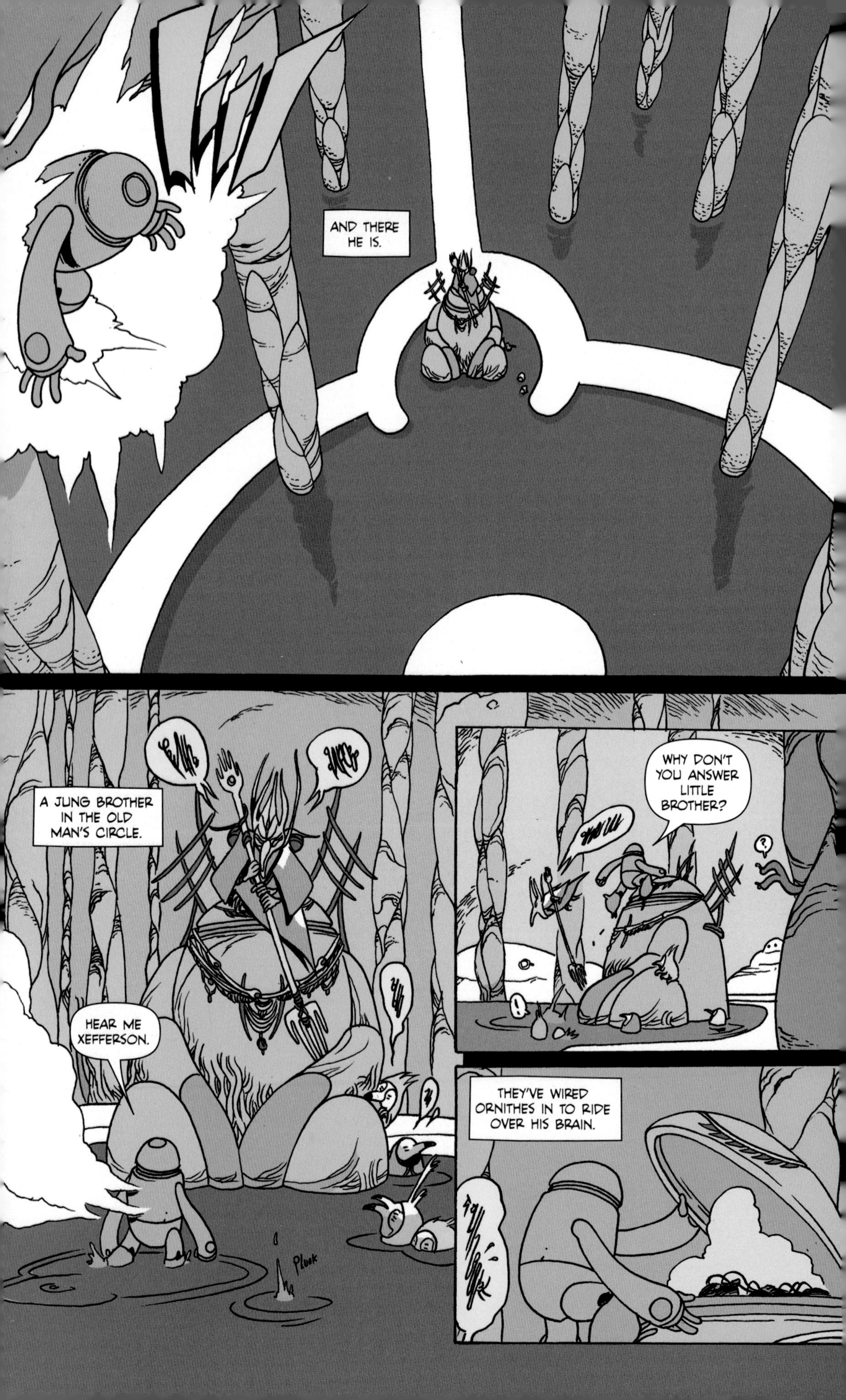
AND THERE HE IS.
A JUNG BROTHER IN THE OLD MAN'S CIRCLE.
HEAR ME XEFFERSON.
Pluck
WHY DON'T YOU ANSWER LITTLE BROTHER?
?
!
THEY'VE WIRED ORNITHES IN TO RIDE OVER HIS BRAIN.

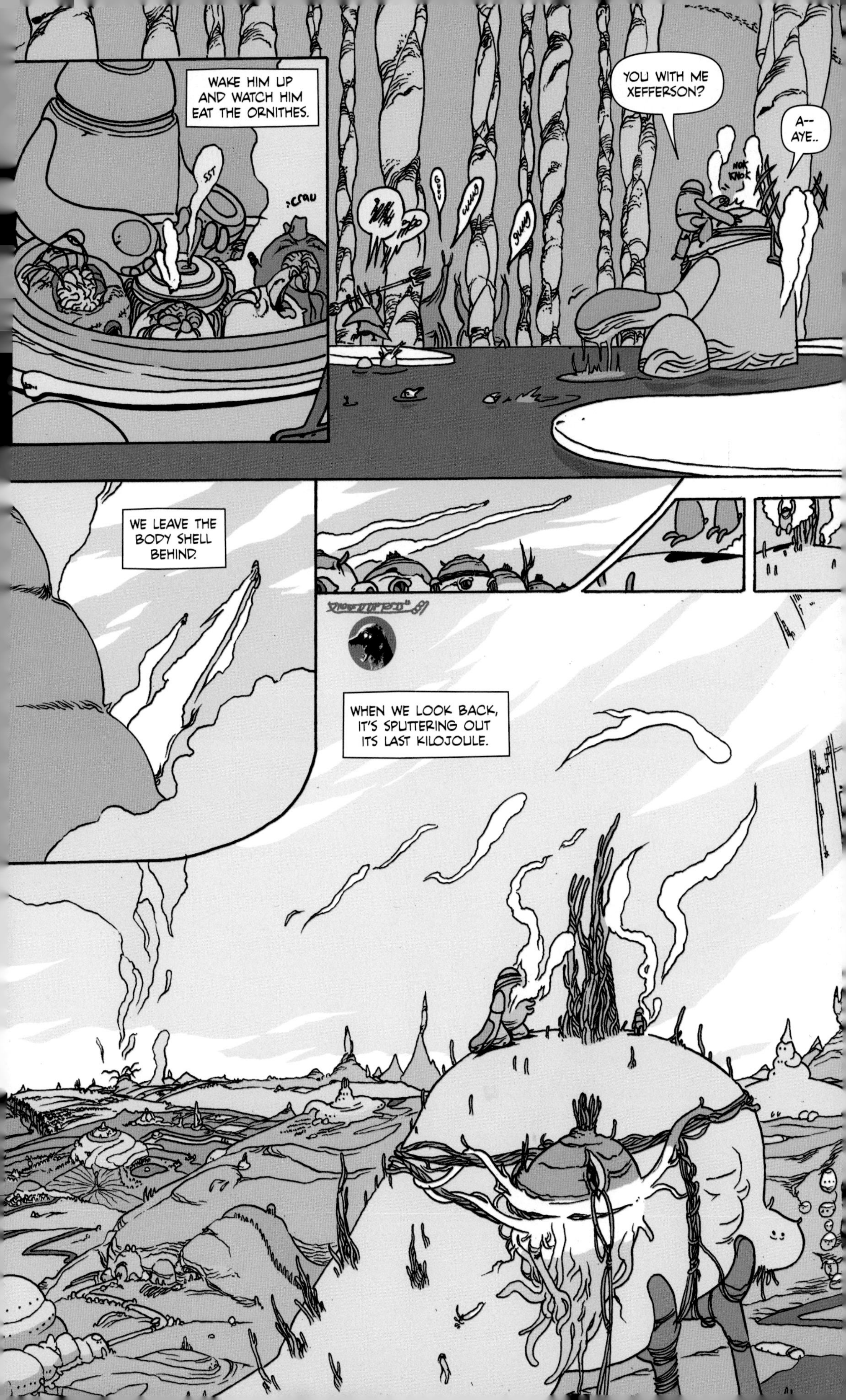
WAKE HIM UP AND WATCH HIM EAT THE ORNITHES.
SST
YOU WITH ME XEFFERSON?
A-- AYE..
WE LEAVE THE BODY SHELL BEHIND.
WHEN WE LOOK BACK, IT'S SPUTTERING OUT ITS LAST KILOJOULE.

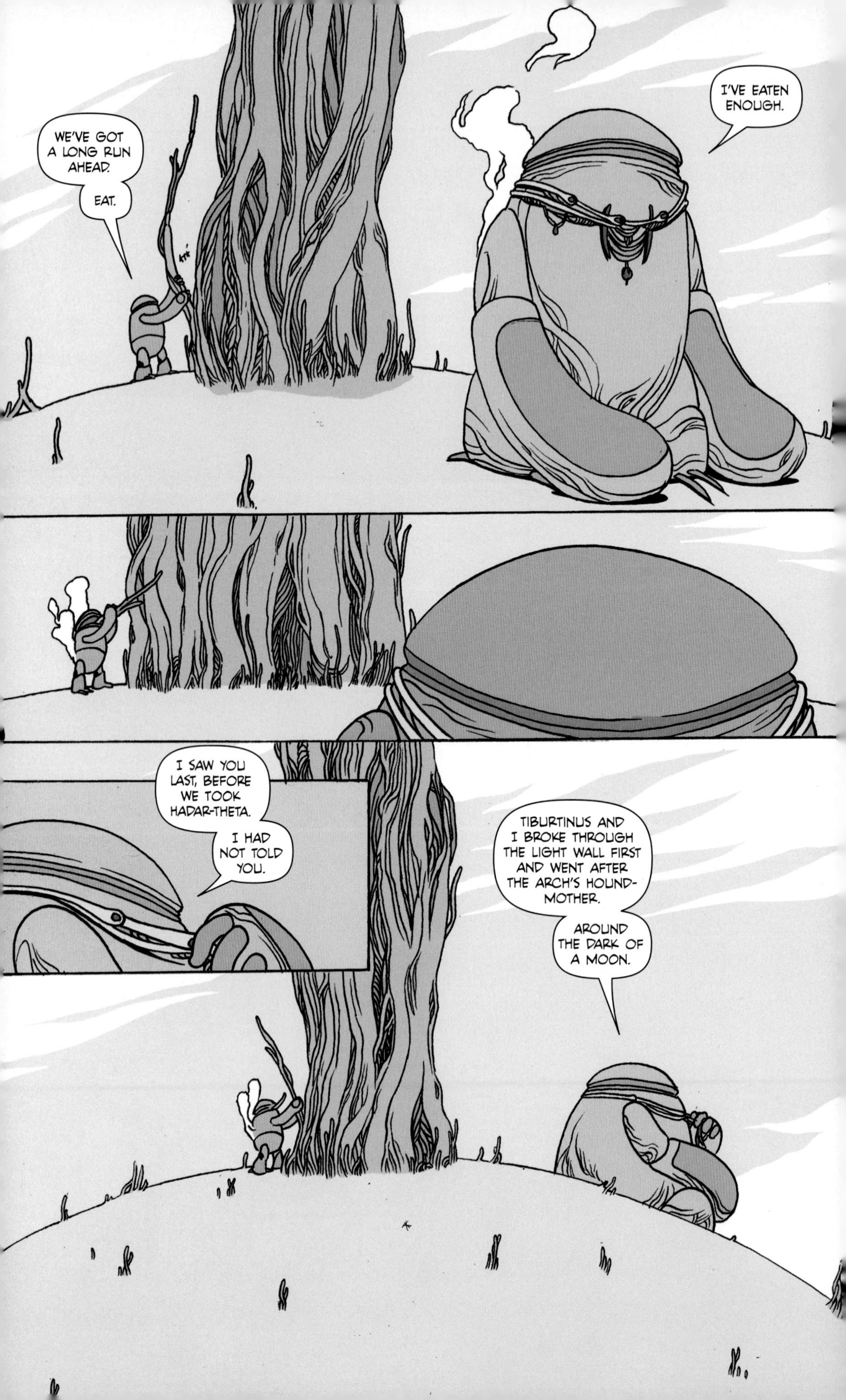

WE'VE GOT A LONG RUN AHEAD.
EAT.
I'VE EATEN ENOUGH.
I SAW YOU LAST, BEFORE WE TOOK HADAR-THETA.
I HAD NOT TOLD YOU.
TIBURTINUS AND I BROKE THROUGH THE LIGHT WALL FIRST AND WENT AFTER THE ARCH'S HOUND-MOTHER.
AROUND THE DARK OF A MOON.

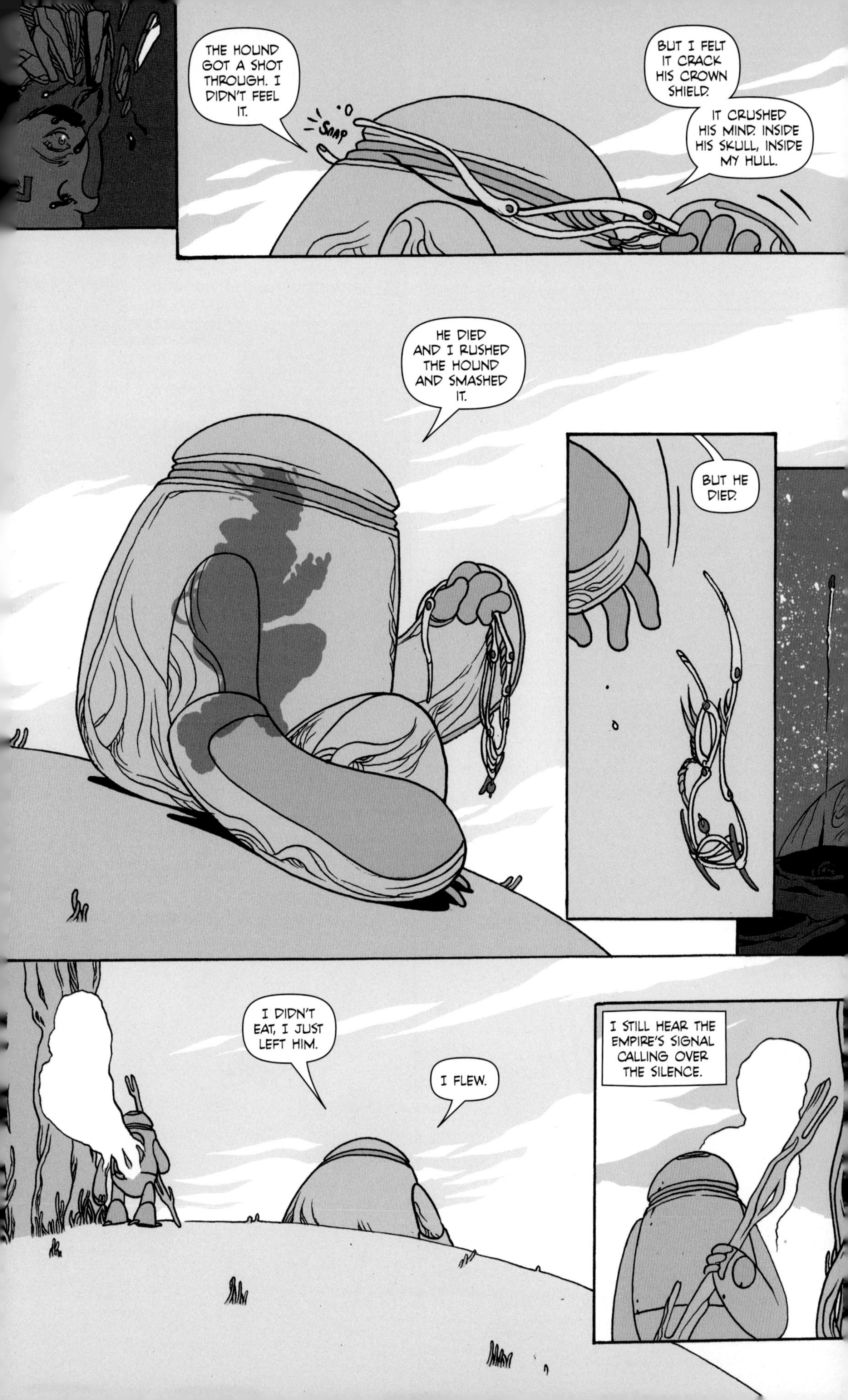
THE HOUND GOT A SHOT THROUGH. I DIDN'T FEEL IT.
SNAP
BUT I FELT IT CRACK HIS CROWN SHIELD.
IT CRUSHED HIS MIND. INSIDE HIS SKULL, INSIDE MY HULL.
HE DIED AND I RUSHED THE HOUND AND SMASHED IT.
BUT HE DIED.
I DIDN'T EAT, I JUST LEFT HIM.
I FLEW.
I STILL HEAR THE EMPIRE'S SIGNAL CALLING OVER THE SILENCE.

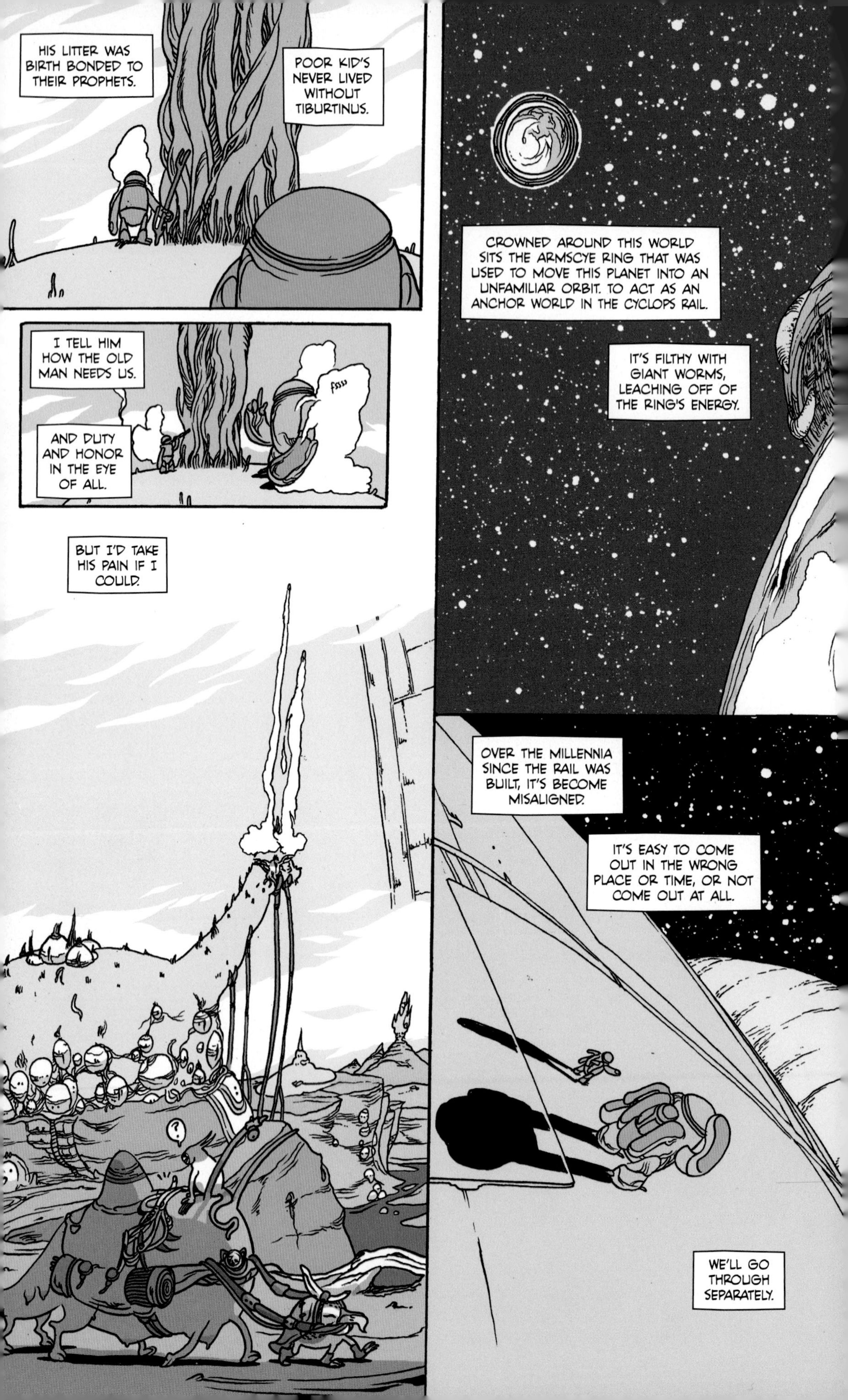
HIS LITTER WAS BIRTH BONDED TO THEIR PROPHETS.
POOR KID'S NEVER LIVED WITHOUT TIBURTINUS.
I TELL HIM HOW THE OLD MAN NEEDS US.
AND DUTY AND HONOR IN THE EYE OF ALL.
BUT I'D TAKE HIS PAIN IF I COULD.
CROWNED AROUND THIS WORLD SITS THE ARMSCYE RING THAT WAS USED TO MOVE THIS PLANET INTO AN UNFAMILIAR ORBIT. TO ACT AS AN ANCHOR WORLD IN THE CYCLOPS RAIL.
IT'S FILTHY WITH GIANT WORMS, LEACHING OFF OF THE RING'S ENERGY.
OVER THE MILLENNIA SINCE THE RAIL WAS BUILT, IT'S BECOME MISALIGNED.
IT'S EASY TO COME OUT IN THE WRONG PLACE OR TIME, OR NOT COME OUT AT ALL.
WE'LL GO THROUGH SEPARATELY.

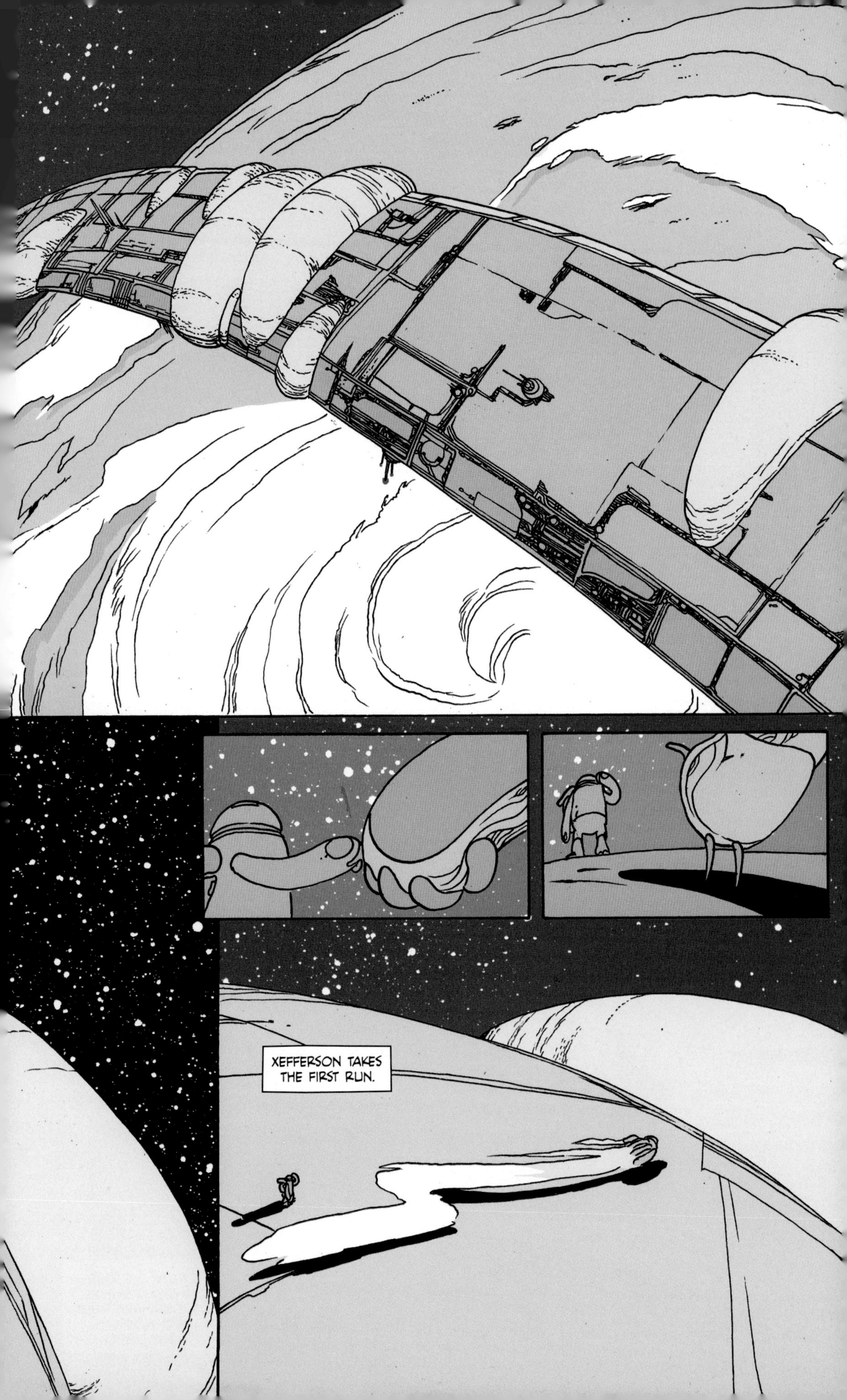
XEFFERSON TAKES THE FIRST RUN.

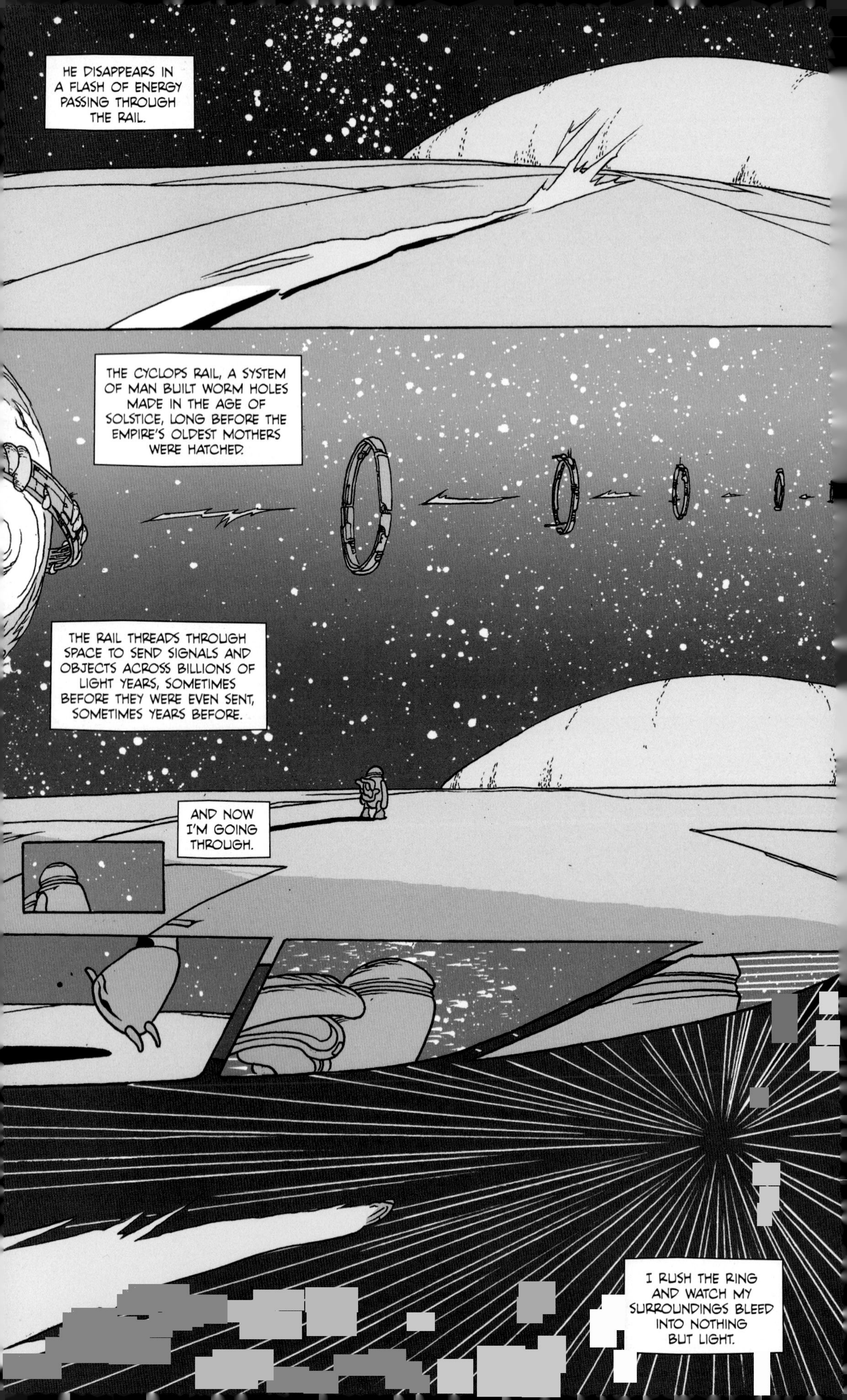
HE DISAPPEARS IN A FLASH OF ENERGY PASSING THROUGH THE RAIL.
THE CYCLOPS RAIL, A SYSTEM OF MAN BUILT WORM HOLES MADE IN THE AGE OF SOLSTICE, LONG BEFORE THE EMPIRE'S OLDEST MOTHERS WERE HATCHED.
THE RAIL THREADS THROUGH SPACE TO SEND SIGNALS AND OBJECTS ACROSS BILLIONS OF LIGHT YEARS, SOMETIMES BEFORE THEY WERE EVEN SENT, SOMETIMES YEARS BEFORE.
AND NOW I'M GOING THROUGH.
I RUSH THE RING AND WATCH MY SURROUNDINGS BLEED INTO NOTHING BUT LIGHT.

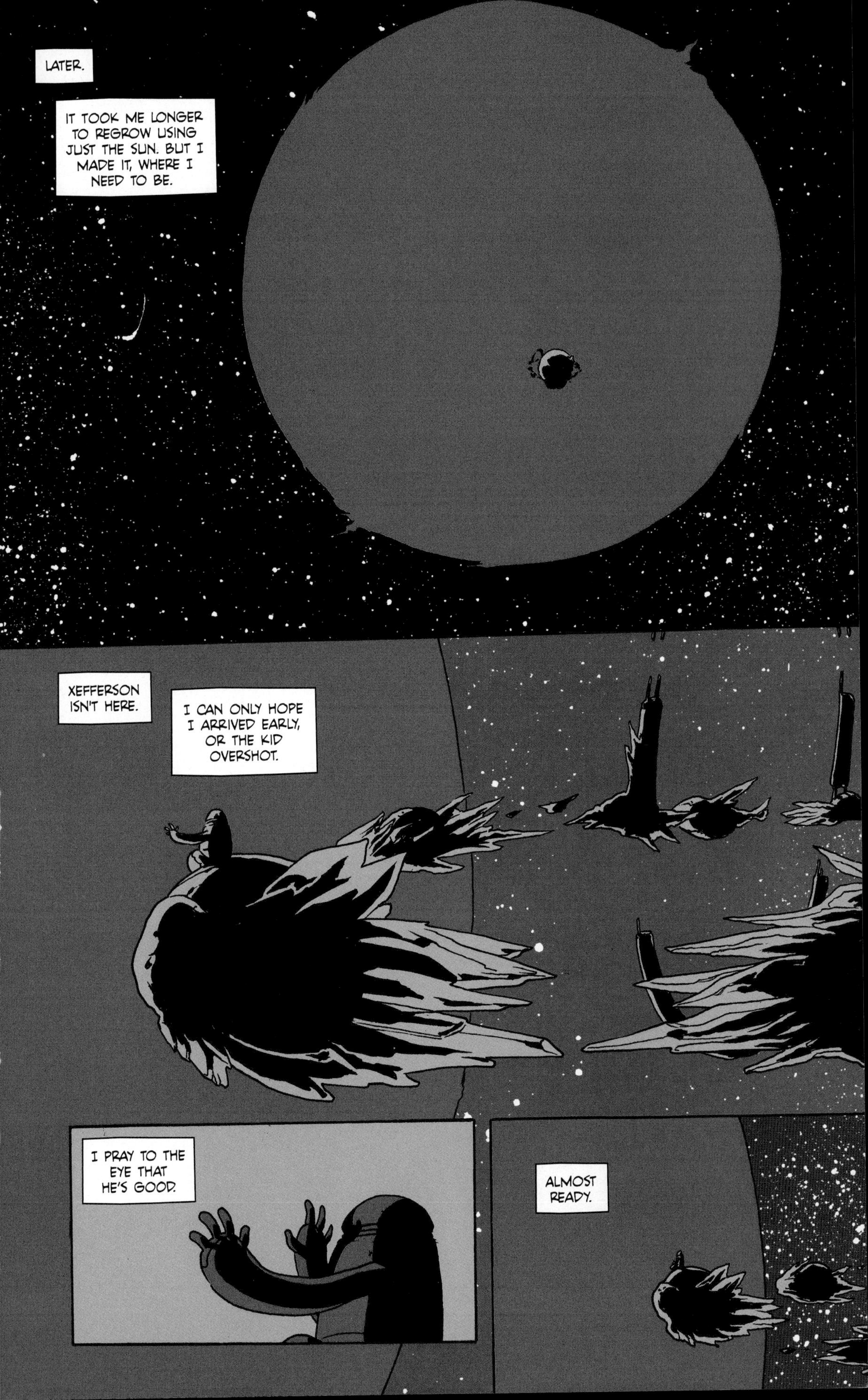
LATER.
IT TOOK ME LONGER TO REGROW USING JUST THE SUN. BUT I MADE IT, WHERE I NEED TO BE.
XEFFERSON ISN'T HERE.
I CAN ONLY HOPE I ARRIVED EARLY, OR THE KID OVERSHOT.
I PRAY TO THE EYE THAT HE'S GOOD.
ALMOST READY.

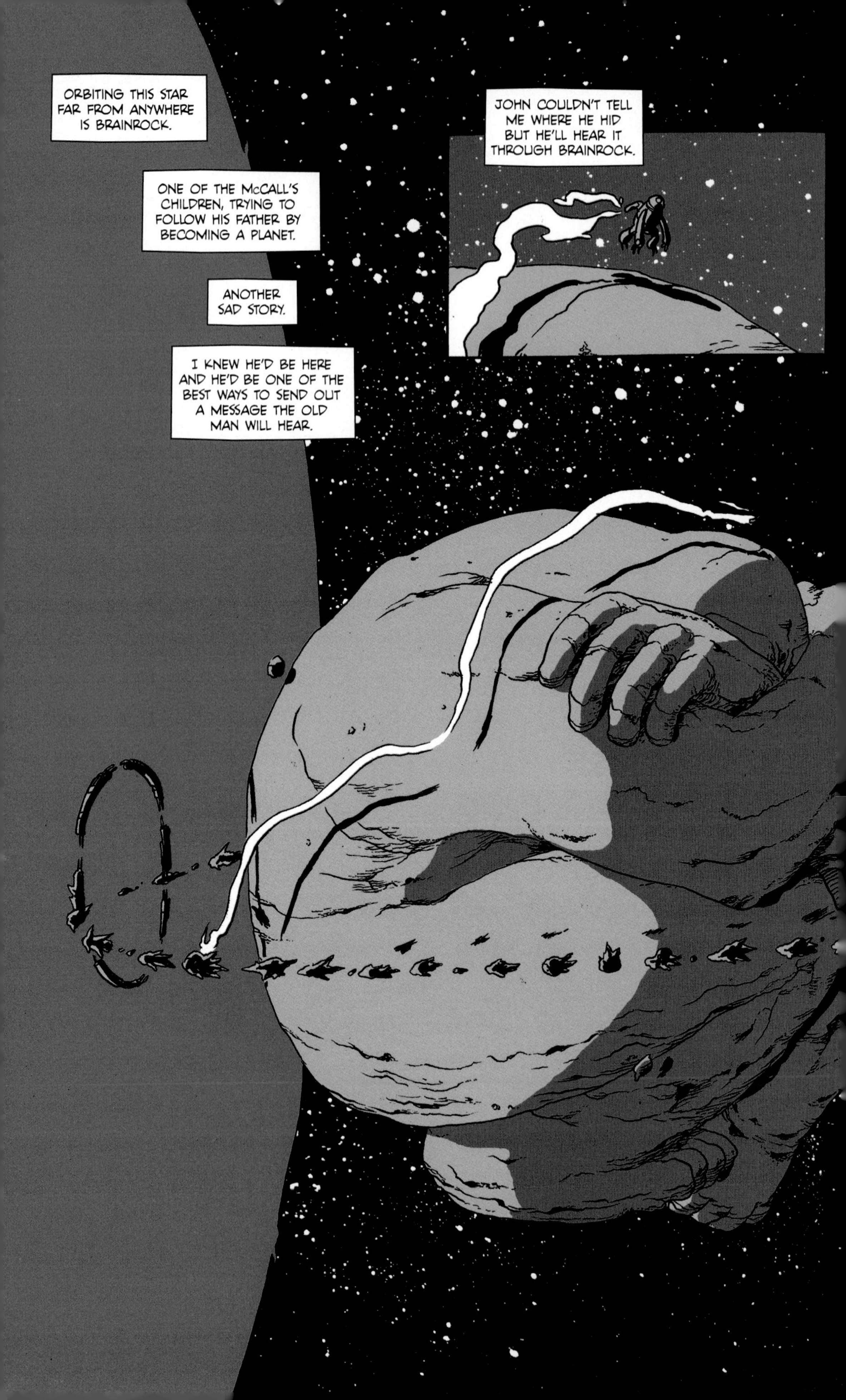
ORBITING THIS STAR FAR FROM ANYWHERE IS BRAINROCK.
ONE OF THE McCALL'S CHILDREN, TRYING TO FOLLOW HIS FATHER BY BECOMING A PLANET.
ANOTHER SAD STORY.
I KNEW HE'D BE HERE AND HE'D BE ONE OF THE BEST WAYS TO SEND OUT A MESSAGE THE OLD MAN WILL HEAR.
JOHN COULDN'T TELL ME WHERE HE HID BUT HE'LL HEAR IT THROUGH BRAINROCK.

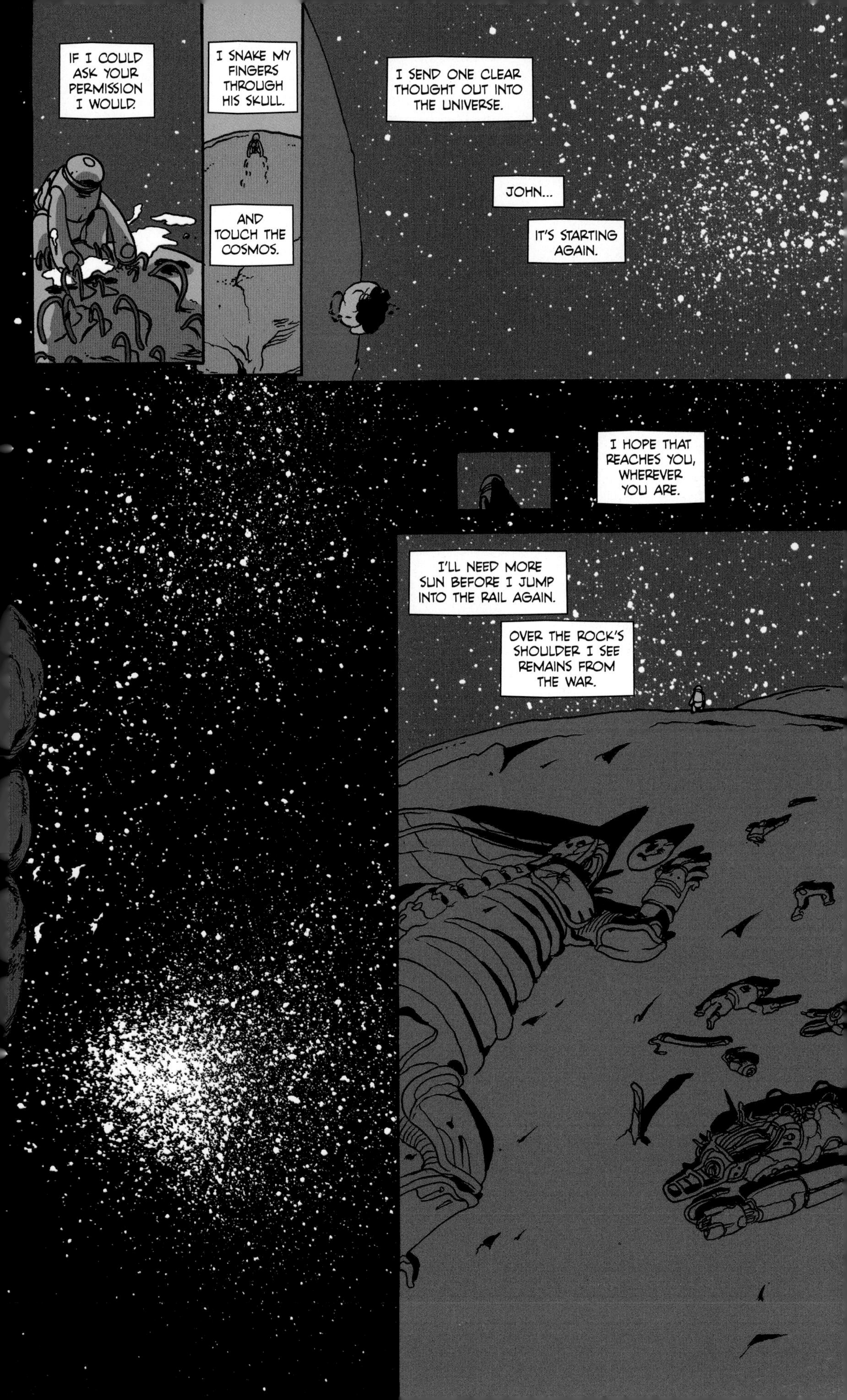
IF I COULD ASK YOUR PERMISSION I WOULD.
I SNAKE MY FINGERS THROUGH HIS SKULL.
AND TOUCH THE COSMOS.
I SEND ONE CLEAR THOUGHT OUT INTO THE UNIVERSE.
JOHN...
IT'S STARTING AGAIN.
I HOPE THAT REACHES YOU, WHEREVER YOU ARE.
I'LL NEED MORE SUN BEFORE I JUMP INTO THE RAIL AGAIN.
OVER THE ROCK'S SHOULDER I SEE REMAINS FROM THE WAR.

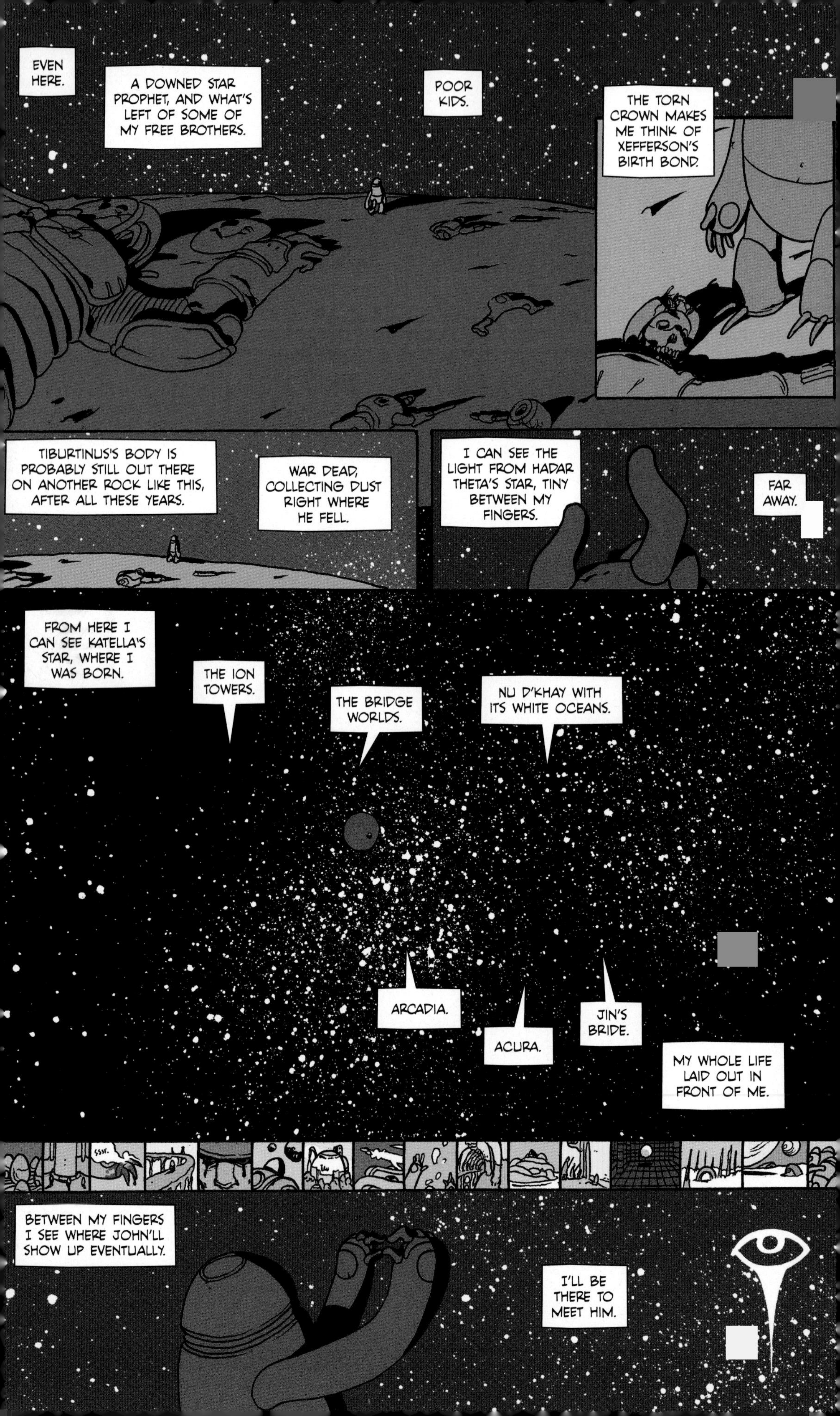
EVEN HERE.
A DOWNED STAR PROPHET, AND WHAT'S LEFT OF SOME OF MY FREE BROTHERS.
POOR KIDS.
THE TORN CROWN MAKES ME THINK OF XEFFERSON'S BIRTH BOND.
TIBURTINUS'S BODY IS PROBABLY STILL OUT THERE ON ANOTHER ROCK LIKE THIS, AFTER ALL THESE YEARS.
WAR DEAD, COLLECTING DUST RIGHT WHERE HE FELL.
I CAN SEE THE LIGHT FROM HADAR THETA'S STAR, TINY BETWEEN MY FINGERS.
FAR AWAY.
FROM HERE I CAN SEE KATELLA'S STAR, WHERE I WAS BORN.
THE ION TOWERS.
THE BRIDGE WORLDS.
NU D'KHAY WITH ITS WHITE OCEANS.
ARCADIA.
ACURA.
JIN'S BRIDE.
MY WHOLE LIFE LAID OUT IN FRONT OF ME.
BETWEEN MY FINGERS I SEE WHERE JOHN'LL SHOW UP EVENTUALLY.
I'LL BE THERE TO MEET HIM.

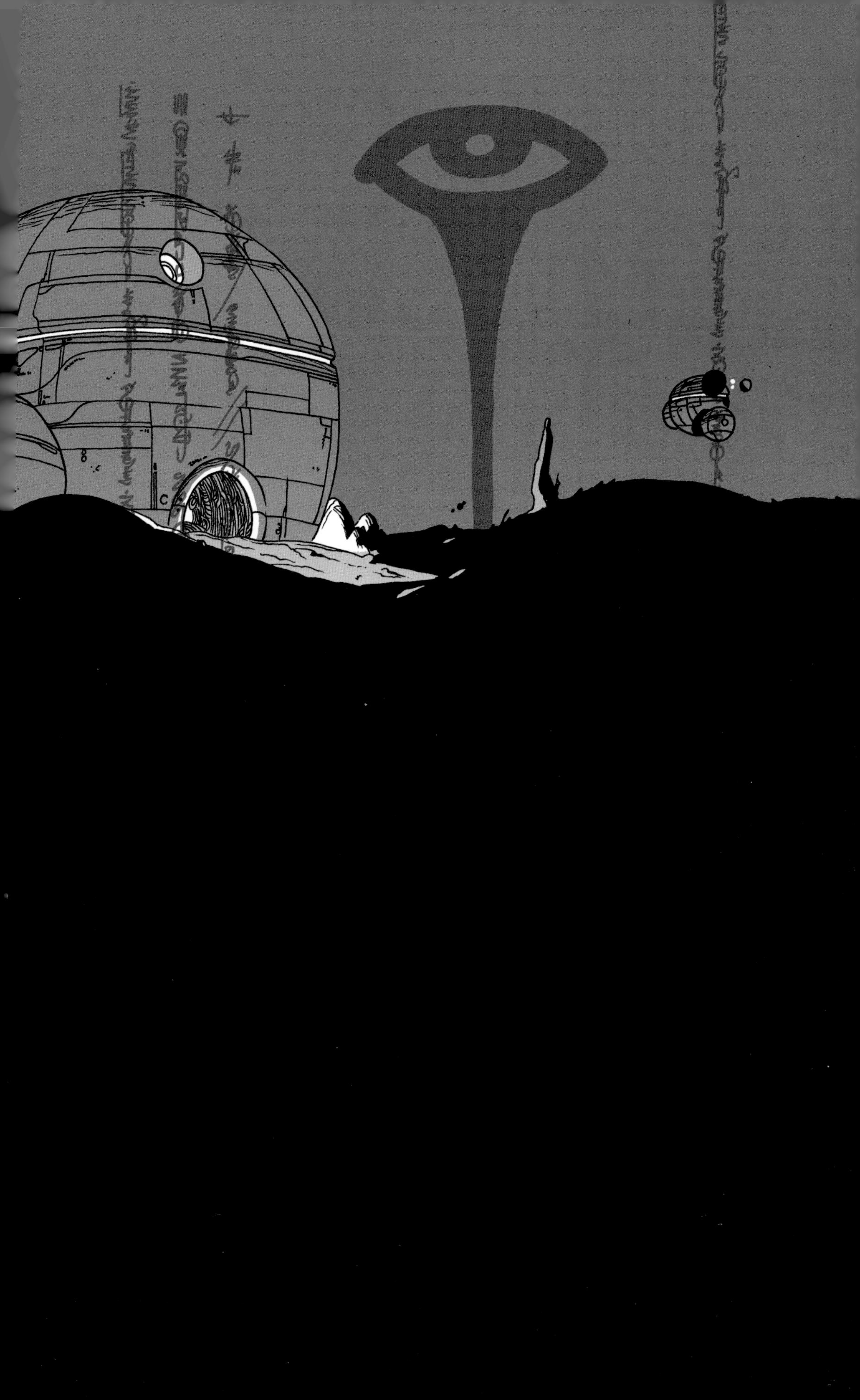

6

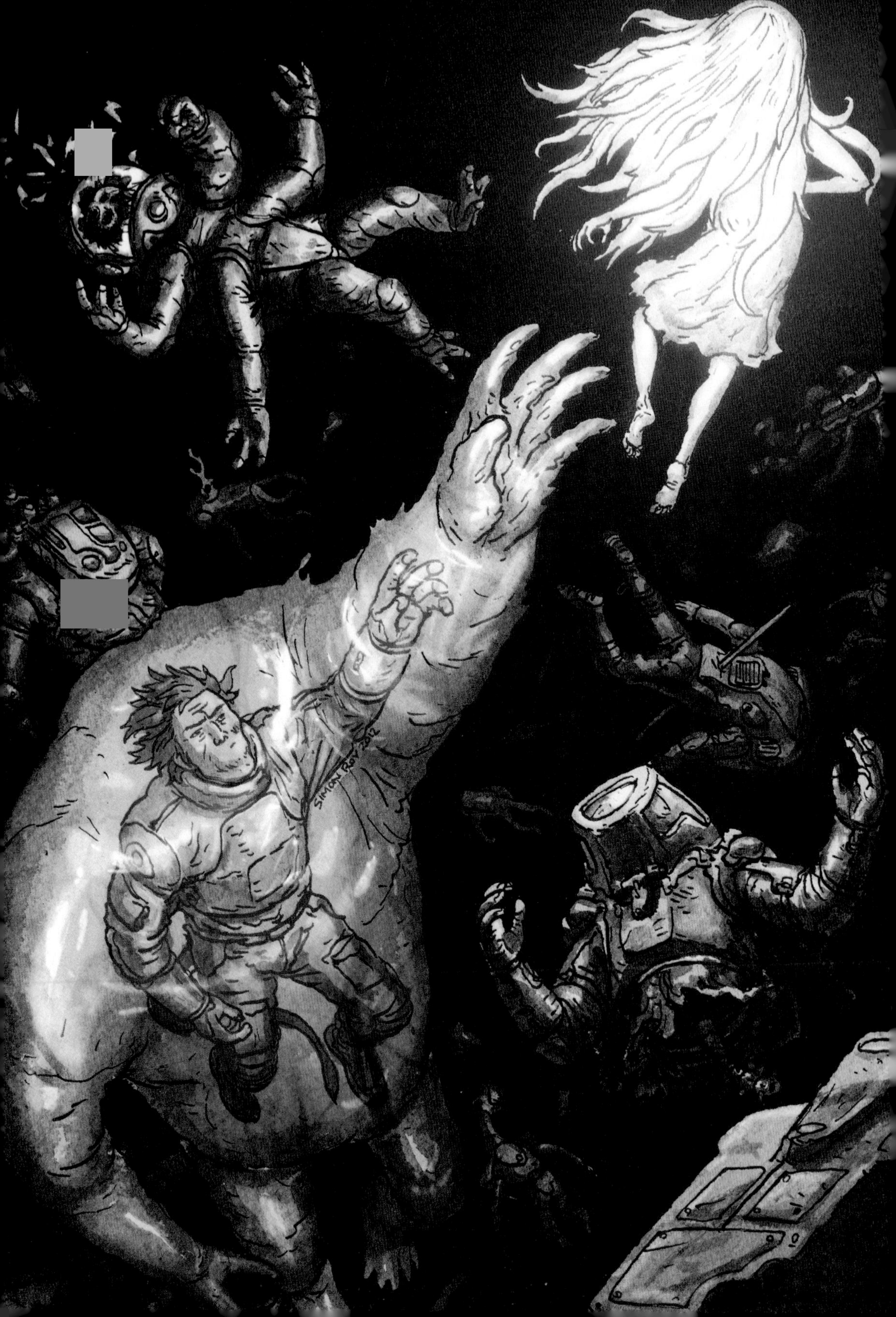
SIMON ROY 2012

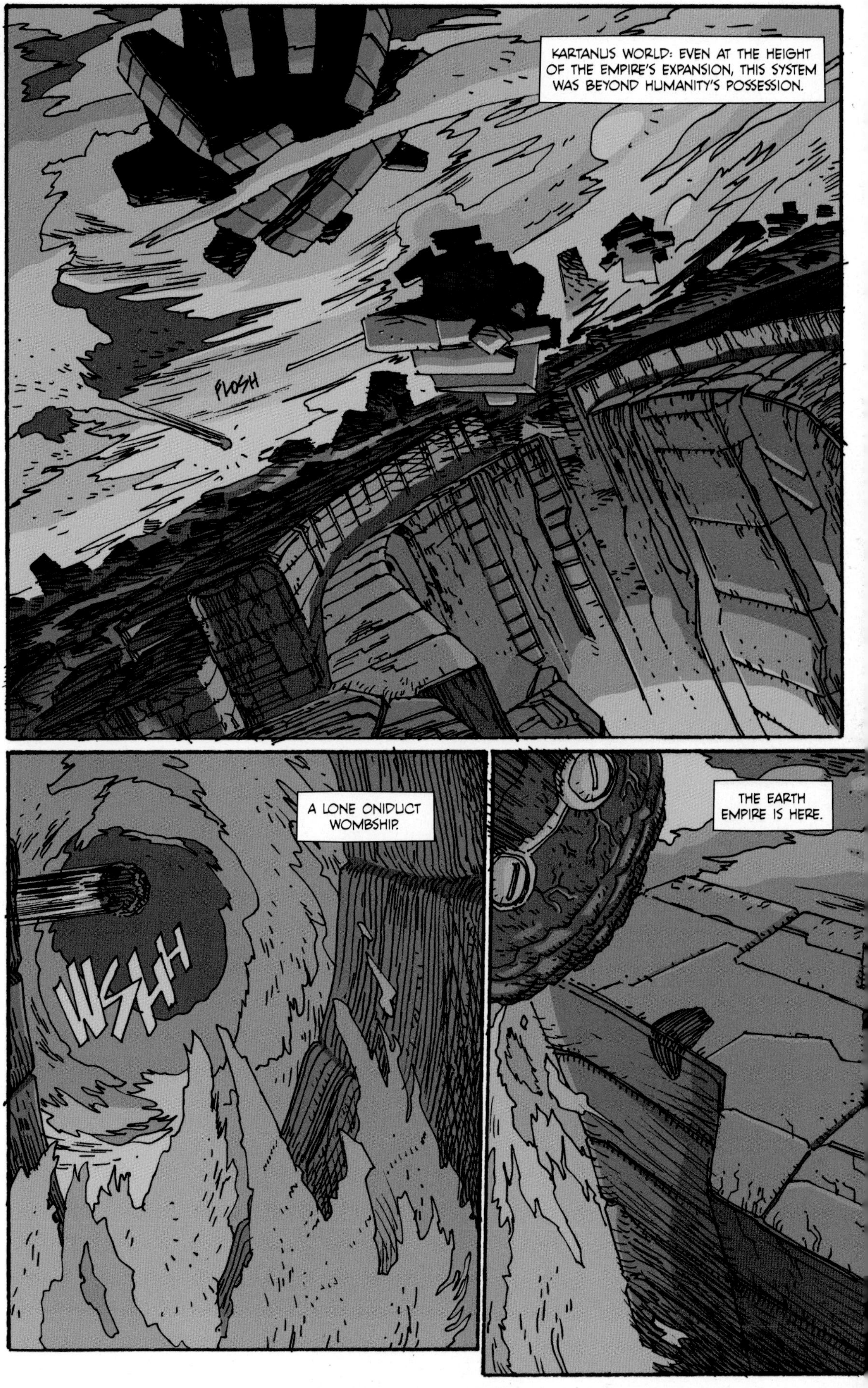
KARTANUS WORLD: EVEN AT THE HEIGHT OF THE EMPIRE'S EXPANSION, THIS SYSTEM WAS BEYOND HUMANITY'S POSSESSION.
FLOSH
A LONE ONIDUCT WOMBSHIP.
WSHH
THE EARTH EMPIRE IS HERE.

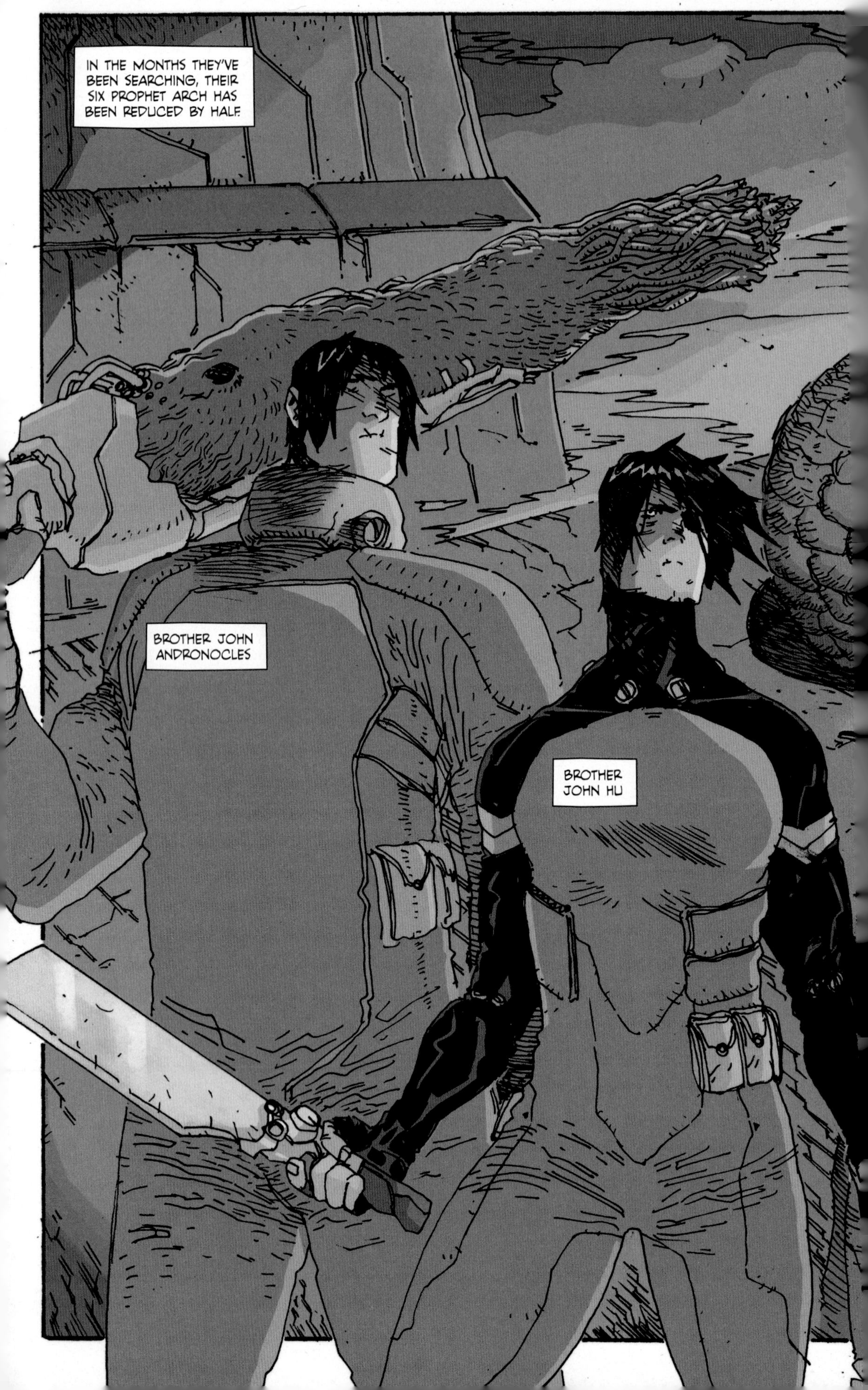
IN THE MONTHS THEY'VE BEEN SEARCHING, THEIR SIX PROPHET ARCH HAS BEEN REDUCED BY HALF.
BROTHER JOHN ANDRONOCLES
BROTHER JOHN HU

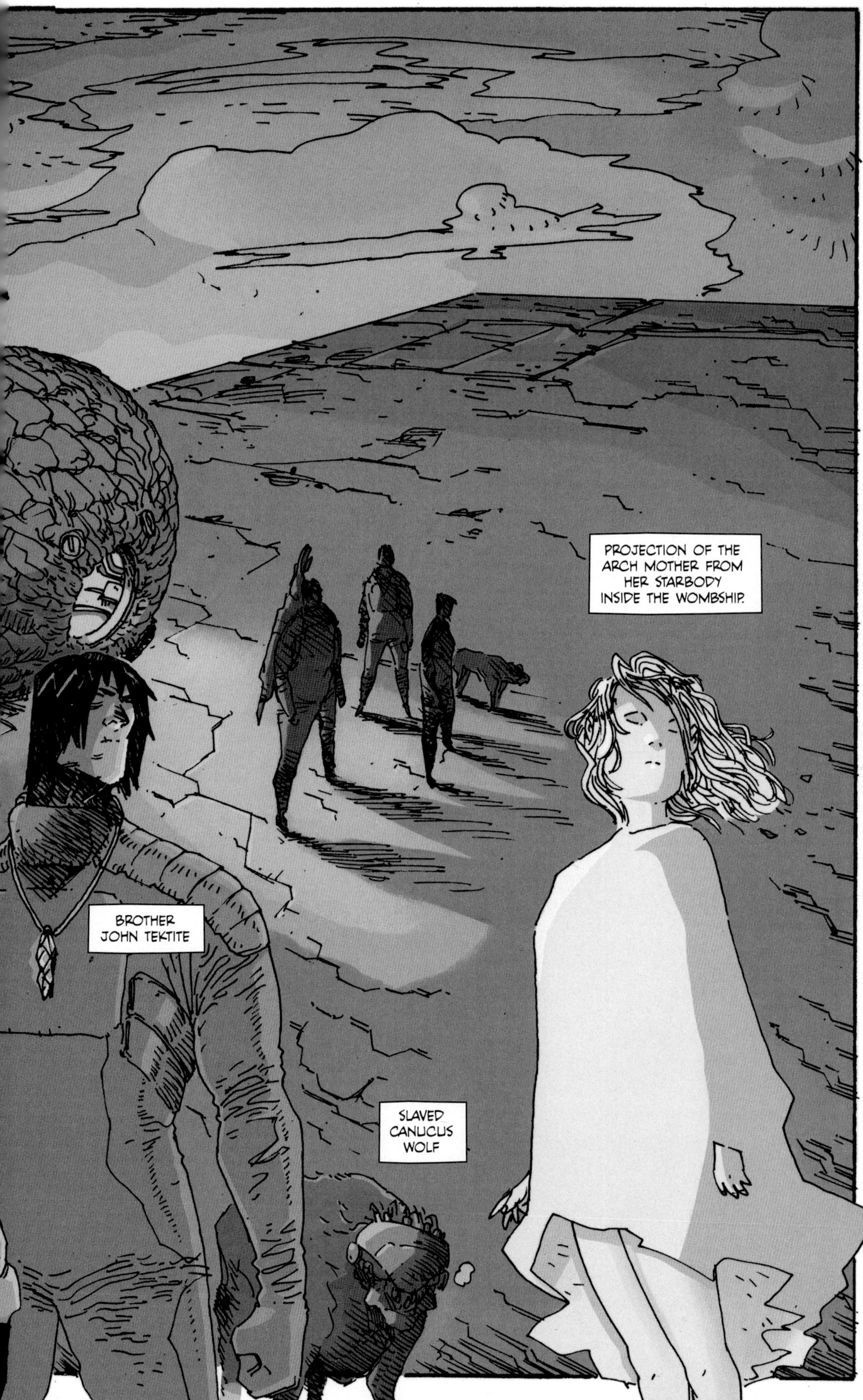
PROJECTION OF THE ARCH MOTHER FROM HER STARBODY INSIDE THE WOMBSHIP.
BROTHER JOHN TEKTITE
SLAVED CANUCUS WOLF

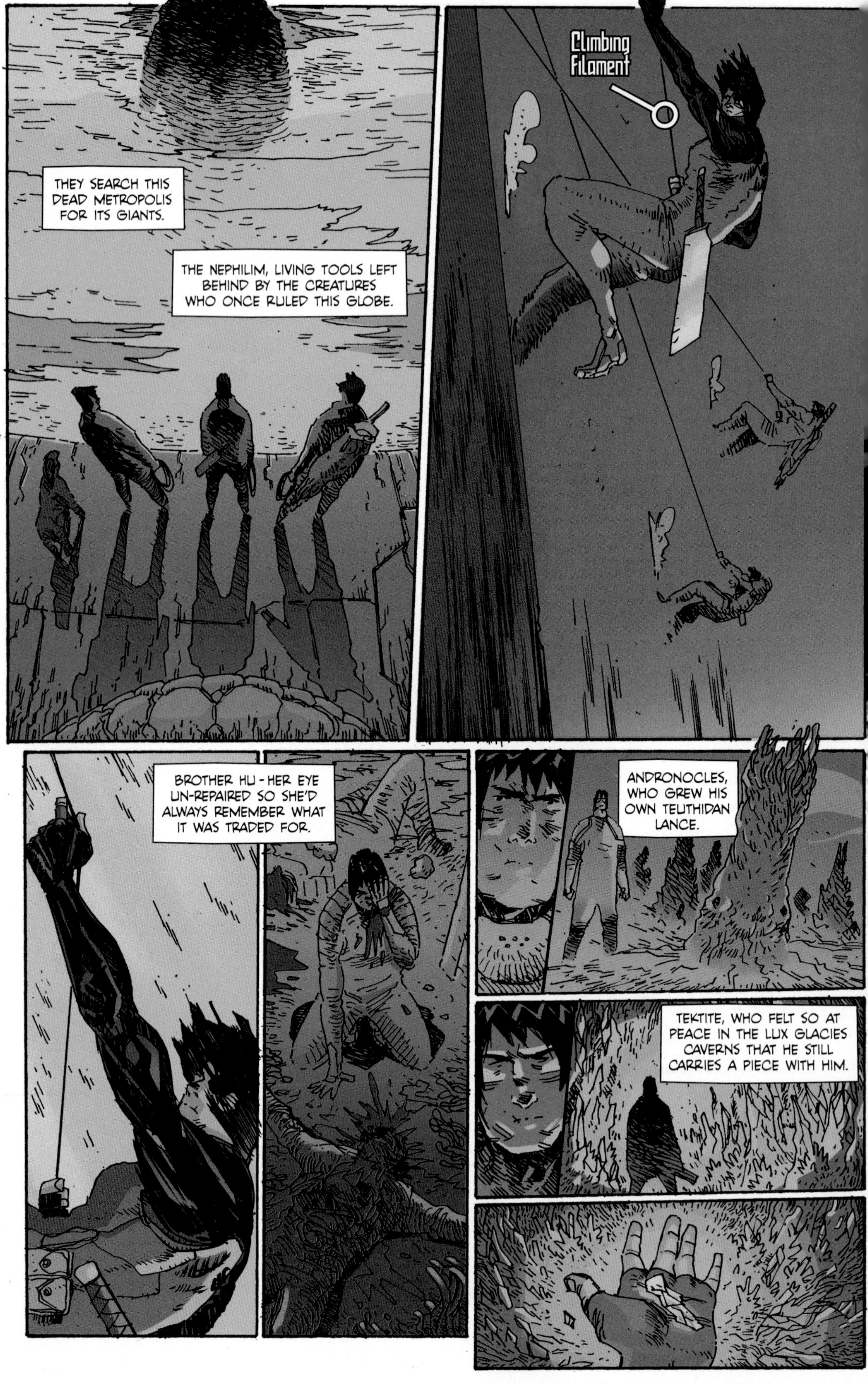
THEY SEARCH THIS DEAD METROPOLIS FOR ITS GIANTS.
THE NEPHILIM, LIVING TOOLS LEFT BEHIND BY THE CREATURES WHO ONCE RULED THIS GLOBE.
Climbing Filament
BROTHER HU - HER EYE UN-REPAIRED SO SHE'D ALWAYS REMEMBER WHAT IT WAS TRADED FOR.
ANDRONOCLES, WHO GREW HIS OWN TEUTHIDAN LANCE.
TEKTITE, WHO FELT SO AT PEACE IN THE LUX GLACIES CAVERNS THAT HE STILL CARRIES A PIECE WITH HIM.

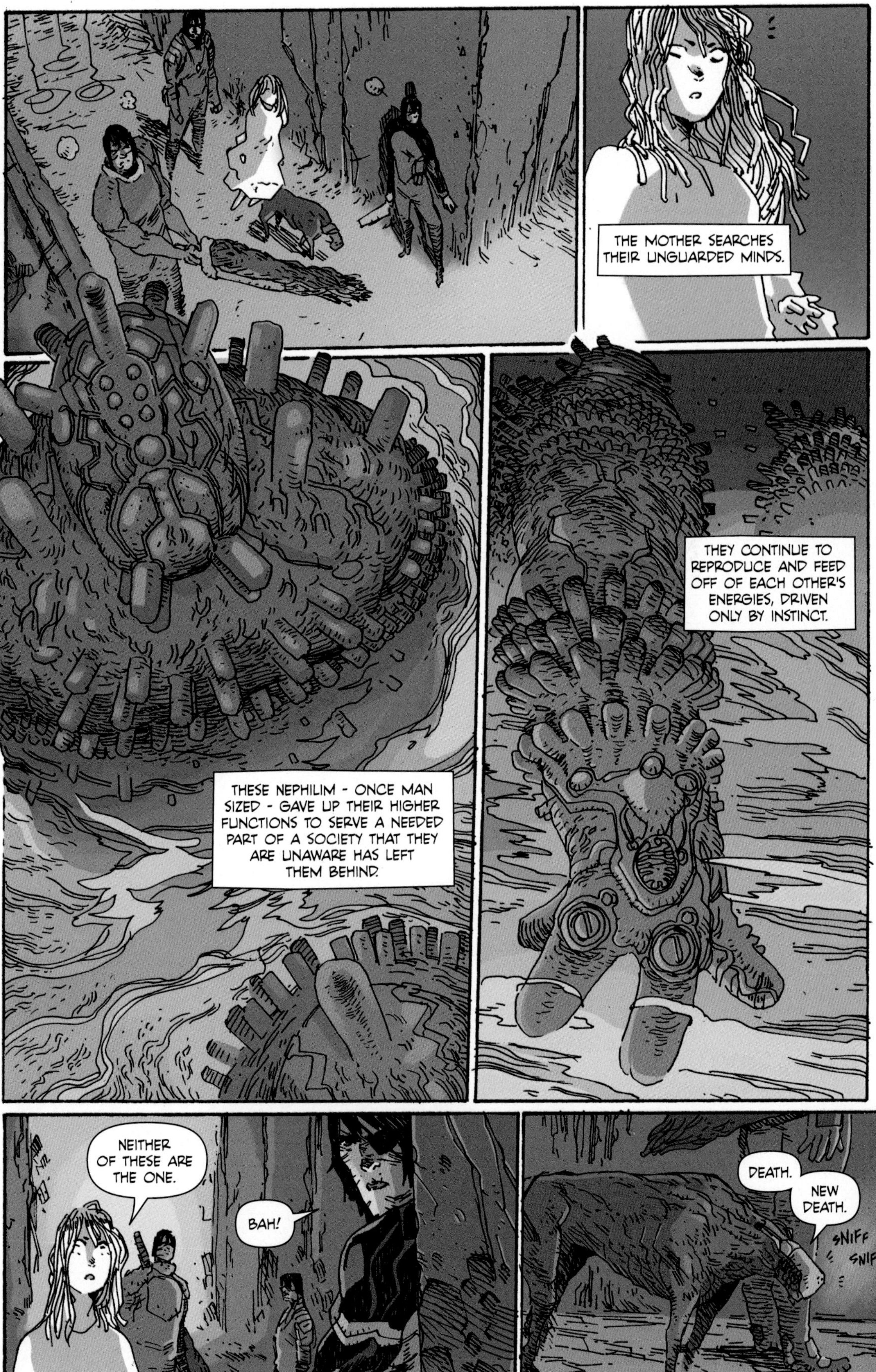
THE MOTHER SEARCHES THEIR UNGUARDED MINDS.
THESE NEPHILIM - ONCE MAN SIZED - GAVE UP THEIR HIGHER FUNCTIONS TO SERVE A NEEDED PART OF A SOCIETY THAT THEY ARE UNAWARE HAS LEFT THEM BEHIND.
THEY CONTINUE TO REPRODUCE AND FEED OFF OF EACH OTHER'S ENERGIES, DRIVEN ONLY BY INSTINCT.
NEITHER OF THESE ARE THE ONE.
BAH!
DEATH.
NEW DEATH.
SNIFF
SNIFF

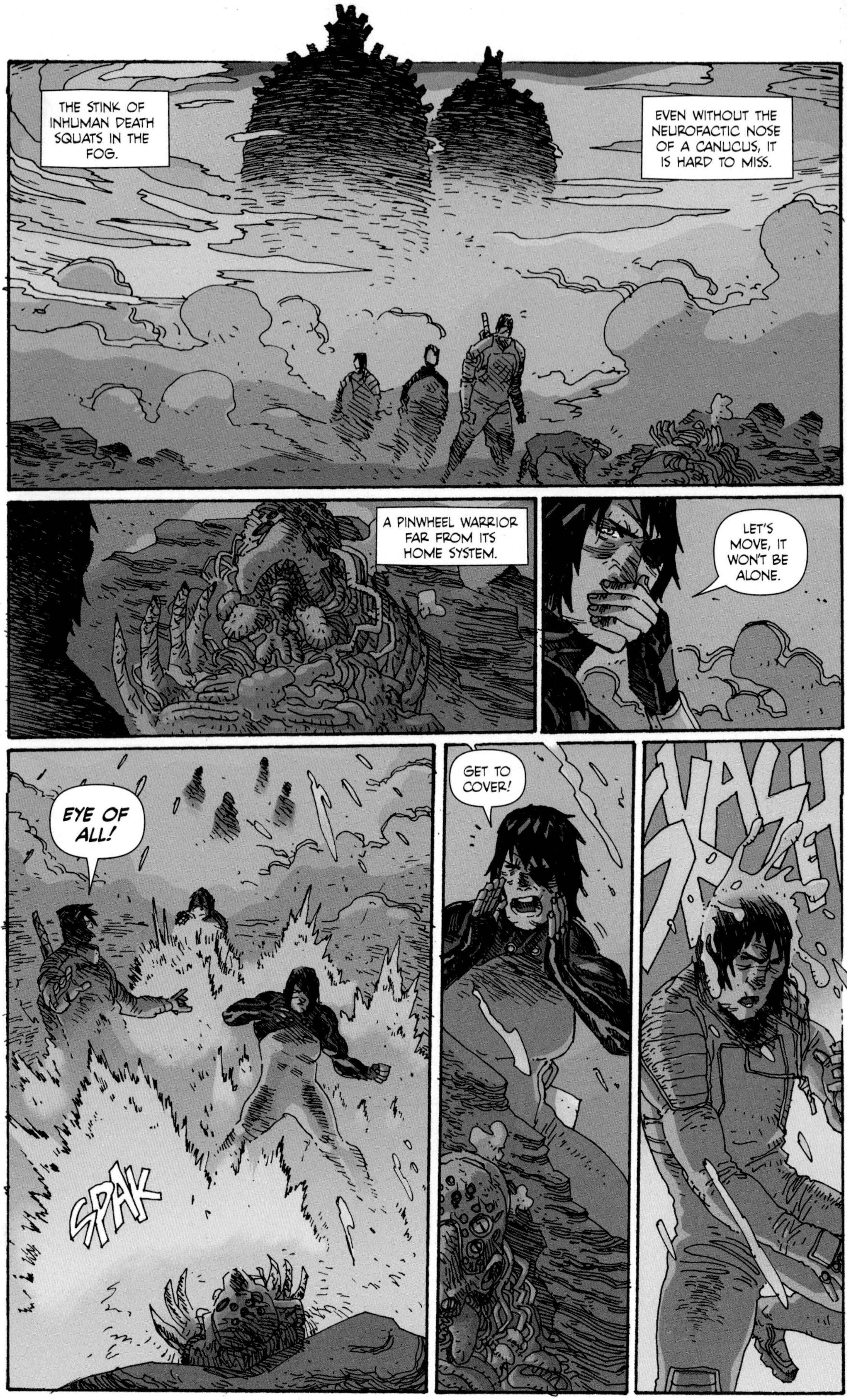
THE STINK OF INHUMAN DEATH SQUATS IN THE FOG.
EVEN WITHOUT THE NEUROFACTIC NOSE OF A CANUCUS, IT IS HARD TO MISS.
A PINWHEEL WARRIOR FAR FROM ITS HOME SYSTEM.
LET'S MOVE, IT WON'T BE ALONE.
EYE OF ALL!
SPAK
GET TO COVER!

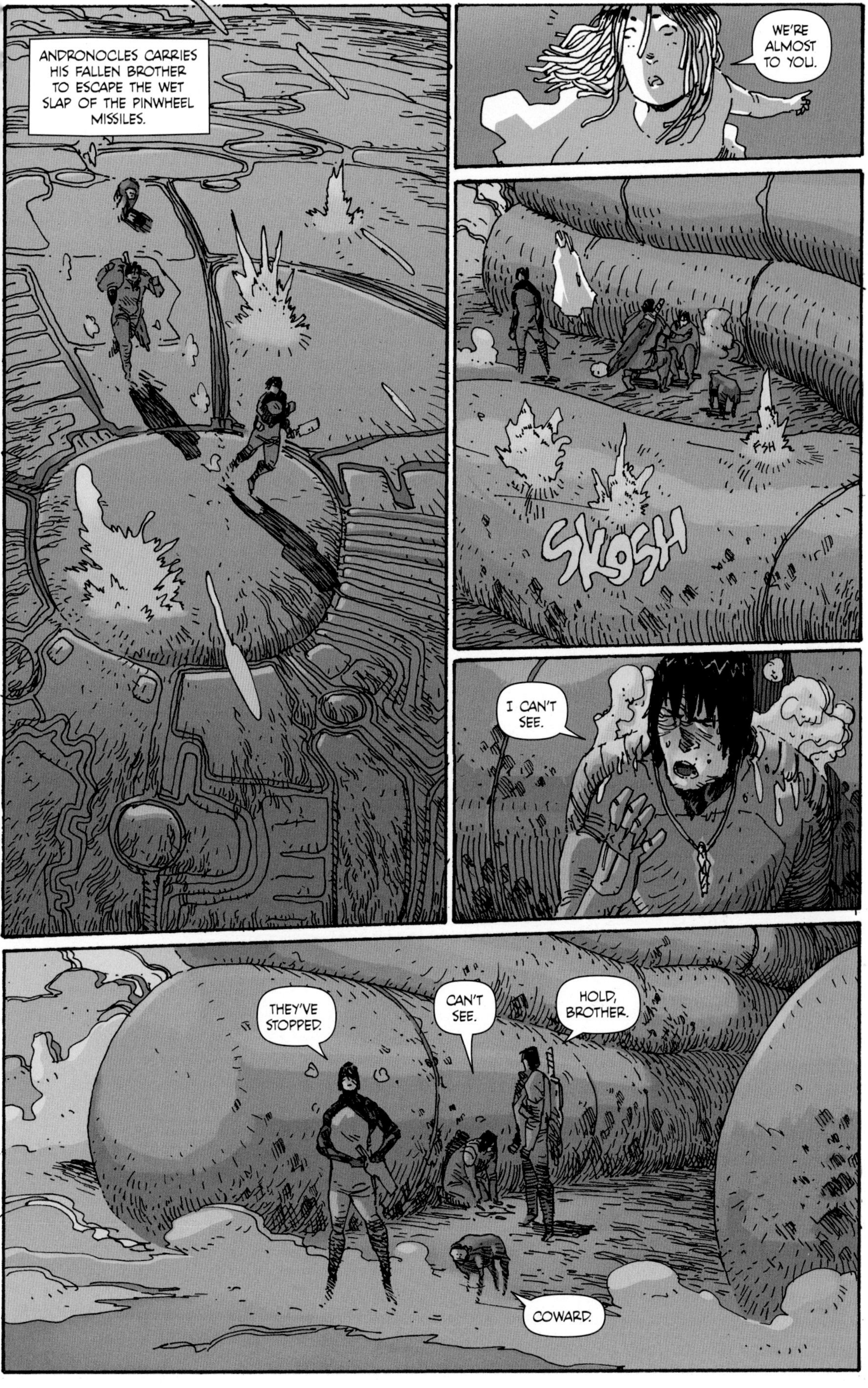
ANDRONOCLES CARRIES HIS FALLEN BROTHER TO ESCAPE THE WET SLAP OF THE PINWHEEL MISSILES.
WE'RE ALMOST TO YOU.
FSH
SKLOSH
I CAN'T SEE.
THEY'VE STOPPED.
CAN'T SEE.
HOLD, BROTHER.
COWARD.

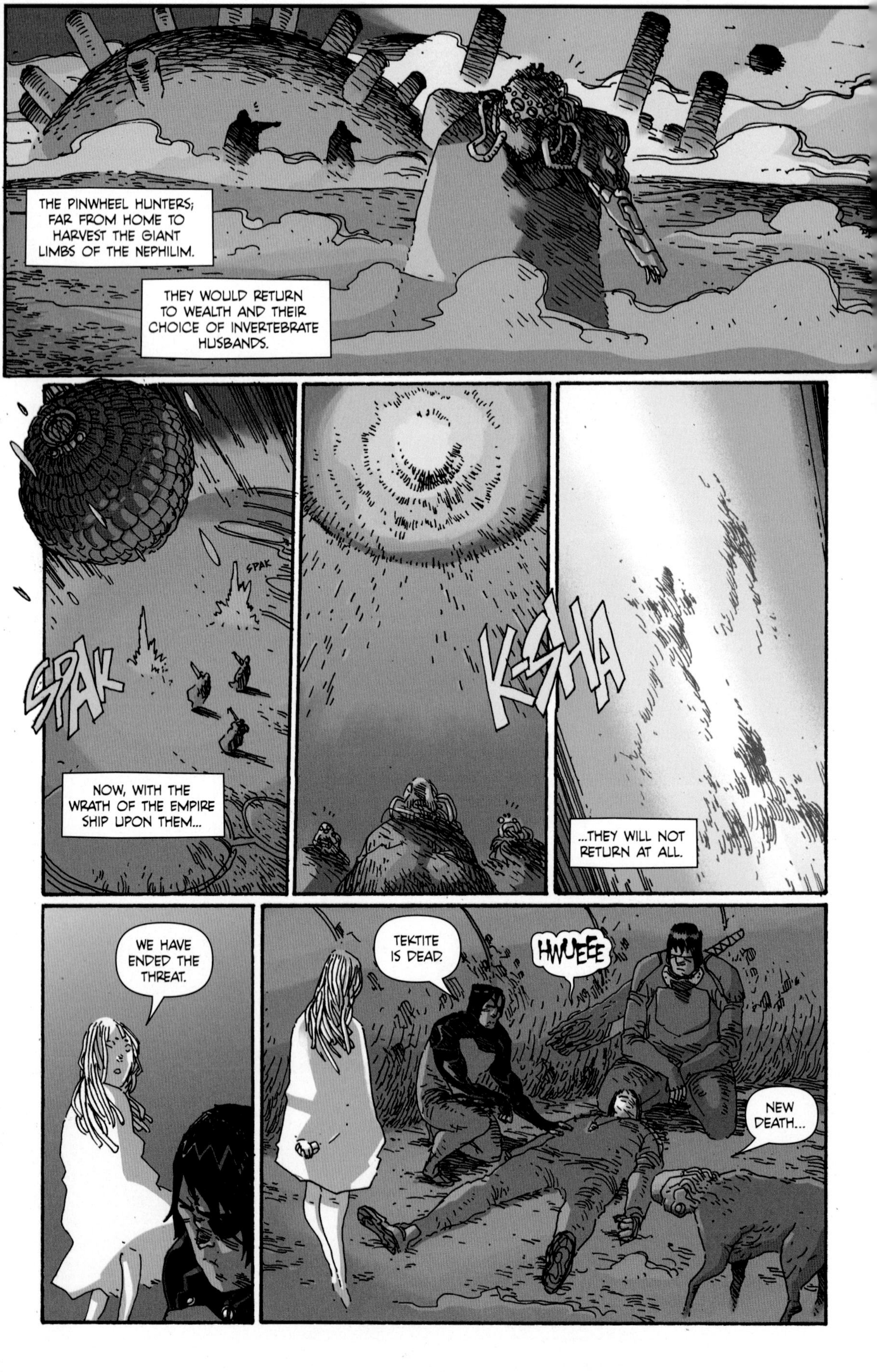
THE PINWHEEL HUNTERS; FAR FROM HOME TO HARVEST THE GIANT LIMBS OF THE NEPHILIM.
THEY WOULD RETURN TO WEALTH AND THEIR CHOICE OF INVERTEBRATE HUSBANDS.
SPAK
SPAK
NOW, WITH THE WRATH OF THE EMPIRE SHIP UPON THEM...
K-SHA
...THEY WILL NOT RETURN AT ALL.
WE HAVE ENDED THE THREAT.
TEKTITE IS DEAD.
HWUEEE
NEW DEATH...

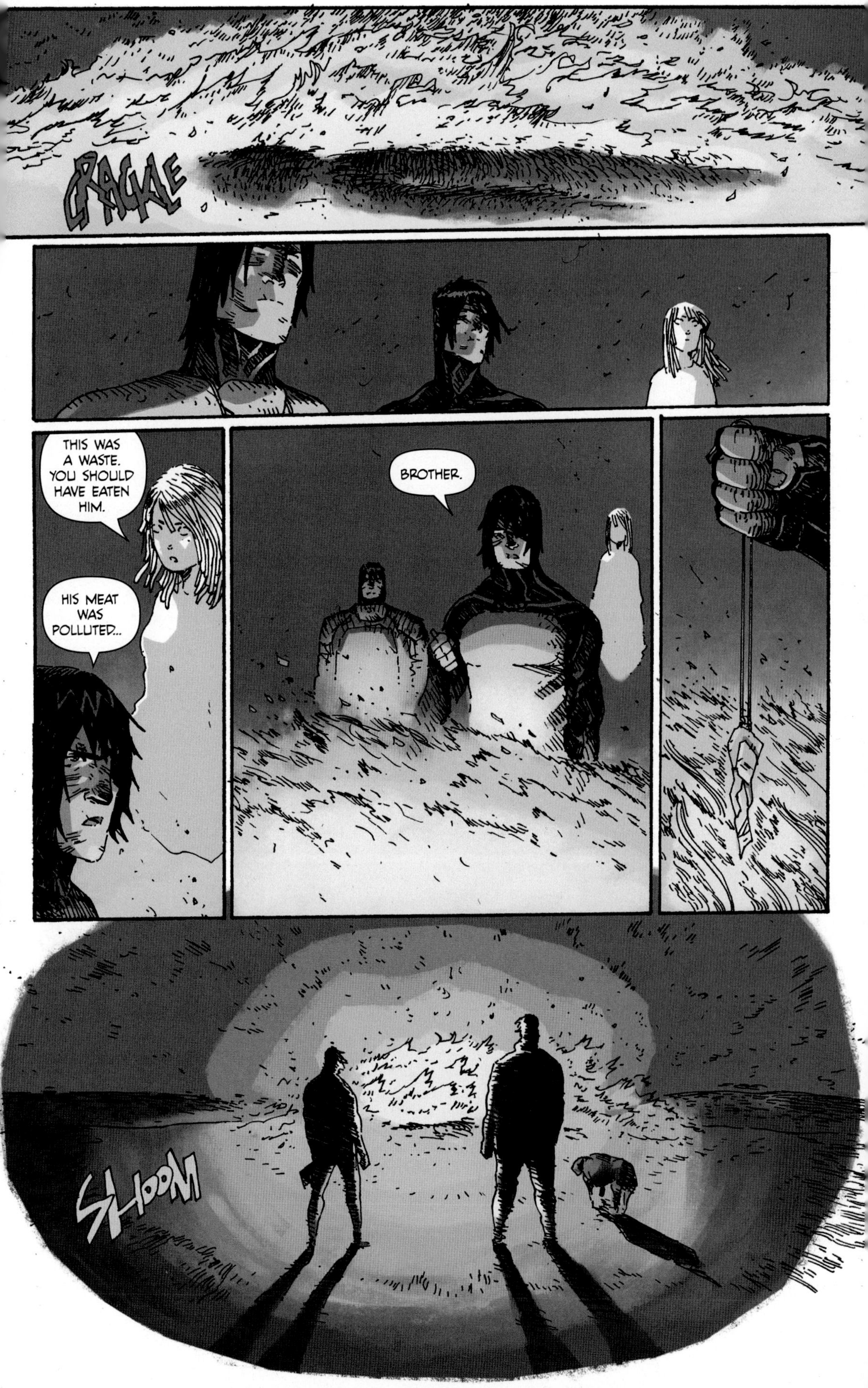
CRACKLE
THIS WAS A WASTE. YOU SHOULD HAVE EATEN HIM.
HIS MEAT WAS POLLUTED...
BROTHER.
SHOOM

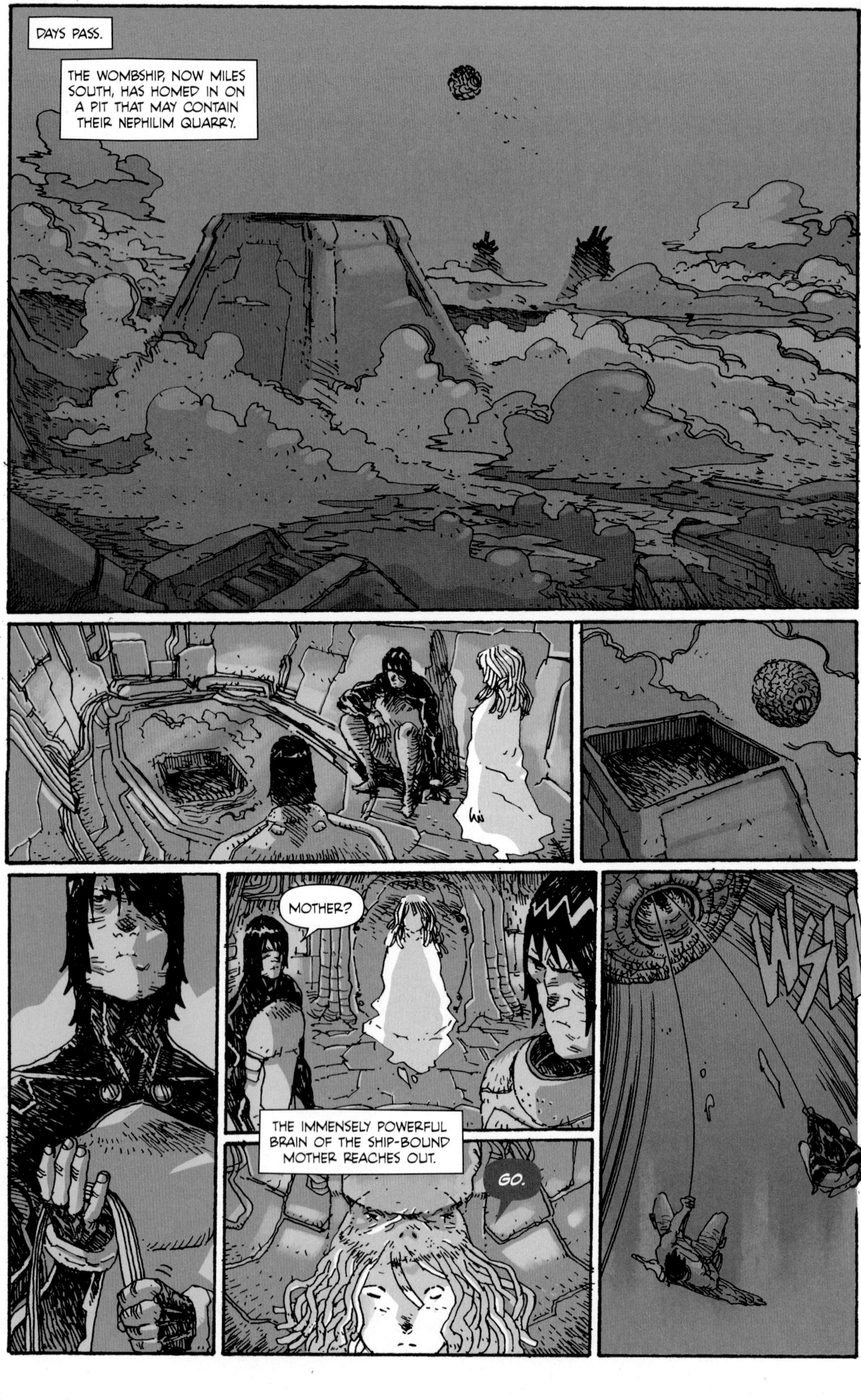
DAYS PASS.
THE WOMBSHIP, NOW MILES SOUTH, HAS HOMED IN ON A PIT THAT MAY CONTAIN THEIR NEPHILIM QUARRY.
MOTHER?
THE IMMENSELY POWERFUL BRAIN OF THE SHIP-BOUND MOTHER REACHES OUT.
GO.
WSH

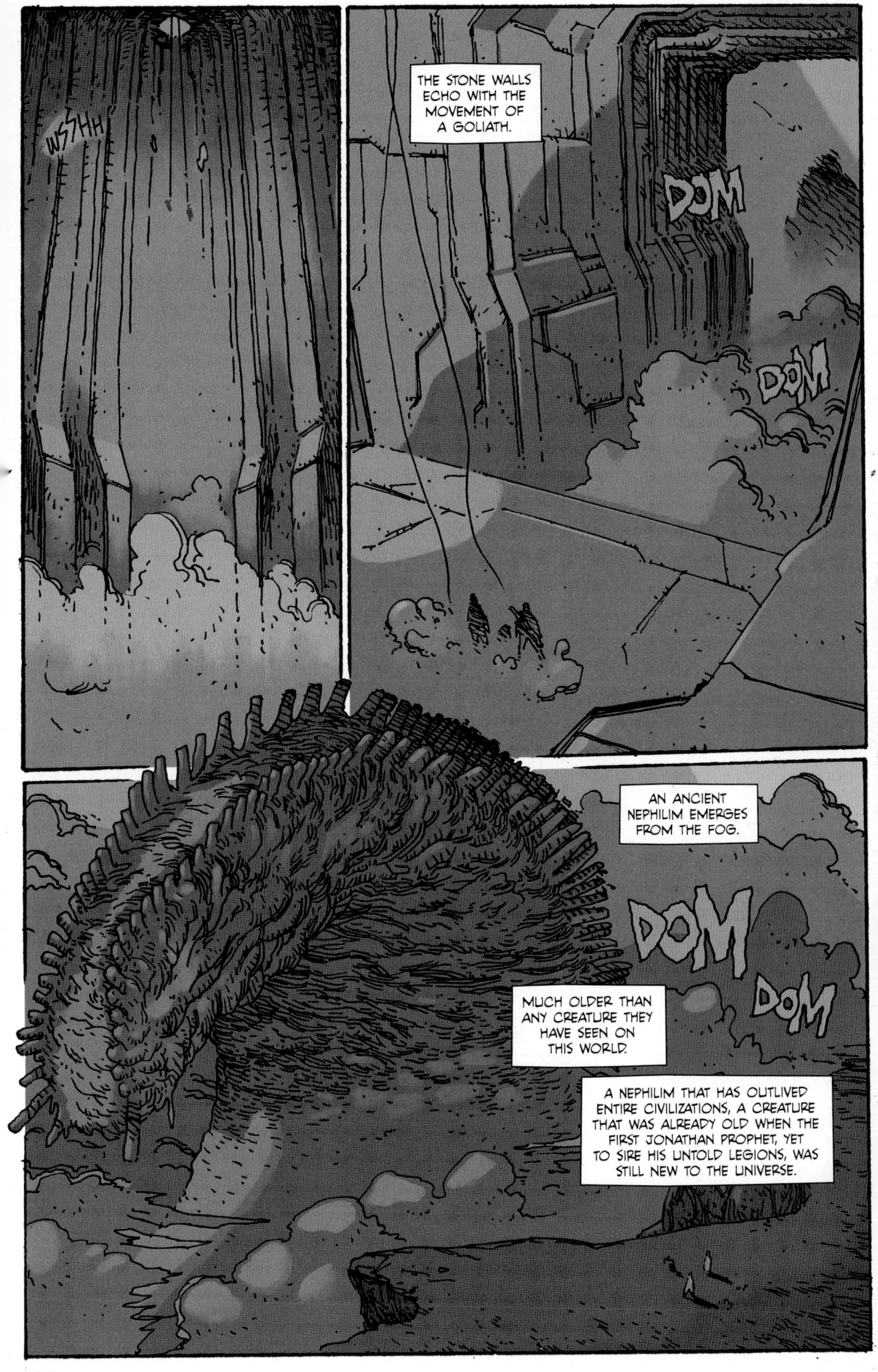
WSSHH
THE STONE WALLS ECHO WITH THE MOVEMENT OF A GOLIATH.
DOM
DOM
AN ANCIENT NEPHILIM EMERGES FROM THE FOG.
DOM
DOM
MUCH OLDER THAN ANY CREATURE THEY HAVE SEEN ON THIS WORLD.
A NEPHILIM THAT HAS OUTLIVED ENTIRE CIVILIZATIONS, A CREATURE THAT WAS ALREADY OLD WHEN THE FIRST JONATHAN PROPHET, YET TO SIRE HIS UNTOLD LEGIONS, WAS STILL NEW TO THE UNIVERSE.

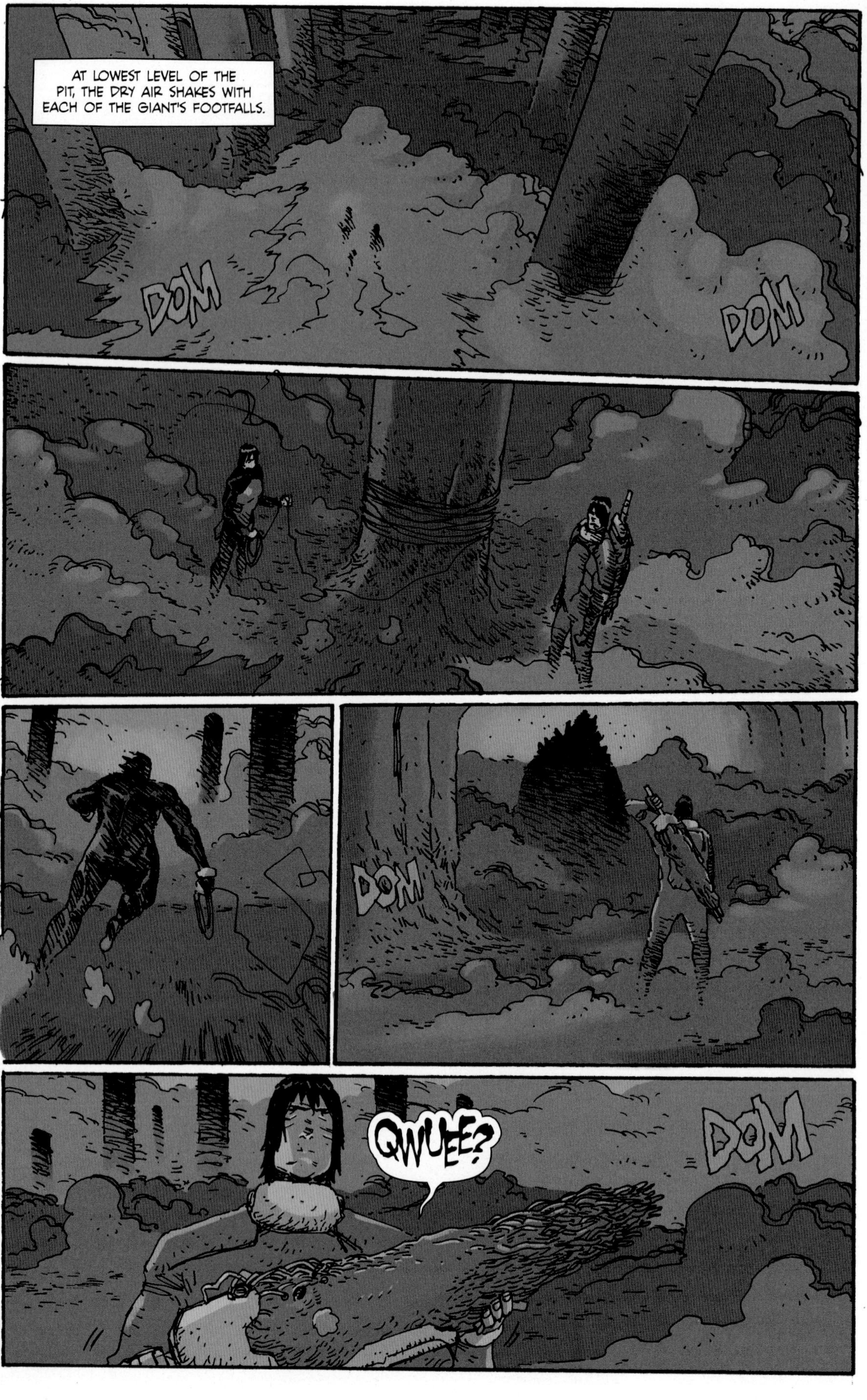

AT LOWEST LEVEL OF THE PIT, THE DRY AIR SHAKES WITH EACH OF THE GIANT'S FOOTFALLS.
DOM
DOM
DOM
QWUEE?
DOM

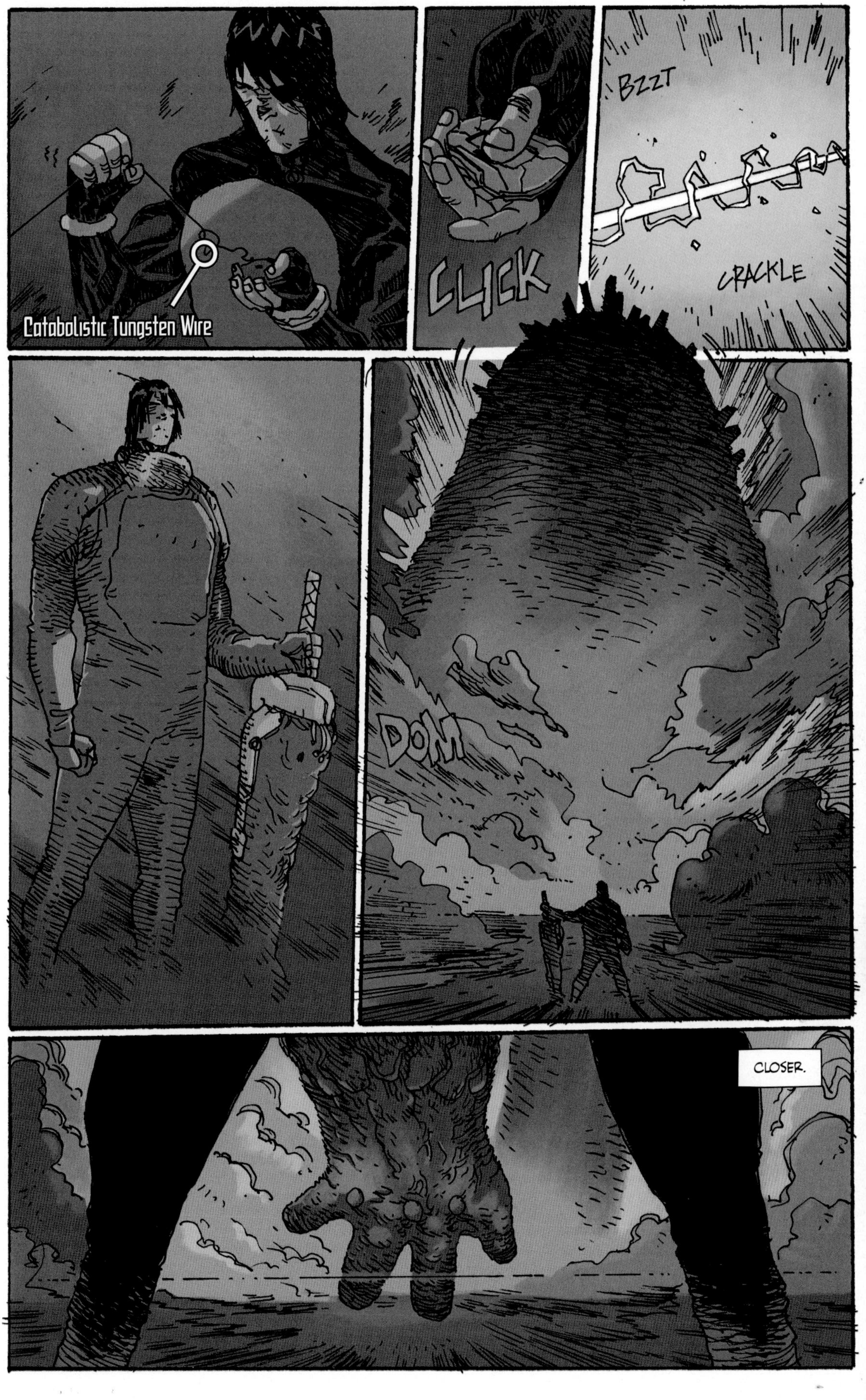
Catabolistic Tungsten Wire
CLICK
BZZT
CRACKLE
DOM
CLOSER.

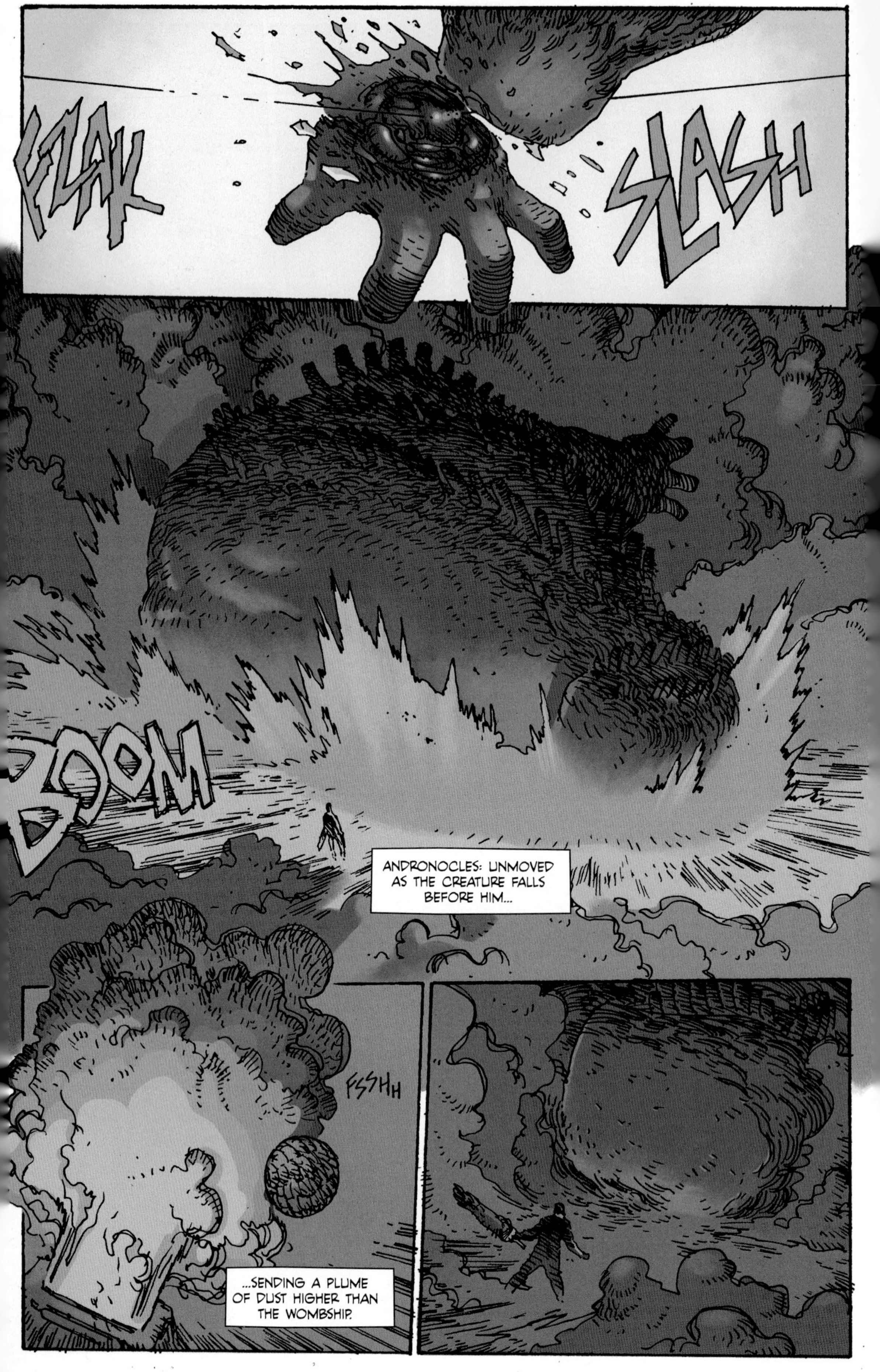
FZAK
SLASH
BOOM
ANDRONOCLES: UNMOVED AS THE CREATURE FALLS BEFORE HIM...
FSSHH
...SENDING A PLUME OF DUST HIGHER THAN THE WOMBSHIP.

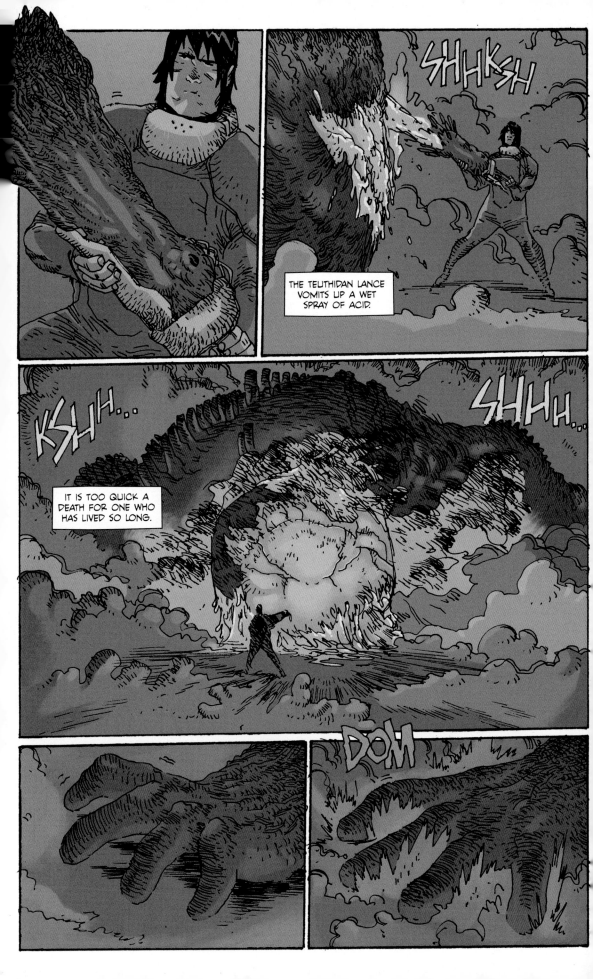

SHHKSH

THE TEUTHIDAN LANCE
VOMITS UP A WET
SPRAY OF ACID.

KSHH...

SHHh...

IT IS TOO QUICK A
DEATH FOR ONE WHO
HAS LIVED SO LONG.

DOM

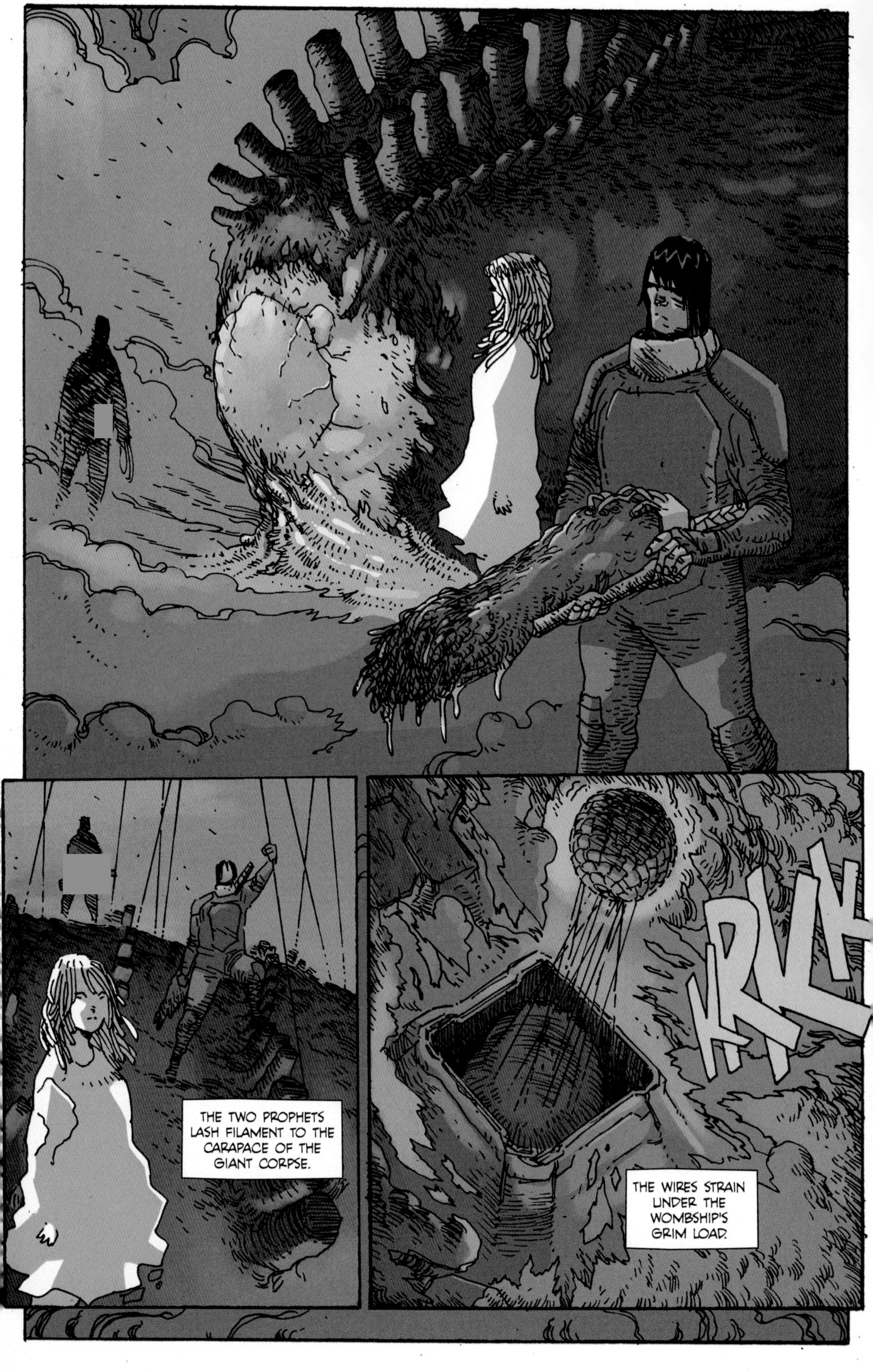
THE TWO PROPHETS LASH FILAMENT TO THE CARAPACE OF THE GIANT CORPSE.
THE WIRES STRAIN UNDER THE WOMBSHIP'S GRIM LOAD.

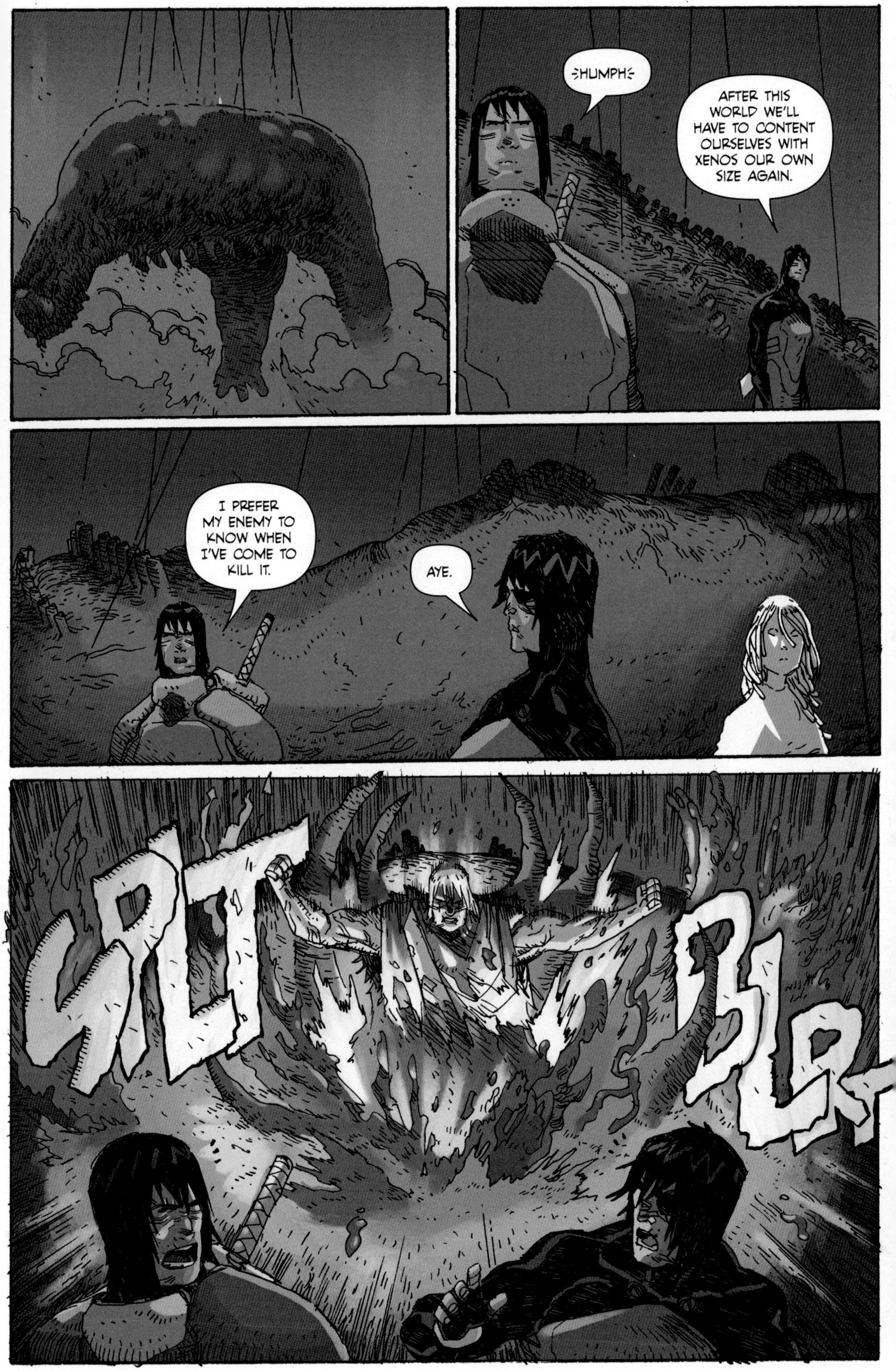

HUMPH
AFTER THIS WORLD WE'LL HAVE TO CONTENT OURSELVES WITH XENOS OUR OWN SIZE AGAIN.
I PREFER MY ENEMY TO KNOW WHEN I'VE COME TO KILL IT.
AYE.

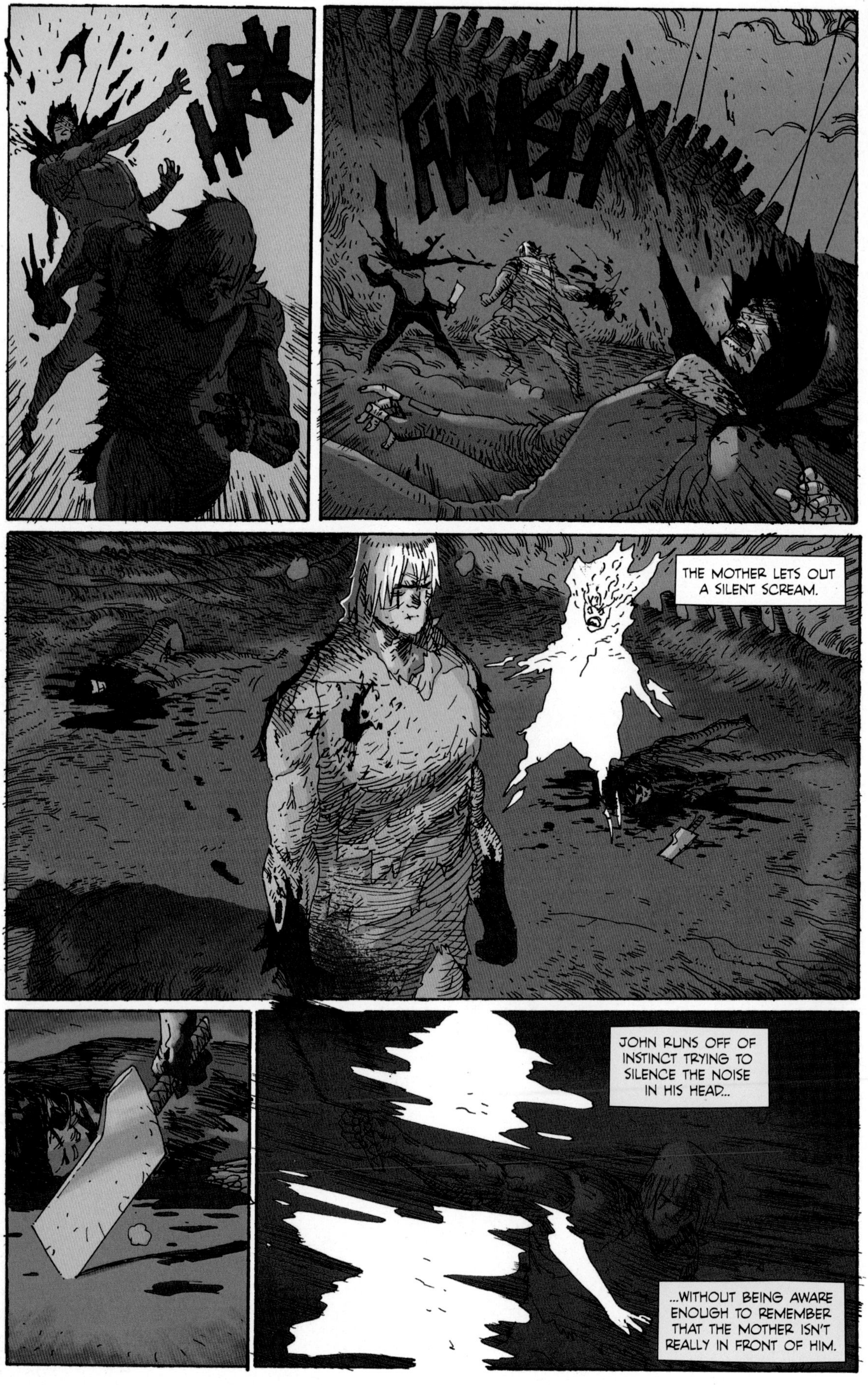
HRK
AAAGH
THE MOTHER LETS OUT A SILENT SCREAM.
JOHN RUNS OFF OF INSTINCT TRYING TO SILENCE THE NOISE IN HIS HEAD...
...WITHOUT BEING AWARE ENOUGH TO REMEMBER THAT THE MOTHER ISN'T REALLY IN FRONT OF HIM.

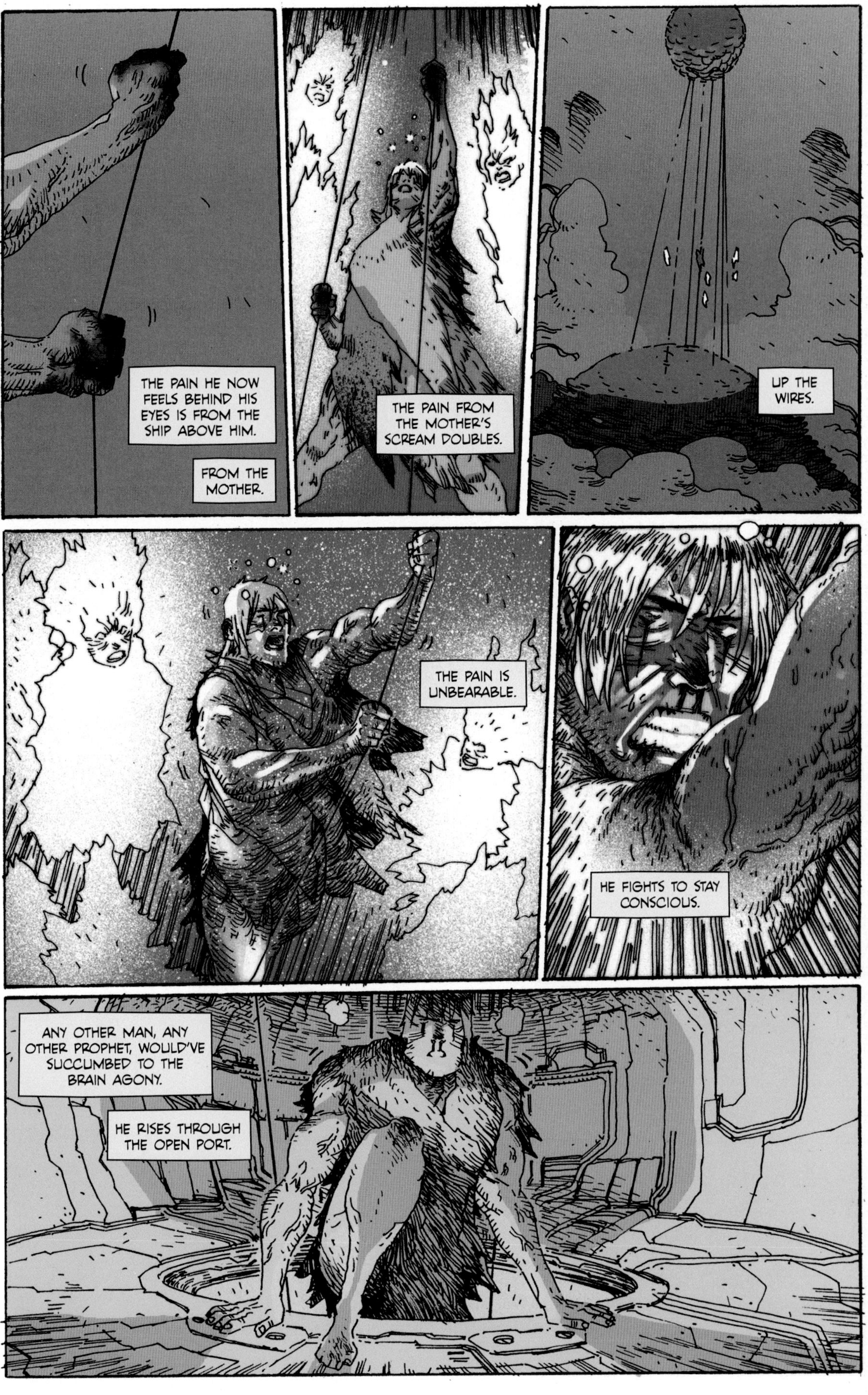
THE PAIN HE NOW FEELS BEHIND HIS EYES IS FROM THE SHIP ABOVE HIM.
FROM THE MOTHER.
THE PAIN FROM THE MOTHER'S SCREAM DOUBLES.
UP THE WIRES.
THE PAIN IS UNBEARABLE.
HE FIGHTS TO STAY CONSCIOUS.
ANY OTHER MAN, ANY OTHER PROPHET, WOULD'VE SUCCUMBED TO THE BRAIN AGONY.
HE RISES THROUGH THE OPEN PORT.

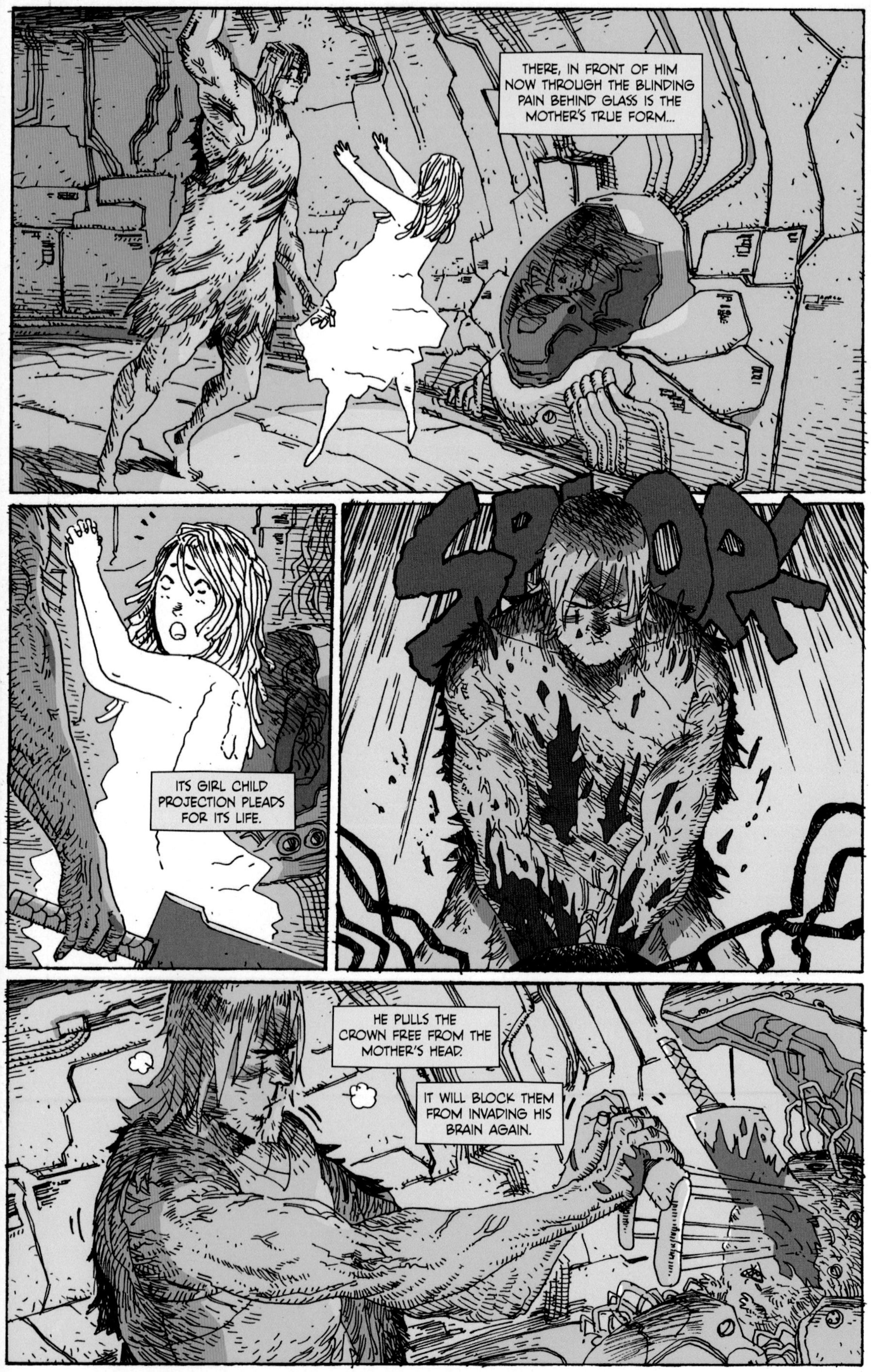
THERE, IN FRONT OF HIM NOW THROUGH THE BLINDING PAIN BEHIND GLASS IS THE MOTHER'S TRUE FORM...
ITS GIRL CHILD PROJECTION PLEADS FOR ITS LIFE.
HE PULLS THE CROWN FREE FROM THE MOTHER'S HEAD.
IT WILL BLOCK THEM FROM INVADING HIS BRAIN AGAIN.

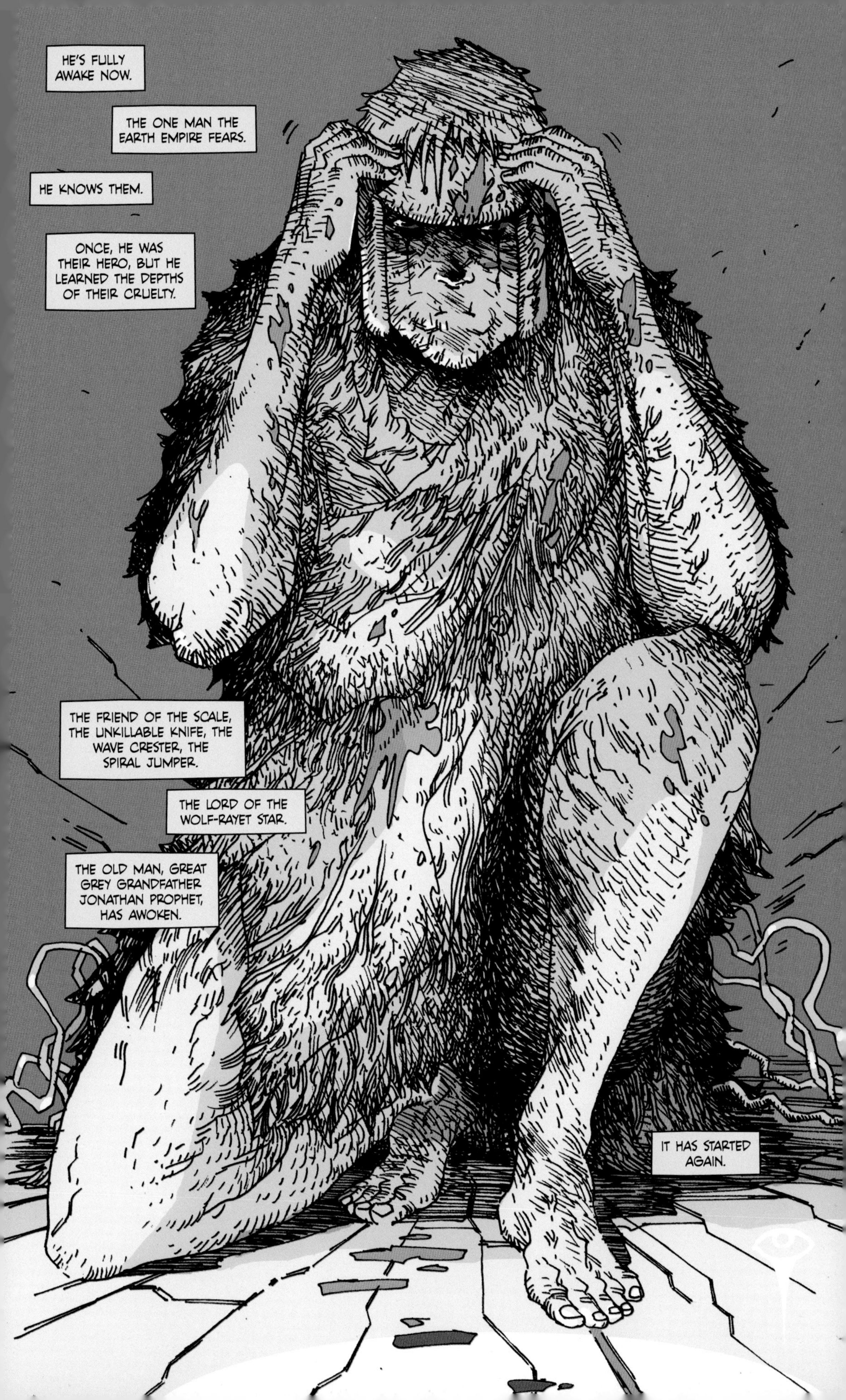
HE'S FULLY AWAKE NOW.
THE ONE MAN THE EARTH EMPIRE FEARS.
HE KNOWS THEM.
ONCE, HE WAS THEIR HERO, BUT HE LEARNED THE DEPTHS OF THEIR CRUELTY.
THE FRIEND OF THE SCALE, THE UNKILLABLE KNIFE, THE WAVE CRESTER, THE SPIRAL JUMPER.
THE LORD OF THE WOLF-RAYET STAR.
THE OLD MAN, GREAT GREY GRANDFATHER JONATHAN PROPHET, HAS AWOKEN.
IT HAS STARTED AGAIN.

COIL: A CLONE STORY

by Emma Rios

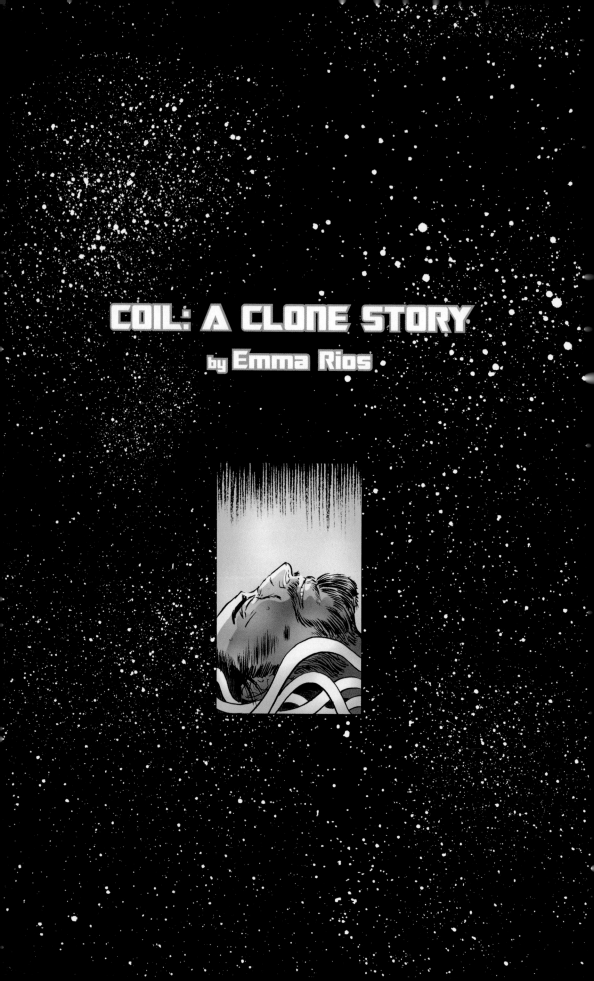

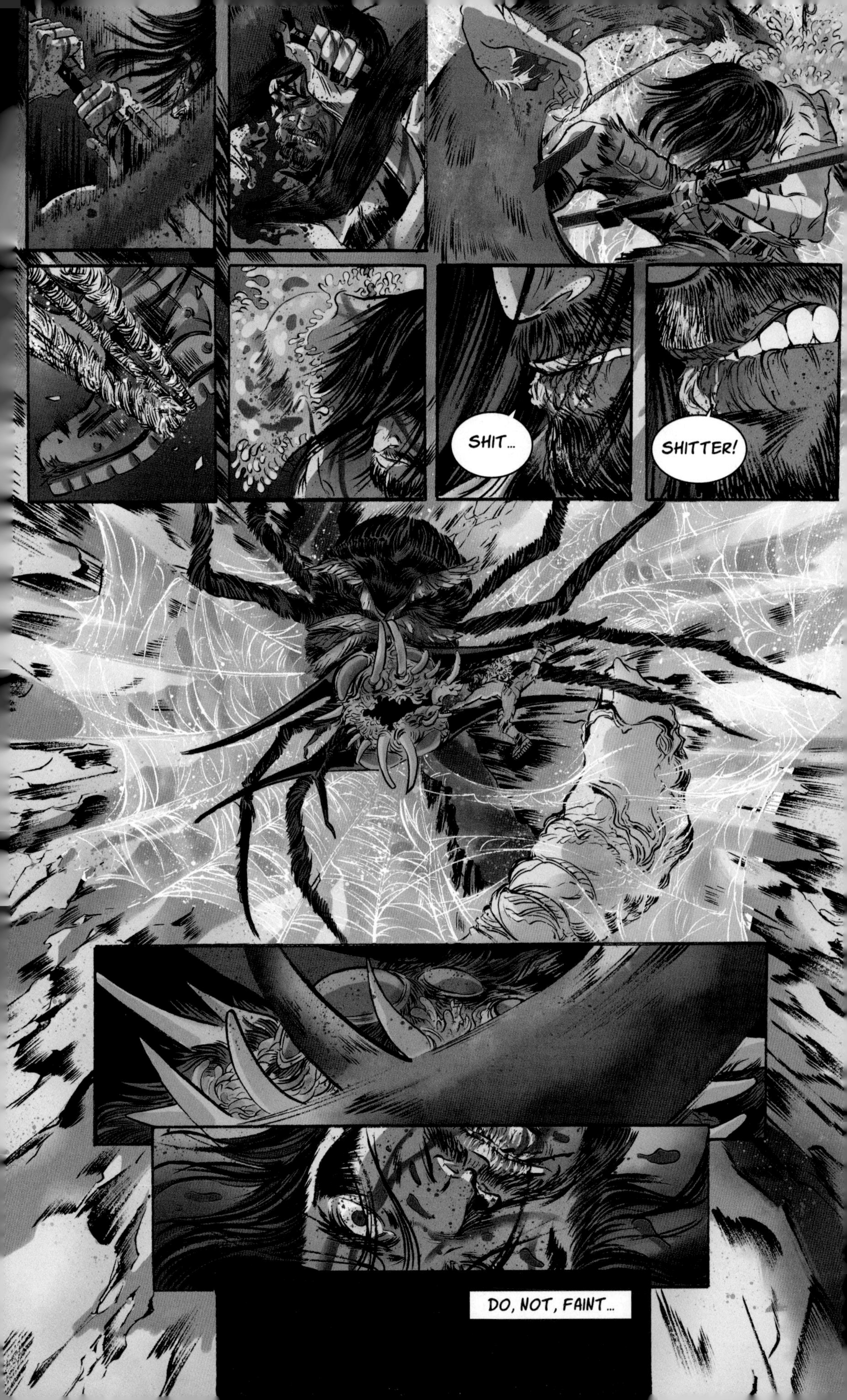
SHIT...
SHITTER!
DO, NOT, FAINT...

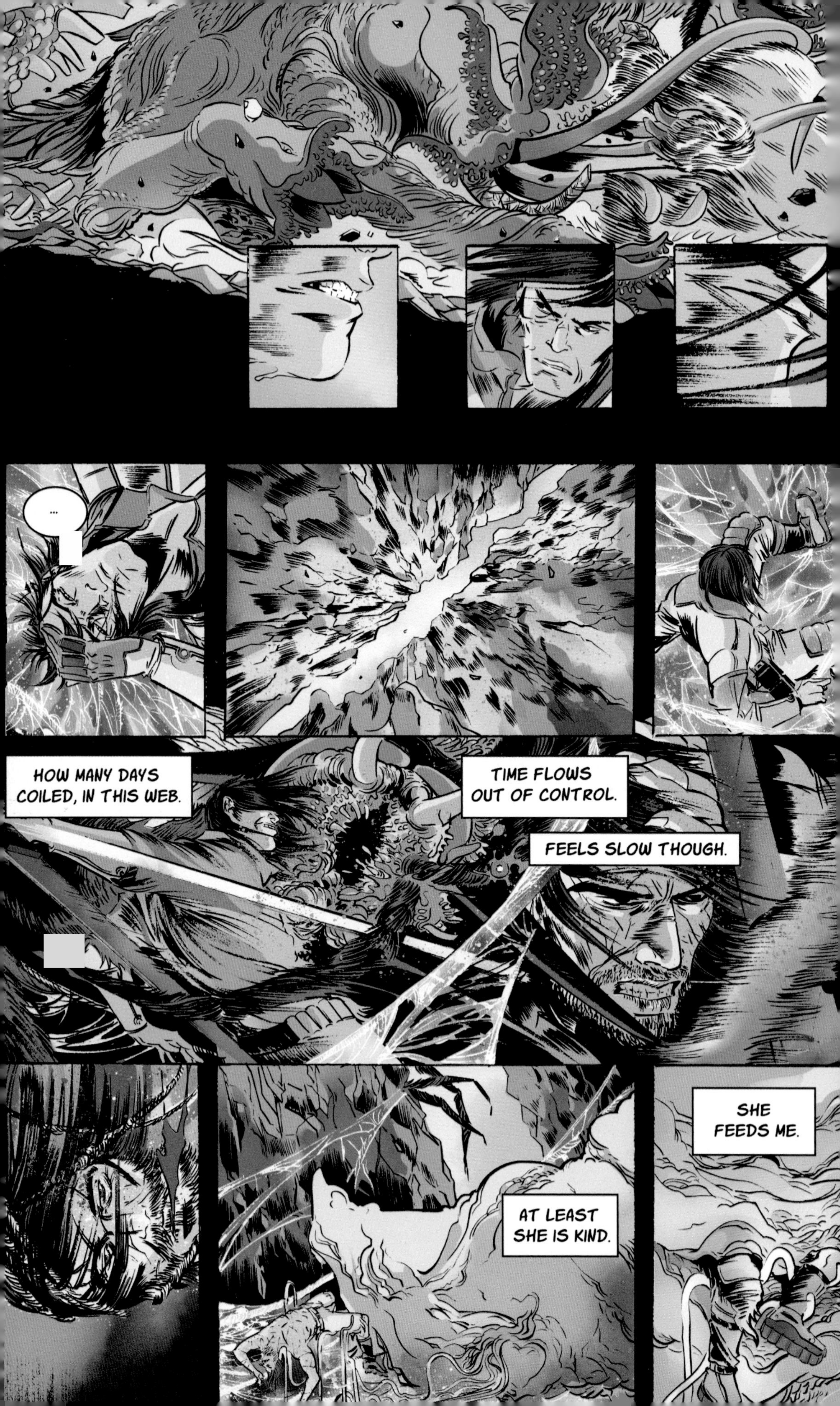
...
HOW MANY DAYS COILED, IN THIS WEB.
TIME FLOWS OUT OF CONTROL.
FEELS SLOW THOUGH.
SHE FEEDS ME.
AT LEAST SHE IS KIND.

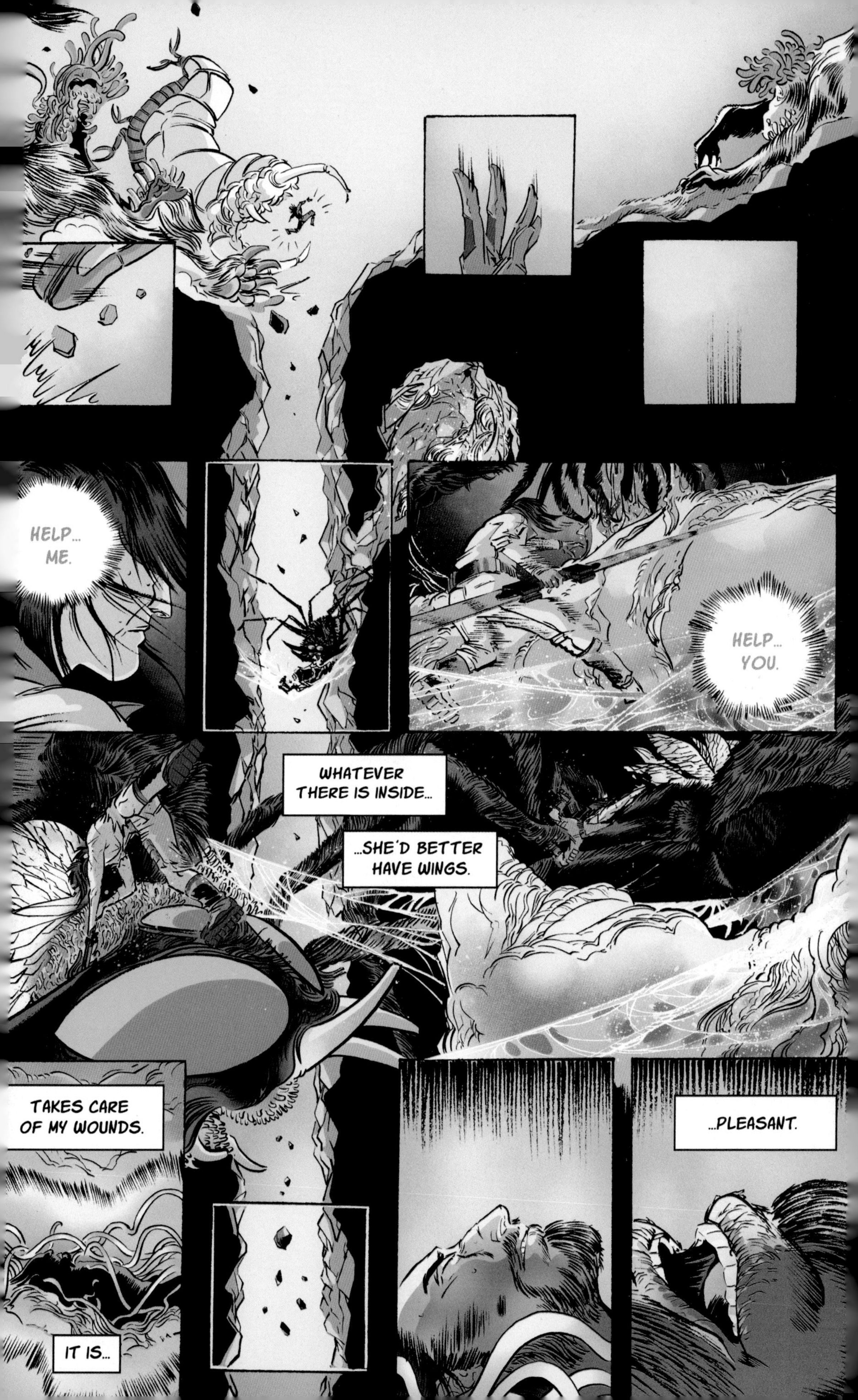
HELP... ME.
HELP... YOU.
WHATEVER THERE IS INSIDE...
...SHE'D BETTER HAVE WINGS.
TAKES CARE OF MY WOUNDS.
IT IS...
...PLEASANT.

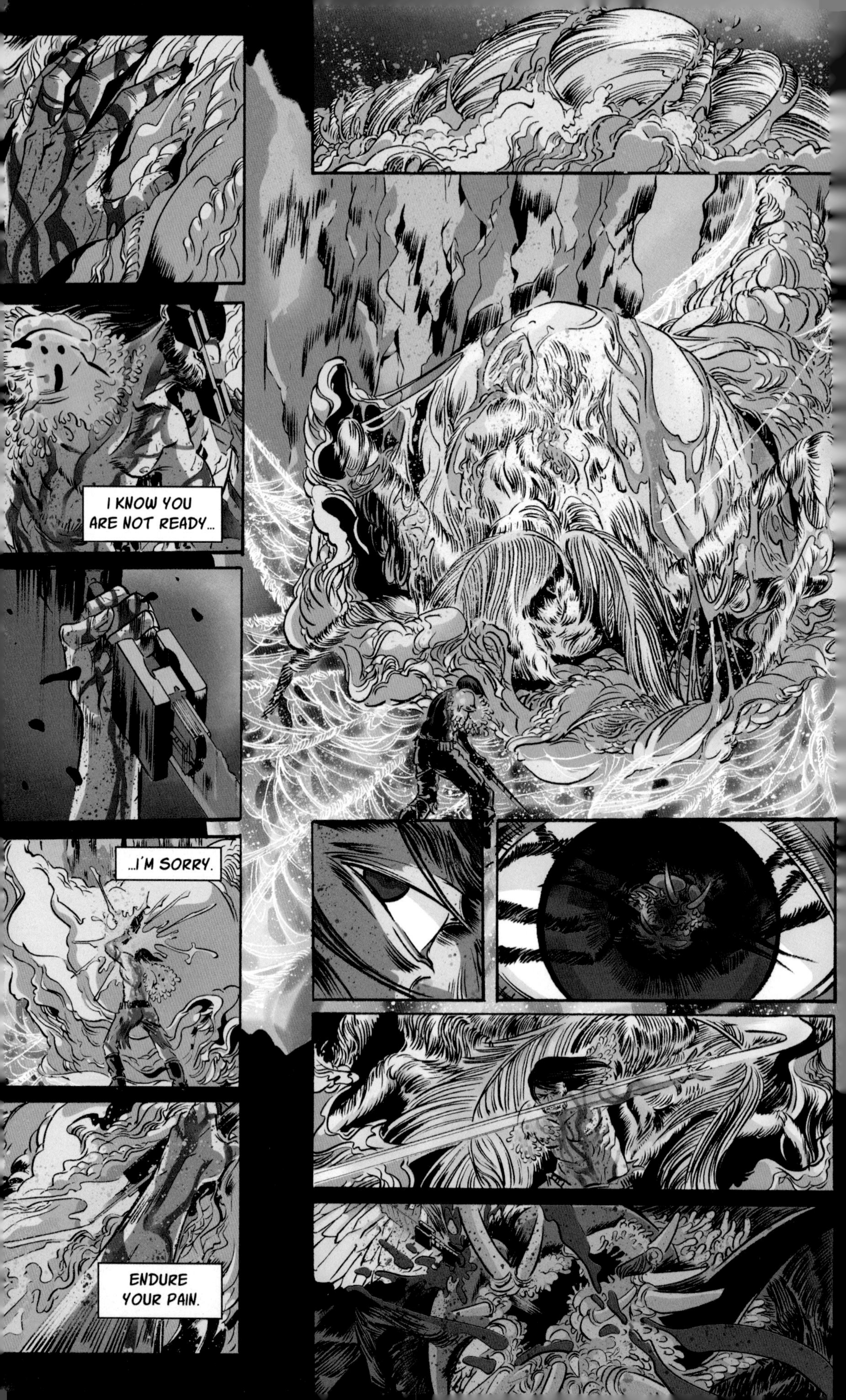
I KNOW YOU ARE NOT READY...
...I'M SORRY.
ENDURE YOUR PAIN.

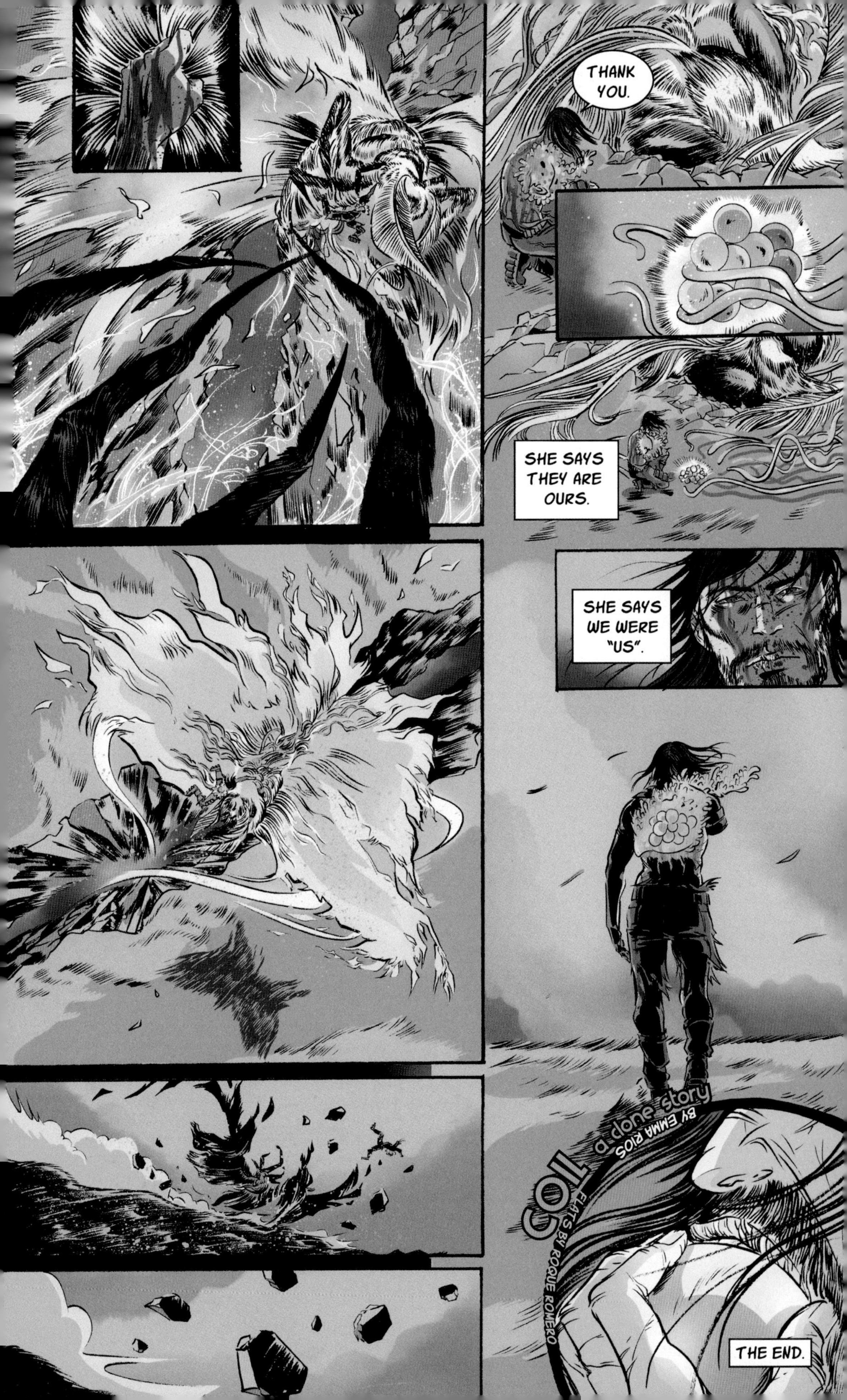
THANK YOU.
SHE SAYS THEY ARE OURS.
SHE SAYS WE WERE "US".
COIL
a clone story
BY EMMA RIOS
FLATS BY ROQUE ROMERO
THE END.

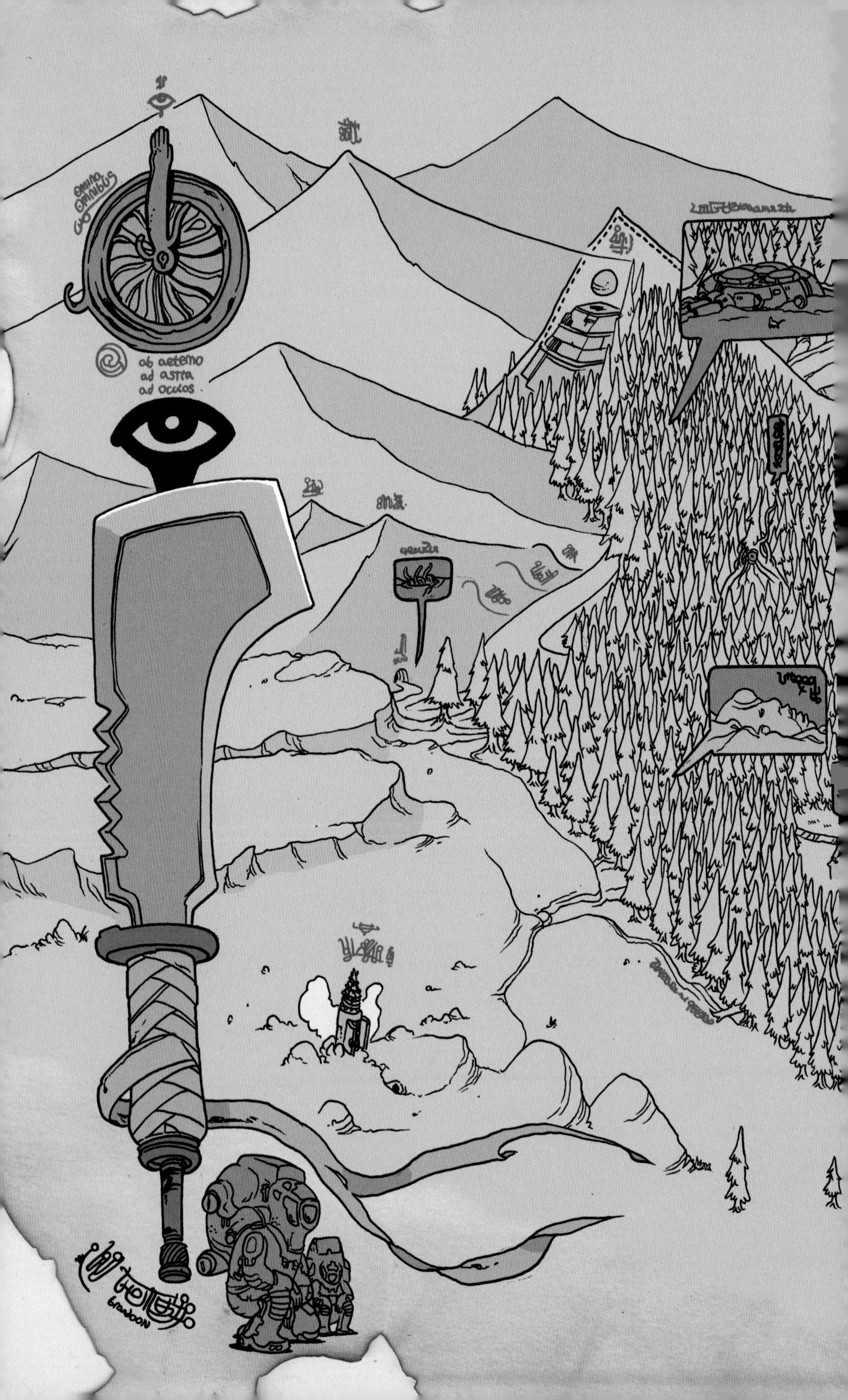
omnia omnibus
ab aeterno
ad astra
ad oculos

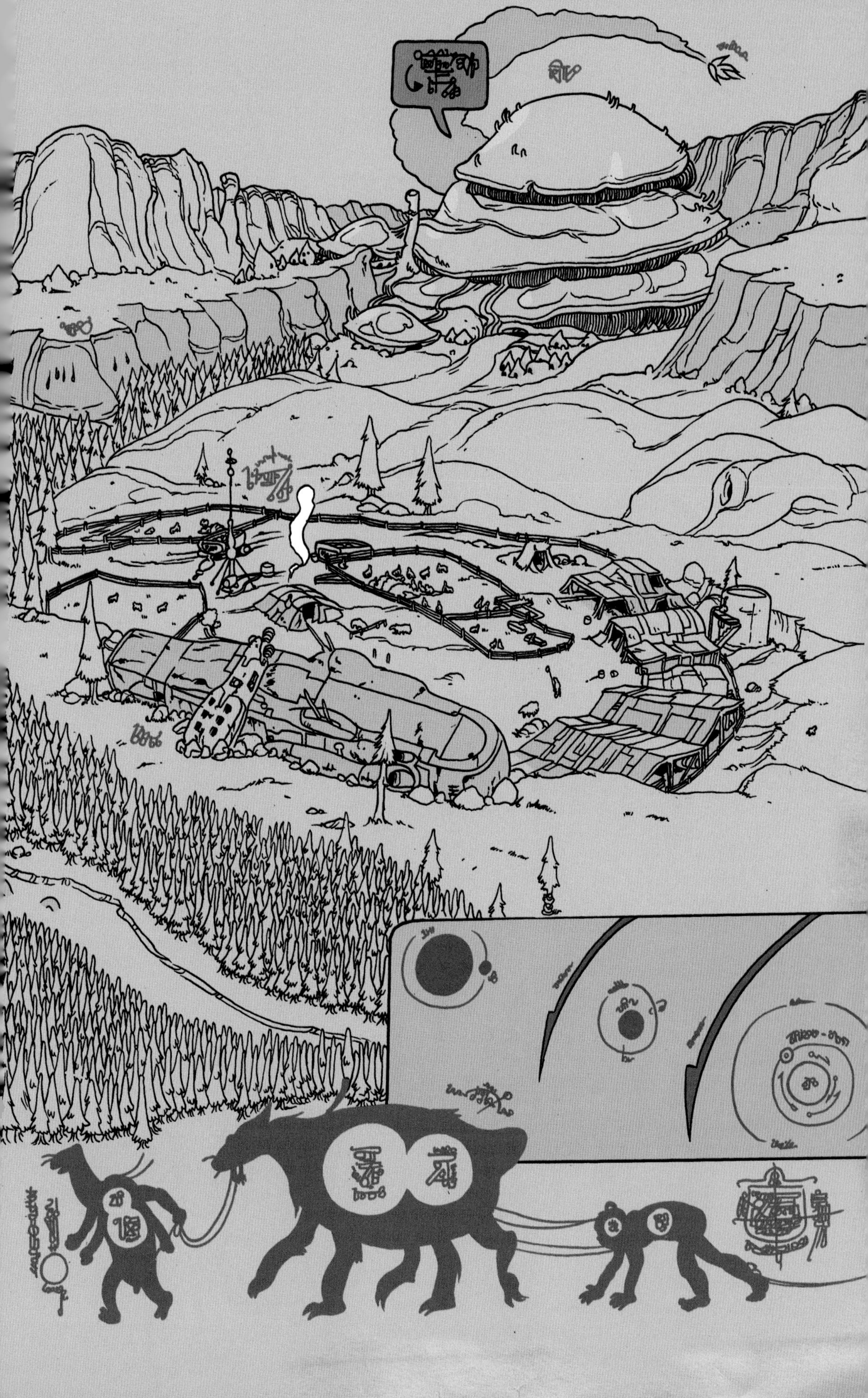

PROPHET EXPLODES INTO HIS ACTION-PACKED REGULAR SERIES!

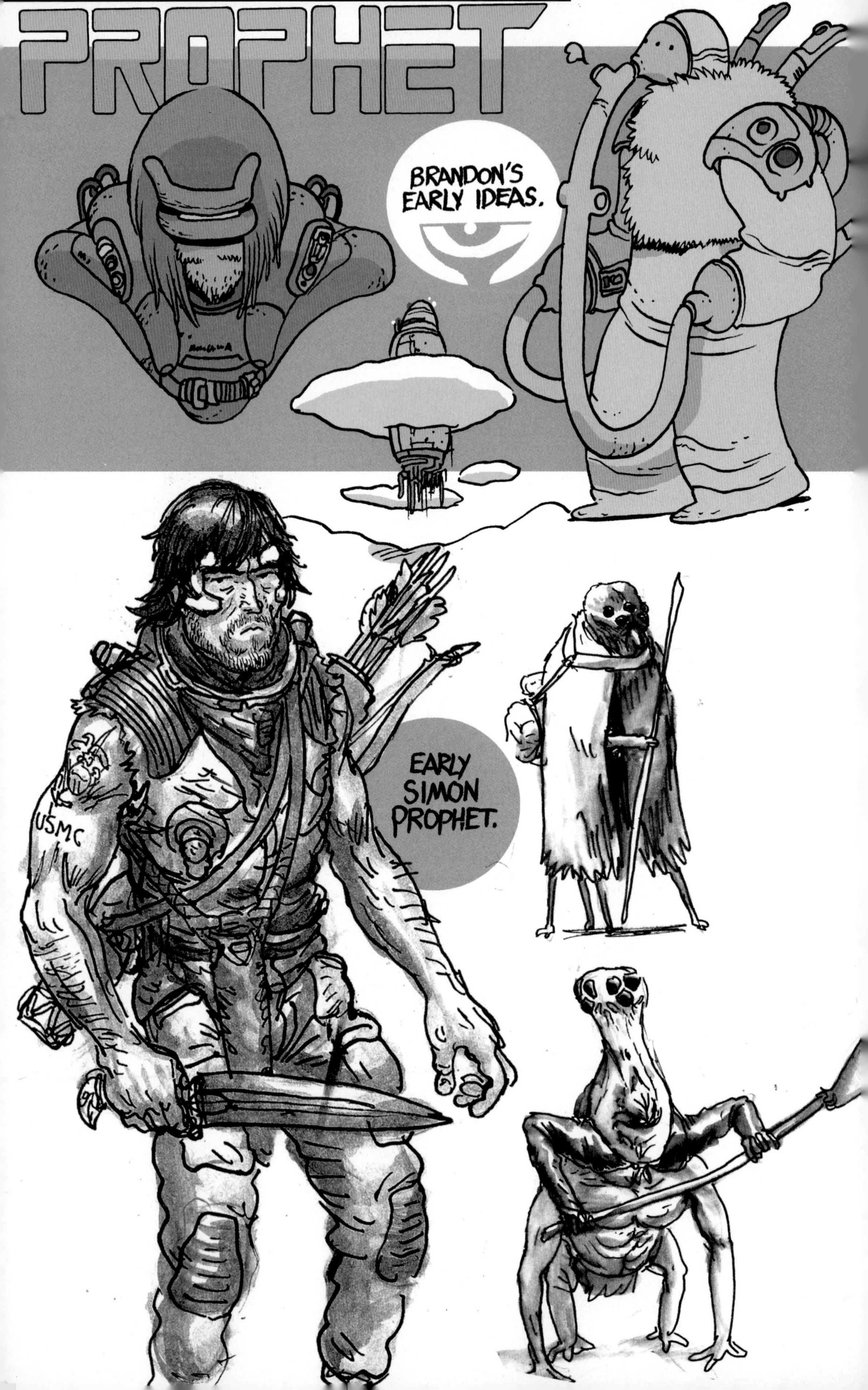
PROPHET
BRANDON'S EARLY IDEAS.
EARLY SIMON PROPHET.
USMC

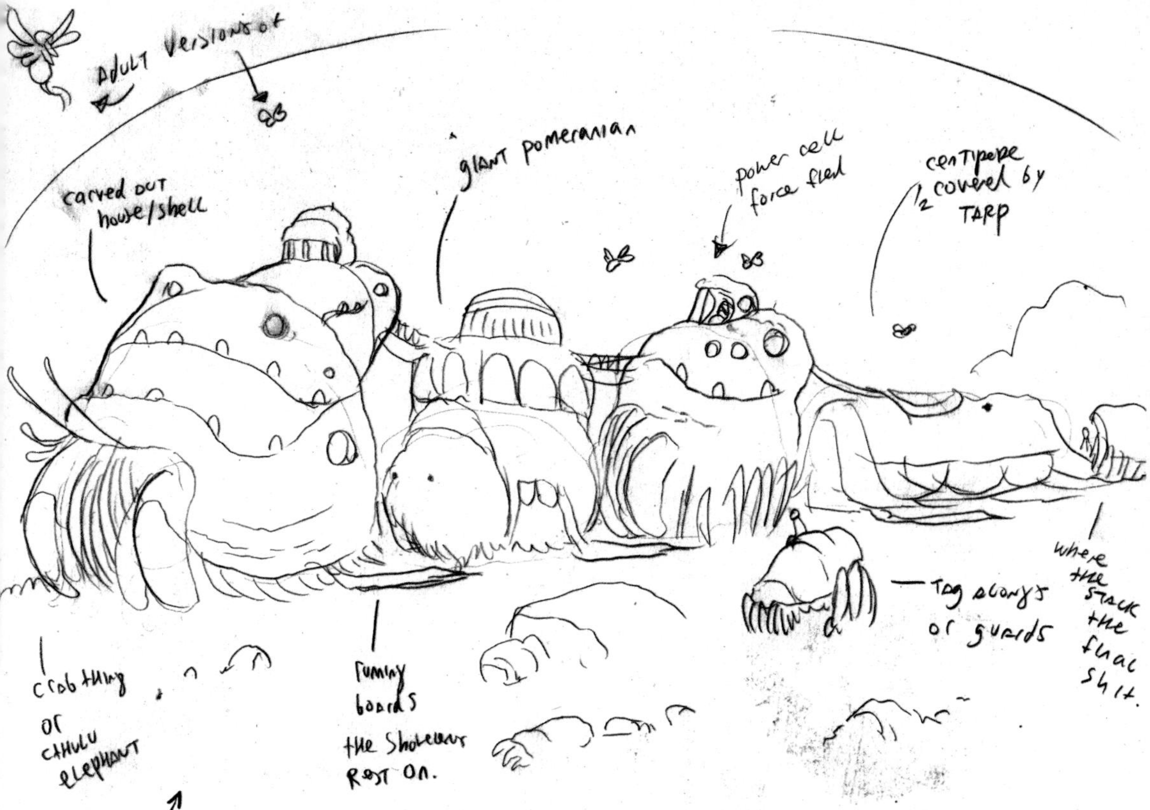
adult versions of
carved out house/shell
giant pomeranian
power cell force field
centipede 1/2 covered by TARP
crab thing or cthulu elephant
running boards the shovelers rest on.
tag alongs or guards
where the stack the final shit.

BRANDON'S TAXA CARAVAN

SIMON'S VERSION

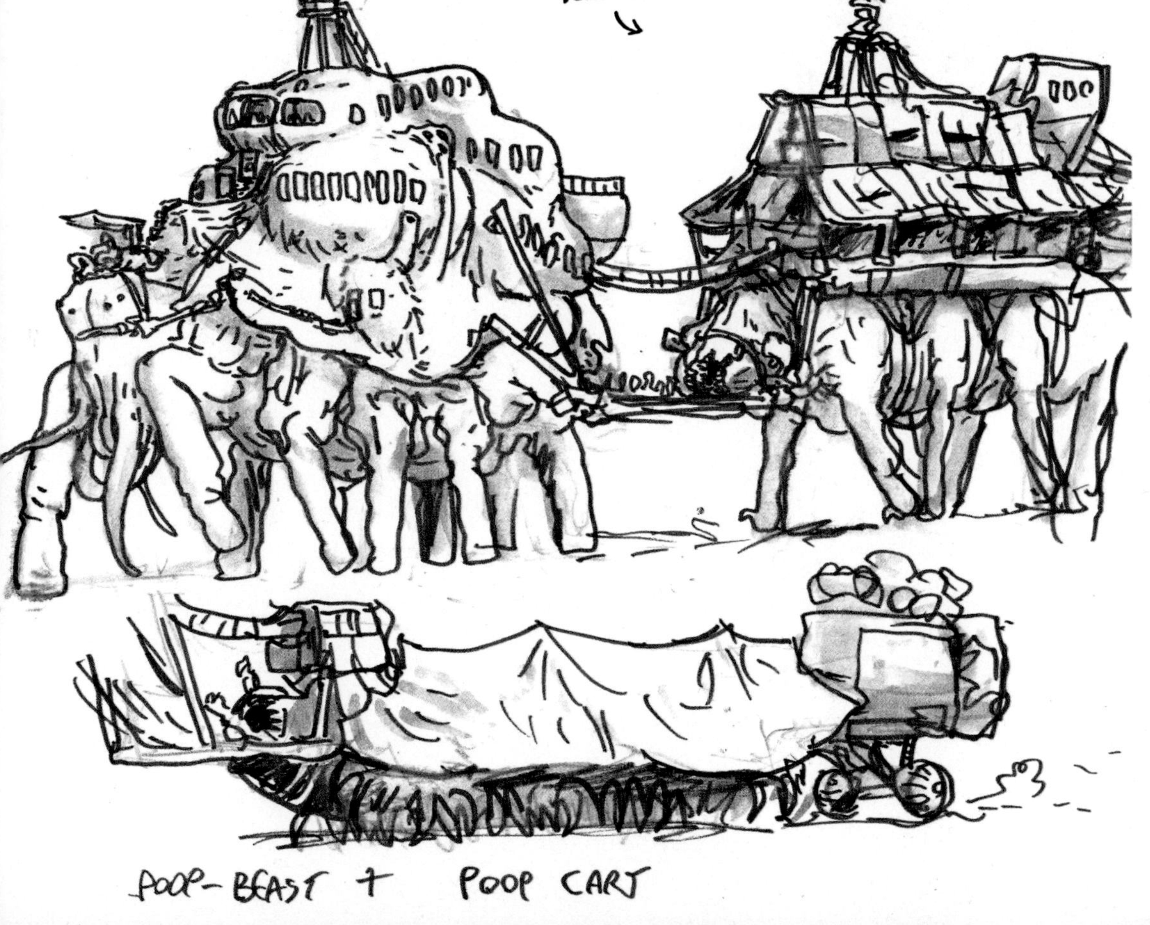
POOP-BEAST + POOP CART

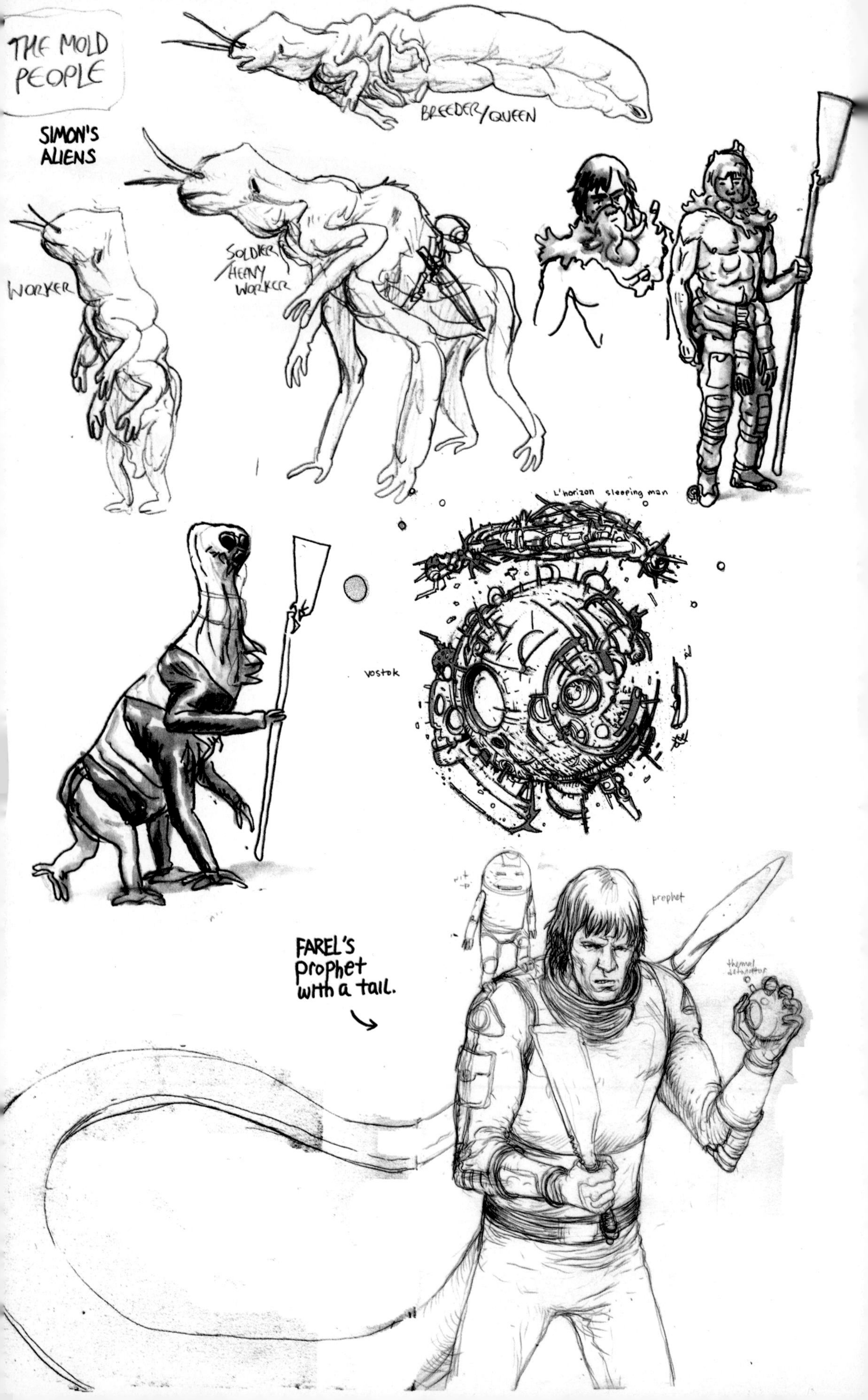
THE MOLD PEOPLE
BREEDER/QUEEN
SIMON'S ALIENS
WORKER
SOLDIER/HEAVY WORKER
L'horizon sleeping man
vostok
prophet
FAREL'S prophet with a tail.

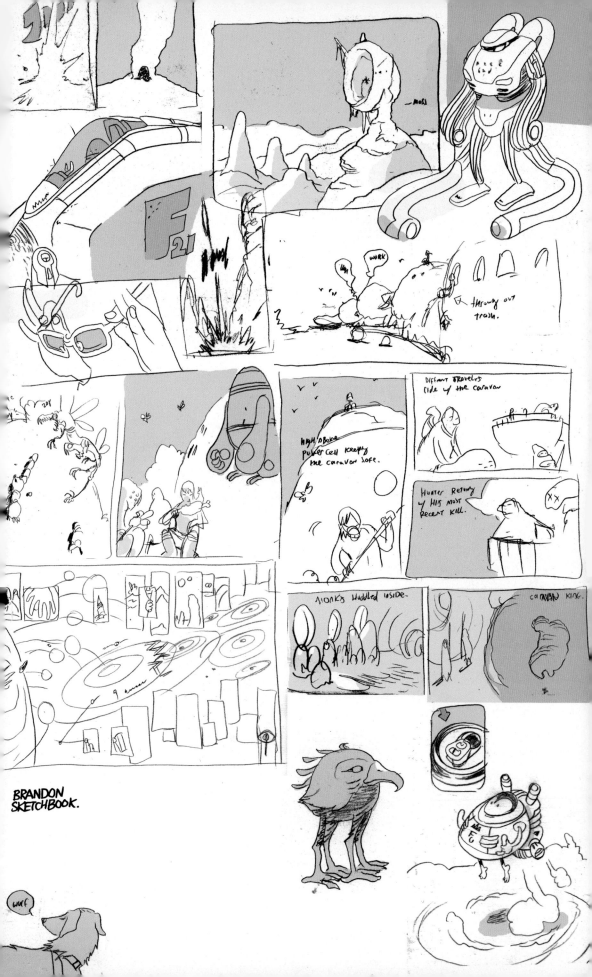

moss

work

throw out trash.

Diffrint travelrs ride w/ the caravan

HIGH ABOVE power cell keeping the caravan safe.

Hunter Returns w/ HIS most recent kill.

100nKS Huddled inside.

CARAVAN KING.

BRANDON SKETCHBOOK.

wurf

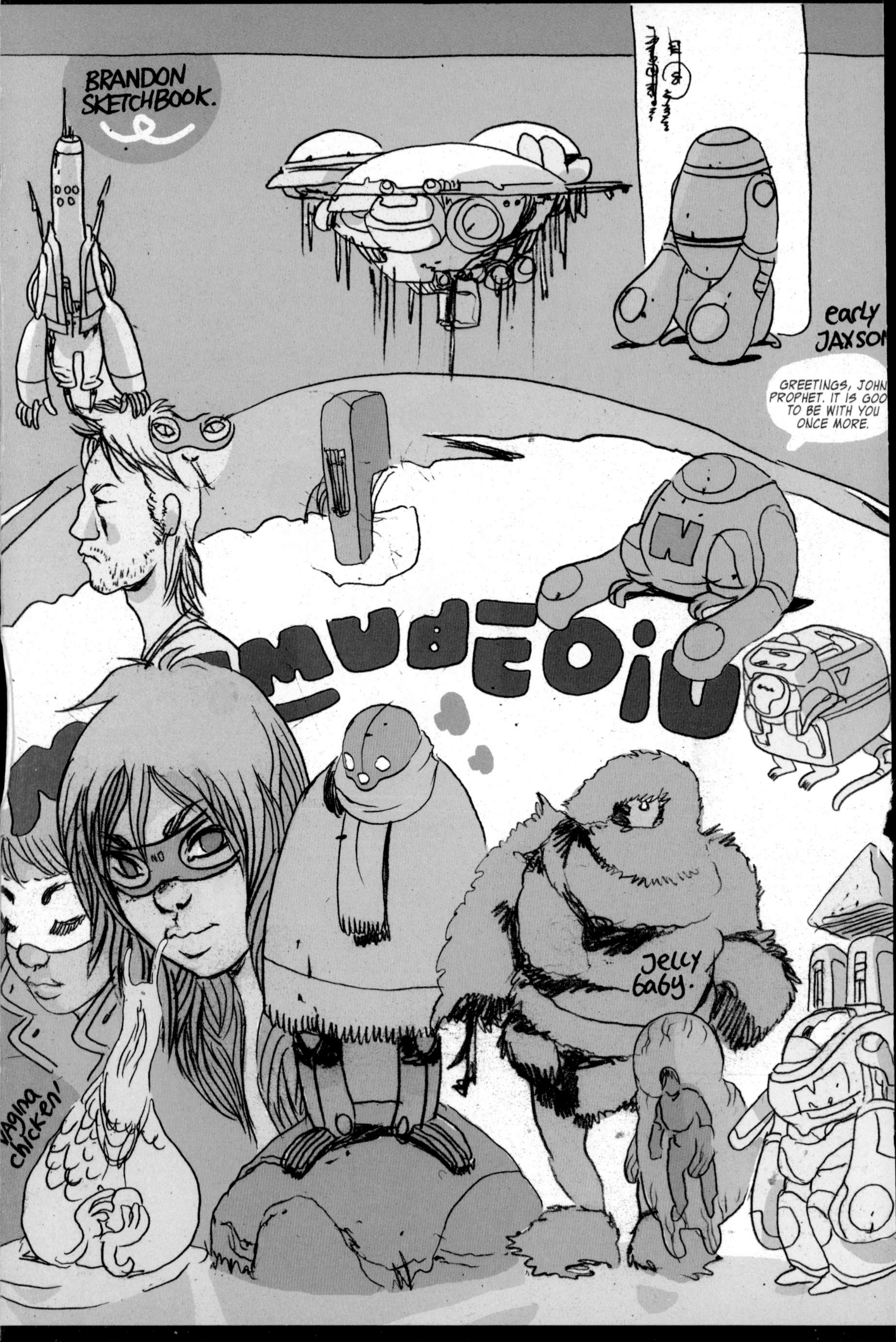
BRANDON SKETCHBOOK.
early JAXSON
GREETINGS, JOHN PROPHET. IT IS GOO TO BE WITH YOU ONCE MORE.
Jelly baby.
vagina chicken!